SCARLET
CROSSES

SCARLET CROSSES

The Truth Lies Within

J. BECKHAM STEELE

Via Press
Pinehurst, Texas

For information, contact:

VIA Press
P.O. Box 180
Pinehurst, Texas 77362

VIA Press is an imprint of Veritas Intus Abscondite, LLC.

Publishers Note:

This is a work of fiction. Names, characters, places, and incidents either are the product of the author's imagination or are used fictitiously, and any resemblance to actual persons, living or dead, events, or locales is entirely coincidental.

ISBN-10: 0997522003
ISBN-13: 9780997522006
LCCN: 2016940655
VIA Press, Magnolia, TX

Portions of the lyrics for two songs are used with permission.

To all of the Megan's out there who fight silent battles to overcome the horrific impact of violence, and to all of the Harris' who fight for justice for them. To all of those who live in fear behind a mask, may you someday feel safe to live without it. To all of those that charted the course, that braved and continue to brave hatred and bigotry, and fight for acceptance of even the smallest parts of our society.

ACKNOWLEDGEMENTS

This book would not have been possible without the love and patience of my wife, my partner, and best friend, Sandra. She has endured so much, listening to so many scene reads, only to have me rewrite them and read them again. She has taken this journey with me, shared the joys, and cried the tears. She is my rock. I love you, Sandra. To my daughters, who have loved me the whole way, thank you for putting up with me. To my family and Sandra's family who support and love me for the person that I am, thank you. To God, for loving me and bringing light into my world, thank you.

To Nicholas Gernon with the NOPD, thank you for taking the time to teach me about the department and the city. To Sarah Balyeat with Tulane Medical, thank you for the tour of the facility. To Christy, who was kind enough to let me tour their offices and gaze out of the window of Megan's conference room in the Place St. Charles building, thank you. To Craig Lambert, thank you for giving me a tour of Megan's home. Thank you, Sanjay, for encouraging me to turn the screenplay into a novel and for beautiful cover art. To Amanda, an amazing editor and one of the most beautiful souls I've ever met, thank you. Thanks to Cathy for her early editing work and friendship. To Deke, Jacob, and Grayson, thank you for being my friend and encouraging me in the ways you all did. To Carolyn for just being an amazing human, friend, and cover model. To Shelley, who read the first (and horrible) version of the screenplay and has read everything since, thank you for loving me as me, thank you for being my friend, and thank you for an amazing pitch poster that inspired me. To Joan, thank you for believing and thank you for your amazing talent in setting up the marketing efforts. To Annie and Ashley, the best friends I could ask for and two of the many "Here, read this" victims. To the city of New Orleans for your beauty, charm, warmth, and awe-inspiring history. Thanks to Tina Sjorgen for contributing a portion of one of Megan's poems. To Lisa Morris for permission to use a portion of her work "Windows in My Walls", thank you. Last but not least, to Tory. She was an angel for me in my darkest days. Thank you, Tory, for saving my life.

Chapter 1

JOUSTING

A lbert Harris pauses three steps shy of the landing. He stares at the aggregation of bodies that lies ahead of him, a confluence of humanity, wandering frantically. He adjusts his collar, loosening his tie a notch, and takes a deep breath. Crowds have have always bothered him, and today's crowd, in this cramped corridor is bothering him worse than most. The unintelligible gibbering echoing off the white marble walls, the scraping of shoes, the clicking of heels, melds into a cacophony. He sighs and takes the final steps into the multitude, wading through the masses that seek a good seat for today's drama. It's a big case, the biggest in years. Ready or not, it's time.

Known as Harris to most except those closest to him, the veteran police detective walks briskly with his partner, Larry Robichaux, through the cavernous second floor of the visage of division that separates those that abide by the law and those that violate it: The Orleans Parish Criminal Court. Ahead of them, past the throng, looms the Section K courtroom in which a judge will sit center between they that would prosecute those violators and those that would defend them.

As the two of them snake their way through the crowd, Harris recognizes many of the faces—he sees them nightly on the news. He knows what they'll say, those talking heads, on the ten o'clock broadcast as they bloviate about the trial of a 'suspected' mafia boss. *Suspected*—it's a word he's heard used in that manner before. It's a manner he hates. Perhaps it's those reporters that bother him most, reminding him of a darker time he prefers not to revisit.

As they reach the eight-foot, wood trimmed doors of the courtroom, Robichaux stops blank, as though he's facing a dragon that could devour him.

"You okay?" Harris asks, turning back to his partner.

"Yeah, just need a second," Robichaux replies, trying to calm his nerves with a series of deep breathing exercises.

Harris watches him for a few moments before softly patting him on the shoulder.

"Listen," Harris says as confident as a knight atop his trusted destrier, "We've been through this a dozen times. She's not gonna be able to make it stick. We've got this son-of-a-gun dead to rights."

Robichaux nods but not so convincingly. "I just want this to be over, Al. I never thought I would be here, not at this point in my career. The worry is killing Mary."

The "son-of-a-gun" that Harris says they have "dead-to-rights" is Victor Donkova, the elder statesman of the local Russian community. At least that's the public image that Victor works hard to portray. Ask anyone within the NOPD, Louisiana State Police, and the State Attorney General's office, and they'll tell you that Victor is the head of the New Orleans Russian crime syndicate.

Harris slides his arm around Robichaux's shoulder. He knows all too well what worry and grieving can do to a person, especially when it's amplified by high-stakes, questions and explanations—and innuendo.

"You know," Harris says, trying to even out the mood. "I love this city. It's been my home for thirty-seven years. She isn't perfect, but she's beautiful. She's ours."

"These guys like Donkova," Harris says, turning to face Robichaux directly. "They come blowing into town after Katrina, taking advantage of the chaos and thinking they can buy their way to impunity. These guys are a blight, a tarnish on a city that's pulled itself up by its bootstraps."

A voice from the crowd calls out a name, one that sends Harris spinning to see.

"Miranda, over here," the deep, male voice repeats. "Miranda."

Harris' eyes widen with anticipation as he struggles to find the voice calling *that* name.

"There you are," he hears, pinpointing its source.

Harris watches as the man shakes hands with a woman, her face hidden from Harris by her hair. Harris' eyes focus, studying her long, brown tresses. His breathing noticeably pauses and his heart races as he patiently waits, hoping that *she* will turn around. After a long, painful moment, she does. Her eyes meet his briefly and she gives him a courteous smile. Harris' expression of hope fades. He sighs softly, scolding himself for thinking the impossible.

He turns back to Robichaux who gives him a compassionate nod and a pat on the shoulder. Harris nods back, scrunching his lips before casting his gaze up and blinking his eyes clear.

"When we lost... a...," he says, squinting his eyes.

"Yeah, Al. You don't have to say it. I know what you're—"

"Since then, it's been hard. There have been times I've wanted to quit, quit everything."

He feels his lip begin to quiver and his breath shorten.

"I didn't think I would make it. I didn't know who I was, who I had become. I couldn't look at another dead body. I couldn't bear the thought of the pain that one human can inflict on another, couldn't hear the stories from their relatives and loved ones, of their loss. I just couldn't do it. I left homicide and joined the task force and—I gotta be honest with you, Larry—it was a move just to finish it all out. I just wanted to coast, to wither away like it all never happened."

"But you didn't. That's the point. You made it through, you stayed the course. When so many jumped ship, you did the right thing, Al."

Harris nods his head and forces a smile.

"You had a lot to do with me staying," he says with earnest, dropping his head a bit to look Robichaux square in the eyes. "I want to thank you for that. This case, this guy, this son-of-a... This case gave me something to hold onto and these allegations, by this...*bitch*, they won't stand."

The mass of bodies pushes closer; a couple of reporters jockeying for position bump into Harris. He turns and looks at them and then sighs heavily, shaking his head in disgust. He raises the security tape and steps under it to a less crowded position near the courtroom door with Robichaux.

"And this consent decree from the DOJ and all the lawsuits and corruption, as a cop I haven't had a lot to be proud of, to hold my head up high. But what we did here, I'm proud of it, proud of us. When we're done with him, there's more fish to catch," Harris says, confidently, with a pat on Robichaux's back.

"Yeah, well the last thing the department needs now is another black eye," Robichaux whispers, as if shielding his words from inquisitive ears. All police activities are under the watchful eye of the federal government— thanks to the new mayor. His request for help from the Department of Justice in reforming a dysfunctional and critically flawed police force resulted in the consent decree.

The Donkova case took an unexpected twist when Victor's defense attorneys accused the department of entrapment and particularly pointed the finger at Robichaux. Of course, the department has come to his defense; they have no choice but to do so in an effort to save the case. Harris and Robichaux both know, however, even if they won't admit it, that the damage has been done and Robichaux has some difficult days ahead.

The problem isn't the accusations; it's the man bringing them—the legendary Max Flannigan and his pack of ruthless attorneys. Flannigan's practice has built a reputation as the law firm of choice for those facing charges for white-collar crimes, and of those so accused, only the ones with the deepest pockets need apply. Leading the defense is Max's big-gun, Megan Callahan, one of the most prominent and successful criminal defense attorneys in the city.

Harris and Robichaux's attention focuses, as if drawn by a magnet on a wave moving through the throng. Harris watches Megan as she strides confidently through the crowd, while three young assistant attorneys struggle to keep up. He studies her as she stops and engages one of them in conversation. The young attorney's eyes widen and her skin flushes as Megan watches her frantically flip through a handful of file folders only to turn apologetic eyes back to her. Harris notices the young woman's lip quiver as Megan berates and humiliates her in front of her colleagues, who look away in fear, sending the scorned counsel hurrying back through the crowd for the forgotten file.

Megan and her remaining entourage turn and push through the crowd, leaving a wake of faces that whisper among themselves of who just passed. As she reaches the door, her eyes catch Harris'. She pauses for a moment then gives him a forced curt smile before entering the courtroom.

Harris turns back to Robichaux, who looks as if he just witnessed the wyvern herself slither past, leaving a trail of death in her path.

"Just settle down. She's not going to eat you," Harris says with a chuckle.

After a moment, Robichaux attempts to shake it off as Harris pats him on the shoulder and throws him a smile.

"You remember Pastor's sermon Sunday?" Harris asks.

"Yeah, the story of Joseph."

"Exactly. That guy had no control of the situation and it seemed his life had ended. But it didn't; it was just beginning. There was a reason for it all. So no matter what happens in there today… trust in Him. He has a reason for everything," Harris says.

"I hope you're right."

"I know I'm right. When this is over, you and I will personally escort Mr. Victor Donkova upriver to Angola. Got it? You can't think otherwise," Harris says pointing to the courtroom. "In there, on the stand, take your time and think it through before you answer."

Robichaux nods, attempting a smile, and then straightens his posture. He opens the doors and enters.

It's the best encouragement Harris can give him. Megan Callahan didn't get where she is for nothing. Harris' words of divine destiny echo hauntingly in his own mind. If only he could believe those words himself.

Harris and several other detectives sit in the courtroom gallery, a sign of solidarity with Robichaux. From their expressions, it's clear the day's proceedings are not going as hoped.

The trial involves suspected embezzlement of several million dollars by Victor's organization. As Harris gazes over at him, he considers how difficult and long the road to get to this point had been, especially considering the overwhelming amount of support for Victor from the local community. He recalls the multitude of large charitable contributions the task force detailed that Victor had been shrewd enough to make to community organizations through a myriad of companies. Add to that key contributions to influential politicians' campaigns, and Victor has recently garnered comparisons to John Gotti, the Teflon Don.

Harris studies him as he sits across the aisle with Megan's team of lawyers and a large posse of supporters who fill the gallery behind him. He can't help but suspect that Victor relishes the mobster analogy. He watches them for a moment then considers that the judge, who sits square in the middle between these opposing forces, is dressed in black. To Harris, it is the defense, with their villainous hearts, that should be dressed in black.

Harris turns and watches helplessly as Megan continues her questioning of Robichaux, sitting under oath, on the witness stand and sweating, perhaps from nervousness, perhaps from the heat that even the ten three-bladed oscillating fans mounted to the walls can't seem to dissipate.

She paces slowly, her long, strawberry-blonde hair pulled into a severe ponytail. She spins a pen in her hand, rolling it through her thin fingers occasionally and then holding it like a sword when she makes a point. Harris wonders to himself if it is the pen, perhaps enchanted by a Voodoo priestess, that has made so many jurors find her legal arguments irresistible. He glances to the juror box where every eye is locked onto Megan's statuesque frame. They seem mesmerized by her, charmed by her elegant, articulate, and practically lyrical speech. He sighs softly in resignation as he wonders if a pit of cobras would fare much differently.

Robichaux squirms in his seat and takes a long drink of water to wash the cottonmouth away while Megan gathers her thoughts in response to his last answer.

"I'm sorry Detective, but I don't believe the jury could hear you. Let me repeat the question: Did you threaten Mr. Donkova that his liquor license could be revoked?"

Heeding Harris' words of wisdom, Robichaux pauses, seemingly formulating his thoughts.

"I didn't put it that way," he finally says.

"No? Well how did you put it, exactly, Detective Robichaux?"

"I told him that he should consider working with Andy, that if the deal didn't go through, he could make both of our lives miserable," he answers methodically.

Megan pauses for effect, letting the answer settle in with the jury. After a few moments she continues.

"Did, Andy, Agent Andrews, did he tell you to say that to Mr. Donkova?"

Robichaux pauses, taking another drink of water before answering. "Not exactly."

Megan turns to the jury and smiles before turning back to Robichaux. She slowly begins to close in on him, her eyes fixed firmly on his—a lioness about to strike.

"Then what, exactly, Detective Robichaux, did Agent Andrews tell you to say to Mr. Donkova?"

"Objection, Your Honor! This is hearsay," District Attorney John Landow says, rising quickly to his feet from behind the prosecution table.

"Your Honor," Megan says as she steps back, respectfully, in front of the bench. "I'm simply asking the witness what was said to him by others he works with, or under the supervision of, in order to establish what effect, if any, it had on him and the actions he took as a result of the conversation in question."

The judge leans forward and peers at both of them as she taps her fingers on the bench. After a short moment of consideration, she looks back at Megan.

"Proceed, Counsel."

Landow, resembling a coach on the sidelines objecting to a referees call, raises his hands in frustrated protest before sitting.

"I'll ask the question again," Megan says while looking at Landow and smiling before turning and taking a couple of sanguine steps towards the witness stand.

"What, exactly, Detective Robichaux, did Agent Andrews tell you to say to Mr. Donkova?"

Robichaux pauses, looking at Harris and the others in the gallery. To Harris, it's a final gaze before the trap door is opened and Robichaux drops, swinging freely at the end of the rope that Megan has very effectively looped around his neck. He can only sit and watch as his partner's career goes down in flames.

Noticing that Robichaux is glancing to Harris, Megan strikes again.

"Detective, I hope you're not receiving some sort of coaching from the gallery," she says as she, and every member of the jury, turns their eyes directly at Harris.

"Please answer the question, Detective," Megan continues, as she positions herself between the two of them.

Robichaux glances to the jury, which watches him intently, then looks back to Megan.

"He said… that Victor needed to feel the urgency of the situation."

Megan studies him for a moment. She turns to the jury, and then, finally, back towards the judge.

"No more questions, Your Honor".

Sitting next to Victor, she whispers into the ear of an assistant attorney. Victor smiles widely, beaming with confidence and apparently sensing another acquittal.

It's a scene that makes Harris seethe.

The trial has adjourned early for the day, and participants and observers are slowly making their way out of the courtroom. Robichaux and the other detectives exit together as Harris hangs back, waiting for the crowd to thin. There's a saying that floats around the legal and law enforcement community of New Orleans: "Don't fuck with Megan Callahan." It's a catchphrase well earned on her part, both from her legal prowess and her reputation of easily defeating all who would challenge her to a verbal joust. It's a distinction that Harris has no intention of acknowledging.

Megan and her assistant stand near the defense table quietly discussing the next steps in the case. Once their conversation wraps up and the assistant walks away, Harris approaches Megan.

"You're ruining a good man's career, you know that?" he says, anger flooding from his eyes.

Megan stops and smiles politely at him.

"Hi to you too, Harris. And I'm not ruining anyone's career. If your partner decided to flush his down the drain, that's not my doing."

"This is *bullshit* and you know it, Callahan. He's a good cop."

Megan strides past him, her ponytail swaying in time with the click of her heels. She stops for a moment, turning towards him before lowering her gaze.

"This isn't about being a good cop, Harris. You're a good cop but... that didn't stop you from getting in hot water with the public integrity bureau, now did it?"

She tosses him a smart-ass smile and leaves him to stand alone, fuming that she had the balls to bring that matter up.

Sometimes it seems the law is not so much about justice as it is about maintaining its divisions. Harris is no stranger to division and its "us versus them" mentality. New Orleans is a city of division. Like the world, separated by oceans, mountains, religions, race, and innumerable schisms, the city he calls home is filled with many discordant states of being. Each of those states is convinced that its esoteric dogma and view of the human condition is the true salvation of mankind. It's a city of East Bank and West Bank, partitioned by the mighty Mississippi, and of Uptown and Downtown, separated by a street named Canal.

As he watches Megan walk away, the divide between those that enforce the law and they that defend those accused of violating it has rarely seemed greater.

Chapter 2

⌗⌗⌗

PHASES

It's not often that Harris picks up his grandson from school. It's close enough to home that he can walk on most days, but today is no such day due to the rain that's moved in. Harris has been trying to connect with an often distant Kyle for some time now, and the early court adjournment has provided him with an opportunity for a small amount of quality time together.

The front door to St. John Community School swings open, and eleven-year-old Kyle Harris steps out. He's a thin child who carries himself cautiously, glancing left and right before heading out and under the awning protecting him from the heavy rain.

He pauses at the top of the steps when he sees that his ride home today is being provided by his grandfather. He sighs and touches his busted lip, today's installment in a continual series of bullying that he endures at school. He looks around, as if considering other options or perhaps going back inside and saying he forgot he was being picked up. However, hesitating is useless, as he sees Harris wave to him from the Crown Victoria. Kyle sighs again, rolling his busted lower lip up against his top lip as much as he can, and proceeds down the steps.

Harris watches Kyle for a moment, focusing on his hair, well-kept but long and draping past his shoulders. That hair is an issue that irritates Harris but one that Andrea, Kyle's grandmother, defends him on. In Harris' opinion, Kyle's mother, Miranda, had been far too lenient with Kyle, spoiling the kid by giving him anything he wanted, or so it seemed. To him, the liberal teachings that Miranda was exposed to at college were the genesis for allowing Kyle to "find himself." How long hair on a boy had anything to do with "finding oneself" remains a mystery to Harris. The only reason Harris hasn't marched him down and plopped his butt in a barber's chair for a good crew cut is his love for Miranda. He pushes the thoughts away, and returns his attention to a phone call before Kyle opens the door to get in.

"Listen Larry, I'm telling you. It will be okay. Just stick to your guns. It's going to break our way. This is a big crock of——," Harris stops himself, not wanting to set a bad example for Kyle. "Let's meet up at Mick's about eight. I'm buying. Okay, see ya then."

He hangs up and sighs, considering for a moment that perhaps his life would have been different, easier, if he had chosen to become a postman rather than following in his father's footsteps. He joined the NOPD a year after he and Andrea married and slowly worked his way up, becoming a detective after ten years as a patrol officer.

He shakes off the frustration and tries to focus once more on Kyle. He looks to him and smiles. Kyle meekly smiles back and then turns his face towards the window.

"Hey buddy! How was your day?" Harris asks, a little too enthusiastically.

"Fine," Kyle answers, still staring at the view outside the car.

"Anything exciting happen?"

"Nope."

One-word answers. That's all Harris seems to be able to extract from Kyle these days. As Kyle stares out the window, Harris studies him, trying to figure out what approach he needs to take to connect with the kid. After a moment, he puts the car in gear, checks his mirrors, and pulls out onto Esplanade Avenue, turning left towards Lake Pontchartrain.

He passes Our Lady of the Rosary Catholic Church, with massive oaks lining the street, extending their limbs thirty feet across both lanes, embracing and sheltering the grounds in front of the beautiful administrative offices of Cabrini High School. He smiles softly, considering those trees' timelessness, seemingly eternal, enduring the many storms that have laid waste to the city. He thinks of his daughter, Miranda, and he checks the smile back in.

He turns left onto Moss Street, traveling alongside Bayou St. John and past the front entrance of Cabrini. It's a school that was an intimate part of his and Andrea's adult lives. She taught art for thirty years, retiring just four years ago, a year before their lives changed forever. He slows, watching the girls of the school run to get into their parent's cars, and remembers the many times he picked up Miranda from that exact same curb.

Harris and Andrea have lived in New Orleans their entire adult lives. A New York City native of Irish decent, Harris met New Orleans native Andrea Dubois while they both attended NYU. Thanks to her southern charm, the hard-nosed son of an NYPD cop was soon putty in her hands. He was obviously willing to follow her to the ends of the earth, because to him, at that time, New Orleans *was* the end of the earth.

It was a bit of culture shock for Harris when he moved from the Big Apple to the Big Easy, transitioning from the fast-paced, time-is-money environment of New York to the laid-back, there's-always-tomorrow spirit of his newly adopted home. But like the city, which has absorbed varied cultures and races since its founding on the muddy banks of the Mississippi River in 1718, Harris eventually blended into the unique and vibrant community.

As he drives the rain-soaked street, he passes the Old Spanish Custom House, a French Colonial style plantation home built in 1784 or earlier as Harris recalls. He thinks back to the Cotillion Ball he attended there with Miranda her senior year of high school. He still doesn't buy the story he was told then: that General Andrew Jackson met there with the Privateer Jean Lafitte before pardoning him and accepting his assistance in defending the city during the War of 1812.

He glances to his right, at Bayou St. John, as the rain falls in sheets across its surface. September rainstorms in New Orleans are a common nuisance. They can also be a cause of anxiety for a city plagued by hurricanes. He's reminded of "The Storm," Hurricane Katrina, and how fortuitous it was for him and Andrea to have purchased a home in the Faubourg St. John neighborhood. It's an area that lies on a small rise known as Esplanade Ridge, a historic overland route from a small outpost on the shores of Lake Pontchartrain to the banks of the Mississippi and the newly founded city of New Orleans. As ridges go, it isn't much of one. Granted, relative to the majority of the city, which lies below sea level in the "bowl," the one-foot-above-sea-level elevation of the ridge can be considered a mountain. That additional elevation prevented their home from flooding during the storm, one of the greatest challenges the city ever faced.

The days before and the months after the storm were harrowing times. Andrea, Miranda, and three-year-old Kyle evacuated early, 275 miles north, to West Monroe, Louisiana where they stayed with relatives until December. Harris, of course, stayed behind and did his part to maintain order in a city laid waste by collapsing levies that flooded eighty percent of the homes and a storm that killed at least 1,800 people along its path—a couple of friends included.

He sighs heavily as he approaches Desoto Street, seeing the road is closed due to construction. He speeds forward and turns left onto St. Philip, which he will take down to North Rendon, then back over to Desoto. Kyle reaches over and flips on the radio, navigating through a few stations before finally landing on one he likes. Lady Gaga's *Born This Way* blares through the speakers, causing Harris to cringe while Kyle keeps the beat and mouths the words. The younger generation's music — it isn't music, not to Harris. He turns the volume down, doing his best to be understanding.

Harris does well for about the first half of the song, but when it reaches the bridge and the radio blares *"No matter gay, straight, or bi, lesbian, transgendered life, I'm on the right track baby, I was born to survive."* it proves to be too much, as frustration washes over him like a wave. He quickly changes the station to local news and weather.

Kyle rolls his eyes, never taking them off the side window. He stares out through the raindrops that stream across the window as Harris drones on about how "the gays" are ruining society and family values. Kyle simply nods and answers "Yes, sir" on cue, all the while searching houses and street signs to see if they are any closer to home.

Harris parks the car along the curb in front of their shotgun style duplex at 3025 Desoto in the Faubourg St. John neighborhood. It's a pleasant area, with oak-lined streets and a mixture of the unique architectural elements of New Orleans including bungalows, center hall cottages, and Greek revival style dwellings. Their home, a modest, light blue, duplex with white, turned-wood brackets on the porch posts, window and door cornices, louvered shutters, and other intricately designed wood embellishments along the porch railings, adds its own unique charm to the community.

There's room for only two cars in the driveway. One is Andrea's and the other is their neighbor's, Nicki Carmichael. Harris and Andrea rented out the second unit of the duplex for years until Miranda moved back in. It was used mostly as storage until last year when Nicki, a single mother of two, asked for help at church. Harris and Andrea heeded their Christian beliefs and opened the second unit up to her. It's worked out pretty well for them, and Kyle has become good friends with Nicki's daughter, Rebecca, a classmate of his.

Harris and Kyle get out of the car and Kyle rushes ahead to the front door. While he still has a bit of Kyle's attention, Harris calls out to him.

"Hey Kyle, the rain's clearing. Want to throw the football in a little bit?"

"I guess so," Kyle answers, without looking back as he rushes into the house.

"I'm never gonna get through to that kid," Harris says to himself as he walks beneath a light sprinkle of the remaining rain and up the sidewalk through the small, well-manicured and fenced front yard. His spirits are lifted when he notices some new blooms on the roses by the crepe myrtles. He's always had a green thumb, and the yard shows it. He delicately tends to the blooms. Pruning off some old branches with his hand, he masterfully avoids pricking himself with the thorns. After a few minutes, and happy with his handiwork, he steps onto the porch, retrieves the mail, and proceeds into the house.

He tosses his keys on the kitchen counter and thumbs through the daily offering of discounts on new cars and fliers proclaiming the greatest back-to-school sales in New Orleans history. Finding nothing of interest except bills, he opens the fridge and pulls out a cold beer. He closes the door and stares at a piece of Kyle's artwork they keep there. It's a female Manga style character with pink and black hair pulled tightly back, large eyes, small face, and a tear on her cheek, standing in a field of flowers. He doesn't understand Kyle's fascination with Japanese art, but he's a good artist; he'll grant him that.

A photo of Kyle's mother, posted on the door next to his drawing, catches Harris' attention. Miranda Harris, the apple of Albert's eye. An only child, though not by choice, young Miranda was the center of Harris and Andrea's lives. They had hoped for three children, or at least two, but a complication during Miranda's delivery left Andrea unable to bear more. Miranda was a wonderful, caring, and delightful child, and grew into a beautiful young woman who studied pre-med at LSU with dreams of becoming a doctor. A doomed relationship with a young man from Shreveport resulted in her being left alone and pregnant. Andrea insisted that Miranda move home, where she could help when the baby was born, and so Miranda could finish her studies. Six months later, Kyle, named after Harris' father, was born into the world, as were two grandparents who proceeded to spoil him as well as any loving grandparents could.

Harris takes a swig of beer and heads into the living room. He settles into the couch amid the iron and wood crosses and images of angels captured on canvas that adorn the walls. He turns on the TV to ESPN Sports Center to get the latest on the prospects for the Saints' upcoming season. After a moment, he glances around, wondering where everyone has disappeared to. Andrea enters from the hallway, leans down and kisses him softly on the cheek.

"How did it go?"

"I got three words. *I*, *guess*, and *so*."

"Nana?" Kyle calls as he rushes in from the hallway.

Harris glances to Andrea as she begins fidgeting with her necklace, twirling the stone pendant. She seems nervous, as if she's trying to divert his attention.

"Yes?" Andrea answers, turning her body and blocking Harris' view of Kyle.

"Can I go to Rebecca's?" Kyle asks.

Andrea turns to Harris, who rolls his eyes and huffs in frustration, clear on what she was hiding. Her eyes turn back to Kyle.

"Don't you want to watch Sports Center with Paw Paw?" she asks.

"Yeah buddy, I'm gonna have some tickets to a couple of games this season," Harris adds. "We need to get all schooled up on the team."

Kyle shakes his head and points towards Rebecca's side of the house. "Can I? Please?"

Andrea glances back to Harris who just turns back to the TV. She studies him for a moment then sighs softly.

"Okay," she says. "But you have to be home by six for dinner."

The words barely finish leaving her lips before Kyle is out the front door. Andrea runs her hands across Harris' shoulders and then sits beside him.

"Babe, he's not like you."

"He doesn't have to be like me, but I would like for him to like to be *with* me."

"You know what I mean, Albert."

He rises and angrily clicks the TV off, pitching the remote back onto the couch by Andrea before heading into the kitchen.

She watches as he paces for a moment and then turns back to her.

"Andrea, I've told you … this is a *phase*."

"And you leaving the toilet seat up or never asking for directions is a phase too. Right, Albert? Babe, you need to—"

"I need to toughen the kid up! That's what I need to do. He needs to quit hanging out with Rebecca. He needs to do boy things. Maybe he needs to be in football, even *soccer* for that matter. He's too soft."

Andrea sighs softly in resignation. She looks at him with disappointment and then properly sets the TV control back on the side table. As Harris paces and finishes his beer, she walks back into the kitchen, calling out to him.

"Are you done for the day, or are you…" she asks, removing a cookbook from a shelf and quickly flipping through the pages.

"I need to meet with Ron and Larry about the trial."

"Will you be back in time for—"

"I don't know."

He watches as she turns back to the cookbook and rapidly flips through several more pages. She slams it shut, closing her eyes and sighing angrily. He steps to the counter, grabs his car keys and jacket and heads out the door.

Kyle and Rebecca sit on the floor in the living room on her side of the duplex, having a good time playing with her collection of Bratz dolls. It's quite the collection—composed of five dolls and enough clothes to put on a fashion show of which any designer worth their salt would be envious. As they put their heads together, comparing their design skills, Kyle's long hair makes it difficult to tell them apart at times.

Rebecca's mother, Nicki, works in the kitchen preparing a dinner of fish sticks and fries and putting the finishing touches on a carrot cake. It can be tough making ends meet as a single mother, and the kindness that Harris and Andrea have shown her by renting her this place, at a discounted rate no less, is greatly appreciated. She is surprised at how strong the friendship between Kyle and Rebecca has become in the last year. She pauses to watch them play, smiling at how they seem to be so bonded.

The front door opens and Rebecca's older brother, Russell, enters in a flurry that causes Kyle and Rebecca to look up and see what all of the commotion is about. Russell throws his backpack on the floor and hurries into the kitchen.

"Hold it right there, mister. Pick that bag up and put it where it's supposed to be," Nicki instructs him, pointing her finger at the discarded bag. "Do you have dirty clothes in there? If you do, put them in the washer. I'm not your maid."

Russell grudgingly does as instructed while mumbling something about washing clothes not being his job either, complaints that don't escape her fine-tuned maternal ears.

"What did you say young man? Not your job? So what is?" she asks.

"Sacking quarterbacks."

"Yeah, well, there won't be any sacking of quarterbacks for you if you don't pull your weight around here," she says, shaking a mixing spoon at him.

Kyle looks back to Rebecca who simply returns to dressing her Cloe doll. He turns back to Russell, watching silently as he puts his finger into the carrot cake, provoking a slap on the shoulder with the wooden spoon and orders to leave the kitchen. Kyle returns his attention to the dolls as Russell enters the living room like he owns the place, stepping over Cloe, Yasmin and the others that silently await their run down the catwalk.

"Hey, ya little troll," Russell says as he pulls Rebecca's hair then plops down on the couch and turns on the TV.

She quickly glances up and sticks her tongue out at him, then returns to dressing Cloe. Kyle looks up to Russell and hesitantly smiles. Russell peers at him for a second, then down at the doll he is playing with.

"Hey, faggot," he says under his breath as he changes the channels, stopping on a commercial for an upcoming MMA championship fight.

Kyle watches the advertisement for the upcoming pay-per-view event and a testosterone-raged fighter gloating over his downed opponent.

"Damn! That guy is such a bad ass," Russell says.

Kyle looks to Russell, examining him. He thinks about the evenings that Rebecca and her family have spent over at his house watching the Saints, and how his grandfather was always so interested in hearing Russell recount his exploits from the previous week's high school football game. He studies him for a few moments more and then returns to the dolls with Rebecca.

The phone in the kitchen rings as Nicki drops the finished fish sticks on the stove. She speaks quietly for a moment then calls to Kyle.

"Kyle, your Nana has dinner ready. You need to head back over."

He scrunches his lips in disappointment, accidentally wiping off some of the makeup that Andrea applied to hide the wound.

Rebecca's eyes widen as she notices the red and purple hue of his busted lip.

"What happened?" she whispers.

"Nothing. It's no big deal," he says as he drops his head and covers his lip with his hand. "Guess I gotta get home," he reluctantly adds as he holds his doll out to Rebecca. She looks at it a moment then back to Kyle.

"You can keep her," she says with a grin.

"Really?" he says, his spirit buoyed by her kindness.

"Yeah. You're better with Yasmin than me anyway."

He smiles and gets up and heads through the kitchen, the Yasmin doll tucked in his pocket. Nicki intercepts him before he leaves and hands him the carrot cake.

"Take this to your grandparents and tell your Nana that I'll give her the recipe for the icing. Found it on Pinterest," she says with a satisfied smile.

His eyes light up as he takes the cake, the best in the world according to him, and heads out the door.

Chapter 3

HAUNTED

While the trial is going well and Megan is confident that the verdict will turn her way, she also knows that juries can be fastidious. She could have gone home and fretted about it, cancelling the evening out she reluctantly agreed to a week ago.

She didn't want to go on a date. She dreaded them. They always ended the same. But "the stars were aligning," her friend had insisted. Megan isn't sure about the stars, but she had decided that after a tough day in the courtroom she could use a night of diversion.

The company, her friend's cousin, turned out to not be as bad as she feared. Maybe she was just being lulled by the romantic atmosphere at Feelings Café or maybe, just maybe, tonight would be different.

"So do you ever get back to Memphis?" Paul asks as they walk down Chartres Street towards the French Quarter, the most famous, and infamous, part of the city. It's practically a living museum where one can walk the same streets and eat, sleep, and drink in the same buildings as the earliest settlers and a favorite of locals and visitors.

"As often as I can, which isn't very," Megan replies. "Work just constantly seems to get in the way."

"Growing up with all those horses must have been great."

"I'll call my mother and tell her you are coming up to muck out some stalls. Then you can tell me how great it is," Megan says with a huff and a roll of her eyes.

"Oh come on. It can't be that bad."

"It wasn't. Getting my hands dirty never bothered me. It's just a lot of work and my sisters and I received no slack because we were girls."

"That's good, though. It taught you a good work ethic."

"Yeah, it did that," Megan says with a nod.

"So do you still ride?"

"Every time I get a chance," she says with a smile.

"What kind do have?"

"A Ford," she says proudly.

"Ford? Are we talking about horses?"

"Sorta," she says with a chuckle. "It's a '71 Ford Bronco."

"Whoa! You have Bronco? Seriously?"

"Yeah. My father and I rebuilt it when I was sixteen," she tells Paul before realizing that he has stopped. She turns back to him as he looks her tall frame up and down in astonishment.

"Yeah, I know. I don't fit the stereotype do I? I hate stereotypes anyway," she says.

"Uh, yeah. I'm sorry. I guess you don't. It just surprised me. You're so beautiful and all."

"Next time I'm changing out gears I'll invite you over and see if you say that," she says, smiling.

'What color is it?" he asks as they continue their walk.

"Moss green and white."

"Cut fenders?"

"They are now. I lifted it after I brought it down here when I bought my place in Marigny," she says, enjoying his expressions as he struggles to put the shattered stereotype back together in some order.

"What about you? Where did you grow up?"

As he begins recounting his childhood in Oklahoma, Megan considers that there are worse potential suitors to be paired up with than Paul. He seems to be a genuinely nice person. He has a reasonable job, he listens when she speaks and actually seems interested in what she has to say. He's a good five inches taller than she is, opening up an assortment of heels that she has had to avoid in the past with others. He isn't married nor has he been. While she realizes that's not the norm for man in his mid-thirties, she's in no position to hold it against him.

A small pack of LSU fans pushes their way past the two of them, carelessly bumping into them as they shout at a group of Texas A&M supporters on the other side of the street. While she has nothing against the Quarter itself, she wouldn't be caught dead on Bourbon Street, choosing instead to leave it for the throngs of football buffs that are beginning to assemble in the city for the coming weekend's games. It's those visitors that caused Megan to give pause before agreeing to take the walk with Paul.

"So tell me more about this submersible you went down in. What was that like?" Megan asks as they finish crossing Esplanade Avenue and into the Quarter proper.

"Yeah, well I was one of the engineers that designed the umbilical connected to the subsea well. So I needed to see the issue first-hand."

"How deep was it?"

"About eight hundred feet."

"Oh God!" Megan says, shuddering at the thought. "I can't imagine being confined like that."

"It was a little… uncomfortable," he replies with a grin.

"How long were you in Houston before you moved here?" she asks.

"About six years, then they moved me to Aberdeen for a year."

"How was that? I've always wanted to visit Scotland."

"Cold and wet, lots of clouds," he says with a frown. "So I got out of there as fast as I could and ended up here a month ago."

"Spend much time in the Quarter?"

"Not much actually. I don't drink a lot and I'm usually too busy with work."

"Well, there's more to the Quarter than drinking," she adds with a smile.

"Like what?"

"We've got Angelina and Brad." she replies, pointing over her shoulder towards the river.

"They live here?"

"They have a place right down here," she answers, turning down Governor Nicholls Street.

They make their way down the block and stop in front of the black and gray, unpretentious, two-story structure.

"This is it?" he asks.

"That's it."

"Hmm, rather nondescript isn't it? I guess I expected more... flash."

"They're good people, pretty down to earth. Brad fell in love with the city when he shot *Interview with the Vampire* here." Megan says with a shrug as they head back up to Chartres.

"Do you ever see them around?" Paul asks.

"They come over to the house for dinner occasionally when they're in town," she answers with a grin.

"You know them?" he asks, wide-eyed and star-struck.

"Yeah."

"Wow, what are they like?"

She looks at him, straight-faced, and waits for him to catch-up, which he does, embarrassingly, and rolls his eyes.

"That's wrong," he says as she smiles and laughs.

They turn back onto Chartres, traveling towards Uptown and into the heart of the Quarter.

"That's where our vampires came from," Megan says, motioning to the Old Ursuline Convent, completed in 1751 and perhaps the oldest structure in the Mississippi valley.

"Vampires? Uh huh," Paul chides.

"That's the story at least. The so called Casket Girls sent here from France in 1720-something to be wives of the French settlers. Supposedly they brought their belongings in small boxes, cassettes, shaped a bit like a casket. The nuns took care of them and put their boxes on the third floor," she says, pointing to the shuttered windows. "When the nuns went to get their belongings, they found the boxes empty."

She glances back to the Convent and the two of them gaze at the finest example of French architecture remaining in the Quarter.

"They say those shutters are sealed with eight hundred blessed screws," she adds before returning her focus to the closed, third-floor windows.

"Blessed screws?" he asks.

"To keep the vampires in, I suppose." she says, turning up Ursulines Avenue. She looks back at Paul who is still a few beats behind her, glancing over his shoulder as if expecting the shutters to burst open and reveal Louis de Pointe du Lac himself standing in the window.

The two of them turn left onto Royal, the original main street through the Vieux Carré. She laughs to herself watching Paul as he hovers near a ghost tour.

"What's the deal with all the ghosts?" he asks. "I mean, even the 'For Rent' signs have 'Haunted' and 'Not Haunted' on them."

"I'm not sure. I don't really believe in that nonsense anyway," she answers, pulling her jean jacket tight and wrapping her arms around her chest on a night that isn't particularly cool.

A city as old as this, she had decided, lends itself to tales of roaming spirits. Any city founded by a mottled group of soldiers, French elite, merchants, trappers, slaves, and free people of color from multiple continents and a history of destruction and rebirth was sure to have a few ghosts and skeletons in its closets.

But the legends of hauntings were just that—legends—that she first heard when she visited the city with her family at the age of thirteen. She smiles as her thoughts fill with memories, always fresh in her mind, of walking next to her father, amazed by the tantalizing facts he seemed to spout forth as naturally and unconsciously as air. It was as if he was a living, breathing encyclopedia. His orations fascinated her.

A light fog-like mist accompanies Megan and Paul on their walk up Royal. They roam past brick and stucco buildings, many dating from the 19th century and some earlier, sitting flush against cobblestone and slate sidewalks, as if clipped directly from Paris with a pass through Barcelona or Pamplona for color. The picturesque second and third floor balconies and galleries are decorated with wrought and cast-iron railings of black and green and adorned with flags.

Behind those railings, hanging gardens of ferns and ivies, bougainvilleas and hibiscus, accent beautifully the pastel and earth tones of the brick and stucco walls, creating a veritable canopy of color.

Paul points in amazement to the shuttered windows, large wooden doors, and carriageways that Megan knows are the result of the rebuilding of the city during Spanish control. She smiles at his enthusiasm; it's nice to walk the streets again with someone smitten by the beauty, and history, of the city that first gave her butterflies as a teenager and that, on nights like this, still does.

"Do you come down here during Mardi Gras?" Paul asks, pointing out lamp posts draped with beads from celebrations past.

"Hell no," she answers emphatically. "I might catch a parade outside the Quarter, *maybe*. But like you said earlier, I'm usually too busy. Don't really care for it all anyway," she adds, contemplating the origins and meaning of the celebration. While she appreciates New Orleans prowess for throwing a good, fun hellacious time, Lent and its period of self-denial is not something that Megan cares to buy into. There's enough repression in the world, it doesn't need celebration.

As cars squeeze down their narrow paths, honking at tipsy revelers too busy chattering to notice them, Jazz music emanates from stages within the clubs of Bourbon Street, becoming the backdrop to another New Orleans treasure: the trove of art galleries that line Royal Street. The two of them stop to admire the artistic genius through the window of a gallery tucked away in a small passage between the Cathedral and the Cabildo, home of the local Spanish government in the late 1700's.

Paul watches her as she gazes through the glass; the reflection of the myriad of pigments seems to make her eyes sparkle even more as she soaks in the creative energy so lovingly imparted into each work by the artist.

"What's your favorite kind of art?" Paul asks.

"All of it," she answers quickly, turning and smiling at him before looking back through the glass.

"It was part of the artist's soul, trapped within. Paint, metal, wood, or stone—it doesn't matter. They've freed something that was inside, begging and craving to live," she adds before turning back to him.

The two of them turn toward the river, down Pirates Alley, home to William Faulkner when he freed the characters from within and wrote his first novel, *Soldiers' Pay*, in 1925. As they pass St. Anthony's Garden, legendary sight of duels of pride and honor, she watches Paul survey the contest between darkness and light as the illuminated statue of Jesus casts its immense shadow onto the back wall of St. Louis Cathedral.

"Do you go to church?" he asks.

"It's been a while," she replies, knowing that it's been at least ten years since she attended mass. "First it was law school, then work. Just lost interest in it, I guess."

"It's beautiful," Paul says, pointing to the statue. "Jesus, welcoming all to salvation."

She ponders his words, considering her relationships, past and present.

"Well, some of them perhaps," she says.

"What do you mean?"

She looks at him and smiles, shaking her head. "Nothing," she replies.

Paul stops in the plaza in front of the Cathedral, gazing up to admire the façade and its three towers extended high, reaching into the sky as if connecting with the Holy Trinity itself.

"This... this is the place I've seen in all the pictures. It's beautiful," he says, glancing back and smiling at Megan. "How old is this?"

"I'm not sure, late 1700's, maybe? It was originally much more Spanish but sometime in the mid-1800's, I believe it was, they reworked it to make it more... French."

"More French, huh?" he says, spinning and casting his eyes back up at the spires with a look of amazement.

She studies him, considering his almost child-like enthusiasm and awe of what he is experiencing. He's different than most men she's encountered. She smiles at the thought that he's slightly vulnerable, willing to just be himself and not hide behind a façade of bravado.

They stroll across the plaza in front of the Cathedral, stopping to admire the work of a lone artist attempting to capture the mystical mood with oil and canvas. The Cathedral's bells, which have tolled hourly over the Quarter since 1819, begin to strike the hour of nine and the romance of the moment seems to take over Paul as he reaches for Megan's hand.

A whisper floats through her mind. *Haven't you learned? He's no different.*

She quickly pulls away, cinching her jacket tightly around her chest and refutes the suggestion, assuring herself that he is different, that this could be different, that he means no harm. The demon prosecutors give opening arguments in a trial of her judgment. *That's what you thought before. He's going to hurt you. That's what they do.*

The two of them turn in front of the Presbytère and onto St. Ann Street towards the river. Paul reaches again for her hand, catching it and clasping it tightly.

He's not so gentle, is he? The voice continues.

She reluctantly lets him take it, attempting to quell the growing chorus of doubt and rebutting her tormentors with memories of Paul's genial nature. As they walk towards Decatur Street and Café du Monde, old fears permeate her mind, ghosts crooning a mercilessly chant.

You shouldn't have come. He's not who he seems.

Her breaths become short and shallow as they make their way beneath the massive oaks that line Jackson Square. Paul stops, pulling her back to him, jarring her a bit and sending a small shiver of pain up through her hand from his firm grip.

It's just like before.

Her heart's pace quickens within a whirlwind of anxiety that she diligently tries to fight. Nearby strangers begin to fade from her vision.

He's a liar.

"It's beautiful here. I'm surrounded by beauty," Paul says, gazing straight into her eyes.

Megan, stop. You're teasing him.

An elderly couple walks past the two of them, seemingly admiring the couple. Megan glances to them. Their warm gaze morphs into a wide-eyed stare, warning of her impending doom.

They see it.

She looks back at Paul who smiles softly at her. He seems so kind, so nice.

Nice? Aren't the guilty ones always nice at first?

She battles to silence the ghostly clamor, roaring above the ringing in her ears, desperately assuring herself this will be different. Paul puts his arms around her and gently pulls her to him. Her body tenses and her heart races. She feels her body flush and her hands begin to tingle.

He's lying. You know what he's going to do. He's going to take you.

She feels dizzy. The sounds of the Quarter begin to fade into a muddled cacophony.

He's strong, too strong. Now you've done it, Megan!

She pushes him away, gasping for air as she glances around, struggling to determine where she is and how long she's been there.

"Did I do something wrong?" Paul asks, concern etched across his face.

"No, you didn't do anything. I'm sorry, it's… I'm… I need to go."

She turns and hurries up the moist sidewalk toward Decatur Street.

He's right behind you.

She picks up her pace, running past the line of mule-drawn carriages awaiting passengers along the banks of the river and quickly hails a cab.

He's going to catch you.

A stunned Paul follows behind, trying in vain to stop her as she climbs in the back seat and closes the door behind her.

Secure the gates.

She reaches quickly and locks the door.

"1924 Burgundy."

"You got it."

Megan tries to hide her panic, but it isn't working. The driver sees her through the mirror. "Everything okay?" he asks softly.

"Yeah, everything's fine," she says. "Just hurry, okay?"

Through the window, she gazes back at Paul, who calls out to her with arms outstretched, another Jesus on the cross. Her tears fall harder and she buries her face in her hands as the cab pulls away. Her prosecutors lay their charge once more:

You can trust no man.

Chapter 4

DIFFERENT

A ndrea sits in the living room of their house in front of a makeshift work-station created from a couple of TV trays and a lamp. She needs a proper work environment but she and Harris are considering moving, taking advantage of a steep rise in property values that has occurred in New Orleans in the last few years. The last thing she needs at this point is another piece of furniture. She carefully strings beads onto a necklace, having already finished the match-ing earrings. It's an activity like meditation; her hands gently move in a rhyth-mic way while her mind quiets. And according to the several recipients of her work, she's actually pretty good at it.

She glances to the clock on the wall, expecting Kyle to be home soon from school. She smiles as she hears the door open. Kyle throws his bag on the kitch-en table and hurriedly walks through the living room and towards the hallway.

"Hey, Nana."

"Allô chérie. Comment était l'école aujourd'hui?" Andrea asks to an empty room in French, still a required subject in many New Orleans schools. "Où allez-vous? Venez discuter avec moi," she adds, calling out to him after looking up to see that he has disappeared down the hall.

"Je dois aller à la salle de bain. Soyez en une minute," Kyle replies before the bathroom door closes behind him.

She smiles and continues threading her next work of art as her thoughts turn to Kyle. She's tried to gradually get Harris to perceive him as the person that he's becoming. She can see that Kyle's different, and she tries to be understanding and patient with him. Harris, however, has refused to even discuss the possibility that Kyle isn't exactly growing up the same way he did, and his father before him.

After a few minutes, she hears Kyle emerge from the hallway. "So... how was your day?" she continues, on beat. "Did you get your grade back on your history test?"

"We were supposed to, but Ms. Randolph was sick and we had a substitute."

"What about your art project? Is it finished?" Andrea asks, looking up to him. His long hair is tucked beneath a baseball cap. He never wears baseball caps.

"I finished it last night," Kyle adds, turning on the TV.

Andrea watches him for a moment. He's acting strangely and seems to be hiding his face from her. She walks to the hall mirror to examine the finishing touches of her necklace, and in the reflection, can see the hidden side of Kyle's face. The hastily, and poorly, applied foundation around his eye is evident. Choosing not to panic, Andrea walks back to her workstation, setting the necklace down.

"Kyle, look at me," she says.

He doesn't. She kneels next to him, takes his face in her hand and pulls it towards her. He tries to hide it, tries to be strong about it, but the shiner is visible. At this moment, so are the tears in his eyes. "Oh honey," she says, hugging him tight.

Andrea kneels next to Kyle in their bathroom, applying concealer on his blackened eye, as he tries to control his crying. His hair has purple streaks running through it, something that wasn't there when Andrea dropped him off at school this morning.

"Paw Paw's gonna see," he says, a little shaken.

"No he won't. Trust me. I've gotten very good at hiding blemishes worse than this over the years," Andrea says, as she continues to expertly apply the camouflage.

"You wanna tell me what happened?" she asks gently.

"After school," Kyle says with a sniffle after a long pause. "Abby and some other girls were putting highlights in their hair. She asked me if I wanted some too, so I said yes. I liked the color. When she was putting it on, Justin came up and started making fun of us."

"Justin LeBlanc?"

"Yeah. Then Matt came—"

"Matt who? Matt Johnson?"

"No, Matt Vincent. So Matt started calling me names so I told him to shut up and he hit me," Kyle says as that last part of the story only serves to bring the tears back, washing away most of her handiwork.

She sets the sponge down and hugs him tightly, softly urging him to calm down. After a few moments, he regains his composure. She runs her fingers through his hair, examining the highlights.

"I'm not gay, Nana. I hate it when they call me that."

The word shocks Andrea's ears. She's never heard him say it before.

"It's 'cause you're different from them, Kyle, and it scares them. And they're just mean little… that Vincent boy, I always knew he was trouble, just like his daddy," she answers as she brushes out Kyle's long, streaked hair.

Kyle looks at himself through the mirror, straight in his light-brown eyes filled with anger.

"I hate boys" he says with a fury. "I wish I wasn't one. Why didn't God make me a girl?"

A worried Andrea stops and stares at him through the mirror, then turns him to face her.

"Don't say that! God made you the way He wants you to be. You're better than they are."

She gives him a hug and a kiss on the forehead, then grabs the sponge and begins reapplying the camouflage to the now dry eye.

"It's your age Kyle. You're just… It's… when you get a little older hun, things will be clearer," she says, finishing the cover up. "There… all gone," she adds.

He examines himself in the mirror and smiles; his purple bruise is no longer visible, even in the sharp bathroom light.

"What about this?" he asks, touching the highlights in his hair.

"That… is the sacrificial lamb," she answers as she runs her fingers through his hair. "Now go on. It'll be fine."

He looks at her with confusion at first, but heads out the door, smiling for the first time all afternoon. She stares at herself in the mirror for a few moments, quietly thinking. This latest incident is only going to intensify Harris' argument that Kyle needs to "toughen up," something that she knows is not the answer

---

While Harris has always said it was her looks, brains, and charms that hooked him, Andrea has often wondered if her cooking had anything to do with it. Tonight, she has prepared a family favorite: Shrimp Creole. It's a dish originated in New Orleans consisting of shrimp, tomatoes, and a smattering of spices all built around a base common to many Creole dishes… onions, celery, and green bell peppers, commonly referred to as the Holy Trinity, with a touch of the Pope, a.k.a. garlic, all served over a bed of white rice.

As she finishes the preparations, she can see him from the corner of her eye, standing and looking at a picture of himself and Miranda at a volleyball game when she was in high school. She knows what he's feeling. She feels it every day, every hour. Miranda was daddy's little girl; she had him wrapped around her finger and she knew it. She knows that Harris had always wanted a son to carry on the family name but the Fates would not allow it. She smiles though, remembering that despite that fact, it did not change the way he felt about Miranda. She remembers Miranda's volleyball games that they attended and how Harris would cheer as loud for her as he would have for a son at a football game.

Harris turns to her and smiles. It's a bit forced and she can see it. She understands why. As she watches him, she considers that despite a few extra pounds that have crept back onto his fifty-eight-year-old frame after his cholesterol scare ten years ago, he's still pretty lean and trim for his age. He even still has most of his hair, even if it's gray. Her heart skips a short beat as she reminds herself that's she's lucky to have him. They've been through tough times together, side by side.

She sees an impish grin creep across his face and blushes. She glances towards Kyle who is setting the table for dinner, then back to Harris.

"Stop it," she says softly and then silently mouths, "You're bad," knowingly raising her eyebrows to emphasize it.

Harris grins and walks to her, grabbing her from behind and wrapping his arms around her while kissing her on the neck. She feigns wanting him to stop and barks orders for the two of them to sit. Harris reluctantly agrees and takes his position at the head of the table as Kyle brings the sweet teas. Andrea brings the main dish then hurries back to get the rice. Kyle sits next to Harris as the Creole goodness gives them both an olfactory workout.

Andrea returns with the rice and looks at Kyle as she sets it on the table and smiles, giving him a wink. His black eye isn't noticeable. They all join hands as Harris prays.

"Dear Lord, thank you for this food which You've so graciously provided to us, and bless it to our bodies. Help us live the life You would have us to and do unto others as we would have them do unto us. Amen."

Andrea takes his plate, piling on the white rice and cheating back on the shrimp, and then loads her and Kyle's. Not much is said, as it is mostly the food doing the talking now. After a few moments of silence, Harris notices Kyle's hair and almost spits out his rice.

"What in the world did you get in your hair, Kyle?"

"Just some color. It'll wash out."

"You mean you did that on *purpose?*"

"Lots of kids are doing it. I think it's—" Andrea adds before Harris cuts her off.

"A lot of *girls*, maybe. Did you do that?" he asks Andrea.

"No, Abby did. At school," Kyle says abruptly.

Harris huffs, giving Andrea a look of frustration. He turns an eye of disappointment to Kyle.

"Well, you tell Abby not to do it again. Tell her you don't want to look like a girl, and make sure you wash that out tonight when you take a shower."

He returns to his meal, his edicts given. Andrea turns her eyes back to Kyle and smiles sympathetically.

"I'm not hungry," Kyle says, putting down his fork. "Can I go watch TV?"

"Finish your dinner fir——" Harris says firmly before being cut off by Andrea.

"Take your plate and set up a TV tray. Just don't spill anything," she says.

Kyle nods, picks up his plate and heads to the living room. Harris looks to Andrea who stares back at him with disappointment.

"What? What did I say?" he asks, confused how he could have ended up the villain in this exchange. Andrea just returns to her meal, silently.

⸺⸺

It's nine o'clock and the onset of sleep draws nigh for the Harris household. Andrea finishes brushing her teeth and makes room for a waiting Harris to squeeze up to the sink. He watches out of the corner of his eye as she pulls the covers back and finds a small gift box. She picks it up and looks to him as he smiles widely at her.

"You didn't think I would forget did you?" he says with a grin.

"I was wondering. You didn't say a word about it this year."

He finishes his nightly oral hygiene and sits on the bed next to her.

"In thirty-five years, have I ever forgotten our anniversary?"

She takes his face in her hands and kisses him softly. "No, you haven't. Thank you."

"Well, go ahead, open it."

She peels off the paper and opens the box revealing a small, silver heart pendant. She gasps as she removes it and reads the engraving '*To Thirty-Five More, Love Albert*'. Her eyes sparkle as she looks up at him.

"Oh Albert, it's beautiful," she says, throwing her arms around his shoulders and hugging him tightly. Jewelry from Albert Harris is truly a special treat, but to have it engraved, something must be bothering him.

"What made you,…"

"I don't know. I've just been thinking a lot, you know? About everything that's going on, Kyle, Miranda. I've just been thinking I need to do more things for you, for us, all of us," he says motioning his hand in a circle to include everyone in the house. "I need to show you more often, not just say it."

"Albert, you show me all the time," she says, blinking tears from her eyes. She hands him the necklace and turns for him to put it on her.

"Yeah, well I need to do better, with you and with Kyle. I need to spend more time with him," he says as he clasps it around her neck.

She rises and admires it in the mirror. She smiles widely, seeing the handsome young man that won her heart thirty-six years ago sitting behind her on the bed. He's a man that has walked by her side through dark and terrifying valleys. He smiles back at her. In that smile, she sees a little glimmer of hope.

Chapter 5

RESUMPTION

M egan clicks a remote on the driver's visor and the gate to the parking area behind her home located in Faubourg Marigny slowly opens. She pulls her Phantom Black, Audi A6 into the lot, watching carefully as the gate closes behind her.

She sighs and clicks the remote again, opening a garage door on the back building. She pulls into the tighter of the two spots available, the wider prime spot reserved for her cherished classic Ford Bronco.

She grabs her bag and shoes from the back seat, and walks in her bare feet through a garage so well stocked with tools, it would make any grease monkey jealous. As she passes the Bronco, she stops and polishes a spot on the hood with the sleeve of her jacket.

She recalls the time she and her father, Wes, mounted the hood on the Bronco. Megan showed an early interest in everything mechanical and she hovered around her father anytime he was repairing or maintaining equipment on the ranch. He was keen to allow her to learn to do things for herself, and he taught her as much as she was willing to learn, sometimes more.

Satisfied that the offending spot has been removed, she smiles and enters the house. She sets her things down on a small table at the bottom of the stairs and resets the security alarm to its 'stay' function, closing the door and locking it behind her. She waits for the characteristic beeping of the alarm to stop before grabbing her things and heading up the steps.

She enters the kitchen and turns on a table lamp, a twisting metal magnolia tree with a soft white light shining through green, muscovite leaves. It's a sculpture created by one of the artisans she rents the first floor to. She doesn't charge him, or the transplanted Californian ceramics artist, market rates. She doesn't have to, and being a bit of an artist herself, she would rather support the local community any way she can, which includes filling her house with its imaginative genius. The creative spirit prevalent in Marigny along with the music, dining, and the laid back atmosphere of the bohemian haven, are the things that attracted her to the area. It is the complete opposite of her law practice.

She admires the lamp, envious of the artistic expression. She dabbled with metal working as a teenager, but gave it up years ago. She thinks to herself that maybe, after thirty-five years on earth, she should take advantage of having such a skilled craftsman downstairs, knock off the rust and give it another try.

Walking through the kitchen and into the living room, she sets her bag on the couch and is greeted by her three-year-old Boxer as he emerges from the hallway, his paws leaving a trail of cat litter behind.

"Oh Frizbee, have you been in the litter box again? Dammit!" she mutters, as he slinks off into the kitchen, guilty as charged. "That's just gross! I'm gonna take you and leave you at Momma's if you keep that up," she adds, shaking her finger at him.

She grabs a broom and, after swatting Friz on the rear, sweeps up the mess he created. Satisfied, she steps into the kitchen and opens a small wine cooler, selecting a favorite chardonnay. As she pours herself a glass, her phone rings.

"Hey, do you want a dog?" Megan says.

"No, I think we have enough. Is he still getting into the litter box?" Ellen, Megan's mother, says through the phone.

"Of course," Megan replies, walking into the living room and stopping at a family picture on a bookshelf.

"Are you coming up this weekend? We're starting on the outdoor kitchen and could use your skills," Ellen says.

"I thought that was next weekend?"

"Nope, this weekend. It's always been this weekend."

Megan sighs audibly through the phone.

"I wish I could. I've just got too much going on, Momma. The Donkova trial is—"

"You need to take some time off."

"I know, I know. Maybe after the trial is over," Megan says with some resignation.

"Don't blame me for caring, Meg. We miss you. I gotta run, talk to you later."

"I miss you, too. Say hello to Rolly for me," Megan says before hanging up.

She picks up the family photo and studies it, smiling as she remembers the day it was taken. In it, she and her sisters sit with her parents, Ellen and Wes, on a stack of hay. She closes her eyes and breathes deeply. She can practically still smell the aroma of the harvest, having unloaded and stacked it earlier that day with her younger sister, Kristi. She opens her eyes and focuses them on her siblings. The smile on her face drops as her gaze remains locked there for a long moment. After a minute she turns her eyes to her father and her smile creeps back in.

She gazes around the room, at the exposed wooden beams that were hidden when she bought the place. She touches the brick walls and remembers scraping the plaster and paint from them herself. She glances down to the hardwood floors, remembering the hours she spent with a sander, breathing life back into the tired planks. The work ethic instilled in her by her father is what got her through law school; it's what got her to where she is now. She looks back at the picture and kisses two of her fingers and softly touches them to her father's cheek.

She picks up her glass and walks through the living room towards her bedroom, recalling the time when she first considered buying the property. The exodus of some who chose not to remain in the city after the storm provided her with the opportunity to take this place and make it her own, to restore it and add her part to the rebuilding of the city, a city she had grown to love.

She smiles remembering that her law partner, Max, had given her grief about buying the 8,000 square foot, 150-year-old "money pit," as he called it.

She laughs, recalling his words. The area was "beneath her." She "needed to stay in Uptown. She had an image to maintain after all." The only image she wanted to maintain was in the courtroom. Some might be surprised to learn that she lives in Marigny, but she feels right at home on this side of town. Anyone that thinks less of her for it, in her opinion, can go to hell.

The beige, two-story Creole-style townhouse, needed work when she bought it, but she wasn't afraid of that. She knows the value of hard work; it's all around her. She poured everything she had into the Burgundy Street property. It was a continuous project, always evolving. Like the artists downstairs, she put her passion into her creation and it paid off. It's her retreat, her solace from the pressure of the practice of law.

She walks into her closet and strips off her skirt and blouse, exchanging them for a sweatshirt, jeans, and a pair of flip-flops. She raises a bedroom window, opening the green shutters to let the cool breeze in from the second floor gallery. She retrieves her glass of wine and heads upstairs to the third floor study added during the renovation.

Opening a set of French doors, she steps out onto a balcony with a view towards the river and the Quarter. Frizbee barrels through chasing Toulouse, her four-year-old Manx.

"Cut it out Friz! Down," Megan says, motioning to him with her fingers which he proceeds to lick. She sighs in disgust, wiping her hand on her jeans recalling where his mouth had previously been.

She sets her glass down on a table and reclines on a chaise-lounge as Toulouse retreats from Frizbee to the safety of the table-top. She waves to her neighbors sitting within the garden on their balcony. She smiles softly, watching and studying the elderly couple; their love for one another still obvious as they sit side by side, holding hands. She looks to her phone, examining it as if using it for the purpose it was designed for were a sin. She grins and dials a number.

"Hey, girl," she says with a smile. "Ha, I thought you'd like that. Can you talk?"

"Okay. Call me when you can," she says after a moment as her smile begins to fade. "I love you, too."

She closes her eyes and breathes deeply, allowing her thoughts to drift to the sounds of Marigny and the bells of St. Louis Cathedral in the distance. Toulouse climbs onto her lap from the table and curls into a purring ball. Frizbee finally gives in and lies down beside her. But her moment of peace is not to be as her phone jolts her back to life.

"Hey, what's up?" she says, rising and stepping towards the French doors. "Sure, come on over. I sent the new gate code in a text. Ciao, Ciao," she says. She takes a sip of wine and smiles at Frizbee. "Your boyfriend's coming over."

Megan opens the garage door just as her best friend, Anna Miller and her dog, a beagle with hormone issues, climb out of Anna's Karmman Ghia. Anna's dog peels out after Frizbee. It's always an odd sight to see a sixty-five-pound boxer running from a twenty-pound beagle. He catches Frizbee at the back of the Bronco and promptly begins trying to mount him.

"Dammit, Rosco, stop it!" Anna yells, chasing after him.

Megan watches Anna as she futilely tries to catch the horny hound. Her eyes focus on Anna's long, dark hair and olive skin, softened by her French, Spanish, and African blood. She smiles remembering the stories that Anna has told her of being able to trace her Creole heritage back to 1820 and Dominique Garnier. She was a free woman of color, consort of Bertrand Cheval, a wealthy French merchant, during the time of Quadroon balls, or so Anna said.

She thinks back to the early days of their friendship, a friendship that couldn't help but turn into more. The first time she saw Anna is never far from her mind; she was volunteering at St. Agnes Women's center where Anna worked. She recalls how her heart seemed to stop in motion, how she was left near speechless by Anna's icy blue eyes. A fire was lit in both of their hearts and followed by a short-lived affair. It's the same fire that Megan still feels the occasional burn of.

"Leave 'em alone, Anna. Rosco loves Friz," Megan shouts as she watches Frizbee snap and bark at Rosco, who incessantly tries to hump him as Anna struggles to pull him away.

Megan and Anna's friendship has endured through the years, despite their sexual relationship ending. Anna simply wanted more than Megan was willing to give her. While Megan loves the female body and spirit, she always felt that someday "he" would come along. She studies the beautiful Anna, as she walks back towards her with Rosco in tow, and considers that perhaps she's fooling herself and in denial like some say. Maybe she should pick a side, the home team, because maybe this "he" is a myth.

"You know it seems appropriate that you would end up with a gay dog," she adds laughing, giving Anna a hug and kiss on the cheek.

"Do you think maybe I shouldn't have self-identified as 'lesbian' on the adoption form at the shelter?" Anna asks with a sigh and a smile.

"I talked to Paul. What happened?" Anna asks after securing Rosco by her side.

"It just..." Megan says, casting her eyes away.

"What?" Anna asks after an awkward moment.

"It just didn't feel right."

She hands Anna a leash. "Let's go," she says, motioning to the dogs.

Anna watches as Megan snaps a leash onto Frizbee's collar, avoiding eye contact with her. After a long moment, Anna does the same and the foursome heads out onto Touro Street, towards the river and Washington Square.

⸻

Washington Square Park, positioned between Frenchmen and Elysian Fields, with its majestic oaks, beautiful central lawn, and once home to the most ignored "No Dogs Allowed" sign in the world, is the centerpiece of the historical Marigny area. As the two friends stroll past the New Orleans AIDS Memorial, Megan throws a tennis ball onto the lawn, causing Frizbee to tear out after it and Rosco to take off after him. The two of them walk without speaking, which is unusual for Anna.

"What's the matter?" Megan asks.

"The usual," Anna sighs.

Said in this context, "the usual" means Michelle, her on-again, off-again girlfriend.

"She's getting possessive again, isn't she?" Megan asks.

"Yeah, and I can't take that. I won't. I love her, but I'm not ready to, you know?" Anna replies as she motions to Frizbee to bring her the tennis ball.

She takes the sopping mess from him and angrily bounces it on the ground several times. She looks back at Megan and then throws the ball back into the field. "See, I've been hanging out with you too long. You're rubbing off on me," she laughs.

"That's not necessarily a good thing. I don't think you want my neuroses," Megan says with a grin.

"Yeah, whatever," Anna says, retrieving the tennis ball from a reluctant Frizbee. "Let's talk about *you*," she adds, tossing her the ball.

"Nothing to talk about," she says, teasing Frizbee with the ball as a frustrated Anna pulls Rosco off of him.

"Oh, I disagree, mon cherie. You're posting poetry like never before, and not your typical dark stuff," Anna says as she makes a gagging expression. "I swear I'm gonna become diabetic reading all that literary sweetness."

Writing is an interest that Megan shares with Anna, having been an avid wordsmith since she was young. Megan is the poet while Anna is the queen of erotica. Megan's love of lyrical verse led her to a website called Poetsbeat a few years ago. Anna joined soon after and began posting erotica under Megan's profile, "Dream Weaver." Anna's reasoning for using Megan's profile was that, even though the website was anonymous, she had shared her own profile with her family, and her mother would die if she knew Anna was writing such scandalous yarns. It didn't bother Megan, since she reaped the benefits of passing Anna's work off as her own. Poetsbeat.com is a place for poets to pour out their hearts, yearning over lost loves and missed opportunities. As with many social websites, it is ripe ground for the formation of online relationships, and Megan had more than a few on the site.

Megan pitches the tennis ball again for Frizbee, who heads off in pursuit, this time sans Rosco.

"Shut up. It's just poetry."

"Who's 'Souls Entwined'…Jennifer? Jen? I mean really, in real life. And don't say 'nobody', cause you know that drives me nuts," Anna adds with a stern look.

"Nobody," Megan replies, tensing up for the arm punch she knows is coming and which immediately does.

"Dammit!" Anna says with a laugh. "I've known the shoe size and how many times a day all your other muses took a crap! Why won't you tell me who she is?"

"Because it's no big deal, okay? She's very protective of her identity, just like I am. But it's cool; I know who she is, and it's all good, so just chill."

"Is she famous?"

"No."

"Is she in prison?"

"No. Will you stop?"

"Can I buy a vowel?"

"I'm going home," Megan answers as she turns and walks away, calling for Frizbee to follow her.

Anna puts the leash back on Rosco and runs to catch up with her.

"Wait up, bitch," she calls.

Megan stops and turns back to her, smiling and cocking her head to the side.

"Don't ask me again."

"Whatever. I'll get it out of you eventually," Anna replies, as they both begin walking back to Megan's place. "What ever happened with you and Veritas?"

"It just didn't work out."

"I thought you guys were hitting it off pretty good."

"We did, it's just…" Megan answers, dropping the rest of the sentence and picking up the pace.

"I can hardly look the guy in the face anymore; I mean, *I* was the one that invited him to join," Anna says, quickly matching Megan's increased clip.

"He's fine. He's a big boy, and he'll be fine. Trust me. I'm fine, we're fine, Jen's fine. Seriously, I'm good Anna. I know you love me and only want the best for me, but I'm fine, okay? What else do you want from me?"

"I just want you to be happy, have a real relationship for once," Anna says. "Not a virtual one. That's worse than long distance."

"I'm trying! I agreed to go out with Paul, didn't I?"

"Yeah, but you didn't even give him a chance."

"It was *just* like all the others. Okay?" Megan says, frustration washing across her face.

Seeing this, Anna quickly hugs her. "It's okay. Damn. I'm sorry, okay? I love you. You know that."

Megan sighs deeply, brushing away the disappointment. She looks at Anna and fakes a smile. "Let's just get home. You can help me refinish those doors."

Megan's shop, in the back building, next to the garage, is nicely equipped with the essentials required by any good do-it-yourselfer. She and Anna are finishing the sanding of a couple of solid-wood doors that Megan picked up from a salvage shop. With goggles, gloves, and hair pulled back into ponytails, the two of them sand away as Rosco and Frizbee mill about, looking as if they have been victims of a wood-dust storm. Megan finishes and moves over to watch Anna, her young Padawan wood worker in training. Anna stops, blows the wood dust away and removes her goggles for a closer inspection.

"Holy crap! That looks good," Anna exclaims of her handiwork.

"See? Daddy always said that to do the job right, you have to use the right tools," Megan says as she picks up the new sander Anna was using and examines it, then smiles as she leans down, examining and running her hand across the doors surface.

"Good?" Anna asks.

"Excellent. You're hired," Megan answers.

"What are you going to do with them?"

"I don't know. I'm thinking a table of some sort."

"Oh, that would be nice. Maybe a long coffee table."

"Maybe. Glass top, perhaps."

Anna's phone beeps with a message from Michelle. She glances back at Megan. The smile and the twinkle in Anna's eyes are a dead giveaway.

"I assume her 'I'm Sorry' text has her back in your good graces?"

"Maybe." Anna answers sheepishly. "She wants to meet down at Three Muses. A friend of hers is performing there tonight. You wanna come?"

"Nah. Gonna turn in early. Got a big day tomorrow."

"You sure?" Anna asks as she dusts herself off heading for the door to collect her things.

"Yeah. I'm sure."

"Suit yourself. We'll miss you. Rosco, let's go boy."

Megan watches the door close behind Anna. She gazes around the shop which is suddenly quiet and cold. She bends down to brush the wood dust from Frizbee. He gazes back with inquisitive eyes. She knows what he's thinking.

"Ice Cream?" she asks, invoking a whimper and a licking of his chops by Frizbee. "Yeah, that's what I thought."

Toulouse has emerged from her hiding place and rests curled up beside Megan, one paw on her arm, as Megan sits in bed, laptop across her lap and several case folders strewn beside her. Frizbee dreams of Rosco, kicking and growling in his bed on the floor. The bedside clock reads 1:30. Megan removes her reading glasses, a recent concession to the aging process, and rubs her eyes. She gathers up the file folders, placing them on the night stand, then logs into the poetry site.

She browses through the new postings by other members and makes a few comments to encourage them in their writing, then navigates to her favorites and selects the "Souls Entwined" profile. She smiles broadly as she clicks on a new posting, entitled "Butterflies".

My Love
from these ashes, this unfulfilled life,
I rise.

A Phoenix seeking to perch
on the arm of its Goddess.
Your voice echoes
in the chambers of my mind.
The sound of my name
crossing your lips
leaves me weak,
butterflies dancing inside.

To my Dream Weaver. Oh baby what you do to me! Love always, Jen.

She smiles and blinks away a few tears then clicks "Comment" and types.

Jen, you always know how to touch my soul with your words. I'm not so sure about the 'Goddess' part, but you can perch with me anytime, girl. I love you. M

She closes her eyes, her thoughts drifting to Jen and their relationship. Even though Anna doesn't realize it, it's more than a casual online romance. Granted, it's not conventional and would be deemed controversial by some, but she makes her laugh; her words stir her heart. Her caress soothes her soul, nourishing a soil she thought barren. They are kindred spirits, speaking a kindred tongue.

She thinks of her father and how he would feel about her relationship with Jen should it move to the next phase. While he certainly wouldn't have an issue with her gender, she can't help but wonder if he would push her towards someone like Paul. Jen isn't exactly the most stable person, bouncing from job to job. She isn't well educated nor does she have a particularly promising future. She can't help but wonder, too, if maybe her father would be right.

She returns her focus to the web page and notices a comment from another user. It's a rambling remark espousing the beauty of the work and how it matches the person it was written for perfectly. She rolls her eyes and shakes her head in disbelief, seeing that the comment is by Veritas, the one with which things "didn't work out," as she said to Anna earlier in the day. She clicks through, opening his profile page.

She slowly scans the titles of the works posted there then selects "Beyond the Fence." It opens and she begins reading the cinquain set beneath its inspiration, Andrew Wyeth's "Christina's World."

Apart,
forbidden love
haunts in silent longing.
He watches her; but he is not
alone.

She sighs softly considering the words and their message. She clicks back to the user's home page and dwells there a moment. A slight smile creeps across her face as she studies the picture of the profile's owner. He's handsome, rugged, and appears to be about thirty with kind, green eyes. The mouse cursor drifts over to "Details" and stops on the status, "Relationship: Married." She looks back at the image a moment then sighs heavily. She cuts her eyes back at that word. Married. She ponders its significance, sitting silently as she seeks answers to puzzles that continue to haunt her. Why was the other half of that relationship able to land a man capable of such beautiful verse? What made *her* worthy of marriage? She grits her teeth and shakes her head, closing the browser.

She looks at Frizbee, then Toulouse, petting her softly on the head, eliciting a fresh round of purring. She closes her laptop, sets it on the floor, pulls the covers up tight, and turns off the lamp.

Chapter 6

RESOURCES

T he courtroom is especially packed today, as final arguments in the Donkova trial have been made. Harris and Robichaux sit with a few other officers in the gallery as the jury returns from deliberation after a surprisingly short amount of time. A very uncomfortable vibe permeates the area around and behind the prosecutor's table where a worried District Attorney Landow consults with an assistant prosecutor. Harris looks to the defendant's table as Megan sits quietly and confidently awaiting the verdict. Victor receives pats of confidence on the back from members of his posse, seated in the gallery behind him. The scene is hauntingly familiar to Harris, who sat in this same courtroom, in this same seat, a few years ago watching Richard 'Dick' Morrison, the most unethical attorney in Orleans Parish, pompously awaiting a different verdict, just as Megan sits there now.

Then, he and Andrea sat surrounded by family, friends, and colleagues. She was a nervous wreck and couldn't bear to watch, instead burying her face in her hands. Harris, filled with hatred, could only watch as the defendant, Phillip, arrogantly chuckled with that bald headed son-of-a-bitch Morrison. Harris struggled inside his own mind to keep his rage from taking control. It welled up like a stone-eyed giant, rampaging from deep within, demanding that he personally pull Phillip limb from limb. He was snapped out of his thoughts and back to his reality by the voice of the jury foreman. He can't remember the man's face, but he'll never forget those words:

We the jury, on the charge of manslaughter, find the defendant not guilty.

Andrea cried out "No!" before collapsing into the arms of her sister. All Harris could do in that moment was watch with stunned disbelief, as Morrison patted a shit-grinning Phillip on the shoulder. Enraged, with the giant inside him now unrestrained, Harris rose and charged the defense table.

"You son-of-a-bitch! He needs to pay!" he cried, as a friend struggled to restrain him.

The judge slammed her gavel down repeatedly, calling for order. The sound of each strike is replaced by the voice of today's bailiff calling all to rise and bringing Harris back to the here and now, at the Donkova trial.

The crowd complies while the judge enters from her chambers. As they return to their seats the judge issues her warnings.

"Let me be clear. I will not tolerate any outbursts in my courtroom, regardless of the verdict," she says, looking directly at Victor and his posse. "Do I make myself clear?"

Satisfied that all parties have been warned she turns to the jury. "Has the jury reached a verdict?"

"We have, Your Honor."

She motions to the bailiff who retrieves the written verdict and returns it to her. She silently reviews it then hands it back for it to be returned.

"Mr. Foreman, will you please read the verdict?" she asks.

"We the jury, in regards to the charge of embezzlement, find the defendant, Victor Donkova, not guilty."

The courtroom erupts with loud shouts from both sides. The judge slams down her gavel repeatedly in anger, calling for order, as Harris watches Megan breathe a sigh of relief and shake Victor's hand. All Harris can do is pat Robichaux on the shoulder and remind himself of the words he spoke to him just a few days ago outside this room—there's a reason for it all.

Harris and a few other officers, stand watching a press conference on the evening news being broadcast on the TV behind the bar as they nurse their defeated
egos, hoping to forget the ass-whipping that Megan gave them today. Mick's
Irish Bar is just the kind of place you would expect members of the NOPD to
adopt as their primary watering hole. It's a popular neighborhood bar not far
from the central office and owned by a retired detective. They welcome the
business and as a result, usually don't have to worry about an unruly crowd getting out of control.

Harris swirls his scotch as he thinks about the futility of months of
work. He wonders about Robichaux and how he's taking it. How could anyone, in good conscience, take the case they presented and flip it, effectively
placing a witness on trial? He's startled out of his thoughts by a familiar
voice from behind him.

"Who's buying?"

He turns to see Detective Sergeant Ron Blanchard, a handsome and dis-
tinguished African-American with a full head of graying hair and prominent
mustache. He's a man who went through the Academy with Harris and they've
remained good friends since. Both Harris and Robichaux are effectively on loan
to the task force but ultimately, through dotted line reporting, they both report
back to Blanchard.

"You are now," Harris says, straight-faced, as the two shake hands.

"How you been, Albert?"

"Been better," Harris says, motioning to the television and the press
conference.

"Yeah, I heard about it."

Blanchard orders an Absolut on the rocks and the two of them watch
silently as District Attorney Landow, in typical politician form with conservative black suit and dark, tightly coiffed hair, stands in front of the camera
and drones on about the "principles that our country was founded upon"
and the "jury of twelve being one of those principles." Harris takes another
drink of his scotch.

"Is it me, or does that guy look like a weasel?" he asks.

"It's not you," Blanchard replies.

When the current state Attorney General announced last year that he would not seek re-election, Landow saw his opportunity for greater fame and power materialize. He has built his campaign around a central theme of "Cleaning Up," touting his successes in Orleans Parish. The loss of the Donkova trial has not helped his campaign. He finishes his speech, smiles his best politician smile, and exits as Megan steps to the podium.

"First, let me agree with one of D.A. Landow's comments. The jury did hear the facts. They also heard the truth. The shameless attempt by the NOPD to entrap Mr. Donkova was—" Megan says before the bartender, sympathetically, changes the channel.

"We had that son-of-a-bitch," Harris says before taking another drink of scotch. "He had a truckload of money and her."

"I really didn't need this shit," Blanchard says as he tosses back the rest of his Absolut.

He looks to Harris and pauses, as if hesitant to say what's on his mind. He pulls a twenty from his pocket and tosses it onto the bar and then turns back to Harris.

"I'm assigning Donaldson to work with—"

"You've gotta be kidding me!" Harris says, cutting him off. He knew this was coming; he just didn't think it would happen so soon.

"Al, don't even think about going there. I've got the integrity bureau so far up my ass right now with Robichaux and this fucking Donkova case, the last thing I need is bullshit from you."

"Come on! What the hell? You know I don't work well with—"

"Don't say it! I swear Al, I love ya like a brother, but if a single *lesbian, dyke, fag, queer, butch* or anything derogatory comes out of your mouth… I won't be able to protect you again."

Harris angrily downs the rest of his drink, slamming the empty glass on the bar.

"I'll see ya later. Say hi to Andrea for me," Blanchard adds with a pat on Harris' shoulder as he leaves.

Harris doesn't look at him. After a moment, he motions to the bartender for another drink and wonders to himself how more fucked up things could get.

On the front steps of the Orleans Parish Criminal Court building, the press conference is wrapping up. As Megan finishes fielding questions from the reporters, John Landow and two assistant D.A.'s make their way down the steps and towards Max Flannigan, who approaches from the sidewalk. As Max draws closer, Landow turns to his assistants.

"You guys go on back. I'll be there in a bit."

Landow watches as they veer to the left towards their office building and once out of earshot range, he takes the final few steps to meet Max, stopping one step short in order to meet him eye to eye.

"What the fuck are you doing?" Landow says through clinched teeth.

Max's physique doesn't match that of a sixty-two-year-old. His shaved head, dark brows, and thin, graying beard and moustache compliment his well-maintained frame. He is an intimidating force, both in and out of the courtroom.

"Nice to see you too, John," Max replies calmly.

"Cut the bullshit, Max! What the hell were you thinking? Threatening me with withholding evidence? Do you have any idea what this loss could do to my campaign?" Max barks, pointing with his thumb over his shoulder towards Megan.

Max looks to the conference, studying the herd for a moment and then slowly turns back to Landow.

"Relax, John. This is just a small bump on the road to your new office in Baton Rouge. Besides—"

"I've put millions in your pocket with those tips. Then you turn around and—" Landow growls before stopping himself as a person approaches.

Max watches as they walk past and after a moment, casts his eyes back to Landow.

"What John? Bite the hand that feeds me?" he says as he takes one step up and closer, his six-foot-three-inch frame now towering over Landow. He glances towards Megan and an assistant attorney who walk slowly down the steps and away from the dispersing conference, then back at Landow and points with his index finger like a professor giving a lecture and making his key point.

"You need to remember who controls your largest contributors," Max says dryly. "Your campaign just got a little tougher. I'll keep my bitch on a leash. You just be careful you don't shit where you eat."

He raises his hand, causing Landow to blink and flinch. He smiles, pats him softly on the shoulder and then turns up the steps towards Megan.

"Nice to see you again, John," he says over his shoulder.

Landow fumes as he watches him meet Megan half way up the steps. He looks around to make sure no one witnessed the tongue-lashing he just received, straightens his jacket and heads down the sidewalk towards his office.

Inside the dark pink granite and glass walls of the Place St. Charles building, a behemoth of power that towers fifty-two stories over the Central Business District, New Orleanian movers, shakers, and power-brokers navigate the treacherous waters of industry, commerce, and law. Within the thirty-third floor executive conference room overlooking Harrah's, the mighty Mississippi, and the historic St. Charles Streetcar, whose wood and brass interior harkens back to the glory days of the city in 1835 when it began service, there's a victory celebration taking place.

"Megan, my dear, you've become the daughter I never had. Thank you so much for what you have done. If I can ever do anything for you, be sure you let me know. Okay?" a very appreciative Victor says, shaking her hand and then wrapping his arms around her.

Megan's body tenses and her breathing stops as Victor hugs her tightly.

"I will Victor, I will," she manages to reply through an inaudible sigh after he releases her.

As he backs away from her, she glances to his hands, noticing a pronounced tremor. While still able to project an intimidating presence at sixty-five, Victor is a shadow of his former self. A life of hard living and a heart condition have taken their toll on him, Megan had decided. Victor coughs and is steadied by one of his bodyguards, the larger of the two that are always on his flank. She watches "The Russian," as Megan had nicknamed him, help Victor into a chair. He's a bear of a man and judging by his stoic demeanor, buzz-cut, and chiseled body, Megan deduced early on that he's former Russian military. The other guard, dubbed "The Persian," with shaved head, a couple of questionable scars on his face, and evil, soulless eyes, quickly pours a glass of water and hands it to Victor.

"Are you okay?" Megan asks in Russian.

"Yes, yes my dear. I'll be fine. I should quit smoking, at least that's what my doctors tell me," Victor replies.

She nods to Max who sighs softly, the concern on his face replaced by relief. She shakes her head knowing that Max's distress has nothing to do with Victor and everything to do with the money that he will pay for his defense in the still pending Federal case.

As she watches Max struggle to communicate with Victor, her mind drifts back to her earliest days in the city. She, like Victor, was an immigrant and she absorbed the diversity that the city offered while struggling at times to understand some of the unique dialects she heard every day. But she never felt the sense of not being welcome, unlike the Americans that arrived after the Louisiana Purchase in 1803. The animosity that existed between them and the Creole population was so intense that the esplanade center of Canal Street was known as "Neutral Ground," separating the Creole old city from the new American city upriver. There in the esplanade meetings between the hostile parties would occur.

Feeling only a slight hint of sympathy for Max, she rejoins their conversation discussing today's victory and what the future holds, or doesn't hold, for the Federal case. Out of the corner of her eyes, she notices the Russian watching her closely as she speaks with Victor. He's been this way since she first met Victor a year earlier. While aware of his admiration, she has little interest in anything other than a professional relationship.

Victor and Megan speak in Russian while she translates as best she can for Max. She's a quick learner, and the linguistic coach Max hired quickly brought her up to conversational level Russian early on in the case.

They all shake hands, and Victor and his guards make their way out, the big guy giving Megan one last look and a smile before leaving. As the door closes behind them, Max turns to Megan.

"Congratulations. Must have been that closing argument."

"Thanks, Max," she replies, waiting for the other shoe to drop. There's always a "but" when it comes to Max Flannigan.

He begins to leave and then, on cue, turns back, not quite so happy this time. "But… don't ever threaten the DA with evidence manipulation charges without clearing it with me first."

"Max, it was a calculated—"

"It was bullshit! It could have backfired."

She grits her teeth, choking back the first words that come to her mind. She looks out the window, choosing her words carefully. She turns back to Max and begins to speak but he immediately cuts her off.

"My firm, my rules. Got it?"

"Got it," she says as frustration with the unappreciative Max washes over her.

"I'm taking you off the Elliot case," he says as he turns and begins to exit.

"Why?" she asks, eyes squinted and brow furrowed as she considers for a moment asking Max to step outside to center of Canal Street.

"You've got it pretty airtight. I think Darby is more than capable of finishing it," he states as he turns back to her.

They exchange a long look and the real reason for this sudden change becomes clear to her.

"Does this have anything to do with Landow and today?"

"This is about resource allocation."

"Resource allocation?"

"Look… you did a great job—"

"You know what Max? *This* is bullshit! I'm the best fucking attorney you've got, and you do this? Your investment in Landow feeling a little risky after that ass-whipping I just gave him?"

"Careful with your accusations."

"Maybe it's best if I just take some time off, get my head together, figure out what I want to do with my life. I'm sure Darby can handle my full case load," she adds as she gathers up her things.

"Megan, I don't think—"

"Because the one thing I don't need right now is to worry whether you're gonna pull the rug out from under me on the next case, too, because you're more interested in getting Landow into office than justice," she says as she begins to leave the room.

"Megan, hang on a sec," Max yells to the door as it closes behind her. He may have just lost his best attorney.

Chapter 7

CONSEQUENCES

In Megan's line of work, it's not uncommon to receive death threats from those who have felt harmed by the ones she defends in court. She takes precautions to protect her identity and address online so it seemed logical to enroll in self-defense training when Anna suggested it to her a year ago. The afternoon dustup with Max has Megan eager to discharge her frustration on the mat inside a gym near Magazine Street and Jefferson Avenue.

"I'm not driving all the way into Algiers just so I can say I'm taking Krav Maga," Megan says with frustration as she leans across an outstretched leg, touching her toes.

"But they've got these bitching shirts," Anna retorts, pulling one leg behind her and mimicking Megan's pose.

"Then go buy the bitching shirt," Megan snaps.

The loud, rhythmic beat of "Elephant" by Tame Impala blasting through the gym's sound system grows louder and louder, while the silence between them becomes the actual elephant in the room. After an awkward moment and feeling Anna's eyes on her, Megan looks over to her.

"Guess somebody got their period, huh?" Anna says dryly.

"I'm sorry," Megan says, switching positions and stretching her other leg out in front. "It's just...I like it here. I like Magazine Street. I like the trees. I like the art. I used to live in Uptown, now I live in Downtown, I work in the CBD. What's next? Should I shop lakeside in Metarie?"

Anna stares at Megan and after a moment, both return their attention to their stretching exercises, mimicking the curving crescent shape of the river, one that earned the city one of its many nicknames, The Crescent City. The tension in the room belies the calm and enchanting atmosphere of the surrounding Garden District, so named for the large and extravagant yards and gardens that surround the Antebellum homes of the 1800's that adorn its thoroughfares.

The beats flowing through the club's speakers fade, and "Habits" by Tove Lo, begins its slow rhythm. Anna smiles widely and jumps to her feet. It's the perfect song to change the mood. Megan, always buoyed by the impulsive Anna, smiles and laughs as Anna begins dancing seductively next to one of the gym's power racks. Anna wraps both hands around one of the rack's vertical supports, using it as an impromptu stripper pole, while singing in perfect time and quickly drawing a small audience.

Anna tugs at the top of her tights, pulling them down, revealing a hip tattoo, an image of the night they both went under the needle resulting in matching marks of a phoenix rising, its beautiful feathers draping down and around the thigh. Memories of tracing those feathers with her fingers flash through Megan's mind, as Anna continues her sultry dance.

At the chorus, Anna reaches down and pulls a reluctant Megan from the floor. Anna slides in close to her, straddling one leg with hers. She wraps one arm around Megan's waist and runs a finger across Megan's cheek as she finishes the chorus.

"*Spend my days locked in a haze, trying to forget you babe, I fall back down, Gotta stay high all my life to forget I'm missing you. Ooh-ooh, ooh-ooh,*" she croons, just inches from Megan's face.

Perhaps it's the crowd, slowly building around them. Perhaps it's the uneasy feeling, the shortening of her breath as she looks into Anna's eyes. Perhaps it's seeing a fire there, one she recognizes, that causes Megan to pull away.

"Stop. Just stop," Megan says through a nervous laugh.

Anna's wide smile droops and her eyes fill with disappointment; the same disappointment Megan saw for weeks after their relationship ended. The touch of Anna's hands on her hips feels suddenly cold.

"I'm sorry, Anna," Megan says with an uneasy smile. "And I'm sorry for snapping at you."

"It's okay," Anna says, raising her hands slightly, acknowledging the 'hands-off' vibe permeating the air around them. "I just thought maybe a change would be good."

Though Megan's sour mood has been successfully expelled, Anna's show has added a new layer of tension. Anna must feel it too, because she changes the subject to a safer topic—work—as the two of them make their way to the class.

"So I guess Max was happy with the results today, huh?" she asks.

"Yeah," Megan replies rather sarcastically.

"That wasn't a very enthusiastic 'yeah'. What was the 'but' this time?"

"The 'but' was… I quit."

Anna stops dead in her tracks.

"You quit?"

"Sorta."

"Sorta? How do you *sorta* quit?"

"I'm just gonna take some time off. Officially, it's a sabbatical,"

"Holy shit!" Anna exclaims, shaking her head trying to imagine the workaholic Megan Callahan not working.

"What are you gonna do?"

"Just breathe for a while," Megan says, as she lets out a heavy sigh. "Maybe I can help out down stairs, take out my frustrations out on some metal."

"Maybe you could open a mechanics shop," Anna jokingly adds as she waves her hand through the air. "Megan Callahan, Grease Monkey."

"Yeah, something like that I guess," Megan says, still not sure what she will do, still not ruling out the possibility that she's made a mistake.

The beckoning of the instructor that class is about to start breaks the conversation and Anna takes the opportunity to bring up a touchy subject.

"I talked to Paul today. He asked about you."

"Anna, I don't think your cousin wants—"

"*Staying in my play pretend where the fun ain't got no end, ooh,*" Anna sings softly.

"Shut up," Megan responds with a slight laugh.

"I'm just saying," Anna says, stepping in front of Megan and throwing her hands up.

"Since you're taking some time, maybe it's a sign from the universe, you know? A new start. Maybe the time's right."

"I don't know. I just——"

"Let's go to Three Muses Friday night, the four of us. Just one date," Anna asks pleadingly.

Megan stops and looks at Anna for a moment. Maybe she's right. Maybe the timing *is* symbolic. Maybe the stars have aligned. Maybe things will be different. Maybe the universe, the fates, or maybe even God if he still cares about her, is trying to tell her something. Maybe it's time to make a change, take a chance, try to live, and trust someone, particularly if that someone is a man.

⁂

Megan and Anna sit at a table for two with four chairs shoehorned in, not far from a small stage inside Three Muses, as Paul retrieves the first of the night's refreshments from the one-hundred-year-old cypress wood bar. The two of them adjust the table closer to the dark, block-paneled walls, attempting to make room for another party that has arrived next to them.

"Look at that line outside," Anna says loudly, leaning into Megan in an effort to overcome the crooning of the musician, an odd fellow from Chile who seems far too old to be wearing a blue do-rag.

"I know. It's not our little secret anymore is it?" Megan replies.

Frenchmen Street has grown in popularity in recent years, especially among locals who are seeking good food, drink, and music away from the overly commercialized Bourbon Street. With The Three Muses having all three of those relished elements, it makes for a crowded scene and Paul carefully weaves his way through tightly bunched tables, balancing three drinks in two hands. He sets them down and heads back to the bar, returning with an appetizer.

The trio nibbles on fried green tomatoes with shrimp remoulade as Paul and Anna discuss the merits of Anna's ailing Karmann Ghia and whether she should sell it. Megan, detached from the conversation, steals glances at the bartender, who occasionally passes the glances back at her, breaking away when they do make eye contact. Someone across the way strains his eyes at Megan, like he might know her, but she can't tell who it is. Anna's phone beeps with a message, which, after reading it, causes her to moan in disappointment.

"Dammit!

"She's not coming is she?" Megan asks

"She had to work late. Again," Anna replies.

Sensing the tension, Paul tries to change the subject, directing his question to Megan.

"So what about you? Do you write on the poetry site too?"

"I dabble. Anna here, she's the real writer."

"Yeah right; I'm a hack," Anna says.

"Have either of you ever had anything published?"

"I don't think I want to. Too many published poets end up dying weird deaths," Anna says.

The man from across the way pushes through the crowd. He bumps into their table, sending their drinks spilling across the top.

"Megan Callahan?"

Anna tenses up; she's seen these occurrences get nasty. Megan straightens in the chair and stiffens, bracing for what might follow.

"Yes?"

"How do you sleep at night?" he asks, anger in his eyes.

Megan looks to Anna and smiles. She's handled guys like this before, and she'll handle this one the same way.

"Oh, mostly on my side, pillow between my legs usually. I just hate it when my knees touch," she says dryly and with straight face.

"You smart-ass," the man snarls, scowling and moving closer to her. Patrons at nearby tables begin to take notice. Paul rises to move between the man and Megan, but she pushes him away. The man moves in close enough that Megan can practically taste the Jameson on his breath.

"Just because Victor Donkova was found innocent doesn't mean he didn't have victims. My wife and I lost everything to that son-of-a-bitch and thanks to you, he's a free man."

Megan looks at Anna, then down at the table, picks up what's left of her gin and tonic and takes a drink. She places her napkin atop the wasted cocktail, pooling on the table surface, then calmly sets the drink down before facing the man once more.

"I don't know who you are, and I don't really care. I did my job and defended a man that the jury—not I—decided was innocent."

The Chilean crooner stops and backs away from the action, protectively clutching his guitar. The bartender arrives, stepping between the man and Megan.

"Let's take it outside, brah," he orders.

"Fuck off!" the man barks back into the bartender's face.

Looking past him and back at Megan, the man shakes his finger in her face.

"I wouldn't expect you to care, you heartless bitch! You should be careful. What you do has consequences."

The bartender grabs the man's hand and twists it down and around then up behind the man's back. He quickly escorts him out the front door, closely followed by the man's female companion who has sat watching the incident in shock.

A patron exits the bathroom, whistling a tune while adjusting his trousers. He stops blank, not expecting to hear his musical melody echo from the walls. His gaze soon matches the others in the room. Megan can feel every eye on her. After a very uncomfortable moment, she grabs her bag and heads out the door. A stunned Anna follows while Paul, confused as hell, throws forty dollars on the table. As Megan exits, the bartender re-enters. He backs up to let her through and they exchange a look, pausing there for a moment. Finally, she mouths "Thank You," and continues out the door.

Chapter 8

APPEARANCES

Two traumatic events with Paul were enough for Megan and she called it an early night, preferring not to stick around for the third strike. She retreated to the safety of her home—and its security system. After a restless night, she finally shook off the previous day's drama.

In the two weeks since, Megan has learned to us a plasma cutting torch in the metal shop on the first floor. She tried her hand at pottery, but quickly determined that wet palms, clay, and a potter's wheel were not her forte. The time away from the soul-crushing environment of the office left her scolding herself for not taking more time off in the past. She's read a couple of novels, spent hours talking with Jen, and written three new works of poetry. But quiet time, introspection, and phone calls could only do so much.

Determined to give the Fates a chance, to listen to the Universe for a change rather than her fears, she wanted to get out, to go somewhere. Her invitation to Jen to go to Key West together fell flat. "The time's not right" and "I'm just not ready" Jen had said. Megan understands fear, but that did little to ease the frustration of having to settle for more of the same. What frustrated Megan further was the sense of relief she felt, whispered upon a stolen sigh.

Today, however, is a new day, a new beginning. Anna was surprised when Megan agreed to go with her to the Alligator Festival in Luling. It was an invitation that Megan had always turned down. Small in footprint but not in attendance, crowds of people fill the West Bank Bridge Park the last weekend of September for food, rides, and some of the best home grown music New Orleans has to offer.

The oppressive Louisiana humidity is in full swing, and while it is the end of September, it is still fairly warm. On the main festival stage, a zydeco band plays as Megan stands in the crowd, cheering and enjoying the music while Anna speaks to some friends as she waits in line at the booth of Bobby's Gator Crew, creator of the finest alligator gumbo in all of Louisiana. While crawfish and alligator provide sustenance for people around the world, few areas can match New Orleans in the popularity of the creatures as a food source. With the abundance of surrounding wetlands, swamps, bayous, and marshes, both species propagate well and their popularity and use in recipes is prolific.

The festival celebrates the end of the annual, thirty-day alligator hunting season. While the alligator is raised commercially for both meat and skin, the large population that lives wild in the swamps of Louisiana must be controlled. They are, after all, predators near the top of the food chain and have been known to kill livestock, pets, and even people. Each year hunters are provided a limited number of tags which allow the harvest of alligators from the wild during a limited hunting season.

Mixed into the same crowd are Harris, Andrea, and Kyle. The festival is an annual event for Harris and his family, albeit a reluctant one on his part. Andrea enjoys the craft booths while Kyle is always eager to ride every ride at the carnival, twice. On the other hand, Harris could do without the heat, humidity, and hubbub of the crowds, who oftentimes enjoy the beverages a bit too much for his taste. He would much rather be home on this Saturday tending to his lawn, but he's being a good sport about it and using the time to try and connect with a still distant Kyle.

As the band finishes their set, the crowd cheers wildly, and one of those over imbibing attendees manages to spill beer on Harris' foot. He resists the urge to arrest and handcuff her for public intoxication, and shakes off the spillage as the woman drunkenly apologizes.

Megan turns to meet back up with Anna and bumps into a man standing a bit too close behind her.

"Sorry," she says as she skirts around him.

"You can bump into me anytime you like, beautiful," the man says, pivoting and studying her as she walks past.

She ignores the man's comment and meets up with Anna and their friends next to the twelve-foot stuffed alligator that is Bobby's trademark. She straddles it, posing for a friend to take a couple of pictures.

"Wow! Those guys were great! Did you hear them?" she asks Anna, adding "Why haven't you ever told me about this?"

"I have, and like you would have come. I've been coming here for years and I always ask you, but you were always too busy."

As Megan rides the beast like a horse; a male friend joins her in the shot by kneeling and placing his head in the enormous carnivore's mouth.

A now thoroughly irritated Harris, along with the rest of his group, emerges from the crowd and makes their way towards Bobby's. The man that Megan bumped into is watching her perform her best cowgirl impression as Harris and crew pass by.

"Fuck! Wish I was that gator. I'd roll over and fuck the shit out of that!" the man exclaims loudly.

"Watch your mouth. There are kids here," Harris snaps as he stops and turns back to the man.

The man, with shaved head and numerous tattoos adorning his body and up his neck, doesn't look pleased to receive instructions. Harris scans him up and down and quickly determines that he is probably a meth addict here to pick a few pockets. After a short stare down, the man holds out both clinched fists, the words 'Fuck' and 'You' tattooed across his knuckles. That's, perhaps, not the wisest thing to do to an already pissed off cop whose .40 caliber Glock Model 27 pistol seems to twitch in its shoulder holster. Harris looks at the bald headed freak and takes a step toward him. Andrea reaches and pulls Harris' arm.

"Come on... let's go," she says softly.

The man laughs, pointing at Harris like he was just schooled, then turns and disappears into the crowd. A frustrated Harris turns back to Andrea.

"Let's just get outta here."

"Let's go see Bobby first. I promised him we would."

He reluctantly agrees, and joins her and Kyle at the edge of the booth, within an arm's length of Megan who has joined Anna in the line. Andrea gives him a smile, attempting to lighten his mood, then closes her eyes and breathes in deeply. Bobby's variant of gumbo includes alligator, shrimp, crab, and oysters. Aromas of the sea, joined by those of the Holy Trinity and the Pope mixed with oregano, basil, and cayenne pepper, fill the air, clamoring with the boisterous sounds of the festival for attendee's attention.

Megan looks at Harris; pretty sure that she recognizes his face, if not his serious demeanor. After a moment she steps over and taps him on the shoulder.

"Harris?"

He turns and focuses, then recognizes her. She's not exactly someone that will raise the spirits of an already dour Harris, but he fakes a smile.

"Callahan. How are you?"

"I'm great. Wasn't sure you would recognize me, no suit and all," she says with a smile.

"How could I forget?" Harris asks dryly.

Megan smiles off the jab, and after a moment Harris remembers his manners.

"This is my wife, Andrea."

"Hi. Megan Callahan. Nice to meet you," she says to Andrea, shaking her hand, then noticing the necklace that Andrea is wearing, her latest creation finished just in time for the festival.

"Where did you get that necklace? It's absolutely beautiful!" Megan exclaims, fawning over the stone and bead work.

"Why thank you. Actually I made it," Andrea answers, blushing with pride.

A normally reserved Kyle has been staring at Megan ever since she tapped Harris on the shoulder. A bit wide-eyed, he walks up to her.

"Hi."

She looks down to him, studying the streaks of gold and red in his hair. An earlier visit to the face-painting booth has adorned his cheek with a butterfly of white, green, and red, trailing golden glitter behind it.

"Well hello. What's your name?" she asks with a smile as she kneels down so she can meet him eye-to-eye.

"Kyle. What's yours?"

"My name's Megan," she answers, a bit taken by the cute kid.

"Is this your…" she asks as she looks up to Harris.

"Grandson, yeah. He's a bit of a mess. Ignore the paint and stuff."

She turns back to Kyle and smiles. She looks square into his eyes, examining, as if studying the intricacies of his essence.

"You remind me of a young version of a very good friend," she says as she runs her hand through his hair, eliciting a smile from him. She studies at him a moment longer then motions him closer to her.

"I wanna tell you something."

He leans in as Megan whispers in his ear.

"I think your hair's pretty, and I *love* the butterfly."

He smiles widely as she rises and affectionately touches the top of his head. Harris may not like her, but she's made a new friend in Andrea who seems truly touched by the kindness that she is showing Kyle. She studies Megan, as if trying to match her up with some vague memory. A loud shout from behind the front table of the booth grabs everyone's attention.

"Albert! Andrea! You made it! Kyle, hey little man, come here," exclaims Bobby Dubois, proprietor of this fine establishment and Andrea's first cousin. Straight out of a Louisiana swamp reality show, Bobby is a bear of man with a thick Cajun accent.

Kyle looks back to Megan, smiles, waves goodbye, and dives under the table and up next to Bobby where they exchange a secret handshake. She watches, wistfully, as Kyle glances back to her then says something which Bobby doesn't quite understand. He leans in closer as Kyle whispers in his ear.

Bobby looks to Megan for a moment, then back to Kyle and nods agreement. Sensing her uneasiness with clearly being talked about, Bobby eases her concerns.

"It's okay missy. He think you pretty," Bobby says with a grin, causing Kyle to slink away in embarrassment and slide under the table and back by Andrea's side.

"How are you Bobby? How was your season?" Harris asks as Andrea and Bobby share a hug.

"Al, let me tell ya, 'd best season I've had in years. Tagged out in twenty-five days. Caught some monsters, ya know."

Kyle has moved next to Harris and tugs on his hand.

"Paw Paw, come on. Let's go ride some rides."

"Al, you better go get that boy on some rides 'fore he pull you finger off," Bobby exclaims.

"We'll stop back by in a bit, Bobby. Save some gumbo for us," Harris says as Kyle pulls him away from the table.

"You got it, Al," Bobby says as he and Andrea share one last hug.

The three of them leave, heading over to the whirling wheels of gastric suicide. Once out of earshot range, Harris touches Kyle's shoulder and leans down to him.

"What did you say to Bobby about Megan?"

"I said she looks like momma."

Harris turns to look at Megan, who watches them as they leave. He had never seen it, but the kid just might be right. He turns back to Andrea who appears to have also put the pieces together. Kyle drops back a bit as Harris and Andrea move ahead. He looks back at Megan. She smiles and waves at him like a kid. He smiles and waves back and then runs to catch up with his grandparents.

Saturday at the festival is marked by a day-long string of performances by several bands from across Louisiana, which runs well into the night, wrapping up around eleven. Megan, Anna, and a late arriving Michelle disperse with the other members of the crowd as Megan checks her phone and casually scans the confluence, as if searching for someone.

Anna and Michelle walk hand-in-hand with Anna carrying a large stuffed alligator, a prize for Michelle's skill with an air rifle.

"What the hell am I gonna do with this thing?" Anna asks.

"Cuddle pillow?" Michelle replies.

"Give it to Rosco. Maybe he can work out some of his frustrations with it," Megan says with a smile as she checks her phone again and sighs when she finds no messages.

"I don't wanna even think about that. You better let me keep it at my place," Michelle says, cringing at the thought of a Rosco-violated stuffed animal ending up as a hastily grabbed pillow. "You guys ready to go?" she adds.

"Please?" Anna, worn out from the day's events, says as she lays her head on Michelle's shoulder.

Megan checks her phone again then scans the crowd.

"You guys go ahead. I'm gonna hang around and check out this last band."

"What are you up to?" Anna asks, her interest peaked by all of Megan's phone checking.

"Nothing. Just wanna hear this next band. I've heard good things about them."

"Are you meeting someone?"

Megan looks away and doesn't answer, prompting the inquisitive Anna to probe deeper.

"Are you meeting Paul?"

"No, Anna. I just want to hear these guys, okay?"

"Yeah, right. I'm not buying that bullshit."

Megan checks her phone again and then gives in.

"It's Jen. Okay?"

"Jen? Who's Jen?" Michelle asks with a smile.

"That's what I've been asking. Oh my God. She's gonna be here? Tonight?" a suddenly reinvigorated Anna asks.

"Anna, please just go home. I'm not ready for you to meet her yet," Megan says, shaking her head in frustration.

"I don't care. I'm ready to meet her. What's the big deal? You ashamed of me or something?"

"Fuck off," Megan answers with a smile. "The time's just not right. She's not ready. So show some respect, okay? You'll meet her soon enough."

Michelle leans into Anna and whispers into her ear, running her arms around Anna's waist and one hand down to her butt. As she whispers, Anna's eyes slowly light up.

"You are one bad Cajun," Anna says, face to face with Michelle while running a finger across her lips.

Michelle smiles to Megan who returns it, thankful for the cover that she just provided.

"Okay, we're gonna go now. *But* you have to promise me that I'll get to meet her. Soon," Anna says half-paying attention to Megan and half already back in the bedroom at her place.

"I promise. Now go," Megan answers

She watches them stroll off towards the parking lot for a moment and then yells out.

"Anna?"

"Yeah?" she replies, turning around but continuing to walk backwards alongside Michelle.

"Make sure you write about it… and post it," Megan says with a grin.

Anna gives her a thumb up, turns, slaps Michelle on the rear and fades into the crowd. Megan's phone buzzes. She looks at it, smiles, then turns and walks away.

Chapter 9

STOLEN

A light rain falls on the moss green Bronco as it sits in the parking area at the festival. Wes and Megan gave it a decent restore when they worked on it together, but she has added a few improvements in the last couple of years. Raised with a four-inch lift and riding on thirty-five-inch Mickey Thompson with Pro-Comp shocks, white accents, and fender flares, it's a beautiful specimen of classic Broncos. While Megan has taken measures to improve the ride and safety of a vehicle not known for road stability, she has left the interior as stock as possible, including newly reupholstered, original, white seats.

She turns the key, firing up the V-8, and wipes her face and hair free of the rain that was an unwelcome guest at this year's festival. She checks her mirrors, and seeing a few other car headlights fire up, smiles, throws the Bronco in gear and heads out onto River Road, then up the ramp and onto I-310.

Halfway across the mighty Mississippi, she's greeted by a string of brake lights that looks to be miles long. She grabs her phone, dials, and listens to the call go straight to voice mail. As the traffic ahead of her rolls to a stop, she turns on the radio and navigates to a satellite station for New Orleans traffic. There's a major accident on 310 just before the I-10 interchange, with traffic crawling by on a left shoulder. With no service road and practically no surface roads in that stretch, this could take hours to get through.

She retries her call, but it again goes straight to voice mail. She considers her options, or option as it is, and takes the exit on the east side of the bridge and down onto 48, the East Bank River Road. She'll take it east until she can cut back up to Airline Drive, then back to 310 and past the accident. From there, it should be a quick trip to I-10 and back home. From the number of cars taking the same route, it seems her idea isn't that novel.

Traffic moves slowly along River Road, as Megan passes the massive and ancient oaks, dripping with Spanish moss, of Destrehan Plantation, a landmark Greek Revival style plantation built in 1790. She thinks of Max and the portrait of the plantations namesake, Jean-Noël Destréhan, which hangs in his office. She shakes her head, remembering a conversation with Max when he stated that if it were not for his ancestors New Orleans would still be a muddy, backwater of a city. She laughs to herself as she thinks of the irony that a man, who can be so sour, lays claim to a family heritage of sweetness, one that perfected the granulation of sugar and paved the way for the explosive growth of the city.

She passes the oil tank farms lining the rivers bank and approaches the community of St. Rose. She re-tries the call from earlier, only to be disappointed again.

"Where is she?" she says with frustration.

It's hard enough to see out of a classic Bronco, and with the increasing rain, the small wipers struggle to clear the windshield for her. She checks the GPS on her phone and sees an option. She turns left onto 626/St. Rose Road. It's a straight shot north, under 310 and then to Airline and, hopefully, that late night dinner she's trying to get to.

Her phone rings as she turns onto St. Rose, as do a few other weary travelers. She picks it up. It's Jen.

"Hey, girl... where are you? Did you get stuck in that mess on 310? Shit, I wish I had known before I got on the bridge. I'm winding through on River Road, should be past it soon. Okay. I love you, too."

She hangs up and smiles, her night back on track. As she drives, she considers what moved the Fates to allow her to meet a woman like Jen. She had never even given thought to meeting someone like her, or that she would have become so smitten so soon. The more she thinks about it, the more it makes sense to her, though; they connect on so many levels.

As she crosses a set of railroad tracks, her pleasant thoughts are interrupted by a truck that rushes dangerously by, forcing her to slow down and ease to the side of the road.

"I hope they find you in a ditch, jerk," she yells through the glass, as the truck speeds ahead into the rain and darkness and the swamp closes in on the road.

She shakes it off and turns the radio back on and smiles as *Saving Me* by Nickleback blares from the speakers, the lyrics of which Jen often sings to her during their late night phone calls.

Her thoughts drift back to when she first met Jen a couple of months ago at a small bar not far from her house after getting to know her through the poetry site. Jen's writings touched a nerve in her, and it was clear that they both had been through some dark days and shared similar demons. That night in the bar, when she first looked into her eyes, she knew there was something special between them. Honestly, it scares her, as she hasn't felt this way in a long time... a very long time.

The rain continues to pour down and the Bronco's wipers sweep as fast they can, while Megan loudly joins Chad in singing the last chorus. Out of the darkness, she sees brake lights on the side of the road. The vehicle lunges into her lane. She screams, jerking the wheel hard to the left, reeling out of control and into the swamp.

The Bronco sits smashed against a tree, taillights blinking and steam pouring from the destroyed front end. The truck that pulled out in front of her rolls to a stop in the middle of the road. The door opens and a man gets out, dashing towards the Bronco while pulling on a pair of gloves. He runs into the knee deep water and up to the driver's door and a bleeding and half-conscious Megan. The broken and bloodied windshield and the bent steering wheel are proof that shoulder restraints were a good invention, as the simple lap belt in the stock Bronco seat offered her little protection.

Barely coherent, with blood streaming from cuts on her face, she looks up to the man and tries to speak. He surveys the road, quickly scanning both directions. He draws back a fist and punches her in the face. Megan doesn't say a word. She can't. The blow knocks her completely unconscious.

Chapter 10

MESSAGES

S unday mornings are a series of rituals for Harris. It's a day of rest, officially sanctioned by God, and the early morning hours allow Harris time to read his Bible, catch up on world events with the Sunday edition of the *Times Picayune*, then breakfast followed by their weekly attendance at the New Hope Baptist Church.

Still in his pajamas, Harris sits in the living room in his favorite chair finishing a story in the sports section of the paper about the Saint's upcoming game against division rival Carolina Panthers. He folds the paper and tosses it onto the stack of unread sections and picks up his Bible from a side table. Raised Catholic, he drifted away from the church during his college years. However, God wasn't done with him and sent an Angel named Andrea whom Harris followed like a puppy into the Protestant faith. While some in Harris' line of work have turned to the bottle as their salvation, he turned to God to help him make sense of the brutal crimes that he investigates, or at least that he used to. He flips open the Bible to a bookmarked page and begins reading in the first chapter of Second Corinthians.

Praise be to the God and Father of our Lord Jesus Christ, the Father of compassion and the God of all comfort, who comforts us in all our troubles, so that we can comfort those in any trouble with the comfort we ourselves receive from God.

He looks up to a bookshelf and a family picture of the four of them, taken when Kyle was just an infant. He gazes at their faces, captured there in that moment of time, a happier time. He returns his attention to the scripture and finds a cross reference. He flips back to the thirteenth chapter of the book of First Corinthians.

> *Love is patient, love is kind. It does not envy, it does not boast, it is not proud.*
> *It does not dishonor others, it is not self-seeking, it is not easily angered, it*
> *keeps no record of wrongs. Love does not delight in evil but rejoices with the*
> *truth. It always protects, always trusts, always hopes, always perseveres.*

His eyes focus on the last verse, the last two words. He stares at them, blankly, as he considers his life the last few years. He closes his Bible and looks back to the photograph for a moment. He smiles slightly, studying Miranda. She has her mother's smile. He sighs softly and sets his Bible on the table. He rises and makes his way to the kitchen. There's breakfast to be made.

The rain has stopped and the sun begins to rise, peaking through a few large oak trees standing guard over a home that at one time was surely proud, but has now been long forgotten. A faint orange glow is visible through a broken window. Inside, within an incorporeal mist, Megan kneels by the edge of a lake on a cool fall evening. She gazes into the calm water and sees the reflection of herself at sixteen years old. She touches it, causing ripples which glow with the light of a nearby campfire. She looks to her right at her father, Wes, who sits, warming himself by the fire.

"There's my angel. Come sit by me," he says as he pats the log he sits on.

Smoke from the fire shifts in the wind and wafts towards her, causing her to cough. She rises and stares at Wes. It's been so long since she's seen him; she really isn't sure it's him. She coughs again as the smoke thickens around her.

"Meg. Over here sweetie, out of the smoke," Wes says, his expression becoming more earnest.

She hesitates, not sure where she is, or why she's there. A loud clap of thunder startles her, and a raindrop falls on her arm. She watches it roll down her wrist, then raises her head, retracing the drops path as another falls and hits her on the forehead. Wes calls firmly to her, causing her to look at him.

"Megan! Wake up!"

The sound of breaking glass jolts her back to her reality as she sits up and gasps for air. She scans a dark and smoke-filled room, struggling to make out shapes and find form in the chaos around her. Her face is bruised and cut, her hair caked in blood. She looks behind her, causing searing pain to shoot through her chest and head. Her equilibrium fails her and she collapses onto an old mattress. She covers her ears in terror, as the crackling flames leap up a nearby wall, shattering another window and sending shards raining to the floor.

As smoke builds around her, she runs her hands below her, and finding a remnant of a sheet, she wraps it around her nude body. She struggles to stand, gasping at the pain and inhaling the searing smoke. She coughs violently as she falls to her knees. She crawls to a wall and pulls herself up to a window. She tries to open it, but its swollen shut by years of neglect. The flames continue their quest, intent to devour the house and all that's inside.

She sees a nearby door, her only hope for passage from the inferno. Her body screams for oxygen and she gasps, scorching her throat. Her lungs convulse, fiercely attempting to expel the blistering air, choking her as she stumbles to the door only to find it too jammed shut. She takes a few steps back, lowers her shoulder and puts her entire weight into the door, breaking it open. With all her strength, she stumbles away from the house and into the cool, wet, darkness of the morning.

The refrigerator door shuts as Harris sets the eggs on the counter. He retrieves a mixing bowl from the cabinet and breaks six eggs into it. He returns to the fridge for the milk and catches sight of a picture of Miranda and newborn Kyle they keep on the door. He remembers that day so clearly, the first time he held Kyle, tinier than any child he had held before in his arms. He was thrilled as he looked down at him. This was no ordinary baby: this was his grandson, the new light of his world.

"Isn't he beautiful, daddy?" he hears Miranda say.

He turns and looks at the table and the chair that she last sat in. He feels a sickening, empty feeling in his chest, as if his heart were gasping for air. He recalls the Bible verses he read and closes his eyes as he reassures himself of their truth. After a long moment, he wipes his cheek on his sleeve, retrieves the milk and returns to fixing the family's Sunday breakfast, a long held tradition in the Harris home.

⎯⎯⎯⎯

An early morning fog blankets Pontchartrain Park not far from the southern shore of Lake Pontchartrain and the industrial canal. A few cars navigate Congress Drive, their drivers on the way to work, or to donuts, or home after a long night.

Along the road's edge, Megan lies within a heavy cover of brush. She hears what she hopes is an approaching car and raises a bloodied arm as high above the weeds as her weak body will allow. For a brief moment, she sees the light from the car illuminate her hand and her heart races, only to sink moments later as the car continues past.

She lies motionless, struggling to control her breathing. She can feel her heart pounding, as if it would burst from her chest at any moment. After what seems like an eternity, she hears another approaching car. She pushes through the pain, again raising her hand as high as she can, only to be disappointed as the light fades once again.

Her heart practically stops as she hears the squeal of tires on the road and the low idle of a stationary engine. She thrusts her arm high into the air, waving it frantically and listens with all of her might, praying to hear the engine draw near. She begins sobbing uncontrollably as light once again illuminates her arm.

"Help me, please," she manages to say, if only in a soft whisper.

She hears the car stop and the door open, followed by footsteps. She can feel the weight of each step of the approaching stranger vibrate through the ground and finally feels a presence next to her. She turns her head, opening her eyes to see a man, grimacing at the sight before him.

"Good God, child. What happened to you?" he says, quickly removing his jacket and placing it over her shivering body.

"Please hel…" she begins to say before slipping back into darkness and silence as the old man dials 911.

Dressed in their Sunday finest, Harris and family settle into their pew at New Hope Baptist Church. The Carmichaels sit one pew back. Andrea and Nicki exchange a hug as Harris gives Russell a punch on the arm, then shakes his hand and asks him how the game went Saturday night. Kyle motions to Rebecca to sit with them and she gladly joins him between Harris and Andrea as the organist begins to play *Blessed Assurance.*

Not far away, at Tulane Medical, an ambulance backs into the emergency area on LaSalle Street. The doors open and two paramedics exit and beginning removing the gurney that carries an intubated and sedated Megan. Several emergency room personnel meet them and begin performing an impromptu examination of her as they roll her through the doors and into Shock Trauma, barking orders to the hospital staff.

Chapter 11

———— ✽✽✽ ————

HEATER

Halfway through the sermon, Harris listens intently as the Pastor, particularly riled by a recent announcement by a major retailer regarding the use of their restrooms and fitting rooms by transgender people, segues to the sanctity of marriage. Andrea sits quietly, her head cocked to side as if draining water, or offending words, from her ears. Pastor Wilton Trudeau stood strong in traditional Southern Baptist theology during the Conservative Resurgence in the 1980's. It was a time in which New Hope lost a few members to the St. Charles Baptist Church in Uptown, a part of the Cooperative Baptist Fellowship, a more liberal organization that fully supported women in pastoral roles, and a more accepting attitude toward homosexuality.

In between Harris and Andrea, Kyle and Rebecca do what most ten and eleven year olds do in church… anything but listen… and for them that means drawing. He puts the finishing touches on a female cartoon character drawn in the style of Manga and hands it to Rebecca and smiles. She takes it, and after admiring it for a moment, smiles back. In the background the Pastor is beginning to hit his stride.

"Marriage is between a man and a woman, ordained by God from the beginning. In Genesis 2:24 we read…"

Rebecca takes her pen and writes "Kylie" at the top of Kyle's drawing then hands it back to him. He reads it, touching the letters, light in his eyes.

Not paying attention in church is something that Harris has scolded Kyle about in the past. Noticing the kids passing the drawings around, he reaches over and takes it away from Kyle, crumbling it in his hand. Kyle looks up at him, crushed. "Pay attention," Harris mouths. Kyle looks back at the pastor just as his sermon reaches a fevered pitch.

"...these deviants. God has no place in His heart for them," the pastor barks, pausing to take a breath and wipe his brow.

"Just as God destroyed the cities of Sodom and Gomorrah, so too will He destroy these gays that pollute His creation. He will cast them into the lake of fire, them and those like them. The L's, the G's, the B's, and the T's. Men acting like women, women acting like men," the pastor continues.

Kyle looks to Harris who intently watches the pastor and nods agreement to the words. He glances to Andrea, who is watching him. She smiles, pats his leg, and then turns away, closing her eyes and sighing softly. Kyle looks back up just as the Pastor's eyes sweep to their side of the chapel and catch his eyes directly.

"God made us all," the pastor says, emphasizing "God" and "all".

"...the way He intended for us to be. Men are men, women are women. God doesn't make mistakes. To think and behave otherwise..." he adds, pausing for effect then finishing the thought with style and emphasis.

"...is the work of the Devil."

Harris' cell phone vibrates and he pulls it from his jacket. He sighs as he reads it, garnering a look from Andrea. Kyle glances at him as he leans over and whispers in her ear. He watches as Harris rises and heads down the aisle, nodding and raising a hand slightly to a few of the congregation's members as he exits the building.

———

Detective Sergeant Ron Blanchard finishes a phone call in his office at the NOPD's central office at the corner of South Broad and Gravier streets. He spins his chair around, hangs up the phone and looks across his desk at Tanisha Broussard, a rising young star in Homicide. She became a detective only six months earlier but has already earned the respect of more senior detectives and, most importantly, Blanchard. However, having earned their respect may not prove to be enough for the current situation. He begins to speak but is interrupted when Harris steps into the doorway.

"This better be good. Pastor was in rare form this morning," Harris says as he steps through the door and begins to close it behind him.

"Leave it open. It's hot as hell in here," a not so amused Blanchard replies, wiping sweat from his brow and rising, exiting past Harris and into the outer office area.

The department is terribly understaffed. It's a combination of budget and the overall situation that the department finds itself in these days. Their reputation has been tarnished by the events that culminated in the consent decree with the Department of Justice. Add to that, continued problems related to the Orleans Parish Prison and other news-grabbing headlines, particularly stemming from gross mismanagement in the sex-crimes unit and all in all, the NOPD is not a comfortable place to work. The budget constraints faced by the city and the department do little to enhance morale.

As Blanchard disappears around the corner, Harris turns to Broussard, extending his hand.

"Albert Harris."

Broussard's eyes widen and she rises, taking his hand in hers.

"Tanisha Broussard. Holy shit! Albert Harris. *The* Albert Harris?"

"I guess that depends."

"I thought you retired."

"Maybe I should have. Guess that depends on why we're here."

"You got me. I got here five minutes ago and he just got off the phone."

"Broussard, huh? I've heard about you. Good stuff. It's an honor."

"Me? You're the one with the highest clearance rate for ten years straight. I'm the one that's honored."

Blanchard arrives in the doorway and sets up an oscillating fan, pointing it into the office.

"Damn budget cuts. We can't afford to turn the fucking air on when our people are in the building on the weekends?" he says as he finds the plug and begins searching for an outlet.

"Don't use…," Broussard says as Blanchard recoils from the sparks that shoot from the wall. The entire floor goes dark.

"Fuck!" Blanchard barks.

"I'll get it. This ain't the first time. I tried to tell ya," Broussard says, exiting the office and disappearing down the hall out the stairwell door to the breaker-box.

Blanchard re-enters his office, giving Harris a look that he's seen before. It's an expression that has nothing to do with heat exhaustion and everything to do with *the* heat, or heaters, high profile cases that require delicate handling.

"This can't be good," Harris says with raised brow.

"LSP found Megan Callahan's car wrapped around a tree on 626 last night."

The men stare at each other, sobering up quickly from the previous chatter.

"By the airport? In St. Rose?" Harris says after a moment.

"Yeah."

"How bad was she hurt?"

"In the accident? Not sure. A motorist found her this morning off of Congress up by Pontchartrain Park."

They exchange a long look, both revisiting a darker time. Blanchard watches him as he turns and stares blankly out the window. He knows what he's thinking. He remembers the story well.

Blanchard was there that night; Harris wasn't supposed to be. Miranda was attending night school and had not come home from class the night before. When the first call came in that she had been found, Blanchard gave orders to keep Harris away, but the entire 4th Brigade from Fort Polk couldn't have stopped him. By the time he got there, the EMT's were moving her from the house to the ambulance.

"Al, you don't want to see her like this. Go to University and wait," Blanchard said as he unsuccessfully tried to hold him back. The site of her battered and bruised body was only the first devastation that awaited Harris in those days.

Blanchard studies him closely, gauging his behavior, his body language. He has to be certain that Harris is right for this case.

"Dead?" Harris quietly asks, continuing to stare out the window.

"Left for," Blanchard replies. "She's in bad shape. Tulane says she was raped," he adds.

Blanchard can only imagine what thoughts are running through Harris' mind right now. He remembers how, after Miranda's death, Harris struggled, burned by the failings of the system. He had reached PO-4 grade, the most senior detective in homicide. He never had an interest in managing people. He solved cases, that's what he did and he was good at it, the best. He personally pushed to have Harris detailed to the joint task force so his friend could heal. But this morning's events are causing him to have to make a very difficult decision.

"Al, I need you on this," Blanchard says quietly.

"If she was raped why not give it to the rape squad?"

Blanchard just looks at him. There's no need for explanation and Harris silently acknowledges that fact.

"It will be Broussard's case. She'll be primary but we need expertise with her. You'll be detailed back in."

"Just put Davis or Dupre with her," Harris says lowly.

"I can't spare them. They're wrapped up in their cases."

Harris turns and looks back out the window and down onto Sirgo Plaza and the memorial to fallen officers.

"Ron, I'm not your man for—"

"Al, I don't have time to joust with you. The Lieutenant's already talked to the Commander, who's already talked to the Chief, both of them. They don't want anything to go wrong. It can't, not now. Not with a heater like this. The spotlight's too bright, especially after the entrapment bullshit she threw at us in the Donkova case. We can't have anything that might be perceived as tit-for-tat."

Harris turns and studies him for a long moment then slowly returns to staring blankly out the window as the lights in the office come back to life.

"He fought me on this one but I want you on it, at least for a while. This is a chance for you to score some points back, Al."

Harris says nothing. Blanchard searches for the right words, hating that he has to do this.

"I know what you're thinking. If this gets too rough, I'll pull you off. But for now, I need my best on this. I need you," Blanchard adds after a long moment of silence.

Harris sighs heavily and turns his eyes back to Blanchard, as Broussard reappears in the doorway.

"What'd I miss?" she says.

Harris studies her for a moment then turns back to Blanchard and silently acknowledges his acceptance.

Chapter 12

REFLECTIONS

The worn pages of last month's *People* magazine flip by at a pace not meant for reading. It's a pace meant to release frustration, and that's exactly what Anna is doing as she sits in the waiting area outside of ICU at Tulane Medical. She tried to get inside, but the nurses and armed officer prevented that possibility. Anna could see Megan through the sliding glass doors, still intubated with bandages on her head, arms, and chest. It was a sight that sent her into tears.

The thought of leaving Megan behind at the festival will not leave her mind. She should have stayed, regardless of what Megan said. If she had, she and Michelle would have been with her on the road home. She left her best friend in an area that she doesn't frequent, to meet God knows who last night, just so she could go home with Michelle, a woman she can't commit to, to have a night of wild sex that didn't happen anyway because Michelle got sick on the way.

All of these irrational thoughts fill her mind as she notices Harris walk past. Seeing the badge on his belt, she gets up and peers through the doors, watching him as he speaks to the nurses then the officer at the door to Megan's room. After a few minutes, he turns and walks back towards her.

"Are you here about Megan?" she asks.

"Who are you?"

"Anna Miller. I'm Megan's friend."

"Albert Harris, NOPD," he replies, stepping to her and offering his hand which she takes.

"Have you found anything?"

"Not yet, just getting started. I'm sorry about this," he says motioning towards Megan's room.

"I can't believe it. I mean, as a woman you can't help but think about it, fear it. But I never thought it would happen, not to her."

Harris silently nods his understanding. After a moment, Anna looks at him closer, recognizing him.

"Hey, I remember you. At the festival, yesterday, she was talking to you."

"Yeah, I guess I was," Harris responds.

Anna watches him as he looks away, seemingly remembering the encounter. After a moment he turns his eyes back to her.

"You got time to talk? Somewhere else?" he says, glancing back over his shoulder.

Her eyes follow his motion back towards Megan's room. She looks back at him, understanding the tone of his question and nods her agreement.

Sunday lunch is finished at the Harris house. The plates are in the dishwasher and Andrea lies on the couch taking her normal Sunday nap, sans Harris. Afternoon nap time means Kyle can do one of two things, either go to his room and be quiet or get out of the house. Rather than sit in his room alone, Kyle usually chooses to go over to Rebecca's and today is no different. The two of them sit in the living room, their favorite spot, and play with her dolls while watching *Project Runway* on the TV. Kyle half-heartedly plays; instead he focuses on the show. But even that has only part of his thoughts.

While he doesn't fully understand some things about himself, he's smart enough, and internet savvy enough, to know he's not like most boys. There's something wrong with him, he's sure of it. Maybe Nanna was right, maybe when he's older things will change and he'll be like everyone else. Paw Paw likes Russell, so maybe he just needs to be more like him.

He tosses his Yasmin doll back into Rebecca's bag and begins flipping through the channels.

"What's the matter? Don't you wanna play?" she asks.

"Nah," he replies without looking at her or seeing the disappointment that washes across her face.

"You mad at me?" she asks.

"No, silly. I'm not mad at you. I just don't feel like playing."

She examines him a bit longer, then puts down her dolls and slides up next to him and turns her attention to the TV. She watches silently as he quickly clicks through the channels, stopping only long enough to determine what is showing. Her eyes widen when the channel lands on the Cartoon Network.

"Oh... stop. Yeah, yeah, yeah. Power Puff Girls," she says.

She smiles widely, only to have it wiped from her face as he changes it after a few moments and stops on Nickelodeon's *The Fairly Odd Parents*, a show Russell would probably watch.

After a moment, Russell walks in and takes the remote from him. He plops down on the couch and changes the channel to the football game.

"Hey! We were watching that. Go watch the one in the kitchen," Kyle says.

"You go watch the one in the kitchen, ya little sissy. That's where girls belong anyway," Russell replies.

A dejected Kyle looks to Rebecca and after a moment, she gets up and heads to the hallway. She stops and turns back to him, motioning for him to follow her.

The food in hospitals has improved dramatically over the span of Harris' life, and Tulane Medical is no exception. While it's certainly not a four-star restaurant, it's not bad. But today, it wouldn't matter how good it is, the food just doesn't interest either Harris or Anna as they sit discussing the events leading up to yesterday.

Sometimes cases like this are easy to crack, sometimes not so much. Harris understands that Megan's situation presents its own unique set of circumstances considering that, being a criminal defense attorney, there are more than a few people in New Orleans who perhaps have felt victimized by her due to a case she defended. Broussard's already putting together a list of cases Megan has successfully litigated in the past few years, as well as the few that she lost. It's not that simple, however, and Harris knows that if the obvious suspects don't pan out, he'll have to get to know Megan, the person, her interests and her dislikes, and as much of her history as he can.

Anna and Harris sit near a first floor window with a view out onto South Saratoga Street. She pushes a half-eaten piece of pecan pie away while Harris makes notes in a small, spiral bound, notebook.

"So the guy gets in her face, you know. He was yelling about a case she tried. I guess he felt cheated out of a lot of money or something."

"What'd Megan do?"

"Handled it like she usually does, bitch slapped him."

"She slapped him? Physically?" Harris asks, astonished at the thought.

"No, verbally. She told him where he could stick it, basically."

Harris nods, remembering the sting of the "bitch-slapping" Megan gave him in the courtroom.

"Did you get a name? Where was this?" he asks after a moment.

"Three Muses, on Frenchmen. No, but he mentioned the guy that Megan defended. It was, umm…. Donco something."

"Donkova?"

"Yeah. Donkova. Victor Donkova. She won that case 'cause the guy was entrapped," she says with a slight smile and bit of pride.

He swallows his words. It's certainly not the time or the person to discuss that case and its merits with. He pauses, collecting his thoughts and forcing his mind back on the case at hand.

"Did this guy threaten her?"

"He said she should be careful. That there were consequences."

"Consequences?"

"Yeah. Do you think he did it?"

"Too early to tell. What happened after that?"

"Jeff came rushing in and bounced his ass out."

"Who's Jeff?'

"The bartender. Used to be like a Green Beret or something."

"Aside from professionally, can you think of anyone that might have wanted to hurt her, an old boyfriend maybe?" he asks as he writes down more notes in his notebook.

"She didn't really have boyfriends," she says, raising her hands to put the quotation marks around that last word.

"So she's a... lesbian," Harris says, rather disdainfully.

"Would it matter?"

Blanchard's words, spoken to him that evening at Mick's, race through his mind as do the words of the lecturer at the seminar on sensitivity that he was forced to sit through. He still doesn't understand why he has to be the one to be sensitive; it's them that are sensitive. It's a life they chose; they should have to deal with the consequences. He stops taking notes, breathes deeply, and aligns his words with departmental policy.

"Of course not. Just trying to——"

"Megan and I both write on this poetry site, poets beat, under the profile Dream Weaver. There are so many lonely hearts on that site, sheez. After we'd been there a while, Megan started getting into online relationships with men, and women, from the site. She's never really had a boyfriend since I've known her and she's always seemed happiest when she had a muse on the site. I've been trying to help her, hook her up you know, with real guys. But... she won't give 'em a chance."

"What do you mean by online relationship?"

"Become involved with them, attached, write love poetry back and forth to each other and stuff. She'd talk with some of 'em on the phone, but it never went past that. If they wanted more, she'd drop 'em like a hot potato," she says, looking away. "She broke a few hearts, pretty sure of that," she adds.

"We'll need to take a look at that site. Can you give us access?"

"Sure."

Harris makes a few notes in his journal then looks back at Anna. He can see the disbelief on her face, seemingly lost in thought, as if the gravity of the idea that one of Megan's muses could be the assailant is sinking in.

"You okay?" Harris asks.

"Yeah, it's just that... do you really think it could be one of them?"

"Anything's possible at this point, Anna. Do you have any names for these... broken hearts?"

"I can get you all of 'em. She ran background checks on them before she'd get involved. She's so serious about her safety, what she does and all."

Harris considers that for a moment. Megan running background checks could mean that she has reason to; perhaps she has been victimized before in some way. Of course, the mere fact that she's a defense attorney should give her ample reason to want to be sure who she was dealing with.

"Can we head back? Don't wanna be away too long, case she wakes up," Anna says.

He closes his notebook and they both rise and head back into the hallway toward the elevators.

"What do you do for a living, Anna?" he asks after a few moments of walking silently.

"I'm a counselor... at St. Agnes Women's center," she says, realizing the ironic tragedy that the woman she met there, that used to volunteer and help so many abused women, is now a victim.

"I've seen a lot, but I wasn't prepared for this. Not this close to home," she adds.

He gives her a sympathetic smile then pats her softly on the shoulder.

"Thank you, Anna, for what you do. You're an angel to many, I'm sure," he says as he pushes the button, calling the elevator.

"I don't know about that. I just try to help, you know?" she says as the doors open and they step inside.

"So which of these guys was her most recent..."

"Muse? None of them," she answers.

"None of them? So she's not in a relationship with anyone right now?"

"No, she is, with Jennifer, Jen. It's been driving me nuts 'cause I kept asking her who she really was and she just kept saying not to worry, that she had it handled and under control. I should have stayed at the festival and met her."

"What do you mean? Megan was meeting this Jen person at the festival?"

"Yeah, Michelle and I were——"

"Who's Michelle?"

"My girlfriend."

He nods and smiles, reminding himself to do just that and only that. The doors open on the fourth floor and they step out. After a brief pause, she continues.

"We were with her most of the night, but decided to leave before the last band. She told me that she was meeting Jen and I wanted to stay and meet her but... we left... and I wish we hadn't."

She stops and begins to cry. She may be a lesbian, but she's human and Harris knows all too well about blaming one's self. He slides his arm around her shoulder and consoles her. She pulls a tissue from her pocket and wipes her eyes.

"I guess I should send her a message on the site and let her know what happened."

"No, don't do that. Don't do anything on that site. We'll need to see all of her communications. We don't want to do anything that might spook someone." Harris says.

She nods in agreement as they begin walking again towards the ICU.

"You don't know anything else about this Jennifer?" he asks.

"Nothing except what's on her profile. I'm sorry, I wish I did." Anna says sadly.

They arrive at the nurse's station outside ICU and check Megan's condition only to learn that she's purposefully being kept unconscious and it will be tomorrow, Monday, at the earliest before he is allowed to interview her and Anna is allowed to see her.

———⁂———

A still sullen Kyle sits on the floor in the middle of Rebecca's room, throwing a tennis ball against the wall and catching it on the rebound. Rebecca plays with her Bratz Styling Head, a Christmas gift from Andrea last year, brushing the hair out, hoping to draw Kyle's attention and possibly cheer him up. It isn't working. She watches him for a minute as he repeatedly throws the ball.

"Momma's gonna get mad if you keep doing that," she says.

"So?"

She studies him, perplexed by the combative behavior so uncharacteristic of him. She stops brushing Cloe's hair and leans in front of him to ensure that he sees her.

"Wanna play a game?"

"Nah."

She scans the room and her eyes widen as she sees just the thing to get his attention. She crawls over to her nightstand and grabs it.

"Wanna play with my Nintendo? Got the new Pokemon game."

He looks at it a moment, offered there in her hand like a precious jewel. It's good bait, but it doesn't work. He shakes his head and returns to his game of catch. She watches him and the ball, gauging his pace and the ball's speed, waiting for the right moment. She dives and catches the ball on the rebound then crawls back and sits by Kyle.

"What's the matter?"

"Nothing."

"Then why won't you play with me?"

"I shouldn't."

"Why?" Rebecca says, a puzzled look on her face.

"Cause it's girl stuff and I'm a boy," he replies with strong words and disappointed eyes.

"So? You have fun don't you?"

"Yeah but…"

"But, what?" she says as she smiles.

He sits, arms crossed, staring at the hardwood floor. After a moment he cuts his eyes up to her.

"Can I tell you something?"

"Yeah, of course."

"You gotta promise not to tell nobody. I mean nobody. It will be our secret. Pinky promise me." he says, extending out his little finger.

"I pinky promise. I won't tell nobody," she answers, wrapping her pinky around his.

He hesitates for a moment, looking away, trying to muster the courage to tell her his secret.

"I wish I was a girl," he finally says. "Cause everything would be easier then."

He watches her carefully, gauging her reaction and fearing the worst.

"And?" she says.

Kyle rolls his eyes, not quite sure how to answer.

"And... that's it. I wish I was a girl."

"Duh! I know that, silly. But I don't care what you are, boy, girl, monkey, frog. You're my best friend. That's all that matters."

They exchange a smile and a hug. She rises and steps into her closet and begins rummaging around as Kyle stands and walks to her dresser, examining all of the girl things she has. He takes a necklace from a holder and places it on his neck, modeling it. She steps out of the closet holding a small backpack, causing Kyle to hastily and clumsily replace the necklace onto its holder.

"I gotcha something," she says.

"What is it?"

"Close the door. Don't want nobody to see."

He does as requested then returns to Rebecca who hands him the backpack. He looks at it a moment, then turns inquisitive eyes back to her.

"Go ahead, open it," she says.

He reaches inside, pulling out a sundress, one of Rebecca's. His eyes light up as he examines it. He turns his eyes to her, not sure what to say or do next.

"I hope you like it. I think it'll fit ya," she says.

He looks back to the dress, tracing one of the shoulder straps through his fingers. A mixture of excitement and relief rushes through him, as if he's found a long-lost treasure. "It's beautiful," he says, holding it up in front of him to check for size. He turns back to her, his eyes glistening and asking the question for him.

"Go ahead, try it on," she says with a smile then walks to the door and locks it.

He quickly pulls off his shirt and slips the sundress over his head. He gazes into the mirror. An eleven-year-old girl with long hair, a beautiful smile, and a new sundress, Kylie, smiles back at him.

Chapter 13

ASSUMPTIONS

B eing the primary detective on a case has its benefits. They're in control and direct the course of the investigation. It also means they usually do all of the paperwork. There are forms to fill out, MORF reports to file, court requests and subpoenas to handle.

As she sits in front of her laptop, working her way through the Dream Weaver profile, Broussard considers that on the first day on the case, it hasn't felt like she's the primary. She respects Harris tremendously, but he seems to be calling the shots. This case is the biggest of her young career and she doesn't want to make a mistake, especially considering how high profile it is and that everyone, from the Chief down, will be watching. So all things considered, she's glad to have his assistance and guidance. Hopefully though, at some point, she'll feel like she's in charge.

In the current case, she and Harris will have files related to cases that Megan has handled to review, websites and phone carriers to subpoena, and eight former muses of Megan's to track down, just to name a few of the tasks to be done.

The lighting in the interior conference room is poor, and Harris seems to struggle with reading the contents of a manila folder, one of the several background check files of Megan's that he and Anna retrieved from Megan's home. It's a tedious process, and while Harris investigates the details of each one,

Broussard reviews the postings and communications with Megan that each of them had on the poetry site.

"Have you seen this Dream Weaver profile?" she asks.

"What about it? It's poetry. Roses are red, violets are blue," Harris says with a smirk on his face.

"You should read some of this. It's beautiful. I bet some of it would even bring to a tear to your eye," she replies, smiling from the corner of her mouth.

Harris huffs, shaking his head. He picks up the next folder in the stack labeled "Jeff Taylor". He looks at that name curiously for moment then opens it to find a picture of the folders subject. "Hmmm," he says as he flips through the contents.

"Hmmm what?" Broussard asks without looking away from her screen.

"I know this guy, Jeff Taylor. He used to tend bar over at Mick's, did a couple of tours in Iraq. Nice guy. Was married last time I talked to him."

"Uh huh… it's always the married ones," she says, glancing at the picture of Jeff that Harris holds. "Don't recognize him. Then again, I don't drink or go to Mick's, so how would I?"

"Stay in this job long enough… you'll drink," he replies.

"Wait a minute, what did Anna say the bartender at Three Muses' name was?" she asks, pieces of the puzzle beginning to fall into place.

"This guy," he says, holding up the picture of Jeff.

"Okay, so… Jeff was in a relationship, online relationship…whatever, with Megan," she states, beginning to lay out the facts.

"Operative word being was. Jen's the latest player," he replies as the two of them look at each other, each of them beginning down the same path of suspicion.

"Jealousy?" she offers, throwing it up to see if it sticks.

"Possible. Honestly, he doesn't seem the type, but I won't rule it out. Did you find anything else in there other than frilly poetry?" he asks, pointing to her laptop and mockingly emphasizing those last two words.

"Yep, once I verified my age," she says, cutting an eye to him.

"Verified your age? You mean there's adult content in there?" he asks, sliding his chair next to hers.

"Megan seems to be the queen of erotica on this site. There's some pretty hot stuff here," she says.

"Porn?" he asks, slipping on his glasses and leaning in to read the screen.

"Literary porn. Short stories and poems."

They each read silently until it's obvious that the graphic content makes each of them uncomfortable.

"Good Lord, this is straight out of Penthouse," he says.

"Got a lot of experience with Penthouse, do we, Harris?" she asks with a grin.

"I was young once. I know you may not believe it, but it's the truth," Harris says blushing slightly. "That stuff is a blight on society. It'll rot your brain," he adds.

He reaches across the table and grabs Jeff's folder; he flips through it, finding his site profile name.

"Anything in there by Veritas, v, e, r—"

"I know how to spell," she replies dryly, navigating through to Jeff's page.

"Let's see... most recent post was a couple of months ago," she says as she scans through the profile. "He dedicated it to her," she adds.

The two of them read silently, only needing a single verse to the get the gist.

Desires
hidden from so many,
lovely, though licentious.
Kneeling at the feet,
kissing,
praising the one served.
Punished upon err,
and erring often.
It is the punishment
that is craved.

"That's—" he says.

"Sadomasochism," she adds, finishing his sentence.

"Print that out for me," he says, garnering a playful glance from Broussard. "Just print it," he adds as she sends it to the printer.

"What are her latest posts?" he asks.

She clicks back to Megan's profile and selects a few works.

"Mostly love poetry. A lot dedicated to Jen… that would be Jennifer, I assume."

She clicks on Jen's profile, hoping to find identifying information.

"Jen's a ghost. Nothing here about her except that she's female and lives in the city," she says disappointedly. "Which means absolutely nothing on an anonymous website," she adds with a look over to Harris.

He nods his reluctant acceptance of that fact then rises and picks up Jeff's folder.

"Okay, I'm gonna stop downstairs, check out her car, then to Three Muses, see if I can catch Jeff there," he says as he heads for the door, turning to look back at Broussard.

She bristles slightly at the comment, reminding herself that she is the primary on the case and to her that means she should be directing him.

"I'll do that. Why don't you loop by Megan's place on your way home, eyeball the area?"

"Nah. You keep working the porn angle. You may be on to something there," he says with a smile before he exits, closing the door behind him.

"Gee thanks," she says sarcastically, sighing heavily and returning to her assigned task.

Harris enters the garage area, recoiling from the wall of heat that greets him from the non-air-conditioned area, and makes his way to a bay containing a BMW 5 series sedan and opens the gate on the ten-foot tall chain-link fence that surrounds it. Crime scene techs are no different than any other group in the department. With the tight budgets, it's not normal procedure to be called in on a Sunday to work a wrecked vehicle. But overtime is overtime and they'll take it when they can get it.

"Lawyers, they make all the money don't they?" Harris asks.

"Doctors don't do too bad either," the tech answers as they shake hands.

"This seems a little big for her. I had her pegged for a Porsche," Harris says, pointing to the car.

"Who?"

"Callahan."

"This isn't hers, that is," the tech answers, pointing to the Bronco being worked by second tech in the adjacent bay. Harris studies it a moment then turns back to the tech.

"Hmm, wouldn't have thunk it," he says and heads out and through the other gate.

Harris walks around the Bronco, admiring it, remembering the times in the late 60's when he road in one much like it belonging to an uncle in Upstate, near Schenectady.

"Haven't seen one of these in a while," he says to the second tech as he enters the Bronco's pen.

"Yeah, shame to see it here and not in front of my house," the tech replies as he gently places a lifted finger print.

"Whatcha got for me so far?" Harris asks as he examines the steering wheel, bent from the impact.

"Not a lot. Lifting prints where we can. Seat belt was cut. Serrated edge, hunting knife maybe."

"Any impact with another vehicle?" Harris asks examining the damaged front end.

"None that I can find."

Harris watches as the tech lifts another print from the door. He walks to the tech's table and notices a broken cell phone.

"Is this hers?"

"Appears to be. Found it on the floorboard."

Harris checks the phone to see if it works. It does, but barely. Through its broken screen he checks recent calls. The last was from Jen. He dials the number from his phone. After a few rings, the call goes to a generic voice mail. He looks to the tech, who simply shrugs and continues his tasks.

"I'm gonna take this with me."

The tech smiles and returns to the table, picking up a clipboard and pen and handing it to Harris.

"As long as you sign for it. Can't have any evidence go missing on my watch."

Harris smiles and signs the release, thankful that someone else working on the case is being diligent. No mistakes.

Harris parks his car along the street, near The Spotted Cat, a popular and smoky Jazz bar, and takes the short walk back down Frenchmen. It's a bit before seven and the street is already showing signs of life as he weaves his way through the crowds and into The Three Muses. Fortunately, it isn't too packed, not yet, so he eases up to the bar and has a seat, inspecting the place as he waits for the bartender. At a nearby table, a young couple sits with friends discussing their pregnancy.

"Welcome to the Muses. What can I get you?" Gabby, an attractive young barmaid, asks.

"Scotch," he says with a smile.

She smiles back and begins to pour his poison.

"You guys got a barkeep named Jeff?"

"Why ya asking?" she says, scanning this stranger up and down.

Harris reaches under his jacket and pulls his badge from his belt clip, holding it for her to see. That's enough explanation for her.

"He's in the back. Let me get him," she says delivering his drink.

As she disappears through a door, he turns and looks at the young couple and their friends going on and on about the pregnancy. He's a thin man, handsome, late twenty's, early thirty's max. His well-groomed beard, clean hands and nails, probably manicured, lead Harris to peg him as a banker, or worse a lawyer. She's of Asian descent, light brown skin, beautiful eyes, and long brown hair. She's speaking of the pregnancy in such medical terms; Harris pegs her as a nurse. He can't help but think of Miranda and what it might have been like when she first told her friends.

His thoughts turn back to Andrew Holland, a fellow from Shreveport Miranda was dating. It seemed pretty serious for a while, like marriage was on the horizon. As happens, carelessness led to an early pregnancy and it wasn't long after that Andrew started acting strangely. Miranda soon found herself abandoned. Harris had decided it was for the better, since Andrew showed his true colors early on. Things got ugly when he started claiming he wasn't the father. They considered pursuing matters legally and forcing a paternity test, but decided all of their lives would be better if Andrew Holland simply disappeared and never darkened their doors again.

As Harris swirls his scotch, his thoughts drift to a happier time when Miranda was on the volleyball team at Cabrini. He and Andrea attended every game they could. Those years of gymnastics training had proved valuable, and he beamed with pride as he sat in the stands watching his daughter make impossible digs and game-saving blocks. How she did it all so effortlessly and gracefully was beyond his understanding. While he was fit as a kid, he could barely do a handstand much less a cartwheel. The loud sound of hands plunking down on the bar in front of him slams him out of his thoughts.

"What the hell do you want? We don't allow cops in this place," the voice, forced and guttural, booms.

Harris slowly looks up and studies the man for a moment. He's handsome and rugged with a heavy five-o'clock shadow and dressed in jeans and long sleeves. He's not a big man, but firm and wiry. He looks tough, but his kind green eyes betray his appearance. Harris is pretty sure he can take him if he has to.

"Well that may be the case, but they obviously hire assholes," Harris says dryly, never smiling.

The two of them stare at each other for a moment, a standoff, and then both break into a smile.

"Albert Harris! How the hell are you?" Jeff says, extending his hand out for a hearty handshake.

"I'm making it, Jeff. Was wondering why I wasn't seeing you over at Mick's anymore."

"Less cops, better tips," Jeff says with a wink and smile.

"Touché," Harris responds, raising his glass to toast that one.

"It's good to see you, Al. How've you been?"

"Been good. You know, staying busy, tracking down bad guys."

"You about ready to pull the trigger on that retirement?"

"I think about it every day. Just not sure what I would do with myself if I did, though."

"I'm sure Andrea can find some things to keep you busy," Jeff says with a grin. "How is she? Kyle?" he adds.

"She's great and Kyle's growing like a weed. I think he's spending too much time with her though. Getting a little soft, if you know what I mean."

Jeff just looks at him and smiles.

"So what brings you into this fine establishment? They throw you out of Mick's?"

"Couple of nights ago, you bounced a guy out of here, yeah?"

"Yeah, Thursday night. Some asshole was going off on a customer. I didn't get his name though. Why? Ahh Fuck me! Did he file a complaint?"

"Wish it was that simple," Harris replies, watching Jeff as he looks away, seemingly lost in thought.

The fact that Jeff referred to Megan as "a customer" does not escape him. After a moment he snaps Jeff back to the here and now.

"You think you can get me a copy of all of the charge customers that night? Maybe I'll get lucky."

"Yeah, sure," Jeff says and then moves down the bar and begins typing on a keyboard, still seeming distracted.

"How's Emily? Your boy?" Harris asks.

"Dustin? He's amazing. I got a great kid there, Al. As for Emily, I don't know. It's pretty bad. It's gotten worse since we last talked."

"That bad, huh?"

"Yeah. I don't know if we're gonna make it," Jeff says as the printer under the counter begins churning out the list.

"Well look, our pastor at church, he's helped several couples that I know. If you want, I can ask him to give you a call."

"Thanks but, I think it's too late for that."

Jeff removes the final page from the printer and hands them to Harris who begins examining them. After a moment, he surveys the room then turns back to Jeff.

"You got a few minutes? I need to ask you some questions."

A few wrinkles of worry grace Jeff's face. After a moment he grabs a bottle of water from a cooler and motions to Gabby that he's taking a break.

***

Harris and Jeff walk down Frenchmen, towards the river and Decatur Street, passing a growing throng of locals mixed with out-of-towners with an inside track to the best music in the city. Jeff opens the water and takes a long swig, washing away an emerging cotton-mouth.

"Listen Al, if this is about those parking tickets... I know I—"

"You got more outstanding tickets? You swore to me—"

"I know. I swear I'm gonna take care of 'em myself this...," he begins to say before sighing in realization. "This isn't about those is it?"

They look at each other for a moment then Jeff turns away. He spins the bottle in his hands and then removes the top and takes another long swig.

"So what's up, Al?"

"I know you're having trouble with your marriage and—"

"I really appreciate you asking and everything but like I said, it's too late... and it's probably for the best anyway," a visibly relieved Jeff says as they round the corner at Decatur and turn uptown towards the Quarter.

Harris simply smiles and nods. The two of them walk silently as they approach Esplanade Avenue and Harris chooses his words carefully.

"Tell me about your relationship with Megan Callahan," he says after a moment.

Jeff takes another long swig of water while watching the approaching traffic. "Who?"

"Don't bullshit me, Jeff. We've known each other too long for that."

Jeff looks at him a moment before the traffic clears.

"Al, what the fuck is going on? Did Emily file some kind of order or some-thing? I swear, we were arguing and she turned to leave——" Jeff says as they begin to cross Esplanade.

"This isn't about Emily. I need you to tell me about your relationship with Megan."

A shaken Jeff takes a long drink, finishing off the bottle of water. He looks at Harris, then back at a wave of boisterous Saints fans approaching them. Harris follows as Jeff crosses riverside to the sidewalk in front of the Old U.S. Mint, and finds a quiet spot near the iron fence surrounding it.

"We've met up a couple of times, well more than a couple. Anyway I met her online on a poetry site. She listened to me. Emily wouldn't. We got to be re-ally good friends and yeah, we've gone out some. How did you find out? I mean, we kept it low key cause of all the shit with Emily. What's..."

The expression on Harris' face says volumes. Jeff's eyes widen and the color rushes from his face as if ice is passing through his veins.

"What's wrong Al? What happened to her?"

Harris looks at him for moment, studying his expression, gauging his sincerity.

"She was raped last night, almost killed."

"What?! Where? Where is she?"

"She's being taken care of," Harris answers as tears build in Jeff's eyes.

Jeff runs his hands through his hair and begins pacing around in a small circle.

"Fuck! I don't fucking believe this!" he says before turning back to Harris. "Take me to her. Please."

"Can't do that."

"Then tell me where she is."

Harris says nothing. He simply watches him. Jeff throws his hands up in the air in frustration and begins pacing again. The next question is a bit harder for Harris to ask. He's, effectively, with five words, about to ask a friend if he is guilty of a crime.

"Where were you last night?"

"Where was I? What, you think I——"

"Where were you, Jeff?"

Jeff looks at him in disbelief and then turns and stares through the iron bars of the fence while grasping them with his hands. He shakes them, as if trying to escape, then turns and sits on the small concrete ledge at the base of the fence.

"I was with her, at least for a while. But I swear Al, you gotta believe me, I didn't have anything to do with this. My God, I would never do that, not to anyone and certainly not to her. You have no idea what she means to me," he says, turning his eyes back up to Harris.

"Okay then, let's detail where you were. Maybe you saw something, or somebody. Where were you? What time was this?"

"She told me she was going to the alligator festival out in Luling. I said I would try to make it by, which I did. So I met up with her there about nine. We stayed a bit listening to some of the music, then left. We were gonna meet up later. I waited an hour, but she didn't show," Jeff says before dropping his face into his hands. "Fuck! I thought she dumped me! I should've gone looking for her. I don't fucking believe this."

"While you were there, did anything happen? Did you get into an argument with anyone or anything like that?"

"No, nothing. We listened to the music and talked. Nothing unusual."

"Was there anything about her behavior that was different? Did she seem uneasy or nervous about being there?"

"She was her normal self, Al. She seemed happy. Fuck! This is fucking unreal."

Harris pats him on the shoulder. It's hard for him to have to ask these questions of a friend. It's something he has only had to do a few times in his career and it's torn him up each time. But he's a professional and its part of the job, regardless of how much he hates it. It's something that must be done. He gives him a moment to collect himself, knowing the questions only get harder from here out.

"What time did you get home?"

"About midnight," a dejected Jeff says, never looking up to Harris.

"Was Emily home?"

"What the fuck, Al? Come on, man! Don't bring Em' into this," Jeff says as he rises and begins to pace again.

"Jeff, I'm doing my job. I don't like this any more than you do. If you say you didn't do it, I want to believe you, but I have to ask these questions," Harris says watching him wear holes in the sidewalk with his pacing.

"Can Emily corroborate what you told me?" he slowly asks.

Jeff turns away, seeking anything but Harris to lock his eyes on. After a few moments, he looks back at him, his sadness having turned to anger.

"Em' moved out a week ago."

Harris searches for the right words. He was hoping that Emily would be able to back Jeff up. Only the most bitter of future ex-wives would leave a guy hanging in this situation. He thinks of a couple from church that he counseled recently, a family broken apart by infidelity. He considers the stack of folders, each a muse of Megan's. He thinks about the erotica she wrote. To Harris, she's obviously not someone that Jeff should have gotten tangled up with.

"Listen Jeff, you do know that you were one of many for her, on that site, right?"

"They didn't matter. We're different," Jeff replies.

He can see the pain in Jeff's eyes. He wants to believe everything Jeff's told him; he knows better than to completely write off the possibilities, but Jeff's probably been through enough questioning, for now. He'll obtain the buccal swab warrant tomorrow and have a tech come by and execute it.

"Look, I'm sorry. We'll leave it here for now. I'll be in touch, so don't go anywhere."

Jeff nods his agreement without looking at Harris as he begins to leave. Harris stops and turns back to him.

"Jeff?"

He looks to him hesitantly, as if expecting to be read his rights.

"I'm telling you this as a friend. Don't go looking for her. You won't find her and if you did, they'll arrest you on the spot."

Jeff shakes his head in disbelief, turns and walks away into the Quarter.

For Harris, it's an odd feeling watching his friend walk away into the night. He's walking away alone. A woman he seems to care about has been hurt and, Harris knows, he feels helpless. Those feelings of loss and help-lessness, Harris is all too familiar with. His heart goes out to Jeff, but his honed and battle-worn detective mind forces him to leave open the possibility of Jeff's involvement. He hopes that isn't the case, but tonight's questioning did little to prove otherwise. He sighs heavily, straightens his jacket, and turns back on Decatur towards his car.

Chapter 14

TIME

L ate at night, while Andrea and Kyle are asleep, Harris sits at the table in their dimly lit kitchen. An antique clock hanging near the doorway reads 11:30 and diligently ticks the seconds away, reminding Harris that time is always fleeting. The only other sounds in the room are those of rustling papers as he works his way through the list of customers that Jeff gave him. For the past three hours, he has persisted and checked them, line by line, comparing them against a long list compiled by Broussard, of individuals that perhaps have felt wronged by Megan's clients. His chosen profession is not romantic. It's tedious, time consuming, and amazingly frustrating. Investigation is a process of reengineering the crime, working backwards until pieces begin to fall in place, if you're lucky.

He takes his pen and marks through a name, moving to the next one. It's a name that sounds familiar. He opens the Donkova case file, flipping through several pages until he finds a listing of several civil suits that had been filed against Victor. His eyes scan through several before stopping. He focuses, studying the name, then casts his eyes back at Jeff's list. The tension in his face eases and he sighs softly, taking his pen and circling the name of Eric Thornton. He sets the pen down, closing his eyes and rubbing his temples.

Though relieved that he found a match, a potential lead, he knows the odds are against him, and the rhythmic tick-tock of the hands of time behind him only grow louder. He knows that he could be dealing with a rescue turned ugly, a stalker that followed her and took advantage of the situation, perhaps a jilted lover, or due to Megan's profession, a revenge driven attempted murder that Megan escaped from. If this is a crime that began as a rape and grew into an attempted murder, he knows his odds improve: eighty-five percent of convicted rapists are men known to their victims.

He opens his eyes and turns his attention to the stack of folders retrieved from Megan's house, her online muses. He thumbs through them until he finds Jeff's. He flips it open, studying the contents. Inside is a summary sheet from Nelson Investigations, a private outfit out of Metairie, run by a former colleague of his. There's the full rundown on Jeff: address, age, military history, employment, and even Emily's details with photos of all of them. Harris continues his scan of the document, pausing on criminal history and noticing several entries for parking violations but nothing else.

A strong yawn washes through him, and again, he checks the time. He flips through the photos of Jeff and his family, and then glances over at the other seven folders on the table. He sighs heavily. There are only so many detectives in the department and only so many hours in the day. He knows how things have a way of playing out, of cases getting cold. New cases come along, new heaters with higher priorities. A detective's personal life interferes; they or a loved one becomes ill, or worse. He knows that one all too well. He shakes off the dark thoughts. He needs to keep working. He can't make a mistake.

He opens his notebook, flipping to his notes from the day. He jots down a few comments relating to his new person of interest. He pauses, the tip of the pen tapping the paper, matching the rhythmic tick of the clock, as he stares into the darkness of the room. After a moment, he writes "36.6%", underlining and circling it for emphasis. He sets the pen down and rests his face in his hands. While technology has grown at an exceptional pace, the clearance rate of violent crimes is actually falling, which means more crimes are going unsolved. He's well aware, painfully so, that things can go wrong. He knows the statistics; he reads them every year. In 2012, the FBI reported that in cities such as New

Orleans, the clearance rate for forcible rape had dropped to 36.6 percent. Just because a case was cleared and the suspect identified doesn't mean there was a conviction. Sometimes witnesses and victims refuse to cooperate. The odds are not in the favor of an overworked and understaffed department.

Add to it the fact that New Orleans' crime lab was destroyed during the Storm and its reconstruction and certification have yet to be accomplished. Fingerprints are still analyzed locally within the department, but DNA and blood samples must be analyzed by the LSP lab in Baton Rouge. The rape kit and samples of blood found under Megan's fingernails will be delivered there tomorrow by Broussard. Hopefully it won't take a month to get the results back like it usually does.

He returns to his notes, retracing what he has learned today. So far, he knows that the Louisiana State Police found her wrecked Bronco in knee deep water along the swampy edge of a desolate road in St. Rose, between the site of the festival and Megan's home. There was blood, a cut seat belt, and no witnesses. It's approximately twenty-seven miles from where she was found. She didn't walk it, so it seems that someone gave her a ride. Question is, was it against her will?

He hears the floor creak directly behind him just as two warm hands caress his shoulders before sliding down his chest. Andrea leans in and kisses him softly on the cheek.

"Hey, you. It's pretty late. Why don't you come to bed?" she asks in a voice as soft as her kiss.

He takes one of her hands, kisses it, then clutches them tightly to his chest as he closes his eyes and leans his head back onto her shoulder. For a short moment, he loses himself within her touch, adrift within the rhythm of her soft breath against his ear supplanting the hands of time.

She kisses him again then slides into the seat across the table. She lays her head on it, placing her arms across the stacks of papers and folders.

"They've already stolen the money. Haven't you worked on this enough tonight?

He watches her for a moment before she turns her eyes up to him and smiles.

"I guess you're right," he says, pulling a folder from under her.

She straightens up and helps him organize the folders. Once everything is tidy, she looks back to him.

"Can I talk to you about something? It may not be the best time, but since we're up and alone." Her voice trails off for a minute before Harris answers.

"Okay, shoot," he says.

"I'm worried about Kyle," she says, her eyes peering straight into his, letting him know that this is something that has been weighing on her. "We thought this year might be different, but it isn't and there are some boys at school picking on him and calling him names," she says, halfway hesitant. Harris knows why; he hasn't exactly been the one wanting to discuss it in a logical and rational manner.

"Uh huh," he replies, his thoughts drifting back to the case as he flips through Jeff's folder again.

"Albert, we need to talk about who Kyle is, I mean who he really is on the inside," Andrea says.

"Picking on him?" Harris replies, about one sentence behind her. "See, that's what I've been talking about. I've got to toughen the kid up. Football maybe or maybe we can enroll him in karate or judo or something so he can learn to defend himself."

"That only addresses part of the problem; it doesn't address the root issue," Andrea says, a bit more stern now.

"What are you suggesting? That..." Harris' phone buzzes with a text from Broussard.

Andrea studies him as he reads it; she's seen that look on his face before. She's lost him. She sighs softly, this time with resignation, gets up and walks to the fridge. Removing the milk first, she then pulls two glasses from the cupboard.

"Is this another embezzlement case?"

As she finishes pouring the second glass of milk, his silence gives her pause. She turns back to him. He looks at her, his eyes giving her the answer she didn't want.

"Albert, you promised. Ron promised," she says with disappointment.

"I know, but this is different. They need me on this, Andrea," he says, his tone begging for her approval.

He watches her as she studies him for a moment, then turns away. He knows what she's thinking. It's too soon. After a long moment, she retrieves two saucers from the cupboard. She opens a small container and places several chocolate-chip cookies on each plate. She's pulling out all the stops. Harris has a weakness for cookies.

She returns to the table and the two of them partake of the chocolate and lactose goodness in silence. He dips a cookie in the milk and smiles at her. She looks at him a moment, straight faced, before finally breaking into a small smile when his cookie breaks off and into his milk. He stares at it a moment, then turns his eyes back to Andrea, shrugs, and proceeds to dunk the remainder.

"So what's so important about this case?" she asks reluctantly.

"High profile victim."

"Murdered?"

"Almost," he says, pausing before delivering the most difficult part. "She was raped," he adds after a moment.

"Oh, Albert," she says, closing her eyes and shaking her head. He watches her silently, giving her time to push the memories, the fears, back into their recesses. After a long pause, she opens her eyes, batting away a loose tear.

"Who is she?"

"Megan Callahan."

"That woman from yesterday, at the festival?" she asks.

"Yeah."

"Oh my God," she says as sadness and shock compete for dominance across her face.

She turns her eyes back to him, as they both relive Kyle's words at the festival, as they both relive Miranda's fate, and the weight of her absence. Harris sniffs and quickly casts his eyes back down to the milk, proceeding to immerse another cookie.

"She was so sweet to Kyle yesterday," Andrea says as her eyes drift away, staring into the darkness of the room.

She turns back to Harris and watches as he takes a bite of milk-drenched cookie with his eyes closed. In the light, she can see the glint of a tear along the lid.

"Albert, are you sure you want to do this?"

He opens his eyes and looks at her a moment, then turns back to the milk with the remainder of the cookie. He stirs it slowly, watching the milk wick into its core.

"Yeah," he says finally.

The tentative tone of his voice registers with her. She remembers the words he used to describe himself and his position on the task-force. He always said them with a laugh, but she knows the meaning of "put out to pasture", at least the meaning it has for Harris.

"You know, since Miranda, I've always felt that I left something unfinished, that I gave up," he says before pausing and looking up at Andrea. "I didn't have to take this case. I started not to, I really did. But…"

Andrea reaches across the table and takes his hand in hers.

"I just hope I have it in me, you know? I can't fail, Andrea. Not again," he says, clutching her hand tightly as tears well up in his eyes.

"Shhh," she comforts. "You didn't fail her, Albert."

He stares into her eyes, battling to silence the murmurings and convince himself that her words are true. After a moment, he crunches his lips together, turning away and shaking his head.

"You won't fail, Albert. You're the best or they wouldn't have asked you."

"Yeah, well. I'm having my doubts."

"Why?"

He glances back down at the milk, swirling it one last time before finishing it off. He rises, taking both of their glasses and saucers and placing them in the dishwasher. He turns back to Andrea and gives her a forced smile.

"I don't know, maybe I'm expendable should anything go wrong," he says.

Andrea huffs loudly. "You're the best, Albert. That's why they brought you back," she says, walking to him and placing her arms tightly around him.

"Do me a favor and tell that to the little voice in my head," he whispers to her.

She looks into his eyes for a long moment then smiles.

"You're the best. Now, pity parties over. Let's go to bed," she says, taking him by the hand, pulling him along with her, out of the kitchen, shutting off the light behind her. The talk about Kyle will have to wait.

Chapter 15

ZOO

While Harris and Broussard intended to visit the offices of the company that provided security for the festival first thing this morning, an interesting bit of information has caused them to take a detour. In the early morning hours of Sunday, the New Orleans Fire Department answered a call at an abandoned house. Megan had been found only a mile or so away not long after the call came in. The fact that Megan has burns on her body and the proximity to where she was found at least opens the possibility that her assailant held her in the house and then tried to burn it down around her. The two of them stand at the edge of the taped-off zone around the house on Debore Drive in the upper ninth ward, while arson investigators probe what little remains of the house.

"I'm gonna go around back, look through the bushes back there towards the direction of the park where they found her," Broussard says as an arson investigator approaches. Harris nods as she heads off to give it her best go at being a tracker.

"You Harris?" the investigator asks.

"That would be me."

"Dale Hartman. Nice to meet you. They told me that you were gonna drop by. I wished I had something to show you but, as you can see, not much left. These old houses, when they go, they go."

"Any idea about the cause?"

"Still working on it but there does seem to be evidence of accelerant. This isn't official, but I'm pretty sure it was torched."

Broussard yells to Harris from behind the house, motioning for him to come there.

"She better have found something and it better not be a snake that she wants me to kill," Harris says with a smile as he motions back to her. "Please keep me posted," he adds, shaking Hartman's hand and heading back to Broussard.

"Might have gotten lucky," she says as he approaches, climbing his way through the over grown yard.

"I hope so. What'd you find?"

"Piece of a sheet perhaps, blood on it, fresh. Also some muddy footprints heading in the direction of the park," she says, pulling a baggy from her jacket and dropping the cloth fragment in it.

"Good work. Let's get some pictures of this while we can," Harris says.

Looking around and examining the environment, they both plot the next course of action, stepping on top of each other with their respective decision.

"I'll call—"

"Let's get—"

Harris looks at her and smiles, raising his hand and yielding the floor to her.

"It's your case. What next?"

"I was gonna say let's get some crime scene guys out here and have them work it over. Maybe there's something in there."

"Sounds like a plan. I'll call it in." he says, laughing to himself as he turns back to the ashes and dials the central office. It's what he was going to say anyway.

Broussard nods approvingly. Finally she feels, even if slightly, in control.

———

Harris, Broussard, and the office manager of Acadian Security, sit in the break room of the company's offices in Elmwood, a New Orleans suburb. Acadian has provided security for the festival for the past five years. They charge half their normal rates since the event is a fundraiser for charitable groups and write off the balance as their contribution to the needy.

The manager has already explained that due to the fact that the festival was held in a public park with no permanent security installations or equipment, surveillance video from the night is spotty at best and key areas only were captured. The rain that set in late that night didn't help matters. The door to the office opens and Justin, a twenty-something guard that worked the festival that night, walks in.

"You wanted to see me?" he asks, nodding hello to Harris and Broussard and seeming a bit uncomfortable that he just walked into an impromptu meeting that involves police officers.

"Yes. Justin, this is Detectives Harris and Broussard with the New Orleans police department. They'd like to ask you some questions."

"'Bout what?" he asks nervously.

"Don't worry. You didn't do nothing, at least not that they know about," she replies with a laugh, enjoying seeing Justin sweat.

"We'd like to show you some pictures, see if you recognize anyone from Saturday night at the festival," Broussard says.

"Oh. Sure, be glad to," a relieved Justin replies, sitting down at the table.

Broussard pulls out two photographs, one of Megan and one of Jeff. She hands them to Justin who studies them closely.

"Did you see either of these two Saturday night?" she asks.

There must have been several thousand people there so remembering one from the masses is pretty difficult unless something happened that stands out in ones memory.

"Yeah. I saw her."

"Where?" Harris asks.

"Near the porta-johns," he replies as he studies the picture of Jeff.

"Saw this guy too. They were in some kinda fight. She clocked him square in the face. Busted his nose pretty good."

Harris and Broussard both sit up in their chairs, leaning forward and exchanging a look of surprise. They hoped to have both Megan and Jeff identified, but they weren't expecting this.

"You saw *this* woman punch *this* guy?" Broussard asks.

"Yeah, she went all Jackie-Chan on his ass. I didn't see what started it. It was in a dark area behind some signs. I ran down there soon as soon as I saw her hit him, asked if she needed help, offered to kick his ass."

"You did what?" the manager asks.

"What did she say?" Harris asks, waving her away.

"Said she didn't need help, that everything was okay."

"Did you file an incident? I didn't see anything like that in your report," the manager asks.

"No. They just walked off, so I didn't bother."

The door opens and another guard, white haired with a beer belly, enters.

"What did I do this time?" he asks with a grin.

"David, these detectives from New Orleans would like to speak to you," the manager answers as she rises. "Are you done with Justin? I need to speak with him if you can spare him," she asks with a stern expression.

Harris is busy making notes and Broussard nods.

"Thanks Justin. If we have any more questions, we'll get back with you," she says

David tosses his cap on the table and takes Justin's chair. Harris looks up and extends his hand which is promptly taken by David.

"Albert Harris, NOPD."

"David Edelston, no pd," he says with a chuckle, which is not returned by Harris.

"David, did you happen to see either of these two at the festival Saturday night?" Harris asks, sliding the pictures in front of him.

David pulls his glasses from his shirt pocket and slowly fits them to his wide face. He examines the photos carefully then sets them down on the table.

"Yep, saw both of 'em."

"Where? What time?" Broussard asks.

"Oh... I had just taken my heart medicine so I guess it was about ten, 'bout an hour before the place closed down. Saw 'em in the parking lot. He had his hands all over her."

"What do you mean, all over her? Was he being aggressive with her?" Harris asks.

"Well, she was kinda pushing him away when I shined my flashlight on 'em. He looked like a deer in headlights. I told 'em to go get a room."

"Then what happened?" Broussard asks.

"She got in her Bronco. Was a nice Bronco, probably bout a '72, something like that. This guy, he heads out across the parking lot. Guess he was going to his car or something."

"Any chance any of this was caught on tape?" Harris asks.

David pauses for a moment, seemingly mapping the festival grounds out in his mind in conjunction with where the cameras were positioned.

"Probably not, plus it was raining and sometimes those cameras get a little flaky."

"Can we take a look?" Harris asks.

"Sure. Follow me," David replies as he rises from the table and heads for the door. Harris and Broussard look at each other. He shakes his head in disappointment. Jeff's deeper in this than he claims, and that's not what Harris wanted to learn.

Anyone who has spent an extended period of time in a hospital will say that it can be a zoo. At Tulane Medical, room 7218 is the lion's den. Megan lies in bed, conscious now, and causing a few around her to wish she wasn't. When the doctors woke her up this morning, the room soon filled with chaos. Megan screamed and cried uncontrollably, a terrified soul unsure of where she was or why. What she was sure of, were the short flashes of what little she could remember about the attack. As she struggled to understand what had happened to her, she was forced to relive those memories over and over again, searching them for any speck of a clue as to what happened, who was responsible and what happens next.

While things have calmed down in the last couple of hours, Megan is still snapping and biting at anything and anybody, a wounded lion striking. Her face is bruised and cut, both eyes blackened. Bandages wrap around her ribs and cover her arms, protecting the cuts and burns. A forty-something Internist examines her, flicking a light in her eyes to check pupil dilation.

"Will you just stop?! I'm fine!" Megan barks.

The doctor scowls at her, then turns the light off and places her finger in front of Megan's face.

"Follow my finger," she instructs.

"I don't want to follow your finger unless it's going out that door."

"Megan, among several things, you've suffered quite a concussion. Will you please just... just humor me and I'll leave you alone," the doctor says, frustrated with Megan's combative attitude.

Megan sighs heavily and reluctantly does so, following her finger as she moves it in front of her face. Satisfied, the doctor backs away and begins making notes on the clipboard. Megan tries to sit up. She cries out as pain shoots around her rib cage. The doctor grabs Megan's shoulders and eases her back into a prone position.

"And, you have a few broken ribs."

"How long am I going to be here?"

"Depends. We'll just have to monitor you and see how you progress."

"Callahan's are quick healers. She'll be out of here in no time," Ellen Callahan, Megan's mother, says as she steps to Megan's bedside and takes her hand in hers. She and Megan's sister, Kristi, drove in from Memphis late yesterday.

Megan rolls her head and looks at her.

"Did you get my laptop?"

"I haven't gone yet. I wanted to——"

"Then fucking go, will you?! I need it."

Ellen ignores the barking. That's not Megan talking and she knows it. It's the medicine, it's the circumstances. She'll gladly let her bark at her all she wants. The alternative is unbearable.

A male nurse enters announcing that he needs to change some of Megan's bandages. Megan watches him suspiciously as he approaches and reaches for her arm.

"Don't! Don't fucking touch me!" she says as the fear and distrust returns.

Kristi steps up to the bed and touches the nurse's shoulder.

"Let me do it. I'm a nurse," she says, taking the bandages from him before he leaves.

"I'll be back in a few hours to check on you. Take it easy on the staff, Megan," the doctor says as she begins to leave.

"Whatever," Megan snarls.

She opens the door just as Harris is about to knock and they pass in the doorway. He steps into the room as all eyes turn to see who the stranger is. Megan glares at him, not saying a word, as their eyes meet. He nods to her, but she doesn't react. She simply lies there watching him with distrust. Seeing his badge, Ellen steps over to greet him.

"You must be Detective Harris," she says, extended her hand. "I'm Ellen, Megan's mother."

"Albert Harris."

"What have you found out? Do you have any idea who the son-of-a-bitch is that did this?" Ellen asks.

"It's still early. Still trying to nail down the facts," he says, and then looks to Megan who extends her claws and strikes.

"I thought you were taking retirement. Couldn't they assign someone that doesn't hate me?" she says with loathing, as Kristi begins to reapply the bandage.

Harris has seen hostile victims before, but he's never had the hostility thrown directly at him and he struggles to gain control of the situation.

"I don't—"

"Oh wait... that would be the whole department, wouldn't it? Guess I'm fucked!" she says cutting hateful eyes to him.

"Be Nice!" Kristi growls softly with a scowl on her face, pulling the bandage tight and causing Megan to flinch.

Harris looks to Ellen who now watches him with the same distrust as Megan. This is not the best way to start the first interview. He glances back at Megan.

"What, Harris?! I thought you would be happy to see me like this? The bitch got what she deserves, right?"

"Megan, you couldn't be farther from the truth," he says, stepping to a side table. He sets his notebook down and removes his jacket. He came here for a reason; he's got a job to do.

When Harris first walked into Megan's room and saw her, he struggled to hold back a flood of emotion. Flashes of Miranda, how she looked that night, the bruises, the cuts, and the blood, rushed through his mind. The situation was compounded by Megan's hostile reaction to him. His thirty-five years of experience as a detective has taught him that he needs to be able to adjust to any situation. Dealing with victims and their families can be difficult, especially early in the investigation and requires a delicate balancing act between the need to obtain information and the desire to be compassionate for those who are hurting. Being a detective is part sleuth and part salesmanship. He knows that those he is trying to help need to feel that he cares for them and their situation. With Broussard on her way to Baton Rouge with the blood samples and rape kit, it's up to Harris to convince Megan that she can trust the department—and him.

He's doing his best. He's taken off the jacket and the tie, changed his tone of voice, made small talk when necessary, and now knows more about a 1971 Bronco than he ever cared to know. He sits in a chair, notebook in hand, next to Megan's bed in which they have helped Megan into an upright position. Kristi stands near him and begins to tend to another bandage that needs changing. Megan's attitude towards him has softened, at least for now. But Harris knows that the right, or wrong, word or phrase can trigger a memory and send her back into the darkness in a moment's notice; he must be careful.

Unfortunately, although some would argue fortunately for Megan, she doesn't remember much after she ran off the road. The mind has a way of shielding the psyche from unpleasant memories. Asking Megan to try and remember what the assailant looked like was a painful and agonizing experience. The only images she can recall involve a white leather mask, akin to something you would find in in a sex shop and favored by those of the leather and bondage crowd, and the assailant's empty, green eyes.

They've already discussed several previous cases that Megan has tried. She positively identified Eric Thornton as the man that verbally accosted her in Three Muses and Harris has already given Broussard the task of tracking him down for questioning. The conversation has moved to the time of accident on St. Rose road.

"So it was pouring rain, and I could barely see out the windshield and some asshole passes me, driving like a maniac. A few minutes later, I see these tail-lights ahead and by the time I saw them, I was right on top of them. The car—" Megan explains.

"Was it a car? What kind?" Harris asks.

She closes her eyes and tries to picture it, culling it from the blurred images of that night.

"It happened so fast, I think it might have been a truck, older model Chevy? I don't know. It just jumped out into the road and I swerved. That's the last thing I remember about the wreck."

Kristi removes the last of the bandage from a wound on Megan's arm causing her to flinch in pain.

"Ouch! Shit! Where'd you go to medical school?"

"Shut up and grow a pair. Hate to tell ya, but you're gonna have to deal with this for a while," Kristi replies before looking at her and smiling sympathetically.

"Sorry. I love you, though," she adds.

"I love you too but you still need to work on your technique," Megan says as she examines the exposed wound. "Is that a cut or a burn?" she asks.

Kristi examines it as does Harris, albeit from a distance. He can't help but notice it, oddly shaped and resembling a crude cross. It's clear to Harris that it's a burn and Kristi confirms it.

"There were flames?" Megan asks, looking to Harris.

"We think you might have been in an abandoned house that burned to the ground the same morning not far from where the motorist found you."

"I can't remember. Seems like... I keep getting this image of smoke and I can smell it but, I just can't tell you for sure. Have you been there?"

"Yeah. Broussard and I were there this morning. Not much left, mostly ashes."

"Broussard? Tanisha Broussard?"

Harris nods and smiles, choosing to not go into detail about his new partner. It might take the mood of the conversation in the wrong direction.

Harris didn't have to say anything; Megan picked up on it right away. She watches him for a moment as he stares down at his notebook. She looks away, realizing that Robichaux has been pulled out of active duty and that it was due to her entrapment tactic in the Donkova case. She usually doesn't give things like this a second thought. Being removed or isolated from the personal side of such an event, it hasn't had much impact on her. She turns back to Harris and though he's good at hiding it, he's not that good.

She has always been able to feel empathy for people around her. But it's more than empathy; she can see right through people, picking up on little nuances that some might call vibes. She can look at someone and quickly make determinations about them and most of the time she's right. She isn't sure if it's a curse or blessing, but right now she's picking those vibes up from Harris.

"I'm sorry," she says.

"She's not that bad," Harris says with a slight smile, attempting to divert the topic. He looks at Megan whose eyes say 'you know what I mean'.

"We've all got jobs to do. You did yours," he says, reopening his notebook before adding "Let's try to get through the rest of these."

Megan nods agreement and watches Kristi finish bandaging the wound.

Harris flips to a page in his notebook, the queue for what he needs to discuss with her, scanning to determine what to discuss next. Actually, he's stalling. He knows good and well what's next and it could become complicated. When the questions get personal, things can begin to get weird. Megan slowly and pain-fully reaches for a water bottle. The ribs are really hurting her. Harris reaches and grabs the bottle and hands it to her.

"Thanks. Never knew broken ribs felt like this," she says as she takes a drink.

"You write on a poetry website, yeah?"

"I dabble. Why?"

"You were in a relationship with Jeff Taylor, an online relationship. Saturday night, you were seen in a confrontation with him at the festival. What was that about?"

Megan squirms, adjusting her position and her expression becomes dour

"It was nothing. How'd you know about Poets Beat and Jeff?" she asks, her eyes beginning to show a hint of suspicion.

"Your friend Anna. We spoke yesterday here at the hospital," Harris replies, unaware of the hornets' nest that he just kicked.

Megan's becomes agitated; picking up the water bottle and spinning it in her hand.

"Really? What else did she say?" she asks through her teeth as she rips the label from the bottle.

"She was trying to help," Kristi says with a look to Megan, puzzled by the sudden degree of animosity.

"She told us about the website, the relationships you had there. It's a legiti-mate lead," Harris calmly replies, clearly seeing the lion crouching, ready to pounce.

"What'd she tell you?" Megan asks with eyes glued to the label being destroyed.

"She provided us with details about a number of them. We've done an initial—"

"So she took you to my house? What else did you do while you there? Did you try on my panties? How'd my shoes fit?"

"Megan, stop it!" Kristi snaps.

He knows better than to reply. He calmly studies his notebook, knowing that even a look can be misinterpreted in these circumstances, and makes a note of Megan's behavior. If she and Anna are best friends, something's wrong. It's not the details that were provided; it's that *Anna* provided them. Perhaps Anna had introduced her to the assailant at some point, and while she can't remember the guy's face or identify him, her mind is still able to make that connection and she's lashing out at her. Perhaps there is a love triangle that he isn't aware of.

After a moment he looks to Kristi who mouths "I'm sorry" to him. He smiles then turns back to Megan who seems to have calmed down.

"Sorry," she says without looking at him as her anger begins to fade.

"Megan, I know this is difficult but no one else can answer these questions."

She doesn't respond. Harris can see her lip quivering ever so slightly as she glances to the door then quickly to the window, the wounded lion seeking to flee.

"We'll find the guy that did this but we have to rule some out," he says, reaching to her hand and taking her little finger in his.

Megan's breathing becomes shallow and her heart begins to race as she looks at his hand holding hers. It's terrifying and comforting at the same time. The trauma that she has been through is churning her mind and the memories are like white capping waves smashing against the wall that she has carefully built around her.

She's taken back to Baptist Memorial in Memphis eighteen years ago. She stood at the edge of her father's bed as his breathing became weaker and weaker. The lung cancer, only diagnosed two months earlier, had proved insurmountable. Wes looked at her, reaching through the guard on the bedside and taking her little finger in his hand.

"I love you Meg. I'll be waiting for you," he said and closed his eyes one last time.

She hears his voice call her name. She looks around, phasing back into her reality.

"Megan. Did you hear me?" Harris says.

"What?" she says, a bit lost.

"Let's pick this up in the morning. I think we've covered enough for today," he says with a compassionate smile and a pat on her hand. She simply nods as he rises and grabs his jacket and tie then looks to Kristi.

"It's been a pleasure meeting you Kristi. Maybe when this is all over we can get up to Memphis and take you up on that night on Beale Street."

He turns back to Megan and smiles.

"Try to get some sleep. See ya in the morning."

She watches him as he leaves and then struggles to shake the memories back into their appropriate places.

Chapter 16

TRAINER

Andrea finishes putting the dishes away as Harris walks into the living room, loosens his belt, and sits in his recliner. The belt loosening is a result of a particularly good meal of stuffed bell peppers. He smiles, thinking about how he always goes on about that dish and how he always says 'I love me some cow,' all the while knowing that Andrea has been using ground turkey in her recipe for a couple of years now, ever since his cholesterol scare. He objected at first, demanding that she switch back and she said she would, but she didn't. She simply changed the recipe. She means well and he loves her so he plays the game. Plus, that new recipe is too damn good.

He turns on the TV to ESPN just as the Saints are kicking off. He begins counting the fifty dollars that Broussard will have to cough up tomorrow as he watches the Saints hold the Dolphins to a three and out. After the commercial, and just as the Saints receive the Dolphin's punt, Andrea walks into the living room and sits on the couch.

"Why don't you go talk to Kyle?" she asks.

"About what?"

"You know what," she says with a tone of admonishment in her voice.

"I'll talk to him at halftime," he says, cheering as Brees completes a long pass over the middle.

Andrea rises and takes the remote from the side table and steps in front of him as he struggles to see the result of the next play. She flips the TV off and turns back to him.

"Go talk to Kyle. Now," she says sternly.

"Well, DVR it so I can watch it when I'm done," he says as he rolls his eyes and huffs.

Andrea flips the set back on and begins the DVR, before turning the TV back off.

"There. Now please, go. You need to help him," she says as she points to the hallway.

Harris reluctantly gets up and walks down the hall to Kyle's room. He opens the door and sees Kyle lying on his bed, working on homework.

"Hey buddy. Can I talk to you?" Harris asks.

"Sure," Kyle says without looking up from his studies.

"Stop your work for a minute and come sit by me," he says as he sits on the bed next to Kyle.

Kyle closes his book, crawls across the bed, and scoots closer to Harris. "Yeah?"

"Nanna told me you're having some trouble at school, that there are some boys picking on you. Is that true?"

"Yeah."

"Who is it?"

"Lots of them. But mostly it's Matt and Justin."

"Matt? The Vincent kid?"

"Yeah."

Harris nods, knowing that name too well. Billy Vincent, Matt's father, is a known troublemaker and had been arrested several times for public intoxication and assault. So it seems the apple doesn't fall far from the tree in the Vincent family.

"What are they saying? Are they hitting you?"

He doesn't answer as he looks away, dropping his eyes to the floor.

"Kyle, answer me."

"They're just mean, stupid boys trying to impress the girls," Kyle says softly.

Harris can sense the reluctance in Kyle, the hesitancy in his voice. He doesn't need Kyle to tell him what they're saying. He knows. He was Matt Vincent when he was a kid, picking on boys that were smaller or effeminate in any way. He remembers Tommy Ells, a boy in his class that bore the brunt of Harris' and his friends' cruelty. He looks at Kyle and wonders how Tommy's parents must have felt. He gazes down at the floor as he thinks about what he should say now that he is on the other side of the fence.

"Kyle, you need to stand up to them, stand up for yourself. Bully's live off of fear. Don't let them intimidate you," he says, patting Kyle on the shoulder.

"They'll back down if you stand up to them. That's what cowards do," he adds, realizing and accepting that he is saying the same of his teenage self.

"I've tried," Kyle says, disappointment pouring from his words.

"Keep trying. They'll eventually respect you for it and turn their attention to someone that they can intimidate. You're a Harris. We face our troubles; we don't hide from them."

He runs his hand through Kyle's hair and kisses him on the head. He pulls the hair back into a pony tail and tugs on it.

"You know, you make yourself a target with this right?"

"Yes, for the hundredth time." Kyle says dejectedly.

"I don't suggest you do this, but if they start it, you need to finish it," Harris says as he rises and stands in front of Kyle.

"Stand up for second," he says, motioning to Kyle and squatting down and holding his hands up like a boxer's sparring partner.

"Give me a punch."

"I don't want to."

"Come on. Just picture their faces on my palms and punch them."

Kyle looks at Harris then away, then back at his hands. A bit of anger begins to build in his face and he punches with his right fist and hits Harris palm. It's not a hard punch.

"Put your shoulder into. Aim and watch for an opening then strike. Try it again."

Kyle focuses and takes a deep breath then punches again with the same effect.

Harris puts his hands down and pats him on the shoulder, realizing that Kyle will probably not become a UFC champion.

"Good job. We'll keep working on it."

As Kyle climbs back onto the bed, Harris walks to the door and then turns back to him.

"Look, if they bother you, move close to a teacher and get their attention," he says, accepting that an ounce of prevention may be better than a pound of cure in Kyle's situation.

Chapter 17

FAULT

The men of New Hope Baptist gather at 6:45 in the morning on the first Tuesday of each month. It's the long held Men's Breakfast that Harris has attended regularly for the past five years, and this Tuesday is no different. Robichaux and his family began going to New Hope about two years ago at the encouragement of Harris. He may be off active duty during the public integrity investigation, but he isn't dead and wouldn't miss the breakfast either. It's something that has become a tradition for both of them.

It's a small group, fifteen on a good day. They gather for fellowship and food, good food with lots of bacon. Since Harris' cholesterol scare, Andrea has banned the substance from the house. But once a month, Harris gets to indulge and indulge he does. Remnants of eggs, wheat toast, and three of what was six slices of good, old time, pork bacon lie on the plate in front of him. Those last few strips of bacon are his morning dessert.

"So how's the case going? Getting anywhere?" Robichaux asks as he mixes several packs of sugar into his coffee.

"It's early, Larry. I wasn't able to speak to Megan until yesterday."

"I feel for you having to take this case. It's gonna be a bitc…" Robichaux says, stopping himself after remembering he's in a house of God.

"It's gonna be *difficult*. Who's *not* on the list of suspects? It's gotta be a mile long," he adds.

Harris shrugs his shoulders, picks up a slice of bacon and takes a bite.

"This is good bacon. Wonder what brand this is?" he asks.

"I don't know. So is she?"

"Is she what?"

"A lesbian?"

"Broussard?"

"No. I know she's a lesbian. Sorry bout that pal. Callahan, is she a lesbian?"

"I don't know. It's not important," Harris replies with a look of bewilderment.

"What do you mean not important? You may need to be hunting for a woman instead of a man. Some bull dyke out there that felt a little jilted," Robichaux says with a chuckle.

"She seems more the bull type, though" he adds with an extra layer of animosity.

"Look Larry, regardless of how you feel about her, no woman should go through what she did," Harris says, setting the half-finished piece of bacon down on the plate.

"May be, but I can't say I have much sympathy for her. I know that's not the Christian thing to say but..."

Harris pushes his plate away and drops his napkin on top.

"No it's not. You need to forgive, Larry. If you can't forgive, you can't get forgiveness," he says retrieving his jacket from the back of the chair.

"I gotta get over to Tulane, talk to her some more. I'll talk to you later," he says as he heads for the door, leaving a sulking Larry to clean up the table.

The lion is up early in room 7218 and she's already chewed out two nurses and threw the cold toast at the nice lady that brought her breakfast. It's been a long, difficult night for Megan. Between the pain and the nightmares, she didn't get much sleep. It's odd how the mind tries to deal with traumatic events, trying to make sense of the madness. Overnight, Megan relived being attacked by Max, the metal sculptor that rents from her, and the guy in the mail room at work, whatever his name is, as her psyche tried in vain to put a face to the voice. His voice, she can hear that very well in her mind. If she heard it again, she would know it in an instant.

When Harris arrived an hour ago, she was at least more cordial than the day before and didn't bite his head off for simply being. Ellen has given him the run-down on the ranch and that their latest stallion, Sein Finn Rocket Bar, a direct descendant of Something Royal, the dam of Secretariat, is throwing off some of the finest foals in all of Tennessee. Once Megan seemed relaxed enough, Harris moved forward with the difficult questions.

The conversation has moved to the discussion of Jeff, and it's not a topic that Megan is reacting well to. She met Jeff through the poetry site, but it was a bit of a caged hunt. Anna knew him from another bar, Anton's, a smoky laid back joint. They held poetry readings once a month and Jeff occasionally tended bar there. One night that both Anna and Megan were in attendance, Jeff hopped in front of the microphone and read a piece he had written. It was brutally dark but hauntingly beautiful and must have struck a chord with Megan. At Megan's encouragement, Anna invited him to the website, and it wasn't long before Jeff was Megan's newest muse.

"Did you ever sense any hostility about your relationship ending?" Harris asks.

"No Harris, there was no hostility. I never felt threatened."

"Why did you agree to meet him at the festival?"

"Because he's a friend. Do I need any other reason?"

"Just trying to make sense of it all," Harris says, holding his hands up defensively to ward away the beast.

"A guard told us that he witnessed an incident between the two of you, that he saw you punch him. What was that about?"

"It was an accident, Harris! He came up behind me and scared me, that's all."

"Another guard said there was another incident between you two in the parking lot."

"Nothing happened, Harris," she exclaims, throwing her hands up in frustration as her breathing begins to quicken.

"Megan, I've known the guy for years. I don't want to think he did it, but I can't rule it out. Your memory of the night is——"

"*He didn't do it*! How many times do I have to say that," she says as she begins to lose control of her emotions, tears streaming down her face.

"This is *not* his voice inside my mind driving me *fucking* insane!" she yells, slapping the side of her head.

Ellen rushes to her side grabbing Megan's hand.

"Stop it! Get the *fuck* away from me!" Megan yells, jerking her hand away.

She closes her eyes, holding both hands out and towards each of them as if pushing them away, focusing, trying to catch the next stone falling from the wall around her while trying to replace the ones that just fell. She breathes deeply for a moment, calming herself and taking herself back to that night in the parking lot.

She received a message from Jeff that he had arrived at the festival, and they met up near the entrance about nine. They listened to the last musical set for about an hour before the rain set in and they decided to leave. They had walked hand in hand to the parking lot, to Megan's Bronco. Her heart had raced the whole time, terrified that the ghosts would come blowing in with a cold wind from her past. Perhaps they were preoccupied and didn't realize she was holding hands with a man, or perhaps there was nothing for them to frighten away.

At her Bronco, she opened the door then turned to look back at him to square up the plan for the evening. He took her hand in his, raised it to his lips and kissed it softly. They stood, oblivious to the rain, and gazed into each other's eyes for what seemed like an eternity.

"How do you do that?" he asked softly.

"Do what?"

"Mesmerize me with those eyes."

Her heart skipped beats as she looked back at him deeply, lost within his eyes before closing hers and inviting him to kiss her and their lips met as he pulled her close to him. It felt like her heart would leap from her chest and she leaned on his arms as her world spun in circles. She had never felt this way before, ever. She could have stood there all night in his arms, it felt so wonderful, so warm and comforting. It was a feeling she had longed for. She melted in his arms and tears flowed freely down her cheeks. She trusted him and she relished in it.

She feels a warm caress on her shoulder. "You okay?" Ellen asks softly.

Megan opens her eyes, tears streaming down her face, and looks at Harris. "He didn't do it," she says calmly.

Megan's lunch tray with a half-eaten meal sits near her bed, on which Kristi is lying. Megan sits, awkwardly due to the pain, with Harris at a small table near the window. She fidgets with a bottle of water from which she has already peeled the label. A few magazines that Kristi brought lie scattered across the top. Lunch for Harris was a Caesars salad with a light vinaigrette dressing as he tried to make up for the decadence of the morning breakfast.

After their meals, Harris moved the questioning back to cases that Megan had tried, figuring that those would be less emotional and allow Megan to think logically. It had worked in that Megan has been fairly calm in the afternoon's session although she's tiring of the questioning. Harris knows he has to circle back to Jen, the mystery woman.

"One last question and I'll leave you be," he says.

"Thank God."

"On the poetry site, your most recent muse is someone named Jennifer, Jen," he gingerly says to her.

Megan shakes her head in frustration. She's done talking about the poetry site.

"So now it's the dyke thing?" she barks.

"Megan, I didn't say that. That's not where I was—"

"Harris, she didn't have anything to do with this. Forget she exists. It's something you're not able to handle okay? Just drop Jen, drop Jeff, and find the *fucker* that did this!"

Harris bulls through with the question.

"Anna said you were meeting Jen at the festival."

He watches her as the mention of Anna's name seems to generate a lot of anger, again.

"She… she couldn't make it. Do you have my phone?" she retorts, shifting the subject.

"I do, but I need it."

"For what? I didn't give you permission to take it as evidence did I? Got something I signed? Give it to me. Get your court order, subpoena my phone records, I hope you do. But you don't need my phone," she barks, holding out her hand.

She's right. Broussard already worked up the subpoena and the judge signed it, along with one for the website, this morning. He smiles a fake smile and pulls the phone from his jacket and hands it to her. A tap on the door breaks the tension as he turns to see Ellen walk in all smiles.

"Look who I ran into," she says.

Anna, carrying the coffees that Ellen had gone to retrieve, steps through the door. Kristi rises and takes the coffees from her, setting them on a counter and then gives her a hug. Harris looks to Megan who stares straight down at the table, breathing rapidly as she squeezes the water bottle in her hand. She looks up and out the window, eyes darting, puzzled, as if she's trying to make sense of a recalled memory.

"Hey," Anna says with tears in her eyes as she steps towards Megan. It's the first time she's been in the room when Megan was awake.

Megan turns quickly to her. Anger and hate fill her face.

"What are *you* doing here?"

Anna stops and glances to Harris, confused. "What? I—"

Megan rises, oblivious to the pain in her chest and takes a step towards Anna.

"Get the *Fuck* out of here!"

Kristi opens the door and yells to the nurses' station.

"We need some help in here!"

"Megan, please, I just wanted to—" Anna says pleadingly as she takes a step back.

"Get out! I don't want to see *you*!"

Anna moves back towards her friend. She just needs to get her to calm down.

"Megan, please…"

Megan's emotions are completely out of control. She's racing between anger, hate, and emotional collapse.

"*Stay away from me!*" she screams as Harris rises and puts his hands on her shoulders, attempting to calm her. She throws her arms back clearing his hands and then turns back to Anna.

"Do you know what he did? *Do you?!* He quoted *your* fuck stories while he was raping *me!*"

Anna collapses into tears as Ellen takes her in her arms. Kristi escorts a couple of nurses into the room.

"*Get Out!*" Megan screams as Harris forcibly takes her in his arms and moves her to the bed where the nurses struggle to administer a tranquilizer. He watches as a destroyed Anna runs from the room with Ellen following and calling to her, while Kristi struggles to calm a hysterical Megan.

Chapter 18

CONNECTIONS

L ate afternoon at Mick's isn't a busy time of day. Things don't kick off until the work day is over since most of their customers are New Orleans
locals. Harris sits at the bar, staring blankly at his drink and lost in thought as
Broussard enters. While Harris was in the lion's den, she was tracking down
Eric Thornton. She walks up and straddles the stool next to Harris.

"Thornton's clean. An asshole, but a clean asshole."

"What'd he say?"

"He was in Dallas with his wife at a high school reunion, tons of witnesses.
You talk to Megan?"

"You could say that."

"What's that mean?"

"Pretty tough sledding but we made progress. She doesn't remember much,
didn't get a good look at the guy. Said she thought he had green eyes but she
couldn't really remember. He was wearing some sort of sadomasochistic mask."

"You mean like bondage?"

"Yeah."

The two of them exchange a look; both of their thoughts go back to Jeff and
the sadomasochistic work he had posted on the poetry site. After a moment, it's
Broussard that breaks the silence.

"What color are Jeff's eyes?"

"They're green, but she swears it wasn't him. I mean she's adamant about it. I've never had a victim become this confrontational."

"Well, considering what she been through I'm sure she's not her normal self."

"I'm sure. Do you know her? I mean, before this case? She seemed to know you when I told her we were working together."

"We belong to the same gym. I've seen her there and we've spoken, but that's about it."

Harris nods and takes a sip of his scotch.

"Want a drink? I'm buying."

"Well in that case yes," she replies and motions to the bartender and orders a Coke.

Harris motions to him to put her drink on his tab then looks back at Broussard.

"So, it seems that Megan isn't the queen of erotica like we thought."

"You been trolling the site looking for more graphic works?" she replies with a laugh.

"Her friend, or ex-friend perhaps, Anna, she wrote those, evidently. She came into the room this afternoon and Megan exploded. I mean completely lost it. Seems our guy quoted something that Anna had written and Megan blames her in some way. I had to physically restrain her; she was that out of control. I felt so bad for both of them. I probably need to check on Anna and make sure she's okay. She took it hard," Harris says, staring blankly ahead as he remembers the chaos of the moment.

"Then that's the key, the poetry site," she replies.

"Yeah. Question is, if that site is anonymous, how did our guy know which account was hers?"

"Who else knew?"

"Except for Anna, only our friend Jeff, according to Megan."

"You don't think Anna's involved in some way do you?" Broussard asks with a twisted look on her face.

"No. I don't think so. Why? They weren't lovers, they were best friends. Anything's possible though. Love triangle? Maybe, but I doubt it."

Broussard thinks about it a moment, taking a drink of her Coke.

"So, do we pick Jeff up?"

Harris turns back to his drink, swirling it around in the glass, thinking that one through.

"It's your call."

She looks away, evaluating her options. Two words that Blanchard said after she returned to his office the past Sunday echo in her mind... "No mistakes." She looks back at Harris.

"What would you do?"

After a moment, he finishes his drink and gets up, pitching a twenty on the bar.

"I'd let him stew. See what the lab comes back with. Watch him and if he starts getting twitchy, we'll bring him in."

"Yeah, that's what I was thinking," she says, nodding her head approvingly.

She downs her Coke and they head out the door into the waning evening light.

"Look, use your excellent computer skills, and see if you can find anything online that could link Megan to that Dream Weaver profile. I'll start working on her other muses," Harris says before turning towards his car. "I'll see ya in the morning. Get some sleep," he adds as he walks away.

She watches him for a moment and laughs to herself. Somehow that old man just took back control of the case. He's smooth, she'll give him that.

⸺⸎⸺

The reason that hospitals are kept so cold has always eluded Megan. She understands that operating rooms are frigid to discourage bacteria growth, but this isn't an operating room. Her search for the thermostat was fruitless and her requests to the nurses have fallen on deaf ears. Maybe that's payback for being such a bitch to them. Adding the cold to the deafening silence creates an environment that, by its nature, can keep a person feeling down.

Ellen and Kristi, at the insistence of Megan, have gone to her house for the night to care for Frizbee and Toulouse. Sleep has again proved elusive for

Megan. She sits, wrapped up in blankets, at the small side table by the window, staring out at the lights of the city. She picks up her phone, broken screen and all, and navigates to her photos, opening it up to some shots she took with Jeff at the festival. The two of them stand with their backs to the stage, Jeff behind her with his arms around her as she leans her head back into his shoulder. The smiles are real and beautiful.

She drops her head as the smile on her face is wiped away by memories of the day's discussions with Harris and his continued probing into her relationships. She built her walls for a reason. They've been breached and her life laid bare for all to see. She feels weak and violated, physically, psychologically, and emotionally. She isn't sure which is worse.

The thought that Harris could consider Jeff a suspect infuriates and terrifies her at the same time. She knows Jeff and she knows he didn't do it, but those ghosts in her head; they won't shut up and are having a heyday planting seeds of doubt in her mind.

She shakes off the bad thoughts and returns to the photos and flips to the next picture, one of Jeff with a piece of tissue sticking out of one his nostrils as Megan kisses him on the cheek, the aftermath of the punch to the face that she gave him. It really was an accident. She had gone to the restroom and Jeff had decided to catch up to her. A crowd of people forced her to take a path through a dark and secluded area raising her alert levels in her mind as she made her way through. Jeff ran up behind and innocently grabbed her shoulder as the music prevented her from hearing his calls. What happened next was pure instinct due to the months of self-defense training, and Jeff was soon sporting a busted nose as Megan dabbed the blood with a tissue from her pocket. She looks up with a smile and stares back out the window and is taken back to a late night call, one of many that she had with Jeff.

It was a Friday night that had rolled into a Saturday morning, another marathon call of baring their souls to each other. She sat curled up on the couch with a blanket as Frizbee laid on the floor beside her.

"It was an '89 Ford F-150," Megan said.

"Four-wheel drive?" Jeff replied.

"Yep."

"With glass packs?"

"Damn straight."

"You really were a tomboy," Jeff replied as he quietly closed the bedroom door after checking to make sure Emily was asleep.

"Closest thing to a son my father ever had. I still wore the dresses and heels, still do, I love 'em, but most of the time it was jeans and boots for me."

"I would have loved to have known you as a kid."

"If you had seen me, maybe not," she replied before shifting the subject by adding "So what's up with you and your last write, the snowbirds one?"

"I don't know. It's just, sometimes I wish I could fly away, start fresh. Leave all the shit behind, you know?"

"Sounds like this might turn out to be your metamorphosis, the emerging from your chrysalis."

"So now I'm a bug?"

"A butterfly maybe."

"Butterflies are nice. Maybe a monarch," Jeff had replied with a laugh before adding "Hey, I wrote you something."

Megan closed her eyes in anticipation of hearing his voice recite words of love to her.

"Yeah? Read it to me?"

"Well, it sucks compared to yours."

"Shut up and read it."

"Okay, okay. Hang on. Let me find the best part," Jeff said as he scanned down the screen on his computer.

"You bewitch my soul as my mind dances on your words, a celestial spirit reading to me the script of my heart," she recalls him saying before she's jerked back to her harsh reality by the wail of an ambulance.

She wipes a tear from her cheek as she looks out the hospital window to the street below. She watches as the ambulance rounds the corner towards the emergency entrance and wonders what horrors were afflicted upon its occupant.

The words Jeff spoke to her that night continue in her mind. "Our love transcends all. There is nothing between us, distance is meaningless. Our souls have melded into one. I close my eyes and you are there," she remembers him saying softly.

She closes her eyes, hoping to find Jeff there in the darkness but is assaulted by images of the attack that race through her psyche, shattering her peace. The cold air of the hospital room sends shivers down her spine as she remembers her flesh exposed and the feel of gloved hands running across her breasts. She can practically feel the restraints on her arms and legs as she hears that horrid voice ricocheting inside her mind.

"So sad you won't be able to write about this," it said, ripping the blindfold from her eyes to reveal that hideous fetish hood of white leather, straps, and zippers for eyes and mouth staring down at her. She remembers the feel of the gloved finger pressed against her lips as the words he ripped from Anna's stories scream through her mind.

"Your lips, lush and soft, meet mine, oscillating moisture and fire co-alesced," it had said before closing on her, pressing the cold, jagged metal of the zipper hard against her mouth.

Her phone rings and she opens her terror-filled eyes, escaping the horror of her memories. She glances to it and sees that it's Jen, as tears flow freely down her face. She drops the phone on the table and buries her face in her hands, crying as the phone rings, and rings, and rings.

The Black Pearl district sits wedged between Audubon Park, the Uptown district, and atop the high banks of the Mississippi River. The ravages of Hurricane Katrina were caused not by the river, but rather flooding from Lake Pontchartrain. The high ground on which the district sits spared the working class neighborhood and its shotgun style homes so common throughout the city. Jeff moved into the area when his final tour of duty in Iraq was finished about five years ago. He had married his high school sweetheart, Emily, who had given birth to a son, Dustin, as Jeff shipped out for a second and final tour. Once his commitment was done, he came home and settled into the house on Garfield Street.

The house is a simple, thousand square-feet, single shotgun-style home with a small backyard. The riverside end of Garfield Street was as close to the amenities of the neighboring districts of Audubon and Uptown as they could afford. Like most parents, they both wanted safe schools and a pleasant area to raise Dustin. But the house on Garfield is also no longer a home to him, not since Emily moved out, taking Dustin with her.

As he lies in his bed staring into the darkness, he wonders how his life could have ended up the way it has. He trusted Emily and shared his deepest desires and fears with her. He had written poetry as a kid and a bout with depression a year or so ago led him to seek an outlet for his pain and returning him to penning verse. He knew Anna from the time he spent tending bar at Anton's, and when she invited him to join Poets Beat, he seized the opportunity, as its online community provided him the avenue to share his writing with the world and at the same time socialize with other hurting hearts, and ultimately Megan.

She saw through his poetry, reading between the lines. They were soon spending countless hours online chatting, which led to countless hours spent on late night phone calls. She saw his soul and loved him for it at a time when Emily was abandoning him for the same reason. Jeff is the first to admit that he became emotionally attached to Megan even though he was still married to Emily. But Emily's hateful words only seemed to drive him towards Megan and her words of love and encouragement.

Their online relationship raged as they each posted romantic and steamy poetry and proclaimed their love to each other for any on the site that would care to read it. However, his carelessness was the catalyst for his current situation when Emily discovered his online postings and threatened divorce, resulting in the online affair coming to a screeching halt. A couple of months of counseling did little to stop a determined Emily who seemed intent on divorce and, in her words, getting away from the freak. The events that followed in the ensuing months have now led him to be top on the list of suspects in the brutal rape of the woman that he has grown to love.

They say time heals all wounds, but Jeff is a slow healer. As the sand grains fall, accumulating higher and higher, the when and where of visual memories fade. However, the spoken word, whether of love or of hate, lives forever. He feels like a failure. He feels beaten. He feels the sickening knot in his stomach as the hate-filled words Emily spoke seem to resonate from the now bare walls and go on to echo inside his mind.

"You can't do this to me, Jeff! To us!" she had said.

"I can't take this anymore! I can't take you anymore! Dustin needs a father," she had screamed.

He wipes the tears from his eyes, rolls over, closes them and thinks of Megan. He can feel her breath and it's as if she is there with him, whispering into his ear.

"Speak to me of dreams and fantasies. When life crumbles, let me embrace you. Let me be eternally with you, our souls speaking as one."

A single tear falls from a closed eye as he smiles softly, comforted, if only for a moment, by the words of the woman that had changed his life. The words of the woman that he fears he will never speak to again.

Chapter 19

FLIGHT

It's been a day unlike most for Harris. It began with Harris witnessing Robichaux mercilessly revel in his contempt for Megan. The hostility of Megan, albeit less intense, continued through the day, climaxing with an emotional breakdown. The hurt on Anna's face, the hate in Megan's eyes, they still haunt him.

Harris sits in his recliner thumbing through the stack of folders relating to Megan's muses. He stops and flips through Jeff's. He sighs in resignation that his friend seems more and more to be involved. In other cases, with other suspects, he would have already arrested the suspect based on the information he and Broussard have gathered. But this isn't another case, nor another suspect. This is a man he considers a friend. Parking Jeff in the OPP, the Orleans Parish Prison, is the last thing, at this point, he wants to do. It's a prison that is widely considered one of the worst in the nation. Beatings and sexual assault are commonplace in the understaffed and underfunded facility. While subject to the federal consent decree and a judge's order for reform, changes have been slow. Violence in prisons is not uncommon, but New Orleans has more than its share. In 2012 in Memphis, a comparable size city and jail, inmate violence accounted for seven ambulance runs to hospital emergency rooms. That same year in New Orleans, inmate violence accounted for more than 300 of the 600 hundred ambulance runs from the OPP.

Harris sets the folders down, removing his glasses and rubbing his temples as a yawn washes through him. He looks to Andrea who sits on the couch, hurriedly trying to finish a new necklace before she goes to bed. Harris checks his watch then picks up the remote and flips on the TV for the nine o'clock news. Kyle enters from the hallway in his pajamas, his hair wet from his nightly shower, and walks to Andrea and hands her a brush. She stops what she is doing and Harris watches as she positions Kyle between her knees and begins brushing out his hair.

"Kyle, why don't you just cut that mop off? Or at least cut it shorter so it looks more like the other boys at school," Harris asks.

"Cause I don't want to. I don't want to look like the boys at school. I like it long," Kyle replies as Andrea gives Harris the "will you stop it?" look.

"Hey... that's the lady from the gator thing," Kyle says, pointing to the TV.

Harris turns and watches in disbelief as the news begins with a picture of Megan, and the breaking story of her injury in a car accident over the weekend and that, sources say, the police are investigating the case as an attempted homicide.

"What happened to her?" Kyle says sadly.

Harris turns the TV off and looks at Kyle.

"She was hurt in a car wreck. That's all."

"Is she gonna be okay?"

"She's gonna be fine. Now you, off to bed."

Kyle turns and kisses Andrea on the cheek then walks to Harris and kisses him on the cheek too and gives him a hug. Harris watches him as he heads for the hall.

"And say your prayers," Harris calls out.

"Yes sir," Kyle answers, disappearing into the back of the house.

Harris looks to Andrea and shakes his head in disbelief.

"If I find out who leaked that, I swear I'm gonna...."

"Who do you think could'a done that?"

"I don't know. Probably one of the processing clerks or somebody like that."

They sit silently for a moment and then Harris picks up the file folder and places it on the table next to him and rises.

"I'm going to bed."

Andrea leans to look down the hall to make sure that Kyle's light is off, and then turns back to Harris.

"Hun, sit down for a minute," she says patting the couch next to her.

Harris sits and she gives him a kiss on the cheek. She peers into his eyes, evaluating his mood, hesitant to bring up the touchy subject of Kyle. It's a conversation that can't continue to be pushed aside.

"Can we talk for a minute? I mean really talk?"

"We can always talk. What do you mean really talk?"

"I mean turn your cell phone off for a minute and pay attention to what I'm saying."

Harris pulls his phone from his belt and flips it off.

"There, you've got my full attention"

She pauses, looking away and trying to gather the courage and the correct words.

"It's about Kyle. I'm worried about *why* he's being bullied at school," she says after a moment.

"That's why I want to put him in football, toughen—"

"You're not listening to me."

"What?"

Andrea takes a deep breath, a final boost of courage to bring up the topic that Harris so adamantly won't discuss.

"I talked to Kyle about it the other day and he asked me why God made him the way he is."

"The 'way he is'?" he asks with raised brow.

"He said he wished God had never made him a boy."

Harris studies her in stunned silence. After a moment, he looks away struggling to understand the meaning of the words she just said to him.

"I just… I just need to talk to him," he says after a moment.

"If you would open your eyes, you would see it. If you ever spent any time with him…"

She senses the bite in her words and stops herself before saying something she would regret. He works hard; it's not his fault that he isn't able to spend more time with Kyle. She watches Harris as he tries to process the thought.

"Kyle needs new shoes. I'm meeting with a realtor tomorrow afternoon so I can't take him. You need to pick him up at school and take him to get a new pair," she adds as she rises and heads to the hallway without looking back, leaving Harris to sit alone.

The room grows eerily silent as Harris contemplates Andrea's words. What has he been missing? What is he not seeing? He casts his eyes to the bookshelf and a picture of Miranda, a school photo from when she was about Kyle's age. He rises and steps over, picking the picture up and smiling as he remembers her youth. He glances to a recent picture of Kyle then back to Miranda's. The likeness of the two strikes him. He stares back at Kyle's image. After a moment, he brushes away the thought of Kyle ending up as anything other than the model of American masculinity. Andrea's right. He needs to spend more time with the boy, quality time to be a better role model.

"I won't fail you," he says softly to Miranda's picture. "Not again," he adds, setting it down and nodding; confident in the road that lies before him.

The third floor of the central office of the NOPD houses the individual offices of the department's supervisors. Outside their doors, in a bullpen layout, are the support staff and detectives' cubicles. It's laid out much as any corporate office environment, with senior staff having the individual offices with windows and everyone else jammed into the noisy and not-so-private center. Harris makes his way down the hallway, coffee in hand to get him started on a rainy morning. From within her cubical, Broussard motions wildly for him to come there.

"You got my money.... sucker?" he says, referencing the Saints 38 to 17 win.

"Did you see this?" she asks.

"See what?"

She turns her monitor towards him. The screen is opened to Megan's Dream Weaver profile. She clicks on a message that was sent to it overnight and labeled 'Road Kill'. She scrolls down and begins reading.

"Risen from the ashes to haunt and hurt again? You're no fucking Phoenix," she says.

She turns to Harris with a look of concern as he leans in to read for himself.

"Seeking safe quarter among those that would protect? Be wise, for they care not. I have failed, for you remain, but the Fates will not wait much longer," he says in shock of what he's reading. He looks to Broussard whose face is panicked.

"He's gonna finish the job," she says.

"Can you block that or something? I don't want Megan reading this," Harris barks as Broussard struggles to find a way to hide the message. It's all for naught. Megan had already opened it by the time Broussard found it.

⁂

The receiving bay at Tulane Medical is pulling dual duty today. Harris hurries Megan out the door, past an eighteen-wheeler being unloaded, and down the steps towards Cleveland Avenue and Broussard's awaiting car. The two of them are followed closely by Kristi and a couple of uniformed officers. Harris thought taking Megan out this way would be the least noticed, but a reporter approaches with cameraman in tow from across the street at the corner of South Liberty.

"Ms. Callahan, can I get a word with you?" the reporter yells as Harris opens the door and eases Megan into the back seat, closing it before the reporter arrives.

It was bad enough that the station reported on the incident, but this is taking it too far. As the reporter steps next the car and taps the window, Harris grabs his microphone and bullies it away from him. He then turns and knocks the camera from the cameraman's hands, sending it crashing to the concrete below.

"What the *fuck,* man? That's a ten-thousand-dollar camera."

Harris reaches in his pocket and pulls out a card and hands it to him.

"Send the department a bill. Now get out of here." he says, turning and handing the microphone back to the reporter and watches them slink away, escorted to safety from the deranged detective by one of the uniforms.

After they are at a safe distance, he taps on the window and Megan rolls it down. He looks at her. She's panicked, white with fear.

"You sure about this? We can protect you here just fine."

"I don't want to be here. I don't want to be in New Orleans," she replies without looking at him.

He studies her for a moment before she finally looks up to him. He can see in her eyes that she isn't changing her mind.

"Okay. Broussard's gonna stay a few days. Shelby County Sherriff's office will have a uniform at your place round the clock till we catch this guy."

"Thank you."

Harris watches her as she looks away, hanging her head. He touches her softly on the shoulder.

"I'll get him," he says.

Not fully convinced, she turns to him, her doubt evident in her eyes.

"Trust me." he adds.

She nods and rolls the window up. He steps to the driver's window and looks down at Broussard as Kristi buckles her seat belt in the back next to Megan.

"Take care of her. I'll see ya in a few," he says to Broussard. She looks at him for a moment, concern on her face, then nods, rolls up the window, and pulls away.

He stands, his hands on his hips, and watches the marked car pull out behind them. He runs his hands through his hair and turns and heads to his car just up the street.

Taking I-55 north, it's a six-hour drive to Memphis from New Orleans and it's been six hours that have been tense for Harris. He wasn't a fan of Megan going into seclusion on her family's ranch outside of Memphis, but he understands why she wanted to. He has no doubt that they would have been able to keep her safe, but knows that it's deeper than that. While it's his job to find the son-of-a-bitch that did this, it's her job to recover, and often times the best thing that one can do in these circumstances is to get away from the place that's so full of bad memories and back to one more pleasant. It's going to make his job that more difficult and will mean more windshield-time if he needs to speak with her, which he knows he will.

Broussard called a couple of hours ago saying that the trip was good so far. Megan had fallen asleep in the back seat, the first time that she has slept for more than an hour since the doctors woke her Monday morning.

After Megan left for Memphis, Harris received a call from the office with some information that didn't make his job easier. Some of the prints lifted from Megan's Bronco were run through IAFIS and the Army's database and came back with a positive match to Jeff. The blood found under Megan's fingernails has yet to be tested, and it may be several days or weeks before the results are back. It weighs heavy on him that he's considering a man he calls a friend as a possible suspect, but he can't simply brush it aside, not at this point.

The department's technology group has been working on the case for a couple of days now. Fortunately, Poets Beat has been very cooperative in providing information pertaining to communications on the website. While Harris was on his way to pick up Kyle from school, they called and informed him that the Road Kill message originated from a mobile device at a McDonalds in Algiers. That meant a public wi-fi and a dead end, at least for now. They also are hoping to have phone records soon from Verizon, Megan's cellular provider, but they aren't known for expediency.

From the school, it's a short drive out Airline Highway and up Causeway into Metairie to the Lakeside Shopping Center, a nice regional mall with the likes of Macy's, JC Penny's, and Dillard's. Kyle sits in the passenger seat with headphones on listening to his iPod as Harris drives in silence. The conversation with Andrea from the night before weighs heavy on his mind. He taps Kyle on the shoulder, motioning for him to take the headphones off.

"So what kind of shoes are we looking for?"

"I don't know. Maybe some Converse or Vans maybe."

"You mean sneakers?"

"Yeah."

"I had Converse as a kid. Loved em. The high-tops, basketball shoes, Chuck Taylors. We called them Chucks. I had the black ones, the originals," Harris says with a smile.

"I don't like black. Maybe I can get a lavender pair?"

"Lavender?"

"Yeah. Or they've got a cool color called peppermint. Ashley has a pair."

"What, red and white? That'd probably be okay," a relieved Harris says.

"No. It's a light green. It's pretty," Kyle says, turning to look back out the window.

Harris knows he needs to discuss things with Kyle, but finding the right words is proving difficult. He knows he can be a bit overbearing at times. Andrea has made sure that he's reminded of that. Being delicate is not his forte.

His thoughts go back to Tommy Ells, the kid he and his buddies bullied in school. He obviously had serious issues or he wouldn't have blown his brains out a few years after high school. He considers that maybe if Tommy's parents had just set him straight, he wouldn't have gone off the deep end.

"Who's Ashley? That your girlfriend?" Harris says with a smile after parking in the first available space. "Is she cute?" he asks raising an eyebrow.

"No, Paw Paw, she's not my girlfriend. We're just friends," Kyle says with a shy smile.

Harris watches him for a moment and his not-so-delicate side has had enough with the beating around the bush.

"Kyle… you like girls, right? I mean, you know," he blurts out.

"Yes, Paw Paw I like girls. I don't like boys, if that's what you're asking," Kyle replies, turning and fidgeting with his iPod.

"I mean, you're a good looking boy, gonna grow into a handsome *man*," Harris says with emphasis. "You're gonna drive the girls crazy," he adds.

The car fills with an awkward silence as Kyle simply stares out the window. After a moment, he turns to Harris.

"Can we just go inside and get the shoes? Please?"

Harris can see the hurt in his eyes. He ponders the situation for a moment and then sighs softly. He turns the car off and the two of them silently make their way across the parking lot.

⎯ ⟞⟢⟞ ⎯

Harris and Kyle walk through the mall to JC Penney's, Harris' store of choice as those other stores are just too damn expensive. The multitude and types of people in the mall, all shapes, sizes, and ethnicities, captures Kyle's attention. He can't help but notice the wide variety of styles available for girls. The women and girls he sees strolling through the mall range from very feminine to masculine, from jeans and boots, to lace trimmed dresses and heels. They wear shorts, t-shirts, and flip-flops and skirts, tights, and boots. Girls with long hair and girls with short hair, even a woman with her head shaved.

He sees the boys, the ones that everyone wants him to be like, and they all look the same. Jeans and a shirt, tennis shoes, or sneakers as Harris calls them, or maybe flip flops. They all seem to match; fitting nicely into a tight definition of male.

There's a voice inside his head that's begging him to stop, to stare through the windows. He smiles softly as he lags behind, gazing at the displays in Justice, Forever 21, and Charlotte Russe. It's the voice of that eleven-year-old girl Kylie that looked back at him in the mirror the day Rebecca gave him the sundress. It's a voice that Kyle fears he will have to quiet if he is to be accepted and fit in. He remembers the feeling of Matt Vincent's fist. So he drops the smile, pushes Kylie back into her recesses, and hurries to catch up with Harris as they walk into the shoe department.

Harris looks around for a salesperson, leaving Kyle to browse the shoes. The display of women's styles proves irresistible and Kyle begins to inspect them, if only for a moment. He surveys what must be a hundred different styles of flats, espadrilles, sandals, and heels. He's lost in thought as he imagines what it must be like to have that much freedom of choice. A sharp pain pierces his ear as Harris pinches it, pulling him away from the displays.

"What are you doing over here? *Boy's* shoes are over there," he says gruffly and with a scowl, pointing to the boys' section.

Harris watches Kyle as he slowly walks to the single rack displaying the ten or so socially acceptable boy's styles in brown, black, white, and a smattering of greens, blues, and reds. He looks back at the women's section, trying to understand what could possibly be going on in Kyle's mind. He thinks for a moment and reassures himself that it's only a phase.

Callahan Farms, a sprawling three-hundred-acre ranch, is situated about thirty minutes outside Memphis in the northeast corner of Shelby County. It's a secluded place, about three miles off of Hwy 205. It's property that has been in Megan's family for three generations, having been purchased by her grandfather in the 1950's.

Broussard walks the perimeter of the area around the house, inspecting and evaluating it from the standpoint of protecting Megan. Near the house, Kristi, Ellen, and ranch foreman and longtime family friend Rolly Davis unload bags from her Ellen's car.

Satisfied with what she is seeing, she dials Harris.

"How's it going? You guys make it to Memphis?" he says through the phone.

"Yeah. They're unloading the car now. Megan's inside."

"How's the place look?"

"Pretty good. Secluded. Driveway's gated and the house sits about half mile off the road. Several full time ranch hands. Shelby County had a uniform waiting when we got here."

"Good to hear."

"I talked to tech. They tracked down Jen's phone. It's a throwaway, one of those pay-as-you-go numbers," Broussard says.

"That figures."

"They also got some data in from Verizon. All calls from Jen that night originated within a mile of the festival grounds, all except the last one."

"Do you need a drum roll?"

"Both phones bounced off the same tower. That puts Jen within a mile of the abduction."

"Why can't this be easy?" he says after a long silence.

"Good question."

"Look, we've gotta find this Jen gal. Have tech keep working it. See if we can get a trace put on that number."

"Already on it," Broussard replies, happy with herself for being one step ahead of the old man.

"Good job. Call me if you hear anything else," Harris says and hangs up.

Broussard looks at the phone in disbelief and smiles. Did he just say 'Good job'?

Being home, this time, under these circumstances, is not something Megan had planned or ever even considered. While little has changed, everything is different. She gazes around the living room, her eyes landing on the grandfather clock that has been in her family for three generations. She watches the pendulum sway, continuing the task it began seventy-five years ago. She recalls the many nights of her youth, lying in bed, tucked securely in by her father, listening to the steady march of time and dreaming of what the future held for her.

She closes her eyes, tears balancing delicately at their precipice, and focuses on the rhythmic tick, slow and methodical, the heart of the home welcoming its child back to its breast. She breathes deeply, taking in the soft aroma of cedar with a hint of jasmine. She smiles softly, recalling the myriad of sachets, candles, and lamps that Ellen used over the years, filling the home with scents, usually with jasmine somewhere in the heart, causing any within to drop their shoulders in ease.

She opens her eyes and steps into the living room. She runs her fingers across the leather of the couch, the one that always slept like a dream. It still does, as evidenced by Toulouse who is already stretched out in the middle of it. She pauses to look at the barber's chair, a relic saved from a dusty, cramped antique store in south Memphis by her father. She envisions him sitting there reading a book, probably historical non-fiction, as he had done so many times when she was a young girl.

She walks into her old bedroom, its vestiges of her youth striking her in a way unlike her previous returns to her childhood home. She steps to a bookshelf and picks up a rustic, wood-framed photograph. It's her and Wes, on a boat dock, fishing. In it, she smiles widely, holding a stringer of several catfish as Wes beams with an even bigger smile. She looks into his eyes, remembering the instruction that he gave her; don't pull the line out of the water too fast. Her heart races a bit, as she feels the anxiety again of waiting, hoping, worrying that she would miss the catch of the day. She focuses, studying his expression in the photograph. She can still feel the pride that smile gave her then.

She sets the picture down and picks up another memory, touching the glass softly. Within it, a teenage Megan stands with Wes next to a large, partially finished statue of an angel built from scrap metal. She can still feel his arm around her shoulders, pulling her tightly to him. She felt so safe there, in her father's arms. He was her biggest fan, her coach, her champion. She remembers cutting every piece of the sculpture herself and welding them together as Wes stood nearby, protectively, encouraging her.

"You can do this, Meg," she can still hear him say, bolstering her spirit when she wanted to give up. Her heart drops in her chest and her breath shudders. If only she could hear him say that one last time.

She sets the picture down and picks up a folded piece of paper, a clipping from Memphis' newspaper, *The Commercial Appeal*. She touches the letters, tracing the title and subtitle of the poem she submitted for a contest, "On Angel Wings. I miss you, Daddy". It was the first time the world would learn that the Callahan's tomboy was a poet. She reads the verse silently, her bottom lip quivering. Gently, she places the paper back on the shelf and picks up a small pair of angel wings made by Wes as a model for the statue. She touches them softly, pulling them close to her chest, as tears flow freely down her face.

Chapter 20

MASKS

Down darkened halls, past rooms built of incorporeal walls and filled with haunts of days past, resides actualities long forgotten—or hidden away. Behind a large, wooden, medieval door bolted from the outside, and surrounded by walls of iron, stone, and glass, a dark haired woman sits crying in the gloom of a poorly lit cell. She's shabbily dressed in dirty and worn fashions, long since out of style. She softly touches a picture frame, which she holds in her lap. As she cries, she looks at the frame, trying to position it in what little light enters the room through the glass wall.

Her chamber is sparsely furnished. A small bed lies next to the stone wall and above it are large wounds, as if the stones have been cut or scratched and healed over. A chair sits near a small table with a smattering of old makeup and a few empty perfume bottles scattered across the top. The walls are adorned with images of masculinity, all of which she has feminized. The poster of Hulk Hogan sports a circle of flowers drawn in bright pastels, while a baseball trophy, with the batter proudly watching the home-run he just hit sail across the outfield wall, sits adorned with a pink bow and wears a dress made from fragments of cloth. A movie poster for *Mr. and Mrs. Smith* hangs from the wall of iron bars, with Mr. Smith having been torn away.

She notices motion through the glass wall, sighs and sets the frame down on a small side table, pausing as she looks with trepidation at a mask that lies there.

Motion in the glass draws her attention as a figure, hazy and obscured, stands on the other side. She picks up the mask and slowly places it on her face, rising and walking to the window as a tear flows down the mask. She slowly wipes her hand across the glass, clearing away the haze, and sees Jeff standing on the other side.

She watches silently as he rolls up his long sleeves and washes his hands, then leans down and splashes water on his face. She stares at the water as it spirals down the drain and thinks of what has become of her life in the last few weeks. She gazes down at the frame, a picture of Megan, whose words reverberate from the cell walls.

"You're not broken, Jeff," she hears her say.

She turns her eyes back to Jeff as he raises his head and looks into the mirror, deep into his reflection, into the eyes that look back at him, her eyes.

"Throw away the mask. I love you for who you are," she hears as again Megan's words ricochet through her world.

As Jeff moves, she mimics every motion, each lean, each turn, and each blink. She slowly reaches to the mask and removes it. A look of fear washes across her face as he stares back at her through the glass. After a moment he smiles then turns and walks away, the light through the glass fading as he does, returning it to opaque and casting her back into darkness.

When Harris and Andrea bought the house on Desoto Street, it was like many others in New Orleans, all house and little outdoor space. When an empty lot next door went onto the market, they jumped at the opportunity to have a little more elbow room and bought it. With sweat equity, they have managed to incorporate the lot beautifully into their property and added a side deck near the back of the house which looks out over a manicured and fenced backyard. It's a place of solace and solitude for Harris. The foul weather of the last few days has broken and he sits on the deck beneath the stars nursing a beer and reflecting on the case which is in a holding pattern until blood and DNA results are returned from Baton Rouge. It's a period of time during an investigation that can be frustrating for a detective, a time when the wheels are spinning but little progress is being made.

His thoughts drift to Kyle and the conversation outside the mall. He isn't satisfied with his feeble attempt at talking with him. He's a better communicator than that pathetic performance in the car. The realization that it's a good thing Andrea wasn't there, as she would have hit him if she had been, is the sole inspiration for a slight smile as he finishes his beer, his one for the night on one of the few nights he has one.

He keeps replaying the conversation in his mind, searching for clues that perhaps he missed. Kyle said he doesn't like boys, so that should be the end of it. But he can't shake the images of the hurt on Kyle's face when he asked him.

He pulls his wallet from his pocket, opening it to the pictures he keeps there. He stares at a photo of Miranda, her senior picture from high school, one of his favorites. He softly touches it, then pulls it from its protective cover and holds it in the palm of his hand, thinking back to when she was born at Charity Hospital. His world changed forever that day as he held all six and a half pounds of her in his hands.

He raises the picture to his lips and gently kisses it. "I miss you," he says softly.

He slides the photo back into his wallet and looks at the next one, of Miranda with Kyle, a church directory picture taken a year before her death. He stares at it, struggling to understand what he should do, if anything. He's a child of the sixties and he remembers well that turbulent time of flower power, hippies, and LSD. It was time of change and society was shaken by the anti-war, civil rights, feminist, and late in the decade, the gay rights movements. He thinks of his father and wonders what actions he would take and what he might say, were he still alive.

He remembers the night when his father, Kyle Norton Harris, was out until sunrise as part of the Tactical Patrol Force on Christopher Street beating back the queens outside the Stonewall Inn. How the next day he had told the stories of using their batons on some of the sissies and faggots and how he hadn't even wanted them to touch him. But that was then and this is now. He isn't his father. He would never treat a gay person poorly, as long as they didn't shove it in his face. Hell will be enough punishment when they get there.

He shakes his head as he considers that his father, the first Kyle Harris, would probably rise right up out of his grave and slap him if he didn't do something to set this Kyle straight. Harris nods as he decides that he must have a firm, manly, talk with Kyle and that he must understand that there are things that are acceptable and things that aren't. He needs to realize that God made him the way he is and that he needs to accept it, drop the girly behavior, and toughen up and be a young man.

He rises and enters into the living room where Andrea sits, working on a new necklace against the backdrop of the nine o'clock news.

"Where's Kyle? Is he still up?" he asks.

"I sent him to bed about ten minutes ago. Why?"

"I need to talk to him," Harris replies as he heads down the hall.

Inside a darkened room with few furnishings and lit only by a light being cast through the window that stands in front of her, Kylie models a beautiful new sundress, admiring herself in the reflection of the mirror. She turns left and right to get a good look at how she fairs in it, her hair swinging as she does. A thunderous boom echoes off the walls.

Harris opens the door to Kyle's room without knocking, cracking it at first, then swinging it open wide upon seeing Kyle standing at his dresser mirror wearing a sundress and white knee socks. Kyle turns and sees him, horror racing across his face.

"What the *hell* are you doing, boy?" Harris barks.

"I'm sorry!" a terrified Kyle yells as he struggles to remove the dress, breaking a shoulder strap in the process.

"Kyle, I've had about enough of this nonsense!" Harris exclaims, unbuckling and beginning to remove his belt.

"I'm sorry. I'm sorry!" Kyle cries as tears stream down his face and he runs to the other side of the room, away from Harris.

Harris moves to him, grabbing him by the arm and swinging him so he can spank him with the belt.

"I'm sorry, Paw Paw. I'll stop!" Kyle screams, crying uncontrollably as Harris raises his arm and strikes him repeatedly, the belt lashing Kyle's skin with each syllable.

"You. Will. Stop. This. Kyle!"

"I'm sorry! I'll be a boy, I'll be a boy!" Kyle cries.

Having heard the commotion, Andrea appears in the doorway, and upon seeing Harris spanking Kyle, yells at him.

"Albert! Stop it!"

Harris stops mid-swing and looks back at Andrea, releasing a hysterical Kyle who runs past Andrea who tries to stop him, out into the hall and into the bathroom, slamming the door behind him.

"I can't believe you!" Andrea screams as she turns back to Harris.

"He needs to be set straight, Andrea! It's my responsibility. He will not grow up gay or transgender or whatever he thinks he is," Harris barks back, confident he's made the right decision.

"It's not his fault Albert! He can't help it. He's Miranda's child for God's sake! Why can't you love him for who he is?" Andrea tearfully replies as she begins softly tapping on the bathroom door.

"I do love him, that's why—"

"As long as he fits into that nice little box, that macho image that you have for all men. Just like you! Just like your father and his father! You love him as long as he's like you, right Albert?" she yells before continuing to knock on the bathroom door.

The door opens and Andrea enters, closing it behind her, leaving Harris standing alone. He looks to the mirror, staring at himself, belt in hand. He glances down to the top of the dresser, to a picture of Miranda that Kyle keeps in his room. He studies it for a moment, her sincere blue eyes beaming from within the frame. He turns his eyes back to his reflection, his own blue eyes. He doesn't like what he sees.

Chapter 21

SECRETS

It's been a rough few weeks since Megan arrived back at the ranch. Sleep continues to elude her and when she is able, it is often fragmented by nightmares. Even the old ghosts have shown up in her dreams. To a large extent, she has withdrawn into herself and often sits quietly in the fetal position, with arms around knees drawn close to her breast. Ellen, Kristi, and Rolly have tried to get her to talk about it, to talk about anything, but they are usually met with requests to be left alone.

There's a lake on the property, down the hill behind the house. It's a lake whose shores are filled with memories of her youth, of the Callahan girls and friends swimming there, jumping from the dock and crashing to the water in cannonballs. She and her father used to love to sit on the very dock that she sits on now and fish. He had stocked the lake with crappy, catfish, and bass, and Megan loved to come down at sunset and feed them. She would tap on the side of the bucket, sending sound waves through the water beckoning the fish to come dine. The water would soon churn with what must have been hundreds of them, taking the floating fish food directly from the surface as Megan threw it to them.

Frizbee lays on the deck next to her as she sits in a chair, gazing out over the calm waters of the lake, as a few ducks swim through the clouds that are reflected on the water's surface. It's a beautiful and calming site that Megan doesn't want to leave. She just wants to sit, think through it all, and one by one, replace the stones in the walls she had carefully crafted over the years to block out the world.

Jeff has tried to call a few times since she arrived, but she hasn't answered. She knows she can't. He's a suspect, even though she believes in her heart that he didn't have anything to do with it. The Jeff that she came to know, trust, and dare she say it to herself, love, is not a person that would do this to her. Perhaps she did trust him too much, though, she considers. There is safety behind the walls.

She searches her memories of the early days of their relationship, seeking small words, phrases, changes of temperament that she might have missed.

She shakes off the thoughts of a nefarious Jeff. She wasn't exactly fair to him early on, hiding her identity well as she always did, yet she knew everything about him. She smiles, remembering how she would yank his chain when he read poetry to her. It thrilled her heart to hear it, but she loved to needle him.

She recalls a late call about four months ago. She was curled up on the bed with Toulouse as Jeff talked about small things, anything, to get her mind off of the nightmare that had awakened her.

"From the light you call, a beacon in the dark," Jeff had said softly as he began to read his latest poem he had written for her.

"Hang on, sister. So I'm in the light or in the dark?"

"Ummm, you are the light. You're the beacon... in the dark. Does that not make sense? Should I rewrite that?"

"No. It's beautiful, babe. Just needed to get it straight in my head. Keep going, girl," she replied with a slight laugh.

She remembers the long pause of silence that followed before Jeff replied.

"Thank you," he said softly.

"For what?"

"For calling me that. It means a lot."

"I'm getting used to it. It's who you are."

"Girl, you have no idea. Okay, where was I? Oh... okay," Jeff said, returning his attention to his prose. "You whisper into my ears words of passion and love that resonate in my mind. Sparrows fluttering to and fro, seeking to perch and nest."

"Where did the sparrows come from?"

"It's a metaphor. The sparrows are the words. Okay fine, I won't read it."

"Sorry," she said with a laugh to herself.

"Whatever. Do you want me to finish it or not?"

"Of course."

"Okay then, shhh. Where was I? Oh, here... such words have seemed foreign to me. Yet, your utterances transmute—"

"My utters do what?"

"Oh shut up. You know what? I'll just post it with the others. You can read it later."

"I'm sorry babe. It's beautiful. It really is," Megan replied laughing.

"So... when am I gonna get a real picture?" he asked hesitantly.

"Here, I'll send it now." she replied, grabbing her laptop and opening it.

"That's not fair babe. I know I was a dufus by putting up a real picture in my profile, but you know what I look like." he replied.

"When I'm ready, and not until then," she had answered as she clicked send and fired Jeff her latest snapshot.

"Does it really matter to you? Are you that shallow?" she adds.

"Well, no... but..." Jeff began to say as his laptop dinged, alerting him to the email.

"I mean, if we can get to know each other with these heart-to-heart talks and tell each other that we love them without knowing what they really look like, without seeing the mask but only seeing the soul, isn't that true love?" she asked.

"Oh great, I'm in love with a sumo wrestler."

"Like that one?"

"Damn. I didn't realize they made thongs that big. You got any in lace?" Jeff replied

"Shut up," Megan said through her laughter.

"Seriously... when?" Jeff asked.

"Babe, be patient. You won't be disappointed. But it shouldn't matter. What if you were blind? Would you need your friends to tell you I was pretty? Would that make me worthy of your affection?"

"No but you can't deny that—"

"I don't deny it, but it shouldn't be that way. That's my point. It's not about the physical; it's about the spiritual, the inside, the soul of the person. That's what makes them truly beautiful."

"I do love your soul."

"And I love yours. All of you, just as you are," she had replied.

The frantic quacking of a duck being chased from the dock by Frizbee, startles her from her thoughts. She admires the tenacity of the fowl, standing its ground as if telling Frizbee to mind his own business, before finally abandoning the dock for the safety of the water.

She did love Jeff and perhaps that's the problem. She loved him and now he's in the middle of all of this. If it wasn't for her, he would still be minding *his* own business and tending bar. But instead, he's living with this constant fear that he's going to be arrested for something she's sure he didn't do. She picks up her phone and dials a number. She turns and watches Kristi approach from the house as she waits through several rings before the call is answered.

"Hey. Yeah, I'm fine. I'll be okay. Listen did you get my message?"

She listens intently for a moment and then scowls, not hearing the answer she wanted to hear.

"I don't care. You owe me. Just do it, alright? Okay, thanks."

She ends the call and stares at the phone for a moment then pulls up her contacts, scrolling through them. She stops, looking away towards the lake, hesitant to dial. After a moment, she looks back at her phone, smiles, and dials the number. The phone rings several times then goes to voicemail and wiping the smile from her face as she hangs up without leaving a message.

"Hey sis. How you feeling?" Kristi asks as she steps onto the dock.

"Okay for now. Ribs still hurt though. How long is this shit gonna last?"

"Could be a couple more weeks, maybe. Momma wants to go eat at McCallister's. You wanna come?"

"Yeah, I don't think so," Megan replies, pointing to her still bruised face.

Megan's phone rings. She looks at it and smiles widely; something Kristi hasn't seen her do much since they got home.

"Hey. How are you?" Megan says, answering the call.

The smile on her face dissipates as quickly as it appeared.

"Who is this?" Megan asks.

"What are you—" Megan says, struggling to get a word in.

Kristi watches as panic washes over Megan's face.

"Wait, let me explain. I didn't mean for this to.... Hello? You still there? Hello?"

Megan falls back into the chair, pulling her knees to her chest and pitching the phone on the dock.

"I can't take this! I didn't want this," she says, dropping her face into her hands.

"Megan, who was that?" Kristi asks as she picks up the phone.

"I didn't mean for this happen. Oh my God. What have I done? I'm so sorry."

Kristi puts her arm around Megan's shoulders and looks at the last call. It's from Jen.

The last couple of weeks have been hell for Harris. Andrea isn't talking to him and Kyle is a sullen, depressed, shadow of himself. He spoke with Kyle, explaining that he was sorry he had to spank him, but he needed to understand there were things he could do and things he couldn't. When he tried to hug Kyle, he pulled away in fear. That look of fear is one Harris has been unable to shake.

To make matters worse, he's now on his way for an additional talk with Jeff. The comparison of the blood found under Megan's nails against CODIS found no matches. It did, however, match back to Jeff's DNA sample. Normally, having a suspect in his sights is a thrilling part of the job. Months of hard work are being paid off. But this isn't a normal case. He doesn't normally prepare to arrest a friend.

He needs to speak to Jeff one more time, to find a good reason he shouldn't arrest him. He has the sadomasochistic poem with him for Jeff to explain and he has a warrant ready to search his house for the white mask. But something in his gut is telling him there's more to this story than he knows.

They've had no luck with the trace on Megan's phone, waiting for Jen to call. They requested a trace on Jen's phone, but were denied by the judge for lack of evidence. Blanchard had overruled the warrantless trace on exigent circumstances. It would have allowed the phone company to ping for Jen's phone every fifteen minutes for forty-eight hours but, such a trace must be followed by a court order. Explaining that action without significant evidence to the Federal judge overseeing the actions of the department is not a conversation he cared to have.

Tech confirmed that all of Jen's postings on the poetry site and email communications to Megan were conducted via public wi-fi or through the mobile phone. They've also exhausted possible leads from the cases that Megan has been part of. They weren't all saints, but they all had alibis.

As he navigated the streets of New Orleans on his way to the Muses to speak to Jeff, he received a call from Broussard regarding the call from Jen and Megan's emotional breakdown as a result. The call was short, but Verizon reported the phone to be mobile on I-10 east bound. It's not an address, but at least it's something. Broussard had tried to return the call but it went straight to a generic voicemail, evidence that it had been turned off.

Harris parks on Frenchmen, a block away from the Muses, hurries down the sidewalk and inside. He sees Jeff on his iPhone behind the bar near the door to the back. Harris straddles a stool and motions to him. Jeff nods, warily acknowledging him. He turns, as if not wanting Harris to be able to see or hear what he says, and quickly finishes his call, slipping his phone into his back pocket.

"Al. Am I still a suspect?" Jeff asks as he slowly walks to Harris.

"Technically... yes. Listen, I need to talk you for a few. Can we go into the back?"

Jeff stalls, taking a towel and wiping the counter.

"I can't, Al. Not without my lawyer," he says after a moment.

"Your lawyer?"

"Yeah. Don't you think I—"

A small flip phone flies through the air past Harris, hitting Jeff square in the chest and dropping onto the bar below him. Harris steps back, turning to see Emily storming towards the bar.

"You lying sack of shit!" she yells at Jeff.

"Em? What the fuck?!"

"I found your goddamn phone and talked to your whore girlfriend... Megan!"

Harris turns and looks at the flip phone lying on the bar as Jeff picks it up and turns it on, checking to make sure it isn't broken. As nearby patrons scatter, Harris' pulse quickens as he is hit with the realization that Jeff has two phones. This could be the unfortunate break he's been hoping for. He steps away from the bar, knowing it's best to let this thing play itself out.

"You're gonna fucking pay for this!" Emily screams as she picks up peanuts and anything else she can reach from the bar and begins throwing them at Jeff.

"Emily, can we talk about this in private?" Jeff exclaims, dodging a shot glass.

"I'm done hiding for you Jeff, you fucking liar. Your whole life is a lie!" she says and begins to storm out before stopping to turn back.

"You know those divorce papers? You can toss 'em. You're gonna get a whole new set, you asshole."

Harris watches her charge out the door. He turns back to Jeff who hangs his head in embarrassment and frustration. Harris takes his phone and dials Jen's number. The flip phone in Jeff's hand rings. He looks at it and selects ignore. Harris walks back over to the bar where Jeff finally meets his eyes with his.

"I'm sorry about that, Al. Fuck!"

"You gonna be okay?"

"Shit! What else could go wrong with my life?" a defeated Jeff asks.

Harris nods then motions to Jeff as if he has a phone call. He turns his back to the bar and dials Jen's number again. Putting the phone to his ear, he turns around and watches Jeff as he looks at the phone again and angrily answers it.

"What?!" he barks before turning his gaze to Harris.

"You should call your lawyer," Harris says calmly into the phone.

The interrogation rooms on the third floor at the central office are located on the other side of the building from their offices and Harris and Broussard walk briskly down the hallway in silence. Harris is glad to have gotten a break but unfortunately, it's breaking to look like Jeff is far more involved than he said, and that's not something that makes Harris happy. But, the cards are not in Jeff's favor and it's enough to bring him in for questioning.

Broussard drops back a few steps from Harris with a look of concern. She seems almost hesitant to continue to the interrogation room.

"Harris, hold up." she says.

"What?" he says as he turns back to her.

"Have you seen his attorney yet?"

"Not yet. Who is it?"

His inquisitive expression changes to one of concern as he studies hers.

"Max Flannigan," she says reluctantly.

They look at each other for moment, neither breaking a smile. After a moment, Harris turns and heads back down the hall.

"That's a good one. I needed that," he says with a laugh.

"I'm serious," she replies, halting him in his tracks.

He turns and stares at her in disbelief.

Chapter 22

⬡

EPIPHANIES

The interrogation rooms are small, cramped spaces with a table and several chairs as well as cameras which capture the questioning in both the visible and infrared spectrums. Max sits next to Jeff and across the table from Broussard. Jeff visibly shakes as he smokes another cigarette, the latest in a chain he has smoked since arriving. Broussard watches silently as Harris paces the room in frustration.

"Shouldn't you recuse yourself? Isn't this interference in the case, obstruction of justice?" Harris asks Max.

"Megan is free to do what she wants. It's unconventional, I'll grant you that, but it's not illegal," Max calmly replies, a true cool customer even under the oddest of circumstances.

"What the hell, Max? Is she trying to sabotage this case?" Broussard asks

"Listen, if you're going to question my client, let's get to it. Otherwise, release him."

Harris and Broussard look at each other, completely frustrated by the situation. They need answers. He has little choice but to move forward.

⬠

The smoke in the room is heavy from Jeff's constant puffing. Technically, there's no smoking in the rooms but Harris has done nothing to stop Jeff from lighting up. If it makes the suspect feel more comfortable, detectives usually have no problem overlooking the violation. Harris has removed his jacket and cracked the door to try and circulate some fresh air. Empty coffee cups litter the table as Max steadfastly reviews his notes of what has transpired.

"Let's go through this again, Jeff. Your prints were all over her Bronco, you were the last one seen with her that night, you were seen in a physical confrontation with her, you can't account for your whereabouts at the time of the crime, *and* she had your blood under her nails. Do you have any wounds on your body that you want to tell us about?" Broussard asks.

"No, I don't have any wounds. If you find my blood it's from when she accidently hit me. I swear I didn't have anything to do with it."

Max has been here long enough and he's already missed his afternoon tee-time. He's ready to cut the bullshit short.

"He's already explained all of this. We've been through it—"

"Tell me why you had a second phone, Jen's phone? Who's Jen? Are you Jen, Jeff? Did you lure her out there because she ended your relationship?" Harris asks.

"She didn't end it. It was stronger than ever. I had the second phone because I had to keep our relationship quiet because of the shit I was going through with Emily. Pay as you go, no phone bill that she could find."

"So the Jennifer profile, that was yours? What was that some kind of disguise to hide who you really were?" Broussard asks.

"No! It's…" Jeff says, dropping the sentence and looking away in frustration.

Harris watches him closely; sure that Jeff is still hiding something.

"It's what, Jeff?" he asks.

Jeff continues to look away for a moment. He turns back toward Harris with tears building in his eyes.

"You know what?" he says, rising and angrily pushing the table away.

Harris instinctively slides his chair towards the door, positioning himself between it and Jeff. Max rises, putting his hand on Jeff's shoulder.

"Jeff, what are you doing? Sit down and relax," he says.

"I can't take it anymore," Jeff says, pulling away from Max and throwing his hands in the air as if surrendering. "I'm tired of this," he adds.

"Yeah? Well, I'm tired of it too. So calm down and let's get this over with."

Jeff stares at him for a long moment, and then turns his eyes to Harris.

"Jeff, sit down and tell me what you want to say," Harris says calmly.

Jeff cast his eyes to floor, then falls back into the chair. He pulls another cigarette from the pack on the table and studies it as he spins it in his fingers.

"I'm tired of hiding," he says softly.

Harris slides his chair back to the table and gives a glance to a relieved Broussard. He opens his notebook; their finally getting somewhere. As is often the case, most people don't have the stamina to endure sustained questioning under this kind of pressure. Max, equally aware of what tired minds can do to a scared suspect, assumes defensive posture.

"Jeff, we should speak in private before you say anything else."

Jeff's broken, tired, and appears guilty. He stares at Max in silence for moment and then turns back to Harris.

"You know, Megan taught me a few things and one was to stop hiding behind a mask. Yeah, I'm Jen. Jennifer, at least to Megan," Jeff says dryly, drained of emotion.

Broussard smiles but it's a bitter sweet moment for Harris. It's the answer he's been looking for and the answer he didn't want to hear. He would much rather have been questioning some piece of shit that ran her off the road as a thrill than sitting here now watching his friend begin to confess.

"So you did lure her out there?" Broussard asks.

"This interview is over!" Max declares, folding his notebook and rising.

"Shut up, Max! Sit down and listen. It's not what you think, any of you," Jeff replies.

Max sighs heavily, checking his watch. He looks at Harris who gives him a forced smile then nods to the chair.

⚬

The confession by Jeff has not turned out like Harris anticipated. Sometimes the search for answers yields unexpected truths. Sometimes that search results in epiphanies, those 'ho lee shit' moments that accompany that unexpected realization or moment of clarity.

Broussard stepped out a few minutes ago after receiving a call that a body had been found in the Mississippi over in Algiers. Considering the direction of the interrogation, she was more than willing to cut out early and let Harris handle the remainder of the questioning.

As Jeff has talked the last ten minutes, Harris' thoughts have moved from the case and closer to home. He's not daydreaming, he's paying attention. But he's not making notes in his notebook as he listens to Jeff explain why "it's not what he thought". There are only two people on earth that Jeff has trusted with what he's now telling Max and Harris. One is divorcing him, and he's accused of raping the other.

Emily was right. Jeff's life is a lie. He's been hiding behind a mask created to satisfy generations of rote societal norms and ideals. Jeff's a great actor, as good as any Hollywood A-Lister. He walks the walk and talks the talk well, faithfully portraying the role that society has defined for him.

As they sit in awkward silence, Harris looks at Max who gives him an "I don't know what to do with this" look. Harris shifts his eyes back to Jeff, watching him as he fidgets with another cigarette, head hanging down, seemingly afraid to make eye contact.

"What exactly does that mean… transgender?" Max asks.

"Outside, physically, genetically, I'm male. But inside, I'm female," Jeff replies, his hands and voice shaking with fear.

When one lives their life to satisfy others, to fit into the norms, playing the role of macho soldier and tough guy, revealing one's self as anything other than the character they've portrayed can be terrifying. Opening up to Emily and then to Megan was difficult, but women tend to be more understanding. Men, on the other hand, often times are not quite as compassionate.

Max looks at Jeff for a moment, studying him, as if he is trying to mentally fit a square peg into a round hole.

"Why would you want to be a woman?" he asks incredulously.

"It's not a matter of want, Max. I don't expect you to understand," Jeff replies, never raising his head or taking his eyes off the cigarette in his hands.

Max sighs and looks at Harris. It's a strange explanation, but an explanation none the less and he'll run with it.

"Harris, it's obvious that you're looking for someone that doesn't exist," Max says, turning to Jeff, who shakes his head, apparently disgusted by the "doesn't exist" characterization.

"I mean she does, but not in the form of the boogeyman…. woman that you're looking for. Whoever did this is still out there."

Harris doesn't look at Max nor does he respond. He's staring down at the table lost in thought. After a moment, he lifts his eyes back up to Jeff.

"When did you decide to be…"

"Transgender? It's not contagious, Al. You won't catch it if you say it," Jeff says, casting his eyes up at him.

Harris watches him for a moment then glances back at Max who expression says "you're on your own".

"When did you decide to be transgender?" Harris says softly after turning his eyes back to Jeff.

"*Decide?* When did you decide to be straight?" Jeff asks. "When did you decide to be a man?" he adds turning to Max.

His questions are met with silence.

"I didn't choose this, Al. My first memories that something was different were when I was about five," Jeff says as Harris drops his eyes to the table.

"Who would? Growing up in a super-religious home listening every fucking Sunday to preachers tell you that you're going to Hell and that God hates you? Live in fear at school that someone's gonna figure out that you're different only to go home to a father that tries to beat it out of you?"

Those last words hit Harris like a hard uppercut to the gut. He looks up and at Jeff.

"The whole time you know in your heart that you're female but, out of fear, you join your buddy's chorus of hate against fags and anyone different so that it won't be turned on you. You mimic their objectification of women because that's what guys do, right? It's what they learn from their fathers and from society. Every night you go to sleep thinking that it will all go away."

Jeff runs his hands through his hair and struggles to hold back tears. Years of pent-up emotions are pouring out, his true-self venting a lifetime of pain, an opportunity she has rarely had afforded to her.

"Do you have any idea what it's like to have everything you see in society, TV, movies, magazines, people, telling you what and how you should be while everything inside screams the opposite?"

Harris doesn't have answers; he's never felt the kind of pain that Jeff describes. He's never even considered that such pain is possible.

Jeff places his left arm, palm up, on the table and unbuttons the long sleeve. He pushes the fabric up to his elbow, revealing years of self-mutilation when he was younger. Harris stares at the scars on his arm, long intertwining wounds healed into Maginot Lines of cells.

"You can hide it from society... but you can't hide it from God. So you have so much guilt and shame that you turn it inside, into self-hate, and try to purge the demons, bleed 'em out," Jeff says, his faced crinkled up.

Harris looks away from Jeff's arms, distressed by what he is seeing. Cutting isn't something that Harris is ignorant of but seeing them and hearing Jeff's story is unsettling.

"When that doesn't work, you take enough tranquilizers to kill an elephant and you become a good liar, living a life that society wants while inside you die," Jeff says, pausing to wipe a tear away.

"When I was in Iraq, I was in a support role. I wanted to be on the lines. It would have been easier just to catch a bullet. At least then I would have gone out a hero," he solemnly adds.

"I'm glad you didn't. It's not worth killing yourself over," Max says after a long moment of awkward silence.

"You live my life and then say that," Jeff replies dryly. He looks to Harris, pulling his attention away from the table top he is staring at.

"When I met Megan, everything changed. She saw through my writing, read between the lines. I trusted her and I eventually opened up to her, terrified that she would run for the hills as fast as she could. But she didn't. She completely accepted me and acknowledged me for who I was... in here," Jeff says, tapping his heart. "It was like she knew who I was inside without me telling her," he adds, then pauses to collect his thoughts as they drift off to her. After a moment he looks back to Harris.

"I guess having both been through hell, we just bonded you know?"

Max has known Megan for eight years and he's pretty sure he knows her fairly well. She's had a good life, a successful life, not this 'hell' Jeff claims.

"What do you mean 'been through hell'? What hell did Megan go through? You mean her father dying?"

"No. When it happened the first time," Jeff answers innocently.

That sentence brings Harris fully back into the room and to the case. He leans forward across the table.

"What do you mean the first time, Jeff? Megan was raped before this?" Harris asks.

Jeff looks at both them, confused.

"Yeah, when she was nineteen. Didn't you know that?" he replies with surprise and disbelief.

"No I didn't know that. There's no record of it," Harris replies as he rises and begins pacing the room.

"Did she tell you a name? Where'd this happen?" Harris asks.

"When she was in college. She didn't tell me a name. We talked about it once and I got the impression it wasn't something she really wanted to talk about."

"Where'd she go to college?"

"Tulane," Max says before Jeff can answer.

Harris continues to pace the room. After a moment he turns back to both of them.

"Jeff, I'm sorry for what you went through," he says, motioning with his eyes to Jeff's arms.

"He's free to go for now," he says to Max. "Just don't leave town," he adds as he grabs his jacket and notebook and exits the room. It's a long shot, but it's a new angle on the case and stranger things have happened.

Chapter 23

ANGLING

Detective work isn't always nine-to-five; criminals don't take the weekends off. Harris needs to speak with Megan about the incident when she was in college. Broussard's doing the preliminary work on the body hauled from the river, so she can't discuss it with her. He wouldn't have wanted her to do it anyway. He's not so crass as to discuss the matter with Megan via the phone. If she hasn't told anyone except Jeff, it's going to be a very sensitive discussion. He can't bring the subject up with Ellen and Kristi. If Megan never told them, their finding out through him could possibly enflame the situation. He needs to speak with her directly and privately, and he needs to do it tomorrow. That's Sunday and he's going to miss church, a rare event. But with six hours of windshield-time between him and Memphis, he's decided it best to drive up in the evening, get a hotel room, and be out at the Callahan place by morning.

Andrea pulls clothes from the closet and lays them on the bed to start packing.

"I got one of the blue shirts and that black suit. Is that okay?" she asks.

"Which one?" Harris asks, turning from his task of packing an overnight bag in the bathroom.

Andrea removes the jacket and hands it to Kyle who is hovering in the room. It isn't often that Harris leaves home overnight on work, so his curiosity is peaked. "Show that to your grandfather," she says.

Kyle takes the jacket into the bathroom and holds it for Harris to see. He looks at it and smiles. "What do you think?" he says to Kyle.

"It's black. Conservative and traditional," Kyle says as he inspects the fabric. Harris watches him, impressed with his language. He looks to Andrea who smiles back at him. He turns back to Kyle then inspects the fabric himself.

"But is it distinctive?" he asks.

"I think so," Kyle replies.

"Distinctive. I like that. Black it is. I'll be distinctive," he says with smile back to Kyle.

Kyle returns the jacket to Andrea who runs her hand through his hair and gives him a kiss on the forehead.

"Kyle?" Harris says, turning back to them. "Will you get that red tie with the small dots on it from the closet?"

Just about every suit Harris own is black or charcoal gray. When he's feeling adventurous, he'll break out the blue jacket or maybe the green one. His ties are traditional, mostly solids with a smattering of stripes and dots. Kyle rummages through the ties that hang on the tie hanger and finds the red one with dots. He continues scanning down to the bottom and finds the one he got Harris for Christmas last year. It's a beautiful silk paisley pattern: burgundy, grey and white on a red background that still has the tag on it. He pulls both ties from the rack and returns to the bathroom door, holding the dotted tie for Harris to see.

"Is this the one?"

Harris turns and inspects it. "Yep, that's it," he says.

Kyle places it back on his arm and holds up the paisley.

"How about this one?"

Harris looks at it, sees the tag and realizes its significance. He fakes a smile, busted for being such a cad.

"It's pretty and a classic actually," Kyle says as he holds it up to Harris' chest.

"You'll look good with it on," he adds with a smile.

Harris takes the tie and positions it on his chest, looking at himself in the mirror.

"You think so?" he says back to the Kyle through the reflection in the mirror as Kyle nods in approval. "Okay, put it in the bag too. I'll have options," he adds, handing the tie back to Kyle who quickly returns it to Andrea so she can pack it.

"You need to go do your homework," she says to him.

"Yes ma'am," Kyle dejectedly replies and turns to the doorway to leave. Before he exits, Harris calls to him.

"Kyle? Come here a second."

Harris meets him in the bedroom, kneeling and looking him in the eye.

"You know I love you, right?" Harris asks.

"I know."

He takes Kyle in his arms and gives him a strong hug and a kiss on the head.

"You're growing up into such a handsome young man," he says, pushing Kyle's hair from his face.

"Just wish you'd cut this so everyone else could see what a handsome boy you are," he adds.

"Well, I like being distinctive," Kyle adds with a smile, the play on the word not escaping him. He's a smart kid, smarter than Harris realizes.

Harris nods and shrugs, signaling a "touché". He gives him another kiss on the head and sends him on his way to his date with his math homework. Harris looks to Andrea who fights the urge to laugh.

"He got ya," she says.

"Yeah. He got me," he answers with smile as he opens the dresser drawer to finish packing.

The beautiful stone and iron entrance of Callahan Farms greets Harris as his pulls into the driveway and up to the security gate. The horse business is twenty-five percent hard work, twenty-five percent luck, and fifty percent image. If you want to sell horses in the high five or six digits range, you'll be dealing with buyers that expect to see a high dollar operation. Ellen Callahan doesn't have a problem with image and Callahan Farms is the envy of many horse breeders.

He enters in the code that Ellen gave him the night before when he called to advise her that he was coming up to talk. As he navigates the winding drive, he's struck by the beauty of the place with its low, rolling hills and groves of oak trees. The paddocks are rich and green. He passes a huge covered arena that he estimates probably cost three hundred thousand at least.

At precisely ten o'clock, he pulls into a circle drive in front of the house, a rustic two-story log home with two stone chimneys. Several barns are visible on the side and behind the house, which sits on a small hilltop overlooking a lake behind it. He gets out and looks around at a sight he rarely sees in New Orleans... space. Horses graze in the paddocks and he hears the quacking of ducks behind the house as he watches what might be a hawk soar through the sky. It's an incredibly peaceful setting; he can certainly understand why Megan wanted to come back here.

"You found it," Ellen calls from the porch.

"My GPS did all of the work, but yeah. What a beautiful place you have here, Ellen," he says as he walks up to meet her.

"Well thank you. With what we spend on it, it better be," Ellen says as the two of them exchange a hug. "Come on in," she says, motioning Harris through the doorway and into the living room, a western themed, horse lover's dream.

"Can I get you some tea?" she asks as she steps over to an island bar.

"No thank you. I just had breakfast. Little place down the road," Harris replies, thinking back to the extra bacon he had ordered, one of the few benefits of being away overnight. "Water, if you have one, would be nice," he adds.

"Was that McCallister's?" she asks, pulling a bottled water from a small fridge and handing it to him.

"Yes, it was. Mighty fine cooking."

"Oh it's such a greasy spoon, but so good. I know it's not good for me but I can't resist their chicken fried steaks, and their pulled pork is some of the best in Shelby County."

The two of them spend the next ten minutes talking about the farm and the quarter horses. She shows him pictures of the champions they have raised and talks about the early days when she and Wes first got into the business. Her eyes sparkle as she recounts stories of Megan's youth.

"Did Megan ever date anybody that you thought might be a danger to her?" he asks.

"You know, Detective Harris—"

"Please, just call me Albert or Harris if you like."

"Okay, Albert. You know, Megan didn't date that often. I mean she had a boyfriend here and there, but she never really seemed interested in them. She seemed more interested in cars and trucks. Good Lord that girl was a mess, never afraid to get her hands dirty when she was working on that Bronco with her daddy."

She leans down and picks up a picture frame from a side table, a photo of the family taken a year before Wes's death.

"That's Wes," she says as she hands him the picture. Her love for him is still evident in her eyes.

"You have a beautiful family, Ellen," he says as he looks at the photo, adding "I'm sorry that you lost him."

"Thank you, on both accounts," she says, taking the picture back and gazing at it lovingly before setting it back down on the table.

"Megan was such a tomboy, Albert. Some of the other kids in school were mean to her, called her names and such," she says, looking back to Harris, her eyes asking for him to hear what she was saying.

"I just wanted her to be happy. I love her," she adds as she turns away.

She walks over to the door to the back deck and looks out at Megan who sits in her place of solace on the boat dock.

"That's all we ever want for our children. Wouldn't you agree?" she says in quivering voice, sniffing and wiping a tear from her cheek as she turns back to him.

He smiles a soft, sympathetic smile and nods then walks to the door.

"How is she?"

"Physically, she's healing. It's the other that I'm worried about. Yesterday was awful. That call from that Jennifer person really upset her. She still won't say what that was all about. My God I wish she had never gotten involved with that poetry site," she adds, shaking her head in disgust.

"How long has she written?"

"Started when she was in high school, for her English class. When Wes died, she wrote a beautiful poem to him. I cried so hard," she says, fighting back more tears.

"She entered it in a contest in the *Appeal,* and it won first place. She was so proud," she recounts with a smile, remembering the happy faced teenager the day the poem was published.

"She wrote some in college, but it was very dark. I hated it. She said it helped her, that it was cathartic for her. I guess someone broke her heart. She wouldn't talk to me much about her relationships."

They stand silently for a moment, watching Megan and Frizbee on the dock as Megan provokes him, encouraging him to get the ducks that swim nearby. After a few moments Harris turns to Ellen.

"Do you have any fishing gear?"

Megan sits in a chair, her knees to her chest, wearing jeans and a sweater to warm her on this cool, late October day. Her back is to Harris as he approaches from up the hill with two fishing poles and a small container of night crawlers. She knows he's coming, but she doesn't acknowledge him. She would much rather sit there and not speak to a soul. She's done this before; she'll get through it.

Harris stops short of the dock and watches her as she looks out over the lake. It's a serene setting that he seems hesitant to disturb. After a few moments, he calls to her.

"Ahoy. Permission to come aboard?"

"It's a dock, not a boat, but..." she pauses for a moment. "Permission granted."

"Any fish in this lake?" he says with a smile.

"Catfish mostly, some bass and perch," she replies with a slight hint of annoyance.

Frizbee greets Harris as he steps onto the dock.

"Nice Boxer. What's his name?"

"Frizbee," she replies, turning her chair towards the other chairs on the deck.

"Yeah? We had a dog named Frisbee when Miranda was young. He was a Beagle, though," he says, setting the bait down in the chair and petting Frizbee, eliciting a fresh round of tail wagging and a curious sniff of the bait.

"Well there you go. We're not so different after all," she says, then calls Frizbee to get away from the worms.

"Can I sit?" Harris asks.

"As long as I don't have to fish."

"Not even if I bait the hooks?" he says, easing into the chair next to her.

She shrugs her shoulders, indifferent to the whole idea. She watches him as he begins baiting a hook and she's reminded of the many times that she's fished from this same dock. She rarely was the first to ask to drop a line and her father usually had to insist, but she always enjoyed it in the end. As Harris finishes baiting the first hook she considers what it must have been like for him to be on the other side of the fence she was on, to lose a daughter.

"I never had a chance to tell you. I'm sorry about Miranda," she says after a moment.

Harris continues baiting the second hook, focusing on getting the wiggling worm onto it just right. He's fighting back the emotions that he always fights whenever the subject is brought up. After a moment, he finishes the threading, looks to Megan and nods.

"That bastard Morrison. One of these days the state bar is gonna grow a pair and disbar his ass. He gives us all a bad name," she says in disgust.

Having his thoughts dwell on how much he hated Richard Morrison, the defense attorney that handled the case against Miranda's killer, Phillip Wiggins, is not the mindset he needs while talking to another defense attorney. He holds one of the fishing poles out to her, shifting the course of the conversation. She looks at it, then back at Harris.

"I'm not fishing," she says defiantly.

"Take the pole," Harris says as he rises and practically places it in her hands.

"Seriously?"

"Seriously. It's therapeutic. Take it."

It's a bit after noon and a couple of empty plates with bread crumbs and scattered chips sit on a nearby table alongside two empty Dr. Pepper bottles. The two of them have sat here for the last two hours talking about anything but the case. She knows he didn't drive six hours just to chat but, she has no desire to bring the subject up. She'll leave that to him. She smiles as he lowers a stringer loaded with two catfish and a bass back into the water.

"Three for you and none for me," he says with a sigh, returning to his chair.

"Best four out of seven?" she asks.

"You up for it?"

"Sure. You need a big fish story you can tell back at the office."

"Yeah, I need to salvage my male pride," he says with a chuckle as she baits her hook and he simply checks his. Seeing that, as before, it's still there, he drops the cork back into the water.

"You know what I like most about fishing?" he asks.

"What's that?"

"The variety. You drop your line and sometimes it's a bass, sometimes a perch, sometimes a catfish. You never know what you're gonna get," he says.

Megan knows Harris' story. He ran afoul of the public integrity bureau after using insensitive language, as the paper put it, around a new department employee who just happened to be gay. It was blown out of proportion but got into the hands of an attorney with an agenda and cost the department a couple hundred thousand dollars by the time the case was settled. She finds it ironic that he would find the variety of fishing to be his favorite part, but has little acceptance of variety in humanity.

"Yeah, like life. It would be pretty boring if everyone was like you, huh?" she says as she cuts an eye to him to catch his reaction.

"Yeah, I guess so," he says after a moment as he pulls his line from the water to find his worm has disappeared. He huffs, catches the cork, and retrieves another worm from the bait can. As he begins threading the poor creature onto the hook, Megan's attention is pulled to a flock of geese migrating south for the winter, their calls beckoning each of them to strive on, to finish their journey.

"If that I could be of down and feather and fly away in times of cold to another place, leaving my troubles behind. Once tempest have passed, I could take wing and fly again home," she says as she watches the snowbirds escaping the harshness of a Canadian winter.

"That's beautiful. You write that?"

"No," she replies before turning her gaze back to Harris. "Jeff did."

Feeling a tug on her line, she turns and sees the cork bobbing. She reacts quickly, too quickly, and jerks the cork out of the water, leaving bait and fish behind.

"Don't jerk it out so quick. Give him time to really take a good bite. When the cork goes completely under, snap it," he with no fish on the stringer says with confidence without looking over at her.

She watches his cork bob in the water, thinking about what he said about leaving the hook in the water. She hasn't been instructed on how to fish in a long time. After several moments lost in her thoughts, she looks at him as he sits, frustrated that he hasn't caught a thing.

"What was the score again?" she asks with a grin.

He simply nods and smiles, never taking his eyes off his cork as she chuckles softly.

"Can I ask you a question?" she says.

"Sure."

"Why you? You draw the short straw or something?"

Harris looks at her for a moment then looks back at his cork.

"I could have refused," he says after a long moment of silence.

"Why didn't you?"

He pauses, continuing to watch his cork bob as he considers the right answer. For some reason, his mind goes back to Andrea. He has always supported his wife's hobbies and encouraged her in every endeavor she undertook. The jewelry though, he sees little value in it. He doesn't understand what women see in all of the beads in assorted colors and shapes. He gave up trying to understand women a long time ago. He smiles, remembering that day at the festival and Megan fawning all over Andrea's latest creation. He looks back at Megan and grins.

"Well, you did compliment Andrea's jewelry."

———

The first annual Callahan/Harris fishing tournament ended in a rout. A nice stringer of five catfish and a couple of bass has been delivered to a ranch hand that is in the process of cleaning them and preparing them for dinner later. At least Harris wasn't skunked; he did finally catch a small bass that will grow substantially over the years to be just shy of the Tennessee state record.

Megan has finished giving Harris the tour of the property where he met Sein Finn Rocket Bar in person, the Callahan's prized stallion. They've migrated into a well-stocked shop and garage where her broken Bronco now resides. It's unusual that a vehicle involved in a crime would be released so quickly but it helps to have some of the best attorneys in the city filing the right papers.

The broken windshield and bloodstained seats have been removed, as has the bent steering column, reminders that Rolly didn't care for Megan to see. The front end is heavily damaged and the battered hood has been removed. Rolly slides out from under the Bronco on a roller and rises. A full head of white hair highlights his small but sinewy frame. A sweeping mustache combined with his gravelly voice has earned him comparisons to Sam Elliot, comparisons that he does little to refute. He wipes his grease covered hands on a rag before offering one to Harris.

"Rolly Davis. Nice to meet you."

"Albert Harris, NOPD."

"So you the guy that's gonna find the son of a bitch?" Rolly says as Megan steps to a nearby tool chest and retrieves a wrench.

"I am. I will find him."

"Good. Bring him straight here. We've already got a tree picked out and I knotted the rope myself," Rolly says, only half kidding.

"I may just do that," Harris replies as he considers that Rolly looks like the kind of guy that wouldn't hesitate to string the "son-of-a-bitch" from a tree limb.

"Meg, I'm gonna go start feeding. I got the starter out. It's over there," Rolly says, pointing to a growing pile of parts as she begins working on a component in the engine.

"Okay. Thanks, Rolly," she replies without looking up.

"Nice to meet you, Albert. When you find him, if you need any help rounding him up, just holler. I'll be down there same day," Rolly says, shaking Harris' hand before heading out the garage door.

Harris watches Megan for a moment, amazed at the ease with which she works on the engine. "So you gonna fix it yourself?" he says.

"Rolly and I. My father was one that taught his daughters to be self-sufficient, take matters into our own hands," she replies, still working the wrench on a stubborn water pump.

"Well, you have the right tools," he replies as he surveys the garage.

"I'll get her running again, better than ever this time. You'd be amazed how handy I am with the right tool in my hands," she replies, looking up to him and smiling as she pulls the water pump from the engine, her hands covered in dirt and grime. She holds it a moment, inspecting it, then tosses it onto the pile of parts.

He notices a tall object standing nearby covered with a dust-covered drop cloth. He steps over to it, inspecting what appears to be some sort of metal sculpture.

"What's this?"

She looks at it, staring through it and remembering.

"Just something Daddy and I were working on," she says, turning her attention back to the engine.

"May I?"

She shrugs, focusing on the engine while watching him out of the corner of her eye as he removes the cover, revealing the partially finished statue.

"An angel," he says surprisingly, pleased with his discovery.

She turns and looks at it for a moment then returns her attention to the engine where she begins working to remove a fender.

"Yeah," she says with a hint of agitation as she works the wrench harder, battling a frozen bolt.

"Nice. I've got a thing for angels," he says as he inspects the work.

"They're among us you know? Watching over us," he adds, turning back and smiling at Megan who is now watching him.

"Yeah?" she says, pausing for a moment. "Then where was mine?" she adds, her words dripping with bitterness.

That didn't go the way he thought it would. He scolds himself for saying it as he walks back to the Bronco. Megan turns and retrieves a hammer from the tool chest and begins pounding on the bolt to loosen it, quite a bit harder than is necessary, as it feels the brunt of her anger. After several hard slams with the hammer, she seems to relax as the tension in her face recedes. She takes a deep breath and sighs.

"That felt good," she says, looking at Harris. She picks the wrench back up and begins removing the now loosened and totally humiliated bolt.

"So did you come here to just to fish or are you angling for something else?"

"I do need to ask you some things."

"Okay, shoot."

"First, I have to say you threw me a curve ball with Max."

"Jeff didn't do it. He also can't afford an attorney and I knew you would hang it on the first viable suspect," she replies without looking up to him.

"Fair enough. But I wish you would have had more faith in me than that."

She looks up at him. After a moment, she nods, silently acknowledging that he's right.

"It's the least I could do now that I've ruined his life," she adds.

He's heard words like that before. The "I've ruined" is the beginning of turning the blame onto herself. That's a road Harris knows all too well and one that he does not want to see her go down.

"Megan, this isn't your fault, none of this. It's the fault of the son-of-a-bitch that did it. Not you, you didn't do anything to deserve or provoke it."

She looks up at him, her eyes exposing her doubt. After a moment, she turns back to the task at hand with the fender, aggressively removing another bolt. Harris pauses, thinking carefully of the words he will use to pull her from the edge of the pit.

"Jeff's an adult. He's makes his own decisions," he says.

"Yeah, well I never intended to cause a divorce, and now I've gotten him tangled up in this fucking shit!"

There's those words again, "I've gotten". He puts his hand on her arm.

"Megan, don't do this. Don't blame yourself," he says, noticing her hazel eyes are glinting with tears.

"When we lost Miranda, I turned it inside. I blamed myself and I searched for answers, reasons, things I should have done or done differently. What did I miss about the bastard when she first went out with him? Why didn't I see something? It ate me up inside. It almost destroyed me."

She wipes a tear from her face, leaving a small streak of grease behind. She turns to the tool chest and begins rummaging through the tools.

"How'd you get through it?"

"Joseph."

"Joseph?"

"From the Bible, the story of Joseph," he replies as she turns to look at him, obviously not following his line of thought.

"You've got a kid, his mother's favorite," he begins to explain. "She makes him a coat, colorful, different than his brothers. So his brothers are out tending the flocks and his mother and father send him out with food. He gets there and his brothers are jealous that he's the favorite, he's different. So they cast him into a pit and then argue about what to do with him. They decide to sell him and tell their parents that a lion killed him. So off Joseph goes to Egypt where he's a slave. Ultimately, he ends up the number two man in the kingdom, controlling the food supply, and saves his family years later when they show up seeking grain due to a drought," he explains.

"I don't get it."

"You know Joseph had to blame himself for a while, thinking he must have done something wrong to end up where he was. Why else would his brothers do that to him? He must have done something to anger them. But he didn't. It wasn't his fault," he says as he looks at her and emphasizes the last sentence.

"He didn't understand why, but he soldiered on and persevered and in the end was there to help his family when they needed him," he adds.

"Well, I'm not sure I buy the 'everything happens for a reason' crap," she replies.

"I believe it does. It helped me," he says with a sincere smile.

They look at each for a moment then Megan returns to working on the fender. He watches her and considers that he needs to lend a hand, to join her in her world, the world she's in right now.

"Can I help?"

She shrugs, turns to the tool chest and retrieves another wrench. She shows Harris a couple of bolts and he rolls his sleeves up and goes to work.

The two of them have managed to remove a few stubborn bolts. Harris has been given the task of removing a fender support while Megan continues working on the fender itself.

"You know, Jeff told me you changed his life, and not in a bad way," Harris says, returning the discussion to the case.

She pauses and thinks of the happiness she felt with Jeff, that moment in the parking lot when she got lost in his eyes and totally trusted him. She loved his green eyes, so full and revealing. She closes hers, seeking and finding his, sparkling beneath the drops of rain that night in the dim light of the parking lot. She smiles, only to have it ripped away by a cool breeze that rushes through her soul—and the room.

She sighs heavily, fidgeting with the socket and removing it several times. She grits her teeth, spinning the wrench in her hand and then scanning the shop to fill her mind with images to flush away her fears.

"Yeah, well. I was there for him when he needed me," she says, lowering her head and resuming her attack on the fender.

"He told me something else," Harris says.

"What's that?"

"That he's Jen. That's he's transgender," he says looking up from the grease and dirt now covering his hands. "Why didn't you just tell me? You left me chasing a ghost."

"Not for me to tell. He trusted me with it. He didn't do it so there was no reason to even discuss it."

"I wouldn't have thunk it, Army and all. He's kinda a man's man," he says.

She watches him for a moment, gauging his reactions and waiting for the bigoted Harris to emerge.

"That make her less of a human?" she asks.

The pronoun switch catches him off guard. He looks at Megan, processing it.

"Well, no. It's just… this whole Bruce, Caitlyn, whatever. Just because you feel like a woman doesn't make you one," Harris says confidently, exerting extra effort against the bolt and spinning the nut loose. With a low grunt, he tosses it into a bowl nestled near the distributor, as if a warning not to challenge him.

Megan shakes her head and sighs beneath her breath. "How long have you been a Christian," she asks after a long moment.

Harris pauses, as if taken aback by the question. He looks up to her with a raised brow that asks the direction of the conversation. "Raised Catholic but got serious about it after Andrea and I married," he finally replies.

Megan smiles softly and nods. She steps over to a small cabinet above a work bench, opens the door and begins searching through an assortment of oils and spray cans.

"I hear Christians going on about God moving in their life," she says, a tinge of bitterness piercing her tone. "What's that all about?"

The sounds of Megan's search through the shelves overtakes the room. She stops and turns to Harris, who studies her, seemingly trying to determine her level of sincerity.

"It's a fair question, Harris. I'm trying to understand. Give me a break, will you? I'm a lawyer. I ask questions for a living."

Harris nods in agreement. "He does. He brings people into our lives, makes things happen."

Megan captures the elusive can of WD-40, closes the cabinet door and steps back to the Bronco.

"How do you know, I mean really *know*, that it's God," she asks as she douses the remaining bolts with the lubricant.

"I can't prove it, Megan. There's no hard evidence. I just know. It's… a feeling, a comfort inside, in my heart."

Megan looks away, focusing on the angel statue. She steps toward it, running her hand across the callous edges of one of the wings. The silence in the room is cut by the flightless creation's song, the metal ringing softly as Megan's fingers kiss its face.

"So I'm supposed to believe that a divine being is moving in your life, guiding you, directing you based on what you *feel*?" she asks before returning to the Bronco.

"You don't have to believe, Megan. You won't until it happens to you. It still can. But for me, I believe. For me it's the truth."

"For Jen, being transgender is the truth," Megan replies, picking up her wrench and returning to the task at hand. After a few turns of the wrench, she casts her eyes back to Harris. "It's a truth that's been there from her earliest memories. She didn't seek it out, or was taught about it. And she didn't get *serious* about it when she grew up. She *felt* different before she knew what different was."

She grabs the can of WD-40 and gives a stubborn bolt a spray. "What do you call a girl that likes boy things?" she asks as she gives the bolt a smack with the wrench before turning her gaze back to him.

"Tomboy, I suppose," he says after looking at her a moment.

She nods and holds up the wrench, motioning to the engine with her eyes as if to say 'like me.' "What about a boy that likes girl things?"

Harris nods, silently acknowledging the answer without saying it.

"Queer? Sissy? That's two of the nicer ones," she says as she returns to the fender with the wrench.

"Girls get all the slack in the world to be who they are. Ultra-feminine or masculine," she says as she exerts extra pressure on the stubborn bolt, smiling as it finally breaks free. "T-shirts and jeans one day, heels and skirts the next. Society never says a word. There's this whole range of expression of one's self that a woman can choose. From one end of the spectrum to the other—or right in the middle," she says, removing the bolt.

⁂

Megan's words echo in Harris' mind. His thoughts drift back to his childhood. Growing up in the 60's, he remembers well that time of change when women were beginning to call for equality. The traditional role of an American woman, that of housewife and mother and not much more, was changing. He can remember watching news reports of protests at the 1968 Miss America pageant where a small group of women filled a "Freedom Trash Can" with bras, girdles, and high-heels, a protest that led to the bra-burning myth so often associated with feminist of that era. He can still see the envy in his mother's face as she watched silently while his father ranted about the collapse of society and a world gone mad.

The clanking sound of a bolt tossed into the nearby bowl snaps him back from his memories. He glances over to Megan. She is watching him.

"What about boys? What do they get? How many options do they have?" she asks.

He doesn't answer. He knows she's not expecting one.

"Boys get two. Either fit into the box of societally defined masculinity or you get the shit kicked out of you and labeled a faggot. Living in the middle will make you the butt of jokes at best. People begin to lose their minds when transgender is thrown into the mix and innocents are murdered for using the restroom. If we can't see it, touch it, hear it, or measure it, it must not exist, right?" she says, her eyes piercing his. "Being transgender is not about walking around in drag and flaming. It's about who's inside, the soul," she adds, tapping her chest and returning her attention the fender.

Harris nods and looks away, a growing sadness in his eyes as his thoughts turn to Kyle.

Megan's surprised by the silence that her words are greeted by. She expected the bigot in Harris to react, to lash out at his fears. After watching the sadness wash over Harris' eyes, she suspects the reason why. Kyle.

At the festival, he reminded her of what a young Jeff might have looked like, had she known him then. She remembers the face paint Kyle wore, the butterfly, the streaks of color in his hair and the soft glimmer in his eyes when she said it was pretty. It was the same glimmer she saw in Jeff's eyes when she first addressed him in the feminine. She wonders if Harris could hear his own words when he told her the story of Joseph and how he was different than his brothers. She cuts her eyes to him, still adrift, and snaps him out of his thoughts.

"How's Kyle?"

She watches him move the puzzle pieces around in his mind then cuts him some slack.

"He sure is a cute kid," she says, finishing off another bolt.

"Yeah, he's a good kid too," he says, wrenching harder to catch up with her.

The two of them work silently for several minutes, ratcheting steel against steel to free the Bronco from its mangled fender.

"That's not the only thing Jeff told me," he says after a moment.

"Yeah? What else did he say?"

He sets the wrench down and pauses, waiting for Megan to look up, for her eyes to meet his.

"That this wasn't the first time, Megan."

Megan's demons howl, relishing in the moment as Harris unknowingly knocks down stones from her walls. They rush in bringing with them memories of a night years ago that she has tried hard to forget. She closes her eyes and breathes deeply, fighting the tinges of panic, she pushes the memories back as she turns to the tool chest and rummages, stalling while she regains control.

"I was nineteen, a freshman in college," she says after a long moment.

"Why didn't you tell anyone?"

"I just wanted it to go away. I wanted to get on with my life."

"Was he a student there?"

She stops and looks up, steadying herself for the second wave attack against the bulwark that kept her safe. She turns back to Harris and begins working the final bolt, a particularly stubborn one, with a zest.

"At the time. He pursued me for a while after that. Then a friend on the rugby team kicked his ass."

"What was his name?"

"DJ. I met him a party. I only knew him as DJ."

He doesn't push for more information. She can see him out of the corner of her eyes as he watches her work the bolt and then glances back at the angel statue, studying it

"Megan, I know this hard. I can only imagine how hard. I don't know if you're religious or not, but based on the angel here, I feel okay to share that one my favorite passages from the Bible is Psalm's 23," he says softly.

"Yeah, the Lord is my shepherd. I learned it as a kid."

"Well, the key is that it doesn't say in the valley. It says walk *through* the valley. That's what you're doing; you're passing through this valley. It is not your final destination. Believe that. Accept that you're passing through, through the darkness to the light on the other side. That and the story of Joseph got me through when we lost Miranda."

In the past, this is a story she might fight with dry or biting humor. But right now, she wipes tears from her eyes, leaving another streak of grease on her face. She looks up to Harris and nods. She removes the final bolt and pulls the fender off. Holding its weight in her hands, she turns her eyes to the angel statue and tosses the fender down in front of it.

"You know," she says, dusting off her hands. "Maybe I can make something good out of all this junk." She turns to Harris, witnessing his smile.

"Maybe some horns to hold up the halo," she adds with a grin.

"I'm not sure about the horns, but I'd like to see what you could do with it. It'll help to keep you focused, give you a positive state of mind. Keep you from dwelling on the negative, you know?" he says.

She smiles softly and sighs, nodding her agreement. "Stay for dinner?" she asks.

"No. I need to get back. Follow up on a few things."

"Bullshit. You haven't had catfish till you've had Momma and Rolly's. We've got an extra room. You can get up early. Momma's up at half past three. She'll have bacon and eggs ready for you."

"I really shouldn't. I need to get started on tracking down this DJ."

"Give it to Broussard. That's what you have a partner for. You can be back by noon, latest." She wipes the grease off of her hands and they begin walking out of the garage.

They look up to see a Sheriff's deputy pull up to the front of house and get out of his car. He's a thin one, and the uniform swallows him. He adjusts his belt, tightening it to the last notch to keep his gun from falling from his waist. She and Harris exchange a look of disbelief and amusement.

"I really would like you to stay. Barney Fife there doesn't give me the greatest sense of security."

Harris watches the young man, considering his options.

"Bacon, huh?" he asks.

"All you can eat."

"Turkey or pork?"

"Turkey's not on the menu for another month."

"Alright then," he says.

Megan smiles widely and heads down the drive. "Come on, Andy. Aunt Bee will have dinner ready soon," she says, looking back over her shoulder at Harris. "And you probably should hold onto Barney's weapon. He makes me a little nervous."

"I'm right behind you, Opie," Harris says with a laugh.

Chapter 24

CROSSES

Ellen's catfish truly was the best catfish Harris had ever eaten. He hopes that the night of sitting around the fireplace with good company was therapeutic for Megan, too. She seemed to enjoy talking about her and Kristi's childhood and she had laughed as he sat in the barber's chair and told stories of growing up in New York.

The breakfast was, of course, grand with plenty of thick, pork bacon—but it was tainted by the memory of Megan's screams during the night from nightmares. He wanted to get up and see if he could help, but he could hear Ellen talking to her. Plus, it wasn't exactly his place.

He called Broussard last night and gave her the new information. She's now putting together a list of students from Tulane, three years either side of the year Megan was raped.

The six-hour drive home has given him plenty of time to think about the case. Even though the blood under her nails matched back to Jeff, he's beginning to believe that he truly had nothing to do with the attack. While he is glad to have new information and a potential new lead, it's a long shot. In many ways, he feels that he's back to square one, the odds growing against him.

Back in New Orleans, Harris turns off of Canal and onto Barrone and rolls to a stop, sighing in frustration. The road is blocked by a film crew moving equipment from a truck to the sidewalk. Due to the growth in the number of films that have been shot in New Orleans in the last ten years, the city has picked up another nickname… Hollywood South. It's a fact that most New Orleanians are proud of, even if it means having to deal with traffic delays and road closures. After a few minutes, the traffic begins to move again. He eases past the Roosevelt Hotel and parks across the street from the Immaculate Conception Jesuit Church, ignoring the "No Parking" sign posted there by the city for the film crew. He exits his car and crosses the street and enters the door at 130 Baronne, an office building adjacent to the church which houses their offices and the offices of St. Agnes Women's Center located on the third floor.

<hr />

In the weeks since Megan was attacked, Anna has struggled with a sense of responsibility for the whole thing. She's convinced herself that if she hadn't written the erotica and published it on Megan's profile, her assailant wouldn't have come after her. She sits in her office at St. Agnes Women's Center, an organization managed by the Jesuit Church which offers assistance and counseling to abused women. It's the same offices in which she met Megan and at which Megan used to volunteer. Working at St. Agnes was an honor for Anna and she felt like she was giving back to the community. Even though she continues to do so, learning that Megan's assailant had quoted her work has left her feeling very unworthy of that honor.

She sits at her desk now, quietly filling out paper work. She watches out of the corner of her eye as her current client, a delicate woman in her late twenties, sits across from her holding her daughter, a blue-eyed six-year-old. She came to the center seeking housing assistance to escape an abusive relationship. Anna looks at the bruises and cuts on her arms and face and remembers the fear in her eyes when she first walked in.

Anna finishes filling out the page then silently watches as her client wipes tears from her eyes. Her daughter tries to comfort her, softly cupping her face in her little hands. Images of Megan race through Anna's mind as they have with each victim that she has helped since the attack. She tries again to talk reason into her client.

"You need to file charges. You can't just slink away into the darkness and let this guy continue to abuse women."

"I can't. He'll find me," she says tearfully. "You don't understand. I have…" she adds, stopping herself as she looks down at her daughter.

Anna studies her for moment, the woman's eyes pleading for her to not push further. Anna closes the file folder and sets it to her right. She opens a desk drawer and finds the correct set of keys, then rises and begins to escort them out.

"It's small, but you'll be safe," Anna says, handing the keys to her.

"Will Donny be there?" the young girl asks fearfully.

"No sweetheart. Donny won't be there," Anna answers, heartbroken by the fear she hears in the innocent child's voice.

"See momma, I told you it was gonna be okay," the child says, sending her mother into tears.

She wipes her eyes with a tissue and turns back to Anna.

"Thank you," she says as she exits the office and into the hall.

Anna watches as the helplessness of the situation washes over her. She forces a smile and waves as the two of them step into the elevator. Once they're inside, she sees Harris step out into the hallway.

"Detective Harris?" she says anxiously.

"Hi Anna. How are you?" he says as he makes his way down the hall to her.

"I'm okay, I guess," she replies wondering what he is doing there. "Do you have any news?" she adds.

"Maybe. Do you have a few minutes? I need to talk to you about some things," Harris says.

Harris came today to ask Anna if she knew anything about the rape that Megan suffered when she was nineteen. Anna was shocked to hear the story and unfortunately could not give him any insight that might prove useful. One half of a box of tissues later, she has collected herself and struggles to understand. This revelation only serves to add more weight to her already guilt-ridden soul.

"You know, you think you know someone. I mean, you spend so much time with them, you know their moods, their likes. You think you know everything about them, then..." she says, pausing as she thinks about the woman she thought she knew intimately. "What kind of friend am I? She didn't trust me enough to tell me something like this?"

She pulls a tissue from the box and dabs away fresh tears.

"I can't believe she never told me," Anna says, drying her nose with the tissue before adding "It all makes sense now."

"What does?"

"Why she couldn't trust men, wouldn't let them get close to her. She would torpedo the relationship if it got physical," she says sadly before resting her head in her hand. After a moment, she looks back at Harris.

"Her relationships on the poetry site were substitutes for the real ones she couldn't allow herself to have. I wish she had told me, I could have helped or found someone that could," she says as the tears flow again.

He takes her hand into his and holds it softly as he sits across the desk from her. Slowly, she collects herself. She dabs the final tears and wipes her nose then rises and begins to pace near the window behind her desk. She stops and stares out onto Barrone Street, her sadness giving way to frustration and anger.

"I don't think I can do this anymore. Every woman that comes in here reminds me of her. Every picture, I see her in that hospital room. I've tried not to blame myself, I have but..." she says to the glass.

After a moment she turns and looks at Harris then at her client's folder laying on her desk. She steps over and picks it up.

"Look at this. She just left here... Bruises, cuts, burns," she says as she flips through the folder.

"She refuses to file charges," she adds as she hands the folder to Harris.

He flips through it, grimacing at the images of abuse. He turns his eyes away and then back to Anna as she returns to her chair and sits.

"Anna, you know, I see a lot of pain in my job too, and it's pretty much only my faith in God that keeps me going. In a hard world, we're to be compassionate. In the darkness, we are to be a light," he says empathetically.

"Every woman that comes in here is a victim, just like Megan. If you walk away, you walk away from her, and from yourself. The monster wins," he adds as he taps the folder and glances back down at the pictures.

One photo in particular catches his attention and he focuses on it. He reaches into his pocket for his glasses and studies the image. Anna motions to the folder.

"He's a monster alright. She's terrified. What kind of man would..." she says, stopping in surprise as Harris quickly rises from his chair, photo in hand, and begins dialing on his phone. Confused, she picks up the folder and starts thumbing through it, trying to determine what he has seen.

"Ellen, are you with Megan? Okay, I need you to take a picture of that burn on her arm, her right one. Yeah, the cross. I need it now. Send it and I'll get back to you," he says into his phone, then hangs up and dials Broussard.

"Hey... I need you to check that list of classmates of Megan's for a..." he says, pausing to motion at Anna to give him a name. She quickly scans the primary information form and finds the full name of her client's abuser.

"Uh.. Donald Herbert," she says as quickly as her nerves will let her.

"Donald, D, Donny, any variation of D. Herbert. Okay, hurry."

He looks to Anna who is totally confused. He steps over to the desk, laying the picture for her to see and points at an oddly shaped cross burned into the woman's arm.

"Megan has a similar burn. We may have just gotten very lucky."

He paces the room in silence, both of them afraid to say a word that might jinx this. His phone beeps with a message. He looks at it, then at Anna. He sets the phone down for her to see and sets the picture of the woman's arm next to it. The wounds are almost identical.

"It's not a burn. It's a brand," he says.

His phone rings and he answers it, placing Broussard on speaker.

"Donald J. Herbert, student at Tulane '96 to '97."

"DJ!" Harris exclaims. "Find him! I'll be in the office in ten," he adds as he ends the call.

He stares at the pictures, severe second degree burns oddly formed into a cross, scarlet crosses. He looks out through the window, sickened by the use of that sanctified emblem, one which he holds so dearly, to inflict such pain. After a long moment, he turns back to Anna.

"I'll need the information sheet and picture as evidence."

"Of course." she says as she hands them to him.

He slides them into his jacket pocket, leans down and hugs her tightly.

"Anna, don't ever quit this job!" he exclaims. "I'll be in touch," he adds as he exits, leaving Anna struggling to understand exactly what just happened.

Harris hurries down the hall of the central office, deftly avoiding a collision with the department's executive assistant. They exchange quick pleasantries before he sticks his head into Blanchard's office.

"Meet us over at Broussard's desk," he says without giving him a chance to reply.

Moments later, he leans over the desk with Broussard as they study her findings.

"There were six guys at Tulane in '97 with first letter D and last name Herbert. Two are dead," she says pointing to a print out.

He pulls the information sheet from his pocket, setting it down beside her print out as Blanchard steps to the desk.

"Whatcha got?" he asks.

"Megan was raped in '97 by a guy named DJ when she was at Tulane. He was a student there," Harris says.

"Is there a record of that?" Blanchard asks.

"No, because she didn't file charges, she didn't even file a report," Broussard explains.

"That's terrible but where are you going with this? The odds of—"

"Hang on," Harris says as he pulls the photograph of the woman's arm from his jacket and lays it on the desk.

"I went by to talk to Anna about it just now, hoping that she might know something. She didn't, but by chance she showed me a file folder of victim that she had just helped."

"Wait a minute, slow down. Where does she work?" Blanchard asks.

"St. Agnes Women's Center," Broussard answers.

"Right, so she was saying that she didn't think she could do the job anymore after what happened to Megan. That everything she sees, every woman that comes in reminds her of her. So she hands me the folder of this woman that sought help but was refusing to file charges on the guy that was abusing her," Harris says before tapping the photo on the desk. "This was burned into her arm."

"Still not following you," Blanchard says as he studies the photo.

Harris pulls his phone out and lays it on the desk next to the picture and opens the photo of Megan's arm.

"Oh my God! They're almost identical," Broussard exclaims. Blanchard leans in for a closer look.

"The guy that did this is named Donny Herbert," Harris says.

"I found six D. Herbert's at Tulane in '97," Broussard says as she begins running the remaining four names through the computer to pull up social security and known addresses. "Including one, a Donald J. Herbert," she adds as she types that name first.

"DJ," Harris says looking at Blanchard.

This sounds promising but Blanchard knows better than to get too excited about something like this. He turns his attention back to Broussard's computer as Donald J. Herbert's details appear on the screen. Broussard checks Anna's client's address against the list of known addresses.

"Bingo!" she exclaims, slapping the desk. "Donald Justin Herbert!" she says, her voice filled with anticipation as she checks the social security number.

"Got him! It's a match. This guy was at Tulane in '97," she says.

Blanchard looks at her a moment then at Harris who anxiously raises his eyebrows as if to say "what do you think". He turns back at the two photographs, studying them.

"So you think these are brands? His mark?" he asks.

"I think so," Harris replies.

"You got anything else to tie this guy to Megan? I mean today, not '97'?" he asks.

"Not yet," Harris replies.

Blanchard studies them both for a long moment.

"Send me the details. I'll get you your search warrant," he says, turning and heading back to his office before adding with a glance over his shoulder, "Good work."

⸺

On their way to Donny's last known address, Broussard informed Harris that the blood she found behind the burned out house had come back belonging to Megan. She spent half a day canvassing the neighborhood looking for any witnesses that might have seen anything unusual. Unfortunately, there weren't too many people awake during the hours in question, but she was successful in finding one witness that claimed to have seen an older Chevy pickup, perhaps a mid '90's model, on the street not long before the house went up in flames. They didn't get a plate nor were they able to discern the color in the darkness.

When they arrived on Cherbourg Street in New Orleans East and knocked on the door, they were greeted by the landlord, and elderly Vietnamese gentleman, who advised them that he hadn't seen or heard from Donny in over a month. He was three months late on the rent and, while he hated to have to do it, he had evicted Donny's girlfriend last week. The landlord did confirm that, as he remembered, Donny drove a pickup truck, a "piece of shit" as he described it.

Harris stops the car in front of 527 Huntlee Drive, across the river in Algiers, a home owned by Donny's mother. It's a small house: wood frame with a carport behind a fenced yard and an old Toyota Corolla sitting on the streets edge. Broussard calls in the tag numbers as Harris gets out and surveys the area, the 15th ward—Old Aurora—as he knows it.

"Corolla belongs to his mother. She also has a 1997 Chevy 1500 in her name," Broussard says, closing the car door behind her and approaching Harris at the back of the car.

"Wonder why she doesn't park under the carport?" he says, motioning towards the house.

"I wonder."

The make their way up the sidewalk and onto the porch as a dog barks at the two intruders from behind the fenced yard. Harris knocks and they wait patiently for someone to answer. He knocks again and this time they hear movement inside. Broussard nervously touches her gun her under jacket.

"You stay here and keep trying. I'm gonna step to the side of the house and watch the side door," Harris says.

Broussard knocks again once Harris is standing near the gate with an eye on the other exit from the house. The door cracks open and a gray haired woman, mousy and thin, peers through the crack.

"What'd ya want?" she asks.

"Mrs. Herbert?" Broussard asks, noticing what appear to be bruises near her eye.

"Yeah. Why ya wanna know?"

"Is Donny here?" Broussard asks as she cuts a glance over to Harris who nods. There's no movement on that side of the house.

"He ain't here. What'd ya want with him? He ain't done nothing!" the woman says, raising her timid voice an octave.

"We need to speak to him. Do you know where he is?"

"I told ya, he ain't here!" she says and shuts the door, locking it.

Broussard looks to Harris, who shakes his head in disappointment. This would have been a lot easier if they could have caught Donny during an afternoon nap.

"Call it in," he says as they make their way to the car.

Broussard dials Blanchard. They'll have their search warrant delivered within an hour.

Seeing the bruises under the woman's eye, Broussard was compassionate enough to call for an abuse counselor when she phoned the details into Blanchard. That counselor, two other officers and the search warrant arrived within thirty minutes. Donny's mother is not happy. The counselor sits with her on the couch, trying to talk reason to her and get her to calm down and let the officers do their jobs.

"He's a good boy! He didn't do anything!" she yells as an officer carries a computer out the front door.

"Put that down, you son-of-a-bitch!" she yells as the counselor restrains her from the officer.

Inside a back bedroom, Harris and Broussard inspect the meager belongings of Donny. A small desk, absent the computer that was just carried out, sits beside a bed. On the wall behind it are print outs of poems from the Dream Weaver profile. On a side table, a small, carefully crafted book—print outs of the erotic stories that Anna wrote—lies next to a stack of DVD's. Harris picks up the disc on top, a film titled *Bound and Dirty*. The graphic image of a nude woman tied to a bed and gagged, with a hooded person standing over her while brandishing a whip, sickens him.

Broussard examines the book of stories, as Harris sets the DVD down and pulls a thumbtack from the wall, removing a piece of paper. It's a poem titled, "On Angel Wings", and written by Megan. As he reads to himself, he can hear a young Megan as she might have read it to her father at his funeral.

She was to fly on alloy wings
a metallic celestial host
an allegory of time together
formation of one
each piece a part of two

But it is you now
that flies with angel wings
my hero, my guardian,
preserving me from above

When as a child with grazed knee
you swathed away the pain
comforted in your arms
as my tears faded away

I am your child
your daughter of mud
your son in pigtails
you are my father, my friend
my eternal champion

He struggles to control his emotions, walking away from Broussard so she can't see him. He thinks of Miranda and what she might have written upon his passing but for that damned day. Megan's words become Miranda's as he continues reading.

Of others you taught me
To love and respect
That judgment was not mine
That in a diverse world
There are many fish in the sea.

So fly now
On Angel wings
Fly over me
Guard me
Prepare for us a place
So that we may be
Together again someday.

I love you Daddy.

He steps into the hall, searching for the nearest way out and finds a back door. He exits quietly to a secluded area behind the carport. He looks to the heavens as tears roll down his face.

"Damn this job!" he says out loud, at barely a whisper.

He wasn't planning on this. It wouldn't be easy, he knew that, but this was supposed to be just another case involving a woman he didn't care for.

He thought he had it all under control, that he had secured away the pain of losing Miranda. He was so wrong. He thinks of the poem, of Megan's father, and prays that as he is caring for Megan, Wes is able somehow to still care for Miranda.

He collects himself and breathes deeply before returning to the back room with Broussard.

"Where'd you go?" she asks

"Had a call from Andrea," he says, looking down at the print-out to hide his eyes. It doesn't totally work; Broussard can see they are bloodshot.

He examines the page closer. In the top right hand corner he can see the website it was printed from, indicating that it was from a December 1994 archive. His mind goes back to the conversation with Ellen in Memphis, about the poem that she said Megan had entered into a contest. He hands the paper to Broussard.

"Look at this."

"What is it?"

"She wrote that when she was sixteen," he says, disappointed by his realization.

Broussard scans the page, seeking within the text the reason Harris handed it to her. He points to the top corner where she reads the web address.

"*Commercial Appeal*? That's the Memphis paper."

"I'll bet your two bits to my dollar that this poem is in the Dream Weaver profile," he says.

That moment of clarity, when it all comes together, hits her.

"If it is, that's how he found her," she says as they look at each other, both disgusted by the thought that he tracked her down through a poem she wrote for her deceased father.

Chapter 25

CONDEMNED

A s Harris drives up North Broad Street, he considers that a detective's job is one of feast or famine. Some days he's eating chicken, a nice fat breast and a thigh, and some days he's left eating the feathers. He thinks about the chicken he's had the last few days.

Donny is a viable suspect, although Harris knows that he'll ultimately have to be able to tie him directly to the rape in order to get a conviction. The print-outs of works from the Dream Weaver profile prove little more than an infatuation. If the computer shows active communication between Donny and Megan, then he has something to work with, and they'll issue an arrest warrant for him on rape charges. They've already issued a BOLO, "be on the lookout", to area law enforcement and the Louisiana State Police for Donny and the '97 Chevy.

But even the most filling day can end in heartburn, and so it has for Harris. He had received a text from Andrea asking him to hurry home, that something had happened to Kyle at school. As he turns off of Esplanade and angles onto Desoto, with Megan's poem weighing heavy on his mind and his paternal instincts kicking in, he recalls his conversation with Kyle; "Finish it if they start it".

He pulls into the driveway as Andrea rises from the rocking chair on the front porch and meets him half way up the sidewalk.

"What happened?" Harris asks.

"It's that Vincent kid, Matt," Andrea says, eyes swollen and red from crying.

"He and Kyle got into a fight. They called me from school and I went to pick him up," she adds as they hurry up the steps.

"Where is he?"

"He's in his room," she says stopping and grabbing his arm.

"He's scared. He's afraid you're gonna be mad at him. Oh, it's so bad, Albert."

She breaks down into tears and he takes her in his arms and holds her tight.

"I'm not gonna be mad at him. Did the Vincent kid start it?"

Andrea nods, wiping her eyes and nose with a tissue.

"He cut his hair, Albert!"

"Who cut his hair? Kyle?"

"No! The Vincent kid! He cut Kyle's hair. He held him down and cut it!" she says breaking back down into tears.

Harris holds her tightly while inside his mind, the giant he learned to hate and numbed to sleep almost four years ago, yawns and rubs his eyes.

Kyle stands in front of a kneeling Harris with Andrea nearby. He's crying uncontrollably as Harris tries to calm him down. Harris' thoughts that perhaps Kyle wouldn't be a UFC champion seem to be holding true. Kyle's eye is swollen and beginning to darken. He has a busted nose and split lip. Harris runs his hands through Kyle's hair, examining the area beginning just below his right ear where the lock of hair that was left on the floor at the school belonged. His breath shortens and jaw tightens at the sight.

"Kyle, calm down. You aren't in trouble. Now just settle down and tell me what happened," Harris says softly and compassionately as he wipes Kyle's face with a wet towel.

"We were in art class, and I was drawing, and Matt came over, and said I draw like a girl," Kyle says, catching his breath every third or fourth syllable.

"I told him to leave me alone and he grabbed my drawing and crumbled it up and threw it on the floor," he adds tearfully.

"Did the teacher see that?"

"No, she had gone for some supplies. So then he said I run like a girl and look like a girl. So I said 'if I want to I can' and said 'what's wrong with drawing, or running, or looking like a girl? Why do you hate girls so much?'"

"Then what happened?"

"Rebecca asked him the same thing, why did he hate girls so much and she said he was gay," Kyle continues to explain.

"What'd he do then?"

"He pushed her, so I hit him, like you showed me," Kyle says as Andrea's eyes widen and her jaw drops open. Harris meets her eyes with a nervous smile.

"Did he hit back?" Harris says, focusing again on Kyle.

"No, the teacher came back in. But he sat over there with scissors and kept looking at me, showing them to me," Kyle says beginning to cry again.

Harris puts his arms around him and hugs him tight then kisses him on the head. He gives Kyle a moment to clear the emotion.

"So when did he cut your hair?"

"After class, I felt sick to my stomach so I went to the restroom and threw up. When I was leaving, him and Justin came in and started pushing me and calling me a faggot. So I pushed him back and he hit me and I fell. He jumped on top of me and I was trying to get him off but he kept hitting me and that was when he…" Kyle says before bursting into tears and burying his face on Harris' shoulder.

Harris turns his face to Andrea. She's seen that face before; the squinted eyes, the flaring nostrils. She hasn't missed it, but she's glad to see it again. She motions softly to Kyle with her eyes. Harris hugs Kyle tightly but he pushes away.

"I hate boys! I wasn't supposed to be a boy!" he cries. "The pastor says I'm going to Hell. Am I gonna go to Hell? I don't want to go to Hell Paw Paw," he says before collapsing back on to Harris' shoulder.

Harris pulls him tightly to him.

"Shhh. Hush that," he says softly as he looks up to Andrea who stands with her hand over her mouth, head dropped and crying.

The giant blinks; pausing from his rampage, as the significance of Kyle's words sink in.

⁂

After Kyle calmed down and finally went to sleep, Harris and Andrea sat in the living room discussing the situation. Not the time for dancing around sensitive issues, the truth came out and they each laid part of the blame on the other. Harris' day of chicken turned into an evening meal of crow as Andrea was keen to criticize him for attempting to teach Kyle to fight. After he apologized, it was Andrea's turn as Harris pointed out that she shouldn't have hidden from him the previous times that Kyle was physically bullied at school.

"I wish you had talked to me about this," Harris says.

"Albert, I've tried so many times. You never want to talk about it. You always blow it off and say 'it's a phase' or 'he needs to be toughened up'. Well you see what that got him, don't you?" Andrea replies, unable to resist the opportunity for a final jab even though they called a truce ten minutes earlier.

Harris sits on the couch, leaning forward with his elbows on his knees. He stares down at the floor, thinking back to the questioning of Jeff with Max, racing through the stories that Jeff told, finding correlations.

"You know, this case... I swear Andrea, it's so bizarre," he says.

"What do you mean?"

"You remember me talking about a bartender down at Mick's? Guy named Jeff? Army guy?"

"Early thirty's? Did I meet him at that fund raiser for that woman from the office?"

"That's the guy."

"What about him?"

"He was my first suspect in—"

"That guy? He said he was married, had a kid. What hap—"

"He is, or he was, I'm not sure what the status is. It's complicated. Anyway, he's not so much of a suspect anymore but that's not the point," he says, raising his hands in the air to indicate "just wait".

"He's transgender. Born male but says he's female inside. His stories are..." he says as his thoughts drift off, remembering the cuts on Jeff's arms when he said he wanted to end it. He thinks of the kid he bullied years ago, Tommy Ells.

He turns his eyes back to Andrea who watches him, a look of shock on her face.

"What?" he says.

"I'm just... it's, you've never even wanted to say the word before."

"Well I'm saying it now, alright? You think I like it?"

"No, I know you don't like it, but we need to face it."

He rises and paces the floor a bit, trying to determine just what he should do.

"Let's ask around, see if there is some kind of therapy or something we can get for him, help him sort this all out."

Andrea puts her arms around his neck. She kisses him softly then hugs him, laying her head on his shoulder, relieved that he is at least, finally, willing to take the first step.

———

When Andrea closed Kyle's door earlier, she thought he had fallen asleep. Actually, he's laid in his bed crying for the past thirty minutes, listening to the argument. As they blamed each other, he blamed himself. If it wasn't for him, they wouldn't be fighting. The tears flowed down his face as he worried that they would get a divorce.

He rises from his bed and walks to his dresser, inspecting himself in the mirror, running his fingers through the gap in his hair, searching for what's missing. In the dim light of the room, he steps to a small desk and opens a drawer and removes a pair of scissors. He walks back to the mirror and Kylie stares back at him. She has the same marks, the blackened eyes, the busted nose, the split lip, and a missing lock of hair. She cries as she watches him raise the scissors and begin to cut the remaining hair even with the shortened locks. As he does so, her hair falls away, drifting to the floor.

"Why are you doing this?" she asks.

He takes another handful of hair, slides the scissors over it, sending it to the floor.

"Please stop," she cries.

He examines the freshly cut hair as tears stream down his face. She watches as he sets the scissors down, her eyes following his as he gazes down at them. She notices something in her hand. It's a mask. She looks back up at him as he stares into her eyes. She slowly raises her hand and places the mask on her face. She has no choice.

"Don't do this," she says as a tear streams down the mask. "Please!"

She cowers in fear, startled by the slamming of iron bars into the floors around her, and finally in front of her, meeting at an ancient wooden door that stands open.

Kyle turns and walks away. The window in front of her begins to fade as the door slams shut, locking her away inside incorporeal walls.

Kyle climbs back into bed and closes his eyes. Inside his heart, Kylie screams and rages against her confinements. She runs to the door and pounds on it, screaming to be let out. In a rage, she takes her nails and scratches the wood leaving deep, long gashes that begin to bleed.

———— ⊱✦⊰ ————

A traumatic evening was followed by a restless night of little sleep. Discovering that Kyle had cut more of his hair during the night didn't exactly start the day off on a good footing. Harris locks his car and walks quickly across the parking lot at Kyle's school. An early morning call arranged an 8:30 meeting with the school counselor. His head hurts and his stomach is sour from the four cups of coffee, and it's only 8:15. Andrea is staying home with Kyle who, according to school policy, has been suspended for two days. She'll take him to have his hair trimmed later this afternoon, knowing that the discussion with the school is in the more than capable hands of Harris.

Harris enters through the front door, turns into the administration offices and signs in. The school counselor, wearing a blouse with a collar tied into a bow, is waiting for him.

"Mr. Harris?" she asks, extending her hand. "Won't you come to my office?" she adds turning and motioning the way.

They step into her office. He surveys the walls, littered with motivational posters. Behind her desk are several diplomas and certificates to illustrate her intelligence and of course, what office wouldn't be complete without the pro-verbial "Keep Calm and [fill in the blank with your word or phrase of choice]" sign. The phrase of choice here is "Dream big".

Harris takes a deep breath. Everything about this woman irritates him. Her blouse got the ball rolling. He cringes at the thought of having to discuss the matter with a Chihuahua. Her smile is unlike any he has ever seen. She squeezes her lips tight against her clinched teeth and the muscles in her cheeks struggle to pull the lip edges into a semblance of a smile. He's not sure if she's smiling or having a bad case of gas.

"Thank you for coming, Mr. Harris," she says motioning for him to have a seat.

"I wish I didn't have to, but we need to talk about this suspension," Harris replies electing not to sit.

The counselor smiles her bitter smile.

"I do understand your concern Mr. Harris, but we do have po——"

"Policies? He didn't start the fight," Harris says, struggling to keep his tone nicely moderated.

"There's no need to get angry. I always encourage our children to be above that," she says as her teeth practically show through her lips.

He looks down and smiles, fighting the urge to pull out his gun and kill her on the spot, thus saving all of the children at the school the trauma of having to deal with her condescending attitude and fashion choices.

"What punishment have you given the little turds that did this?" he softly asks.

"I'm not at liberty to discuss the terms, but they have also been suspended," she replies.

"Suspended?" he says, leaning in and placing both hands on her desk.

"Yes, Mr. Harris they were——" she says, pushing her chair back a bit with her feet.

"My grandson was beaten. They cut his hair. They should be facing a minimum of aggravated battery charges and be in the juvenile system," he says calmly with a slow and forceful meter.

"Mr. Harris, please. These are children. Boys will be boys. We don't need to damage them perm—"

"Damage them... are you kidding me? Who are you protecting here?"

"I'm trying to protect them all, Mr. Harris."

He throws his hands up in frustration, turns around and his eyes land on that damn stay calm poster. He stares it a moment, wanting to rip it from the wall but instead choosing, for the time being, to heed its message instead.

"Mr. Harris, have you considered moving Kyle to a different school, Lusher perhaps or the school of art? They both have wonderful theatre and arts programs," she asks before qualifying it with "It's only a suggestion... for Kyle's benefit."

He turns around slowly and glares at her for a moment as he replays her words in his mind.

"Change schools? You want me to teach my grandchild to run from his problems? To crawl into a corner every time someone doesn't like the way he looks or what he wears? Because he's... *artistic?*" he says, adding the quotations around that last word with his fingers.

"I didn't mean anything by—"

"I know exactly what you meant!"

"Mr. Harris, I'm only trying to help."

"You're no better than those two punks! Kyle is different but that doesn't earn him a beating!" he says as he steps towards the door, done with this conversation. He opens it then pauses and turns back to her.

"You said you want to protect all of them. You need to protect Kyle when he's on this property. If you can't, I'll bet your two bits to my dollar that I know an attorney that would love to come down and rip this school a new asshole," he says calmly and forcefully before exiting, as the giant laughs behind the wheel of the bus that just ran over her.

Chapter 26

DETERMINATION

With Kyle weighing on his heart and the school counselor raising his blood pressure, Harris has leaned heavily on Broussard the last couple of weeks and she came through like a true champion, working the case and beating the bushes to find Donny. The computer's hard drive was imaged and technicians were able to confirm that someone using it had several profiles on the poetry site, including one named "Lace Lady" created to appear to be Gloria, Donny's mother. All of the profiles had varying degrees of communication with Megan through the site. A warrant was issued for Donny's arrest and both he and the '97 Chevy were registered in NCIC.

Yesterday, he and Andrea visited a few therapists and settled on one that Kyle will begin seeing twice a week. While Andrea is concerned that it could do more harm than good, Harris is confident that the good doctor will be able to help Kyle get things straight in his head. He is, after all, the doctor that helped the Williams family at church when their son thought he was gay.

While the last couple of weeks have been a mixture of feathers and crow, today has been a day of chicken. Sometimes Hollywood takes liberty with things and exercises their artistic license. Two way mirrors in interrogation rooms is one of those things. Some police departments have them but New Orleans is not on that list. Harris and Blanchard stand in a small office watching thirty-six-year-old Donny Herbert on the video feed as he sits in a chair, hand-cuffed to the table, in the adjoining interrogation room.

When questioned, his mother had insisted that she hadn't seen Donny in three weeks and for the two weeks after they searched her house, it seemed that Donny had disappeared into the under belly of New Orleans, or worse still, had left the city or perhaps even the state. The Louisiana State Police had searched for him and his truck to no avail. A trace on the truck within the OMV had been triggered when someone called the office requesting to transfer the title. Normally, this is a two-sided operation where the seller must file a form and the buyer must do likewise. If the seller doesn't file, the owner can't get clear title without jumping through hoops.

The result of the thirty-minute trip to Kenner to visit the new owner was disappointing to say the least. Donny sold the truck a month earlier to a drinking buddy for five hundred dollars. The guy purchased it as a sixteenth birthday gift with the intention of putting a little elbow grease and sweat into it and turning it into a father/son project. The two of them had already spent considerable time working on it and potentially damaging any evidence that the techs guys might be able to glean from it.

Harris' break came this morning when Donny attempted a withdrawal from Gloria's bank account. It wasn't the withdrawal itself that got him caught; he did that regularly. It was the alert that had been issued to all financial institutions in the state through MOBSA, the Metropolitan Orleans Bank Security Association. Having spent time on the organized crime task force, it was a tool that Harris had learned while tracking money. Donny was arrested in the lobby of a bank in Slidell, on the north side of Lake Pontchartrain, after a quick thinking teller flirted with him long enough for officers to arrive.

It seemed that Donny dropped out of Tulane in '98 and had led a life marked by drugs and violence ever since, wandering from job to job up and down the Gulf Coast. Most of those jobs had been in construction, one of many in a highly transient work force. His record shows that he's been arrested a couple of times in other states for marijuana possession and a few years ago was arrested in Alabama for beating his then girlfriend who, much like Anna's client, had refused to testify so the charges were dropped.

The erotica that Anna posted on the site and the often sultry messages that Megan would write to potential muses created a vixen-esque persona for the Dream Weaver profile. While none of the profiles managed from Donny's computer were on the list of Megan's muses, she had exchanged those sultry communications with several of them. Most troubling was a message from Megan to Lace Lady in which she innocently mentioned that she would be attending the Gator Festival.

Donny sits alone in the interrogation room, his court-appointed lawyer having not arrived. He's skinny, ratty, with a shaved head. He appears to have not bathed in days and has worn the same clothes for just as long. From the way he wipes his nose on his sleeve, it seems clear to Harris that this is his normal appearance and not the result of being on the run for three days. They watch him as he leans back in his chair and casts smart ass glances at the camera. There is something oddly familiar about him to Harris but he can't put his finger on it.

"Gloria knows nothing of the Lace Lady profile," Broussard says as she approaches from the outer room. "Megan was catfished," she adds with a look of disgust.

"Catfished?" Harris asks, unaware of term.

"Fooled. It means using a fake online profile to get close to her. Like Manti Te'o," she says.

Harris nods, astonished by the creative use of the name of type of fish. He tries to work the logic through to see the correlation between a fake online profile and a catfish, but it eludes him and he refocuses on the tasks at hand.

"The lab drew a complete blank. There were no traces. They said a foreign object was used during the rape," Harris explains to Blanchard, grimacing at the thought.

"Sick bastard," Broussard says as she turns and looks at Donnie who smiles for the camera.

"I don't want to look at him. I'm gonna go find out when his attorney will be here," she adds, turning and exiting the room.

Harris and Blanchard watch as Donnie flattens his hands on the table, moving his fingers as if he's trying to get their attention. Harris taps the keyboard, focusing the camera onto Donny's hands. The words 'Fuck' and 'You' are tattooed across his knuckles; a cross is inked onto the top of his right hand.

"I'll be damned," Harris says, his expression going blank as he remembers Donny and the confrontation he had with him at the festival near Bobby's booth.

"What?" Blanchard asks.

Harris' own demons begin raging in his mind, accusing him of failing, of not being the strong, hardnosed cop he used to be, of becoming weak and timid, of failing Kyle.

"Harris? What?" Blanchard asks again, touching his shoulder and snapping him out of his thoughts.

"I saw this piece of shit at the festival that day. He was making crude comments about her," Harris says as his demons demand judgment for his inaction.

"That's perfect! You can place him there," Blanchard says.

"Yeah," Harris says softly, still staring into nothingness as he counters the charges against him in his own mind.

"I should have shot him," he says dryly as he turns back to Blanchard.

Blanchard was there when Harris lost Miranda. He was there that day in the courtroom, holding him back when he charged the defense table. He feared this case might turn out the same way: futile. He watches Harris for a moment; by the sober look on his face, he knows that if Harris could go back to the moment he saw Donny at the festival, he might just have done it.

Blanchard focuses on the monitor and the antics within the interrogation room. "How you holding up, Al?" he finally says, apprehension clinging to his words.

"I'm fine. I'm fine."

"You done good on this. I'm bringing Jonas from the rape squad in. I told you—"

"Ron, I'm fine. I can handle it."

Blanchard studies him, reading his expression, trying to calculate if he is really fine and capable of handling the case the rest of the way through.

The two of them stand together, quietly watching the freak show continuing inside as Donny sneezes and wipes his nose on his hand, then his hand on the table and finally his sleeve.

"That night, when they brought Miranda out of that house, it felt like my world had ended," Harris says quietly without looking at Blanchard.

"They give us guns. They teach us to use them. It's ... a license to kill. I've always prayed that I never have to use it. I never wanted to kill someone," Harris says pausing before turning his eyes back to him. "But I wanted to kill him," he adds.

"When he walked..." Harris begins to say before turning away, obviously struggling to abate the pain.

"Al, you don't have to—"

"When he walked..." Harris says again, voice cracking from the anguish Blanchard knows is rushing back to the forefront of his memory

"I sat outside his house. Had it all figured out, how I was gonna do it," Harris says, his expression going blank as he relives that time.

Exactly what happened the night Miranda was killed may never be known. There were mistakes made during the investigation and scumbag attorney Richard Morrison had used that to his advantage to obtain a not guilty verdict. It was a heart breaking case that seemed so clear cut. Phillip Wiggins killed Miranda. Harris knew it. The department knew it. They just couldn't prove it to the jury.

After the trial, Harris had taken a leave of absence from work, questioning himself if he could possibly continue at all. His world had been destroyed and while his daughter, the light of his life, lay entombed in granite, the man responsible walked free on the streets of New Orleans. Harris considers himself a good man, a godly man, but sometimes things just go too far. They did for Harris and that night outside of Phillip's house plays over and over again in his mind.

He had staked out Phillip's home for weeks and knew his every movement. Most nights Phillip would go for drinks with friends after work then arrive home about eight, park his car in the private lot at the corner of Barracks and North Rampart then walk the block back down to the old Morro Castle building where he had an apartment. The building was rumored to be haunted, as are the majority of buildings in New Orleans as far as rumors go. Whether it was or not, Harris had decided to add one more departed soul to the mix. Phillip needed to pay, and if the the "system" couldn't do it, he would.

What he was planning went against ever thing he believed in. He knew the verses.

It is mine to avenge; I will repay.
In due time their foot will slip;
their day of disaster is near
and their doom rushes upon them
Deuteronomy, 32:35

That night he would be the angel of the Lord, with Phillip's doom rushing upon him. It made no difference to Harris if he were caught.

It was a night like the others. Phillip's car passed Harris as he stood in the small alcove across from the Center of Jesus The Lord Church, with its century old walls that enclosed the goodness of God that had been taught to so many over the past one hundred years. There were no lights on in the Church and little from the street. The additional shadows cast by the Crepe Myrtles along the street's edge made for the perfect den from which to strike. Harris owned a 9mm Luger, a gift from his father that he had taken off of German soldier in WWII. It was more than sufficient to finish the job.

Harris heard the gate to the parking lot open. He scanned the street up and down, looking for possible witnesses and found none. He glanced to the Church; the lights were still out. He breathed deeply as Phillips footsteps approached, readying himself. He would wait for him to pass, step behind him, place the barrel at the base of the skull and pull the trigger.

As Phillip passed in front, between Harris and the street and under the Crepe Myrtles, Harris saw her. She wasn't there moments before. A figure, whose features were obscured by light from behind her, stood inside a normally closed and locked door in the walls of the Church. She was staring directly at him. Harris froze as he studied what he could see of her features, her hair, her height, her shape. She could have been Miranda.

Harris glanced back to Phillip, who was several steps ahead and out into what light there was on the street. He turned his eyes back across to the Church. The door was closed and the woman was gone. He surveyed the street, struggling to find her. In the blink of an eye she had vanished, and thus began Harris' belief that angels walked the earth. He hated himself at that moment.

———

Blanchard watches silently as Harris wipes his eyes with a handkerchief.

"I just couldn't do it. Somebody, some *thing*, stopped me," he says.

Blanchard silently and sadly looks at his friend, feeling his pain.

"I need this, Ron. Let me do it," Harris says through clinched teeth.

Blanchard quietly processes his thoughts. Everything he knows professionally is telling him to pull Harris off the case. But his friendship with Harris is telling him something else. Their silence is broken by Broussard, who enters from the outer room.

"He'll be here in ten," she says, her exasperation evident in her voice.

"Who is it?" Harris asks.

Broussard pauses, hesitant to answer. She glances to Blanchard for help, but gets none. She takes a deep breath.

"Richard Morrison," she says with a slight grimace, as if she's pulling the trigger in a firing squad.

The room goes deathly silent for what seems like an eternity. Harris slowly turns to Broussard, who mouths "Sorry," then to Blanchard who runs his hands through his hair in frustration.

"That's it. I'm taking you——"

"Ron! I've got it! Let me do it," Harris says, taking Blanchard by the arm and adding, "I need this."

Blanchard studies him. He hasn't seen this kind of determination in Harris' eyes in quite a while. It's risky. It's too personal. But Harris is his friend first, and he knows what Harris needs. Blanchard nods and says to Broussard, "Go stall him when he gets here."

Broussard smiles and leaves the room as Harris and Blanchard return to watching Donny through the monitors.

"It's hot in here, don't you think?" Harris asks while keeping his eyes locked on the monitor.

Blanchard doesn't speak a word. Seeing Donny through the monitor, Harris breathes deeply while Blanchard turns and leaves the room.

Harris paces the interrogation room next to Donny who still sits, his right hand cuffed to the eye-bolt in the middle of the table. A picture of Megan from the hospital lies on the table in front of Donny. Harris glances to the surveillance camera, its red light glaring, filming the proceedings.

Harris stops and watches him for a moment, then reaches into his pocket and removes the key for the handcuffs.

"That looks uncomfortable and I don't want that. What kind of host would that make me?" he says as he unlocks the cuff.

Donny rubs his wrist with his hand and leans the chair back on two legs, stretching his back.

"What? No 'thank you'?" Harris asks after a moment.

Donny stares straight forward, gritting his teeth.

"You think you're a smart guy don't you, Donny?" Harris asks.

Donny just sits staring straight forward, emotionless, a burning cigarette in his hand.

"You sold the truck. We found it. They're ripping it apart as we speak, searching for hairs. Did she lose any hair when you threw her inside?"

Donny twists, adjusting in the chair and gritting his teeth, but still remains silent. Harris looks at Donny's right hand and the tattoo of a cross emblazoned across the top. The ink is bright and the skin is still enflamed.

"That cross you burned in her arm, same one you burn on all your women, isn't it? What's that all about Donny? You like to mark your victims? You a saint or something? Leaving the mark of God behind?"

"Fuck You!" Donny says, finally cracking.

"Fuck me? Oh, I don't think you could do that if you wanted. What happened? Your coke habit make you a eunuch? Can't get it up anymore... *Donna?*" Harris says, leaning down towards Donny's ear and stressing the last word.

"Man! Fuck You! I didn't rape that bitch!" Donny says angrily as he turns to Harris.

"Now I don't believe that for a minute, *Donna,*" Harris says, stressing 'Donna' knowing that it's getting under his skin.

The room, and entire floor, suddenly goes dark. Shouts of frustration can be heard from within the department as someone is scolded for using "that" outlet, the same one Blanchard used the day he put Harris on the case. Harris smiles slightly. He and Blanchard have always worked well together.

He steps to the door, opening it slightly to let a bit of natural light into the room. He looks to the camera and sees that the red light has gone out. He reaches into his pocket and pulls out a printout of the poem that Megan said Donny recited when he was raping her. He lays it on the table in front of Donny. She may not have seen his face, but she'll recognize his voice.

"You like poetry, Donna? You must. You had five profiles on your computer for that poetry site," Harris says as he lays his phone on the table beside the poem and taps record.

"Read that for me, Donna. I forgot my glasses," he says as steps around next to him.

Donny stares at the poem for a moment, and then smiles a smart ass smile. He picks it up, moving it back and forth away from his eyes, mocking Harris.

"Let's see. There once was a man from Nantucket, whose dick was so long he could suck it," Donny says with a smile, then laughs and sets the paper down.

He leans back in the chair, tipping it back on two legs, and grins at Harris. Harris kicks the legs of the chair, sending Donny to the floor. He grabs him by the collar, pulling him up and violently slamming the back of his head into the bottom of the table. He pushes Donny's face hard against the surface and leans down close to his ear.

"Don't fuck with me, asshole! I know people that will do shit to you that would make Satan flinch! Read the fucking poem!"

Donny's empty, green eyes just glare.

A few minutes later, the door to the interrogation outer room opens and Harris steps out into the hall, sliding his phone into his jacket pocket with a satisfied smile on his face. Richard Morrison is steps away, looking back as he walks, with Broussard trailing him to get his attention.

"I really don't have time," the slimy, bald Morrison says, turning his head and almost running into Harris who doesn't bother to get out of the way.

"Dick Morrison. I thought you got disbarred?" Harris says, making certain to stress the first name longer and louder than most would.

"It's Richard, and *fuck* you, Harris. I was cleared and you know it," Morrison says as he motions for Harris to get out of his way. "Have you been fucking with my client?" he adds.

"Me? Nooo," Harris says innocently. "We've just been reading some poetry. Thought it might calm his nerves a little," Harris adds with a smile.

"Well, if you'll excuse me, I need to start planning my next victory," Morrison says as he pushes on past. Harris watches him until the door closes, then turns back to Broussard to exchange a smile.

Chapter 27

COLLAPSE

In the days since Harris was last in Memphis, almost two weeks now, Megan has spent a lot of her time doing the one thing she can control, something that she can trust: working on the Bronco with Rolly. In many ways the Bronco represents who she is and where she came from. The memories of spending time with her father working on it years ago had been something that she relished. To leave it in the state it was in after it was wrecked would have been tantamount to abandoning a part of herself. To let someone else repair it when she is capable was not something that she would even consider.

In the hour since Harris arrived, they have all sat around the kitchen table as he explained the development of the case in the past week. He made sure to emphasize that the break came as a result of Anna's compassionate heart and had she quit due to her self-imposed guilt, Donny would most likely not be in jail today. The call yesterday with the news that Donny had been arrested came as a relief to Ellen and Kristi and to some degree to Megan, but for her it's been difficult. The dreams last night were worse, compounded by the memories of the first rape.

When they first sat down, he had shown Megan a picture of Donny, his mug shot. Megan stared at it in disbelief as she remembered turning and bumping into him at the festival. Ellen and Kristi listened intently as Harris explained the evidence they have against Donny. It's precious little but it's enough to hold him.

Listening intently was not something that Megan could do as her thoughts drifted back to those darks days. Since learning of Donny's arrest, she's had to force herself to enter many dark rooms and search through things that she had locked away. All the while, fearful that she might confabulate a memory, just to have it all make sense.

As Harris explained the chain of events to Ellen and Kristi, Megan drifted into herself, searching the day at the festival for any clue she had missed. He was there and he had watched all day and into the night. Maybe it was that she met Jeff there and seeing him, Donny's rage grew. Did she speak to him more than once? How long had he been following her on the site? Was he one of her muses? How she could have been so stupid, so foolish she wondered. Her demons begin to thoroughly indict her in a trial of self-guilt convening within her soul.

A sudden feeling of confinement races through her limbs and she begins pacing. She breathes deeply, to shake off the restraints from her hands and feet, still feeling his body on her. The new memories mingle with the old and she can see him in her mind now, the twenty-year-old Donny, atop her.

She didn't know whose house it had been. It was a party that she was invited to somewhere in Uptown. She met him beside the pool when one of her friends introduced them, then disappeared with some other guy. They had talked for hours. Maybe it was the alcohol. Maybe it was stupidity. Maybe she trusted him and she shouldn't have.

One thing led to another and soon she had gone with him to a back bedroom. They kissed in front of a fireplace where he began to unbutton her shirt, taking it farther than she had wanted. She resisted, while he insisted. He had pushed her down, putting all his weight on top of her, holding her hands down with one hand and unbuttoning her jeans with the other. She struggled and freed one hand, grabbing a fire iron and struck him in the head.

He rolled onto the floor in pain and then went still as Megan crawled away and cowered against a wall. She watched him for several minutes, afraid that she had killed him. She slowly crawled across the floor towards him, calling his name, but he did not respond. She reached him and hesitantly rolled him over. His eyes opened and he quickly rose up; he grabbed her by the throat, choking her, pushing her onto her back and striking her head hard on the floor. As she drifted on the edge of consciousness from the blow, he raped her. When she regained full consciousness, he was gone. She collected herself, hailed a cab, cried all the way back to her apartment, and began quarrying the stones that would protect her from that day forward. At least they had until now.

She hears her name and turns to Harris who stares protectively at her.

"Megan, you okay?" he asks.

She wipes a few tears from her eyes, then wraps her arms around her chest and nods her head.

"I'm fine."

"I need to play something for you," he says looking at her compassionately as he sets his phone on the table.

She watches it with fear, as if Donny himself might rise straight out of the phone and pull her back inside with him. She turns back to Harris who nods.

"You can do this," he says adding "I need you to identify him by his voice".

Megan paces a few times then sits. She wipes her face and pushes her hair back.

"Ok."

Harris puts his hand on top of hers and she clasps it tightly. He hits play. She listens to the hideous sound of his voice and cringes. It may as well be the hiss and rattle of a poisonous snake. She pushes through a few verses, leaning in to hear it better, listening for inflection and pronunciation.

"Your lips, lush and soft, meet mine, oscillating moisture and fire——" the recording says before Megan hits stop.

"It's him," she says, turning her eyes to Harris.

"Are you sure?"

"It's not oscillating, it's osculating," she says as she begins to drift away.

"I don't know why that word stuck in my head but he mispronounced it that night and just now. It's him," she adds dryly and then turns back to Harris.

"He spoke to me at the festival. I can't believe I didn't recognize him," she says, further laying the blame on herself rather than Donny.

"Megan, he doesn't look anything like——"

"I should have recognized him," she says, cutting him off as she pulls her knees to her chest, wrapping them tightly with her arms.

"How did he know Dream Weaver was Megan's profile? It's anonymous," Kristi asks.

Harris reaches into the file folder in front of him and pulls out the printout from Donny's wall. He looks at it a moment, then at Megan. He recalls how he felt when he first read the words, how he could hear Miranda saying them. He knows how much Megan's father meant to her, how much she misses him. He knows it's going to be very painful to learn that the poem she wrote out of love and loss was the key to her present pain. He hands the paper to Kristi then places his other hand on Megan's shoulder.

"That was found in his house," he says, looking back to Megan who turns to see.

"A printout from the *Commercial Appeal* website," he reluctantly adds.

Kristi only has to read the title. She drops the paper on the table and begins to cry.

"What? What is it?" Ellen pleads.

"Daddy's poem," Kristi says as she turns to wrap her arms around Megan, hugging her tight.

"What does that mean? How did he..." Ellen says, her eyes begging for an explanation.

"It was published in her profile on the poetry site," Harris says reluctantly.

Megan barely reacts. She looks past Kristi's arms and at the paper lying on the table. The trial of her self-guilt that has raged in her mind draws near to a close as the prosecutor rests his case with a smile.

Chapter 28

VERSES

On his way home from Memphis, Harris is haunted by the look on Megan's face when she realized that it was her own words of love that led hate to her. He can only imagine how difficult it must be for her, but he is sadly aware of how painful the next few months will be. He knows all too well the frustrations of a victim and a victim's family. The justice process is not known for expediency and the time it takes to bring a case to trial can be overwhelming and disheartening for the victim, often resulting in them feeling abandoned or forgotten by those they are trusting to obtain justice for them.

There's little danger of Donny being released any time soon. In the state of Louisiana, a District Attorney has up to one hundred and twenty days to file felony charges. Louisiana's unique legal system and often underfunded public defender systems can result in some suspects sitting in jail for months before ever seeing or hearing from an attorney. Richard Morrison's arrival so soon after Donny's arrest was a rarity, but it wasn't by chance. Blanchard made a few phone calls to ensure that Donny wouldn't be able to claim he was being denied legal representation. There can be no mistakes on this case, he owes that to Harris.

An accident on I-55 south of Jackson, Mississippi has traffic now at a near standstill. The stop and start nature of the traffic for the past five miles reminds him of the days ahead of them. The periods of excitement, when progress is being made, will be peppered among an abundance of days waiting for the system to, hopefully, work.

The case file will be due at the District Attorney's office on December 6th, twenty-eight days after Donny's arrest. This is one time that he is glad he isn't the primary detective because that responsibility will fall squarely on Broussard's shoulders. He hopes that they will be able to find some form of evidence either at the house that burned or Donny's truck that will tie him directly to Megan.

Once the file has been submitted, the D.A.'s office will call for a charge conference two or three weeks later. He does a quick calculation and realizes that time period will fall during the Christmas holidays, further delaying the conference until after the first of the year and only adding to the agony of the wait.

He passes the site of the accident, where a mangled Toyota lies wedged beneath an eighteen-wheeler's trailer, with fire fighters using saws to remove the victim's body. He thinks of that person's family being told of their death this close to Thanksgiving and Christmas. He thinks of Ellen and Kristi, how they were spared that pain, how he wishes he had been spared, too.

—⊰⊱—

In the two months since the assault, Megan has struggled to rebuild the walls that she had so carefully constructed the previous sixteen years. Five weeks ago she reluctantly gave in to pressure from Ellen and Kristi and began seeing a therapist in Memphis. Two weeks later, fed up with her prying questions, Megan ended their professional relationship with a torrent of choice expletives. Since then, she and Rolly made great headway with the Bronco and it sits now, stripped to the frame, awaiting its resurrection.

Six months ago, Ellen brought Pharaoh, a five-year-old white Polish Arabian that had been rescued from an abusive and neglectful owner, onto the farm. Proper feeding and care are beginning to hide the ribs and pelvic bones that once showed through his skin. Megan has spent a lot of time with him, bonding in many ways with a kindred soul. While he is fearful of most on the ranch, he follows her around like a shadow, the bridge of trust between them evident.

Equine-facilitated Psychotherapy is a medical field recognized globally for helping people with, among other things, anxiety and post-traumatic stress disorder. It made no difference to her what it was called; it just felt good to be with him. They needed each other.

But the most cathartic therapy for Megan, as it had been through her life, is writing. Each phrase is a cry of anguish; each verse a lamentation. Each piece, filled with those pain and fear-laden words encased in ink on the page, mollifies her haunted spirit.

A thunderstorm has set in on the ranch and Megan sits quietly on her bed in her old room. The thunder and lightning replay that night in her mind as she forms the words and drops them onto paper through teary eyes. She stares at her reflection in a mirror, as she's done many times tonight, seeing a shell of the person she used to be. She turns back to her laptop and continues typing, her nauseated soul heaving away the pain.

Forgive me father for I have sinned.
Odium has slain me of this world.
Inhumed in the blackness,
the loneliness,
the malady of my soul.

And darkness rots.
Buried in this grave,
I am entombed
in the afterbirth
wrought of my own hands.

Demons taunt,
dancing in my psyche,
they smash lucidity,
leaving shards
that eviscerate my consciousness

Enshrouded in this anguish of silence,
muted by the retch of my iniquities,
time flees.
Each second a shattering in my mind.

She wipes her eyes and clicks "Publish". She begins to close her laptop when it beeps with a message from Jeff, saying he has posted a new piece. She clicks the link and silently begins reading "One More".

One more
talk,
breath,
touch.
Your voice a symphony
to my soul.
three syllables
tracing passages through my mind.
If only that once again,
I could hear you say,

I love you.

Please talk to me.

She stares at the words, tears streaming down her face practically mirroring the rain drops on the window. She closes her laptop, flips off the light, and burrows her body beneath the blanket, sobbing.

A loud clap of thunder startles Megan from her sleep. She rolls over, clutching a pillow close to her chest, and watches the shadows thrown on the wall by the lightning flashing outside. She thinks of Jeff and the times he has tried to call.

She has wanted to answer, but her fears and the guilt that she crucifies herself with have stopped her. She thinks of his words, of Jen's words, in the poems that she wrote to her. She thinks of the trust they had in each other, of the heart-to-heart talks, of the times they were together, of looking into his eyes and seeing her soul. She remembers how she melted in her arms, how safe it felt, how she loved him and accepted her.

Another loud clap of thunder and the light is driven out by the darkness. She considers what he has been through because of her, because of her foolishness. She tells herself that she's ruined his life, caused a divorce, and gotten him arrested. He trusted her and she failed him. She's afraid of the future, afraid of the uncertainty, and she doesn't want to burden him with her troubles when he is just beginning to live his life for himself, for herself. She picks her laptop up from the floor, opens it and begins typing.

A week after Donny was arrested, Harris went by Jeff's house to let him know that he was no longer officially a suspect. As the day wound down, they sat on Jeff's back porch and talked about life, his divorce, and Megan. Jeff had always enjoyed talking with him at Mick's and it was nice to just sit and visit without the cloud of suspicion hanging over his head.

Since that time, Jeff has tried to call Megan every day. She has yet to answer. He can't understand why he's been shut out of her life when he wants so badly to be there for her, to hold her hand, to whisper into her ear as she had done for him so many times.

He's up early, hoping that Megan replied to his latest posting, praying that there is a message from her waiting for him when he logs in. If only that message, when it comes, says she loves him, that she misses him, and asks him to come to Memphis, he will drop everything, quit his job if necessary, and make the quickest drive from New Orleans to Memphis ever recorded.

He logs into the site and his heart leaps when he sees a message from her. He stares at the notification, the mouse cursor hovering over it hesitantly. He knows that clicking that link is a point of no return. His fate lies within, guilty or acquitted, worthy or worthless. He takes a deep breath, clicks it and silently reads:

Jen

I never dreamed that I would meet someone like you. When I say that, I mean someone with the inner strength that you have even if you didn't or still don't realize it. If you still don't, you should. You are a beautiful soul Jen, please accept that and believe it.

It's so easy to lose sight of who we are, becoming entombed in a world created for us that we allow and succumb to. It's easy to feel that we are simply a veneer, a mask, and that no one ever truly sees the real person within. So often our lives are orchestrated by others and we are but puppets, kites on a string made to dance, living a life that someone else dictates.

Then one day, the chrysalis opens and the metamorphosis begins. We find who we are deep inside and gather strength to be that person and be proud to do so. Jen, your chrysalis is opening with a rebirth of spring so that you may find yourself and be who you are, the woman that I know you to be, breaking free of the binds. I'm so happy that I was there to witness it Jen, to be part of it with you.

It is time to cut the strings Jen, to realize how strong you are and that dreams do in fact come true if you believe in yourself and them. One of those strings is me. I'm broken Jen and I will only serve to hold you back, an anchor that will drag you down.

If you ever loved me, let me be. Fly, my butterfly, fly. I love you too much to pin you to a board.

M.

Tomorrow is Thanksgiving. He will not participate. He has nothing to be thankful for. His mournful cries will not wake his son, taken by Emily to her parents' place in Atlanta, hours and miles away. Even further, it seems, is the one woman who truly accepted him, the one woman who loved him for who he is—that woman just floated away.

The previous night's rain has cleared, and Thanksgiving Day has turned into a beautiful one in Memphis. The family gathered, along with an assortment of aunts, uncles, and cousins, at Ellen's house to partake of the traditional meal of turkey, dressing, green bean casserole, and candied yams. Megan could feel her arteries harden as she walked through the kitchen with its culinary assortment. She had provided the yams even though she really didn't feel like participating. How could she not? After all, family had driven in to tell her "She looked great!" and "They had been praying for her." She was sure that was the most that Ellen had allowed any of them to say and had instructed all of them beforehand not to mention the rape.

She quickly grew tired of the reminiscing of days gone past that is taking place right now in the living room and sits instead in the barn working on a stubborn differential cover on the rear axle of the Bronco. It lies on blocks in front of her and next to the unfinished statue, re-covered with the drop cloth. She sits on a cinder block and lights a cutting torch, adjusting the oxygen to give it a red flame with an ample amount of smoke. She isn't trying to cut the cover, just trying to heat the stubborn bolts. She waves the flame across them for a few moments then turns it away without shutting it off. She takes a wrench and tries to loosen a bolt while the flame from the torch ignites a grease-covered rag lying next to her.

She shuts off the torch, scolding herself for the unsafe move, and then uses her gloved hand to tamp out the rag as smoke rises and rushes across her face causing her to cough.

"Meg," she hears a voice say.

She looks around behind her, expecting to see Rolly or a relative standing there, but finds no one. A slight breeze brings more smoke wafting across her face. She coughs again, waving her hand in front of her face to clear the smoke. She hears her father's voice.

"Megan, wake up."

She stares blankly ahead, remembering for the first time when she awoke inside the burning house and the moments that preceded it. She sees the drop of water from the rain-soaked roof as it falls towards her. She hears the thunder clap that immediately followed. She sees again her father sitting on the log by the fire. She sees him smile at her.

She rises and paces, realizing that it wasn't by chance she woke up, that her angel had indeed been there. She closes her eyes tightly, rebuking herself for doubting.

After a moment, she opens her eyes and looks at the statue. She steps over to it and removes the drop cloth. She runs her hand across a partially finished wing and smiles softly. She turns her eyes to the pile of discarded parts from the Bronco and picks up the fender she removed when Harris was here. She holds it up to the statue, analyzing it, then returns to the cinder block and replaces the differential with the fender. She puts on a pair of safety glasses and relights the torch, adjusting the oxygen to create a sharp, bluish white flame. She smiles as it hisses loudly, rendering the fender into useable form.

Chapter 29

TWISTED

The last six weeks has been everything that Harris expected it to be as far as the case is concerned, mostly waiting. In the last few days, there has finally been some forward progress and he is on his way back to Memphis to see Megan and ask one of the most difficult questions a detective has to ask of a rape victim.

When he passed the site of the accident that he saw the last time he was on this freeway, its concrete still scarred from the flames, he remembered his thoughts about death during the holiday season. He wondered if the Callahan Thanksgiving had gone well, hopefully better than the one at his house which was a bit different this year. As had been the tradition since Nicki moved into the duplex next-door, she, Russell, and Rebecca had joined the Harris' for the feast. While they enjoyed their visit, the troubles that Kyle has been going through, though not discussed, weighed heavily on the mood of the occasion. Kyle had hardly eaten a thing, sullenly picking at his food and electing not to have a piece of Nicki's carrot cake.

The change in Kyle's behavior had not gone unnoticed by Andrea and Harris but they disagree as to its meaning. Kyle has been seeing the therapist for three weeks now. Andrea has begun to express concern that the therapy may not be what Kyle needs, but Harris is confident that Reparative Therapy, as he has learned it is called, is helping Kyle. He has pointed out to her that Kyle is gaining much needed male confidence, noting that Kyle rarely plays with Rebecca any more, even though she still comes over and ask him to, although that itself is beginning to decline. He has also pointed out, much to the disagreement of Andrea, that what she calls "talking back" is actually Kyle become more self-assertive. Regardless, Kyle does seem focused on school more than before, often retreating into his room soon after dinner to complete his homework and go to bed early.

The examination of Donny's truck ultimately yielded two key pieces of evidence, hair that was determined to be Megan's and one leather glove, a right glove, with a small blood stain that tested back to her. That find was the last bit of evidence that Harris and Broussard added to the case file, which was delivered on schedule to District Attorney Landow's office on December 6th.

In years past, the Christmas season was something that Harris endured. While it is a celebration of the birth of Jesus, a person of utmost importance to him, he hasn't been drawn into the season from that perspective. He doesn't need a predefined holiday to celebrate the birth of Jesus. Christmas was, for many years, a rote repetition of gift giving and salutations of good cheer. This year was different. He actually took the entire week as vacation to spend quality time with Andrea and Kyle and he made a concerted effort to purchase gifts with meaning, gifts from the heart, and in the case of Kyle, a light blue pair of Converse sneakers. It was as close to lavender or peppermint as he could stand.

At the encouragement of Andrea and with the help of her talented hands, Kyle took an art project from school and turned it into a tie as a Christmas gift for Harris. He isn't sure that the woven pink roses and vines on a burgundy linen and silk background is right for the workplace, but he was truthfully touched by the gift and will eventually find a place and time to wear it.

Harris smiles as he pulls through the gate at Callahan Farms. He stops and rolls down the window before turning off the engine. He sits for a moment, listening to silence, absorbing the serenity that drew Megan back here. His soul needs a bit of that serenity at the moment.

As he had expected, the charge conference was delayed until after the first and occurred a few days ago on January 7th. While he is confident they have the right guy in jail, the actual evidence they have against him is thin. They have a witness that can place a truck *like* Donny's in the area of the house before it burned. They have Megan's blood found on the sheet behind the house. They have the hair and blood sample from his truck. They have the computer, the profiles, the evidence collected at his mother's house, but what they don't have is something to tie him directly to the rape.

Donny's attorney, Richard Morrison, once a prominent legal counselor, had fallen on hard times in the past couple of years after letting his penchant for alcohol take control of him. Some questionable litigation led to ethics charges of which he was ultimately cleared. However, the damage had been done and he was now largely a public defender. Descriptive terms for those that practice law are plentiful and often unfounded. But the terms "ambulance chaser" and "bottom dwelling scum sucker" are quite applicable in this instance.

Morrison is already making the case that it was a rescue gone bad. Their story is that Donny happened upon the accident and was forced to cut the seatbelt to remove Megan from the Bronco. He put her in his truck with the intention of taking her to the hospital, but panicked and left her at the house with the hopes that someone would find her. He's even taken it as far as to challenge jurisdiction, arguing that the scene of the crime itself could not be firmly established in Orleans Parish, especially considering that her ordeal began not far from the concert grounds in St. Charles Parish.

The charge conference was heated to say the least. Landow and his assistant attorneys insisted that unless Megan was persuaded to testify, they will only be able to charge Donny with simple battery since there was no weapon found. If she is willing to testify then, and only then, will they charge him with sexual battery, a felony offense.

Harris pulls into the circle drive in front of the house and kills the engine. He stares at the house for a moment and then says a quick prayer asking that God will guide his words and soothe Megan's spirit.

The conversation started out well enough with the group spending the first thirty minutes talking about Thanksgiving and Christmas. Later, he and Megan walked to the barn to see the progress she was making on the Bronco and he used the opportunity to attempt to buoy her with his faith as he had tried to do when he first visited her here. He can only hope that something he said will be a lifeline to her, a rock to grasp in the torrent.

They returned to the house and were joined by Ellen and Kristi as Harris began to explain the current state of the case. The conversation at hand is the need for her to testify when, and if, the case goes to trial. With no charges or report ever filed about the first rape, there is little hope that any of its details would be allowed in as evidence. The hard line that Landow is taking regarding charges leaves Harris little room. If he wants a conviction for anything more than a misdemeanor offense, he needs her to testify.

While Megan was in the room, she was largely absent and lost in her thoughts. When not apathetic and staring blankly, she would oscillate between helplessness and rage, withdrawing into herself or storming around the room demanding vengeance. Harris was glad to see that she was capable of rage. She needs to blame Donny. He's the one who did this.

When he brought the subject of testifying up, it first sent Megan into her apathetic phase, followed shortly by grief and fear, and now by rage. This, however, is a rage that Harris wishes she wasn't showing. She's directing it at him. She paces the living room quickly, arms protectively clasped around her chest.

"No! No! You do your fucking job and find the evidence!" Megan yells at Harris who stands near the couch that Ellen and Kristi sit on.

"Megan, you know he did it. We know he did it. But we'll have to convince the jury. Nothing or no one will do that as well as you," Harris says.

Megan continues to pace, shortening her circle to only a couple of steps in each direction. She clinches her chest tightly, worry and doubt sweeping across her face.

"I can't," she says softly after several moments.

"Megan, you've been there a thousand times. You've done it," Kristi interjects.

"You're damn right I've done it!" she barks at Kristi, stops pacing and looks to her.

"A thousand times I've done it!" she exclaims throwing her arms into the air demonstratively.

"I've stood in that courtroom and made the strongest witness fade and melt into a fucking puddle," she says as she begins pacing again.

"I've taken good, honest people and twisted them like taffy, shaping the syllables they spoke into the words I needed to hear," she says stopping and turning to Harris. "The words the jury needed to hear to win the god-damn case," she says to him with tears in her eyes.

"Then you'll be prepared for it, beat them at their own game," Harris says.

"I know how they play the game, Harris. I know what they'll do to me," she says as she sits on the couch and pulls her knees to her chest, clutching them with her arms. She looks back up to Harris.

"I will *not* go through that. You find the fucking evidence!"

Harris watches her as she looks away and rocks back and forth on the couch. Ellen heads towards the patio door and stares hopelessly through the screen. Harris sits down next to Megan, leaning forward and placing his elbows on his knees. He stares down at the floor searching his mind for the right thing to say. He doesn't need a commitment right now, but he does need to get her moving in the right direction.

"Megan, if Miranda had been able to, if she had lived, I know she would have testified. She didn't get a chance to and that son-of-a-bitch walked free to hurt God knows how many other women," he says with his eyes still locked on the floor. He blinks the tears away when he looks to her, but she can still see them, glistening around the edges.

"You lived, and thank God that you did because you now have that chance," he adds.

She watches him for a moment then turns away and begins rocking again as fear, rational or not, takes back control.

"I can't. I can't."

Harris feels a hand on his shoulder and looks up to see Ellen wipe tears from her eyes. She doesn't say a word—she doesn't have to—her expression says "Please stop" well enough. He sighs softly and nods. Megan's been through enough. He'll try again another day.

Chapter 30

WINDOWS

In the week since he returned from Memphis, Harris hasn't exactly been a joy to be around. It didn't help matters that his beloved Saints lost their divisional playoff game last Saturday to the Seattle Seahawks, ending their season. Since then, Andrea has been careful to let him work things out. She's seen him like this before, a period of quiet reflection interlaced with a general sour attitude about everything. She realizes that it's primarily Megan's case that is bothering him, and the unsettling fact that another rapist might go unpunished. He'll work through it, he always does. She knows that if he needs to talk about, he will bring the subject up.

Kyle has retired to his bedroom early, again, and Harris sits in the living room watching the NFC Championship game between the Seahawks and the San Francisco 49'ers, rooting for a 49'ers win and yelling at the officials for a questionable call. She smiles as she listens to him. At least he isn't worrying about the case.

She raises the lid on the washing machine and begins placing dirty clothes into it. She picks up a long sleeve shirt of Kyle's, examining the shirt pocket for any debris that might clog the washers drain. She notices a dark stain on the left sleeve. She turns the shirt inside out and finds a blood stain on the inside of the long sleeve. Concern washes over her as she sorts the pile of clothes searching for other shirts of his. She finds one, also a long sleeve, and upon turning it inside out finds another blood stain. She runs possible scenarios through her mind that could explain their existence. She sets the shirt down and hurriedly makes her way through the living room and down the hall to Kyle's room

She knocks on the door and opens it after Kyle answers. He's sitting at his desk, drawing, wearing a long sleeve t-shirt and shorts.

"Kyle? Did you scratch your arm or something at school?"

Kyle's expression goes blank and he hesitates.

"Umm, yeah, during gym," he finally replies.

"Let me see it," she says as she steps over to him, reaching for his arm.

He pulls away, clutching his left arm with his right.

"It's fine, Nanna."

"Nonsense. There's blood on your shirt sleeve. I need to see it," she insists as she pulls his arm away and pushes the sleeve up.

"Nanna don't, it's fine," he says as he struggles to keep her from seeing his arm.

She pushes the sleeve up to the elbow. Her eyes widen and her jaw drops as she sees several long, deep cuts beginning at the wrist and moving half way up the elbow. They overlap several more that are various stages of healing.

"Oh my God!"

"I'm sorry, Nanna!" Kyle says as he breaks into tears.

"Albert! Albert, get in here now! Hurry!" she says before rising and rushing into the bathroom. Harris meets her in the hall as she emerges with alcohol and cotton swabs.

"What is it?"

She doesn't stop nor look at him. She rushes into Kyle's bedroom as Harris follows, completely lost. She kneels next to a sobbing Kyle and begins to wipe down the wounds. Harris' eyes see the cuts on Kyle's arm.

"I'm sorry, Paw Paw. I didn't mean to do it," Kyle says as Andrea turns fear filled eyes up to Harris.

Harris sits in their darkened bedroom, lit only by a small lamp that sits on his bedside table and the television, tuned to the ten o'clock news. The lead story is about the main prosecution witness in the Caleb Elliot drug trafficking trial, the same trial that Max pulled Megan off of, one Mikhail Levokova, being killed while in the Orleans Parish prison.

If Harris were listening, he would hear the reporter say that the death of the main witness could adversely affect the outcome of the trial and District Attorney John Landow's campaign for Attorney General. But he isn't listening. He sits clutching a picture of Miranda that he keeps by his bedside. He grimaces, trying to comprehend how his world has become so upside down. He considers how he, at least in his mind, failed Miranda when her killer escaped justice and how he feels now, that he has failed her once again by failing to prevent this from happening to Kyle. Hearing Andrea approach in the hall, he sets the picture down, not wanting her to see him in this state.

She enters the bedroom, herself drying tears and wiping her nose. She walks quietly through and to the bathroom, turning the water on to wash her face.

"How is he?" Harris asks without looking up at her.

"I don't know. I bandaged them, but he doesn't want to talk about it."

"Why do you think he's doing this?"

"I'm not a therapist; just know a little about cutting from when I taught. It happens for a multitude of reasons. Could be for attention but I don't think that's it. Could be a control thing and it's the one thing he has control over. Could be self-hate," she says as she dries her face.

"Is it related to the transgender thing?"

"Possibly. Maybe guilt for not being able to feel like he fits in."

He turns the TV off and stares blankly at the screen, replaying the days since Miranda's death, searching for clues, something he said or did perhaps. The words that Jeff spoke in the interrogation room when he relayed the story of his youth echo in his mind.

Andrea returns to the bedroom and sits by him. She puts her arms around his neck and her head on his shoulder. That moment of connection is too much for him.

"I don't know what to do," he says, breaking down into tears.

She runs her hand across his face and pulls his head to hers. He sobs uncontrollably for a brief moment then struggles to pull himself together.

"Why is this happening? Did I, or did we, do something wrong? Something that would make him this way?" he says.

"Shhhh. We didn't do anything," she says, kissing him softly on the forehead before adding, "It's just the way he is."

Harris drops his head and closes his eyes tightly as he takes Andrea's hand in his and begins to pray.

"Dear Father, please help us. Please help me. I've tried to live my life for You, follow Your word. Lord we hurt. We hurt for Miranda and we hurt for Kyle. Please help us. Show us what we should do, what I should do," he says through the tears.

He looks up to Andrea who smiles at him and kisses him softly. He wipes his eyes and sighs deeply. He rises and slowly walks to the door.

"I'm gonna go work for a bit."

She nods agreement then calls to him before he exits.

"Is Megan still refusing to testify?"

He gazes down at the floor, thinking of the times she's refused despite his best efforts.

"Yeah. She's got a wall a mile high."

"To protect her soul," Andrea says as she considers that perhaps Kyle has begun to do the same thing.

"I think we should start paying attention to the soul, to the heart, to who Kyle is inside and I don't want him seeing that nut anymore," she adds confidently and somewhat defiantly, expecting Harris to react negatively.

He doesn't. He just looks at her and nods. After a moment, he turns to leave and she calls to him again.

"Read her poetry. Maybe you'll find something there."

He forces a smile and exits into the hall and to his small office. He sits at his desk and turns on a lamp and fires up his computer. He needs to be thinking about the case but he can't get his mind off of Kyle. He thinks back to the interview of Jeff and the scars on his arms. "Bleeding the demons out," as Jeff had put it. It's only eight-thirty but it feels like midnight.

Once the computer boots up, he opens a browser and rather than opening the poetry site, he types in "transgender". An article on suicide rates catches his eye. As he reads, he learns that a recent study found that among Americans that identified as transgender, the attempted suicide rate is forty-one percent, twenty-five times the national general population percentage. As he reads further, he learns that of those that identified as transgender and who had experienced domestic violence at the hands of family member, sixty-six percent had attempted suicide. He drops his head into hands, praying that whipping a child doesn't fall into that category.

He continues to read and learns that another study found that LGBT youth who experienced rejection from family members are eight times more likely to attempt suicide than those who experienced little or no rejection, are six times more likely to suffer from depression, and three times more likely to use illegal drugs. He sits quietly, staring blankly at the desktop as his mind processes the epiphany of the risk that Kyle could face. His thoughts drift to Tommy Ells, and guilt washes over him.

———

For the first time in his life, Jeff spent the holidays alone. A divorced father, even a soon-to-be divorced father, has the cards stacked against him by the system. The mothers almost always get custody of the child. It hasn't helped matters that Emily is threatening to expose Jeff as transgender during the custody hearings. She's taken it as far as charging that Jeff's online purchase, and subsequent use, of female hormones, not uncommon among transgender people who are struggling to equalize their external image with their internal, is tantamount to illegal drug abuse.

Needless to say, the last six weeks have been a difficult struggle for Jeff. Feeling abandoned by Megan and hated by Emily, he's drawn into himself. He sees Dustin once a week, twice if he's lucky. He quit working at the Muses a few weeks ago, deciding he needed a change of environment and something closer to his house and picked up a couple of bartending jobs off of Magazine Street.

The silence of the empty house is deafening to him. He walks the hall and stands in the doorway to what was his son Dustin's room, empty except for a few discarded stuffed animals that he has carefully arranged along the wall. He walks back to the vacant living room, sits in the sole chair and turns on the TV, rapidly clicking through the channels hoping to find something to occupy his mind but finding little that can pacify it.

He turns the TV off and walks to the bathroom where he rummages through a drawer and finds an old bottle of Xanax. He used to take them regularly before meeting Megan. Over the course of their relationship, he slowly weaned himself off of them. But now they're all he has and his old demons are back.

He removes the top, pours out two pills, and drinks water directly from the faucet. He throws his head back to wash down the pills, then looks into the mirror.

On the other side, entombed in her cell, Jen stands staring back at Jeff as she holds the mask that is his face.

"Please don't do this," she says softly to the glass.

He stares deep into his reflection as she smiles tentatively back. He doesn't return the smile but casts her back into the darkness, as the mirror becomes opaque.

Harris opens a new browser window, then navigates to the Dream Weaver profile, sees Megan's last post, and begins reading. He Google's a word he doesn't recognize: odium— "the state or fact of being subjected to hatred and contempt as a result of a despicable act or blameworthy circumstance."

He considers Megan's use of the word. The hate and contempt is the internalized self-hate that she must be inflicting on herself. He thinks of Kyle and how he must be doing the same thing. He returns to reading and finishes the poem, then works his way through her posts, looking for the clues that Andrea suggested might be there.

It takes about thirty minutes for the Xanax to kick in and those thirty minutes feel like thirty days to Jeff, who paces the kitchen, phone in hand. He doesn't want to be alone. He's desperate for something familiar. He dials Emily.

Emily stands at a folding ironing board in the living room of her small apartment as Dustin sits nearby playing a game on his Xbox. Her phone's ringing, and it's Jeff. She looks at the time, nine-thirty, and sighs.

"What do you want?"

"Nothing, just wanted to talk, that's all," Jeff's voice says through the phone.

"*I* don't want to talk to *you*," she says. Noticing that Dustin is watching her, she turns her back to him. "Did you sign the papers?"

"I don't want to talk about the papers right now. How was Christmas?"

"Fine, no thanks to you. Sign the fucking papers, Jeff."

"Did you go to your mother's?"

"Why do you care?"

"I'm just, I just want to talk okay? Like adults."

"Sign the goddamn papers. If you don't..." she says as she turns to look at Dustin.

"Is that dad?" Dustin asks.

She turns back away from Dustin. "I swear, I'm gonna——"

"Can I talk to him?" Dustin asks pleadingly.

"Em, please don't," Jeff says through the phone.

"I'm done with you, Jeff. Dustin has a mother. He doesn't need another one. He needs a father, and you can't be that," she says as she shields the phone with her hand.

"Let me talk to Dustin."

She walks over and turns the TV off, motioning Dustin to his bedroom.

"I know he's right there, Em. I could hear him playing Halo."

"He's taking a bath. Sign the fucking papers," she says as Dustin disappears into the hallway.

She hangs up the phone, sits on the couch and runs her hands through her hair as she begins to cry.

Jeff slams his phone down on the counter. He's crashing. He opens a cabinet door and pulls out an unopened bottle of whiskey and a shot glass, and begins pouring.

To say Megan is a prolific writer is an understatement. There are a total of two-hundred and twenty-two poems in the Dream Weaver profile, not counting the erotica. Harris has worked his way through twenty. So far, he's found little more than obscure phrases and metaphors that he isn't sure he understands.

He sighs heavily and clicks a link to comments that Megan has left for other writers. A third of the way down the page, something catches his eye. It's a comment on a work titled "Windows In My Walls", a comment in which she tagged Jen.

Babe, these words have been ripped from my soul. It's as if the author danced within my mind, coaxing my heart to confess its true feelings and what you mean to me. I love you. M

The name of the work alone makes him sit up straight. He opens it, adjusts his glasses and begins reading.

When we met, my innermost substance
was your newly discovered country
and you reveled in it.
Late at night, you lay awake
turning all of my pages,
reading cover to cover.

It was a fearful thing
to be really known,
and I pulled heart curtains
over your windows in my walls.

Patiently you opened them,
searching my inner rooms
for the pain I'd hidden away.
I began to trust
and the disconnected part of me
slipped back into place.

I loved you guilelessly,
without secrets.
and I saw
that I had never loved before.

He clicks print and the printer whirls to life. He picks up his phone and dials Jeff's number, but it just rings and rings and goes to voicemail. He rises and hurries back to the bedroom to grab his wallet, keys, and jacket.

"What's going on?" Andrea asks, confused. She sets her book down and removes her reading glasses.

"I think I found the key," he says as he leans down and kisses her on the cheek.

"The key? Key to what?"

"Megan's walls," he says before heading toward the doorway.

"Where are you going?" she asks as he hurries out of the room.

"To see a mason," he says from the hallway.

Andrea looks around, perplexed by his comment.

"A mason?" she says softly. "A metaphor? Albert?"

Jeff raises the zipper on his jeans, a surprisingly difficult task when one is in the early stages of intoxication. He clumsily flushes the toilet and walks to the sink. He isn't feeling well and he washes his hands and face.

With the mirror now translucent, Jen stands watching him as he takes a towel and dries himself. He stares into the mirror with a rage that sends chills down her spine. She watches in fear as he reaches for the bottle of Xanax. She looks at it warily, then back to Jeff.

"They don't work on me anymore," she says softly, pleadingly.

He angrily opens the bottle and pours out two more and downs them with his drink. She turns away, disappointed and broken as Jeff leaves and the mirror fades.

It's a short drive from Desoto Street to the Three Muses. It may be the middle of January and cold, but there was still a crowd on Frenchmen Street. It is New Orleans after all. He was disappointed to learn that Jeff had quit, so now he's making the fifteen to twenty minute, with no traffic, trip over to the Black Pearl area and Garfield Street. It's a long shot and a risky one, but if Jeff, or Jen, can put windows in Megan's walls then perhaps he, or she, can talk sense into her about testifying.

Jeff sits on his back deck with his laptop across his knees. The almost empty whiskey bottle sits on a table by his side as does the bottle of Xanax. He alternates between smoking a cigarette and finishing a poem he has been working on. He crushes the cigarette out in an ashtray and rubs his eyes, then struggles to regain his focus as he looks back to the screen. He types a few more words, and then gives the work a final read, squinting and struggling to see the screen clearly. He shakes his head to clear the cobwebs, and then publishes it to the site.

He sets the laptop on the table and lights another cigarette. He leans back, taking a long drag and listens to sound of the cool wind blow a wooden wind chime that hangs above the deck. He's tired and his eyes are heavy. He doesn't feel like getting out of the chair. He pictures a skeleton with sun bleached bones hanging in a tree, as he listens to the sound of the hollow bamboo on the wind chime clack together.

His thoughts turn to Dustin as the sounds of the chime fade away and are replaced by his voice.

"You're the best daddy ever," he hears him say.

The pleasant and peaceful moment is shattered by the voice of Emily.

"He needs a father and you can't be that," she had said.

A tear forms in the corner of his closed eye. He wants to reach and wipe it away but he can't muster the strength. The voice of his angel and her words of love replace Emily's words of hate.

"Through it all, stay with me."

He can feel her breath on his neck, her lips against his ear as she softly whispers to him again. He can see her face so clearly.

"Stay with me," she says softly.

Her face begins to fade away and he struggles to recall it. As she fades into darkness, her words fade with her. "Stay with…"

From within that darkness, Jeff is stirred. He hears those words again but it's different, lower. They are there but for a moment, followed by total blackness and total silence.

"Come on buddy, stay with me!" Harris says, as he struggles to hold Jeff after finding him lying unconscious on the deck. He dials 911 and calls for an ambulance. He pulls Jeff's limp body up and against his chest as he sits on the deck behind him.

He looks to the table and sees the whiskey bottle. He sees the Xanax. He's reminded of the horrible statistics he just read about, of the forty-one percent of transgender people that attempt suicide. He stares at the scars on Jeff's arms and sees the cuts on Kyle's. He looks down at Jeff's short hair and see's Kyle's long mane. He turns his face to the heavens with tears in his eyes as the wails of an approaching ambulance pierce the night.

"Stay with me! She needs you! I need you!" he yells.

He looks back down and sees the limp, dead body of Kyle and cries.

Chapter 31

FEAR

I t's a bit past nine Saturday morning and Harris stands in the kitchen pouring pancake batter into a mixing bowl, making more of a mess than normal. He could have used an extra couple of hours of sleep this morning. He was at the hospital until midnight last night, hanging around until the doctors were able to stabilize Jeff. He called to check on him about an hour ago and was told that he may be there a couple of days—for observation.

He examines the instructions on the package of mix, reminding his tired mind of the necessary ingredients. He opens the fridge and then returns to the counter to begin adding the eggs and milk. A sleepy Kyle enters the room, pulls out a chair at the table and sits.

"Morning."

"Hey buddy. How'd you sleep?"

"Fine. What are you doing? It's not Sunday."

"Wanted to make you breakfast. How many pancakes you want?" Harris says pointing to the bowl of batter.

"Pancakes?"

"Yeah. I can make you pancakes, right? I mean, I'm a little messy I'll admit, but I make a mean pancake."

"Two's enough. Do we have any blueberries?"

"Blueberries? Maybe," Harris says, opening the fridge door and rummaging around. Sure enough, there's a fresh package.

"Blueberries. Got 'em," he says returning to the counter.

"Can I help?"

"Absolutely."

Kyle walks over to the counter. Harris watches him as he begins to pour the berries into the mix.

"Don't pour too many in there."

Kyle turns his eyes to him, as if to say 'seriously?'

"Put as many as you want. The bluer the better," Harris says with a smile.

Harris studies the bandage on Kyle's arm, remembering the cuts and the fear in Andrea's eyes. After a thorough stirring, Kyle finishes and looks up to Harris and smiles.

Harris kneels and turns Kyle around to face him.

"You know I love you, right? That we love you, your Nanna and I."

"Yeah I know, and I love you, too."

"Kyle, you're a wonderful kid. You're kind, caring, talented, good-looking, smart."

"I don't know why I did it," Kyle says as he begins to cry. "I'm sorry, Paw Paw."

Harris hugs him tightly and kisses him on the forehead.

"We'll get through this, all of us, together. Okay?"

Kyle nods and wipes the tears away.

"Okay. Let's make some pancakes," Harris says after giving him another kiss on the forehead.

The sun shines brightly across the ranch and the air is sharp with the cold front passing through. There's a light fog rising from the lake. Megan shivers and zips up her jacket. It's cold, but not cold enough to go inside and miss the view. She sits for a while, watching the ducks swim across the lake, playing a game of peek-a-boo with her as they fade at times behind the mist as it rises from the surface. She never truly realized how peaceful it was here. Gazing out across the pastures as the horses graze in the distance gives her soul peace.

SCARLET CROSSES

She picks up her laptop from a side table and logs into the poetry site. She sees a new posting by Jen titled "Rebirth". She opens it and begins reading.

Now to the young they do opine,
live your life and paint it fine,
Pigments of actuality
on canvas of reality.

And that dye smothered me.

This paint by numbers is so trite
as masses chant their ancient rite.
These are the colors you will use,
this is the form that you will choose.

Take this brush and paint you fair,
with mallet chisel chin so square.
Don this enameled shell of lies
that you may please our blinded eyes.

So I wrecked me.

With time worn and whetted claws,
born of cruel, cold cell walls
I drew his blood, his truth belied,
and cried that it was I inside.

From below the waves my voice did shriek,
drowning in the havoc wreaked.
Silenced by a sedative sea
in which he sought to bury me.

So the masses could see,

the me,

that was not me.

And you, looking within his eyes
and saving me from my demise.
On first embrace, with breast to breast,
our hearts did burst from out our chests.

From sodden lungs you heard my plea,
beyond this shadow cast for me.
From haunted path on which I tread,
on borrowed breath a whisper fled.

See me.

And you with hammer swung with might,
did smash away the plastered blight.
My soul did leap from solvent bath
and I was free to breathe at last.

I miss you.

She sets the laptop down and closes it, turning her gaze towards the lake and the ducks, which she can see clearly, no longer hidden by the thin vapors of the fog.

"Dammit," she says as she clinches her fist tightly. "Why do you do that to me? Why can't I just forget you?"

She wipes a tear from her eye and rises. Walking to the edge of the deck and breathing deeply, she shakes her head to try and clear her thoughts. Through the steamy vapors of her breathe she notices Rolly in the barn. She steps off the porch and heads his way. They have an engine to mount.

Harris exits the patient pickup area of Tulane Medical, hurrying to get to his car parked along the street. Jeff follows closely behind, squinting from the glare of the mid-morning sun off the windshields. He looks a bit ragged and pale, still weak from his ordeal. They arrive at the car and get in.

"You gonna be okay?" Harris asks as he cranks the engine.

"Yeah, I think so."

They pull away from the hospital in silence and onto Tulane Avenue, then left onto South Claiborne.

"You know it was an accident, right?" Jeff asks. Harris looks at him, smiles slightly and nods. "Thank you," Jeff adds.

"Pay me back by getting her to testify," Harris says.

"What makes you think I can?"

Harris reaches into his coat pocket and pulls out the poem that Megan commented on. He hands it to Jeff who opens it and begins reading.

"'Cause you put windows in her walls," Harris says.

"She won't even talk to me. She won't answer my calls."

"She doesn't have to. We're going to her," Harris says with a look to Jeff.

"Seriously? Now?"

"As soon as you get cleaned up and a change of clothes."

Jeff thinks about it a moment, worried that perhaps it isn't a good idea. But then again, he'll get to see her and he's sure that's all it will take.

"Thank you, again."

"When we get there, let me do the talking. And... if you get goofy on me, I'm not above shooting you," Harris says then looks at Jeff and smiles.

"Okay then, I'll try not to get goofy," Jeff says as he turns his attention to the poem.

⁂

The other times that he has driven the six hours to Memphis, Harris wished someone had ridden in the car with him. For the first three or four hours, he might as well have been driving alone, as Jeff slept most of the way. It only took the first two hours of Jeff's snoring for Harris to regret the thoughts of wanting a travel buddy. Jeff's awake now and they have been chatting for the last hour or so. They've talked about the Saints and their season, about politics, about Jeff's experiences in Iraq and how difficult it can be for a veteran to integrate back into civilian society. Harris has been looking for an opportunity to bring the subject up, and perhaps gain more insight into Kyle.

"Can I ask you a question?" Harris asks.

"Sure."

"If it's too personal just say so."

"Just ask me."

"You know how you're transgender, right?"

"Yeah, I know that well."

"Okay, well, Andrea and I, we think maybe that Kyle might be."

"What makes you say that?"

"The way he is. He's..."

"Effeminate?"

"Yeah, well, somewhat. He told us he wished God hadn't made him a boy; that he wasn't supposed to be one. He likes girl things, dolls, wears his hair long, most of his friends are girls. He's really having a hard time at school; some little punks beat him up pretty bad a couple of months ago."

"Is he alright?"

"Yeah, well... we aren't sure."

"What do you mean? They beat him that bad?"

"No. Physically he's fine. It's a..."

"Oh."

"Yeah," Harris replies.

They sit silently for a moment, Jeff uneasy to ask and Harris unsure how to say it. Harris begins to speak and feels his voice quiver. He swallows and reminds himself that Jeff is the perfect person to speak to about it and that he'll understand. He sighs heavily.

"Andrea found cuts on his arm last week."

"Oh shit! I'm so sorry," Jeff says as Harris nods appreciatively and feigns a smile.

"She bandaged him up and… he's having a lot of trouble, Jeff. He's changed. He's withdrawn. And I'm wondering if, since you, you know, since you've got experience with this maybe you could talk to him."

"Wow. Never been asked that before," Jeff says as he struggles to come up with an answer. After a moment he adds, "While I would love to be able to help, Al, I don't think it would be appropriate. He doesn't need anything from me. He needs it from you. You need to talk to him. I mean I suppose I could talk to him about the cutting, but not about being transgender. He may not be transgender, Al."

"But he said he wasn't supposed to be a boy."

"Okay, well he may be trans, but I didn't really understand this till I was grown. I mean, I think I always knew, but was in a state of denial. I certainly couldn't talk to *my* father about it. When I finally told my parents a couple of years ago, my father tried to cast Satan out of me."

Harris looks at him and thinks back to some of the sermons at New Hope and how the pastor had said gays were possessed by demons.

"It didn't work. He was never in me. It's who I was, who I am. I always thought maybe I would grow out of it, that it was a phase. Point is… Kyle's what? How old?"

"Eleven, be twelve in March."

"Eleven. Okay, he's young, Al. He may be trans; he may be gay. I know that isn't what you want to hear. But he may turn out straight as a board. But you gotta let him figure that out and be there for him. He needs to know that you're not gonna abandon him or shun him no matter what. A parent shouldn't do that, ever."

As Harris takes in the things that he said, Jeff's words drift back to his parents.

"You know, I haven't spoken to my father in a couple of years. My mother, she refuses to discuss it or even acknowledge that such a thing exists. A couple of therapy sessions and I was fine as far as she was concerned."

They ride quietly for several miles before Harris hears him sniff and looks over and sees him wipe tears from his eyes.

"You okay?"

"Yeah. I'm fine. Sorry. It's just that..."

"What?"

"It's just that... a... I've always felt like a leper Al, someone to be avoided, that God hated me and condemned to hell by virtue of birth."

He stops, looking away out the passenger's window, fighting back the tears. He's not very successful.

"I've never considered the idea that I might be a help to someone because of *who* I am. It's such an alien thought to me to think that I could..."

Harris glances over at him, not sure what to say or if he should say anything at all. But he realizes that Jeff is sharing some very intimate details and fears and he must say something, it's his obligation.

"God doesn't hate you, Jeff. He's not a God of hate. He loves all of His children."

"Yeah, well you wouldn't know it by reading the news would you?" Jeff says, bitterness piercing his words.

As they ride quietly, Harris considers that, six months ago, he might have answered Jeff differently. To be totally honest with himself, he would have answered differently, always quick to throw stones until a loved one becomes the target. After several minutes, Jeff breaks the silence.

"Can I ask *you* a question?"

"Sure."

"What is it about Kyle being transgender that scares you?"

Harris thinks for a moment. He hadn't thought of it as fear, but he's right, he does fear it.

"Several things, I guess. His safety, for one."

"That's legitimate. Things are better, but there's still a lot of misguided hate out there. What else?"

Now that they've been acknowledged, the fears swarm inside Harris' mind. He listens as they howl, deriding him with predictions of calamities to come. Tears well up in his eyes as one specter, standing dominant over the others, casts its judgment on his soul.

"I'm supposed to teach him to be a man. He's my grandson Jeff, my boy, the son I never had. I don't want to lose him." he says, scrunching his lips to fight back the emotion and looking away to hide his eyes.

"I've heard that before," Jeff says, pausing and staring out the side window for a long moment.

"That's what my father said... then he disowned me," he adds soberly.

Designers at Ford Motors never dreamed the interior of a Crown Victoria could be so silent. It's deafening. Jeff rolls the window down and lights a cigarette and Harris fights the urge to light one up himself.

"He's still the same person, Al. The only way you'll lose that person is if *you* push them away."

Harris watches Jeff as he stares blankly at the cherry of the cigarette, its smoke rising and wafting out the window.

"You know I'm on the other side of that coin. I've never felt qualified to be a father, to teach Dustin to be a *man*," Jeff says, stressing his words by dropping his voice an octave on the last three words before pausing and adding "Not sure what I'm supposed to teach him."

"What are you talking about? You teach him to be strong, stand up for himself, stand up for others, to be kind, treat women, everyone for that matter, with respect, to believe in himself, that he can do anything he sets his mind to."

Jeff's silence captures Harris' attention and he glances at him. Jeff stares down at the floor, as if trying to grasp what, to Harris, should be an easily understood tenant of being a man. After a moment, Jeff takes a long drag on his cigarette and blows the smoke out the window.

"Yeah, I guess. I think most parents would want those things for their child... did you teach that to Miranda?"

"Of course."

"But she was a girl right?" Jeff says, turning to look at him.

The thought settles in to Harris' mind. He looks at Jeff a moment, and then nods his understanding before turning his attention back to the highway... and the road that lies before him.

Chapter 32

TRUTH

There's a surgery being performed in the barn on the Callahan estate. Two skilled surgeons carefully lower a new heart into the patient. It has a displacement of 351 cubic inches and has been lovingly reconditioned by one of the best speed shops in Tennessee. It's referred to as a 351 Windsor, so named because the family of engines that it hails from was originally built by Ford in their Windsor, Ontario plant. This one however, is American through and through as Ford moved production of the engine to Cleveland, Ohio in 1969. Once installed and tricked out, the engine will generate four hundred horsepower. It will get horrid gas mileage, but it will sound and feel good doing so.

Rolly lies on a roller under the Bronco and prepares a mount to accept the new engine. Megan is manning the hoist. Behind her, the angel statue stands proudly with two complete wings. Megan's still working on the horns and halo.

"So then Billy looks at the guy and says, 'Let's take it outside'," Rolly says from beneath the beast, continuing a story from his wilder days.

"Wait a minute. You said there were three of them," Megan says with an air of disbelief.

"There were. Let it down a little."

Megan takes the chain and slowly lets the engine down slightly. She looks up and notices Harris' car pulling into the circle drive. She watches as he parks and both front doors open.

"A little more," Rolly calls out.

She doesn't hear him. She's watching Jeff walk towards the house, and then be instructed by Harris to stay back by the car. He looks around, taking in the site of the place.

"Meg?" Rolly says, realizing that his fellow surgeon is not paying attention. He barks loudly. "Meg!"

She snaps out of it and returns to lowering the engine.

"That's good. Perfect."

He rolls out and rises, dusting off his jeans. He sees Megan has already walked to the garage door and stands now watching somebody down by the house. He walks over himself to have a closer look.

"Who's that with Harris?"

"A friend," she says with a smile as she slowly begins making her way down the driveway.

⸺⸳⸺

Jeff stands next to the car trying not to "get goofy" as Harris said. He watches Harris step towards the front porch then calls out to him.

"You sure about this, Al?"

"It will be fine. Just stay there and don't do anything stupid."

Harris knocks on the door and breathes deeply, sighing away the tension. Hopefully everything will be fine. He closes his eyes and says a quick prayer to increase the odds. Kristi opens the door and steps out, followed closely by Ellen.

"Detective, you made it," Kristi says with a smile as she takes a glance over his shoulder at Jeff.

"You're just in time for dinner, Albert," Ellen says as she steps past Kristi and onto the porch. Her mood shifts quickly when she sees Jeff at the car.

"Who's that?" she says suspiciously.

Harris looks to Kristi. "You didn't tell her?"

"I didn't get a chance. I'm sorry. I got hung up at the hospital."

"Tell me what? Who is that, Albert?"

"Ellen, that's Jeff Taylor."

"Taylor? From the poetry site?" she says as she eyes Jeff up and down.

"From New Orleans and yes, from the poetry site. He's a friend of—"

"I don't want him here, Albert. I want him off my property right now," she says calmly, turning back to Harris.

"Momma, I think it's a worth a try. He may be able to get Megan to testify," Kristi says as she puts her hands softly on Ellen's shoulders.

"I know it's unconventional Ellen, but I'm here. Nothing's gonna happen. If Megan doesn't want to see him, we'll leave."

"Albert what if you've got the wrong guy? What if this guy did it?" she says looking back towards Jeff or at least where Jeff was.

Following her eyes, Harris turns to see that Jeff has abandoned his assigned position. His heart leaps through his chest as he quickly makes his way off the porch, looking both directions, fearing that he may have to shoot him after all.

He looks to his right, towards the barn, and sees Jeff and Megan walking towards each other. He relaxes, just a little, when he sees the slight smile on her face. He follows a number of paces back, as Jeff and Megan approach each other.

⸺⸺

As Rolly busies himself outside the barn, watching Megan closely and ready to intervene at a moment's notices, Jeff approaches her, hands clenched in his pockets. She steps towards him, her arms protectively clasped around her chest. She watches his expression, studying him, remembering her. Her pulse quickens and her heart seems to skip beats. He looks anxious, as if he fears she will tell him to leave or worse still, turn and run.

"Hey. It's good to see you," he says with a smile once they are close enough to speak.

She glances to an approaching Harris then back at Jeff and smiles.

"Good to see you too, Jeff," she says before catching herself. "Jen. Sorry, I'm a little out of practice."

Jeff looks at her and smiles. "It's okay."

He looks away, out across the paddocks. She sees the glint of tear before he wipes it away.

"I haven't heard that in a long time," he says before turning back to her. "It feels great. Thank you."

"It's who you are," she says with a shrug and a grin.

"How are you feeling?" he says after a moment, shifting the focus back to her.

"I'll be okay."

Harris pauses, a few yards away, trying to allow a little personal time between the two of them but close enough that he can act if necessary.

"I'm making it through the valley," Megan says, cutting her eyes back to Harris and nodding to him.

Harris nods back, picking up on her reference to his words of guidance. He steps back a couple of feet but still within earshot range.

"So do you always accept rides from strange men? Is there something I should know about, Jen?" she says with a grin.

"Yeah, I met him at a bar last night. He's cute, don't you think?"

Jeff turns to look back at Harris who casually moves his jacket so Jeff can see his gun. He turns back to Megan and smiles.

"No sudden moves okay? I don't want to get shot."

"Yeah, between him and Rolly you wouldn't stand a chance," she replies as she looks back over her shoulder at her protector.

Jeff looks back to Harris and smiles then turns back to Megan.

"He's a good cop. We've gotten to know each other quite a bit better these last couple of months."

"I'm sorry it all went down like it did, Jen. Sorry you got caught up in this."

"Sorry? Don't be sorry. I got a free trip to Memphis out of it. We're going to Graceland tomorrow. Wanna come?"

A sudden, alien feeling washes over her, one she hasn't felt in months. She laughs, a hard belly laugh, and it feels wonderful. That was one of the things she loved about Jen, her ability to make her laugh. It's one of the things she still loves about her. She drops her arms, putting her hands in her pockets.

"I'll pass. But make sure to see the jungle room. It's *amazing*."

"I'll do that," Jen says with a grin, then calls out to Harris. "Hear that? Graceland. Tomorrow. Jungle room."

"Yeah? Well you're buying the tickets," Harris says as he smiles and begins walking back to the house, giving them ample quiet space.

The two walk slowly, drifting towards the barn, unsure of the path before them.

"I'm really sorry for everything. I ruined your life," she says.

"Ruined? Are you serious? Meg, you saved my life, you gave me life. I was slowly dying and then you..." Jen says, pausing and searching for the right words. "You changed my world, Meg. You didn't ruin it. You fixed it. It's a world I want so badly, a world with you in it."

She looks away, gritting her teeth as her demons mock her, whispering words of fear, of emotional cataclysms, that drag her back before the court of self-punishment.

Jen watches her, visibly struggling with her decision.

"Meg, I don't know what the future holds for me. I don't know if I'll transition or if I'll stay like..." she says, motioning down her body. "But I do know this; when I'm with you I'm in a good place because of you, because of who you are. I'm comfortable when I'm with you and I've never been comfortable with who I am until you came into my life," she says softly.

Megan turns and looks at her, peering through the window that she just pulled the cover from. She steps closer, looking deep into Jen's eyes. She's missed her.

"I can make no promises to you, except for one and that is to love you with all of my heart. You deserve love. Please don't lock me out," Jen says.

The demons present their evidence, sending flashes of Donny racing through her mind. She rebuts with memories of the comfort of being in Jen's arms. She retorts their argument, remembering how her face would hurt from smiling and laughing when with her, how Jen's words calmed her soul late at night. The demon counsel lays one final charge: she can trust no *man*. She counters with a confession: Guilty as charged.

After a moment, she smiles and tugs Jen's shirt.

"Yeah, well I'm not sure you know what you're getting yourself into."

"I'll take my chances."

She looks into her eyes for a moment then scans her up and down.

"I don't know... you've got better legs than I do."

"Well, you've got bigger tits," Jen says with a smile.

"You know that skirt you've got? The one with the turquoise conch belt?"

"Yeah. What about it?"

Megan shrugs her shoulders. "I'm taking it," she says with a grin.

"Come on, not that one."

"Sorry. I have my price."

"I'm not sure," Jen answers, shaking her head before casting her eyes back to Megan.

"Fine. It's a small price to pay."

They stare into each other's eyes for a moment, each of their hearts racing. Megan reaches out to take her hand. Jen looks down at it but doesn't accept it.

"No... first you've got a butt-chewing coming."

"For what?"

"For that message you sent me."

"I'm sorry, I was just——"

"It's not the message, well it is, partly. How dare you lecture me about living a life orchestrated by others, being a puppet on a string and becoming entombed in a world that someone else creates for us?"

Megan's a little confused. She thought if anyone would understand those metaphors it would be Jen.

"I meant it as encouragement."

"And it was. But the whole time you sit up here refusing to testify, letting that mother-fucker create your world and entomb you? Are you *really* going to let him control you like that, be your puppet master and orchestrate your life?"

Megan doesn't answer, but she knows Jen's right. She doesn't need anyone running her life, especially that asshole Donny. Her silence, and the slight fury in her eyes, is the all acknowledgement that Jen needs.

"I love you, Megan Callahan. I'll be there for you, right beside you, if you'll let me."

Megan smiles tentatively then sighs, nodding her head.

"Know much about engines?" she says, motioning over her shoulder back to the barn.

"A little. Is it an MRAP or at least a Hummer? A real one, not one of those pansy-ass civilian ones."

Megan laughs, turns and begins walking towards the barn. She stops for a second and holds out her hand. Jen smiles, this time grabbing it tightly, as they both walk up the driveway.

Harris looks to a still distrustful Ellen and a smiling Kristi then up to heavens to thank the Lord that no one was shot.

Chapter 33

INJUSTICE

J en's talk served a larger purpose for Megan than she realized. That night, as they sat around the living room, Megan realized that she needed to make amends with Anna. She called her the next day, after Harris and Jen left for New Orleans, and apologized to her for being distant and, most importantly, for blaming her. It was good to hear the voice of her friend again and it strengthened her newfound desire to go back to New Orleans to live life on her terms, but not until Mardi Gras was over. Festivities were not on her agenda. The last thing she wanted to see was a lot of people in masks. She thought it appropriate to return during Lent, a flipping of the finger to the man that sought to deny her happiness.

Megan and Anna are unloading her things from Kristi's car outside the garage of Megan's home on an unusually warm March day. Rolly came down yesterday with his truck and trailer and brought the almost rebuilt Bronco and the newly finished angel statue. Jen fights gravity and physics as she attempts to balance the statue on a cart and move it inside. Rosco pulls against his leash which Anna has tied to a post, not wanting to deal with his incessant chasing of Frizbee, who roams freely, passing in front of Rosco occasionally and sending him into howling fits.

It's the first time in slightly over five months that she's been home. She hadn't realized how much she missed the place. It was if she had been lost in a fog for that time, a fog that is now lifting. She carries an arm load of clothes into the house, through the kitchen. Anna follows closely behind carrying a couple of bags and watching Megan anxiously, waiting for her to see the surprise she has left in the living room. Megan steps into the room and drops the clothes onto the back of the couch. Her eyes widen as she sees a beautiful coffee table, with glass top and wrought iron base.

"Do you like it?" Anna asks.

"I love it! Is that one of the doors?"

"Yeah, well I didn't do it all. Got some help from those two downstairs. He built the base and she and I painted the designs," Ann says proudly.

"Oh my God, you guys didn't have to do that."

"I know, but we wanted to. "

They share a hug and Megan begins inspecting the latest piece of artwork for her house.

"Meg? Where you want this?" Jen asks, carefully navigating the cart and angel through the kitchen

Megan looks around, visualizing it in several locations. She finally settles on one and points to an area near the staircase to the third floor.

As the city filled with revealers and floats and bands paraded down the streets, Donny was charged with sexual battery, a felony offense, on February 19th and trial was set for June 23rd. While Harris and Broussard hoped for additional charges such as kidnapping, they'll take the single felony charge.

Persuading Megan to testify has been the highlight of a difficult five months for Harris. He and Broussard sit, all smiles, in Blanchard's office. Blanchard looks uneasy and occasionally glances out his office window as if looking for someone.

"They said that Morrison turned white as a sheet when Landow told him Megan would testify," Harris says with a laugh.

"Would have loved to have been a fly on the wall, see that guy crap his pants," Broussard adds.

Blanchard laughs but only half-heartedly.

"Is she ready?" he says to Harris, studying him, gauging his reaction.

"Yeah, she's ready."

Blanchard doesn't look convinced. Harris looks to Broussard for support and after a moment, she nods.

"She'll be fine, Ron. Trust me," Harris says.

Blanchard looks back out his office window and see's the person he's been looking for. He looks to Harris, making eye contact, and then looks away as Harris turns to see Landow standing in the doorway. Blanchard can hardly look Harris in the eye.

As Landow sits calmly in a chair across from an upset Blanchard, Broussard stands quietly by the window looking out on the park below. Harris paces the room behind and around Landow, demonstratively speaking with both his mouth and his hands.

"A plea deal? The only pleading should be him for his life!" Harris says.

Landow rises and straightens his jacket. He certainly can be a pompous ass when he wants to be and right now, he wants to be. He takes one threatening step towards Harris.

"Last time I checked, Harris, it was still my office that determines the charges and tries the case."

Harris, his anger rumbling within, grits his teeth and takes a step towards Landow.

"She's testifying, John! She'll—"

"Do you think we are too stupid to realize what that son-of-a-bitch Morrison is going to try and do to her on the stand? Do you really want that for her? One chink in her armor and—"

"It won't chink!"

"*How* do you know?"

"Because I know her! She's got bigger balls than any of us!" the giant roars directly into Landow's face.

Broussard pushes between the two of them. Harris glares at Landow over her shoulder, and then returns to pacing the small office.

"What charges are they agreeing to?" Broussard asks.

"Second degree battery, time served and three years pro—"

"Are you *fucking* kidding me?! He raped and tried to burn her alive!" Harris explodes as people passing by the office stop and peer into the window.

"Harris, I'm not going to debate this with you. It's done."

Broussard sees the rage in Harris' eyes and steps back between the two of them.

"You have to give her a chance!" Harris cries out. "You have to let Miranda testify!"

The room goes deathly silent. Harris looks to Broussard who looks back at him with an astonished, empathetic look on her face. He turns to Blanchard then realizes what he said. Landow unsympathetically smiles.

"I would think that you, of all people, would rather see a plea than see him walk."

That's too much for Harris and he charges Landow, attempting to push through Broussard.

"Fuck this. Come on, let's go," she says quietly to him, holding him back.

He pulls away from her, face red with anger, and gazes back to Blanchard who can give him no support. There's nothing he can do.

"Come on Harris. Fuck this shit. Let's go," Broussard says to him in a whisper.

He gives Landow another look, piercing him with his eyes. Finally, after a long tense moment, he relents and he and Broussard exit.

Landow begins to exit behind them. As he gets to the door, Blanchard calls to him.

"Are you sure this isn't about Baton Rouge?"

"This is about *justice*," Landow says, turning back to him.

"Really? What about justice for Megan?"

"We got a conviction. That's all that matters."

"No. You... you got a conviction that looks good for your campaign. That bastard got a get-out-of-jail-free card and Megan got fucked... again."

"Ron, you know how—"

"Get the fuck out of my office, John," Blanchard says pointing to the door.

Disgusted by the system that he is a part of, he watches Landow leave. Plea agreements are the most common settlement of cases, but this one smells to high heaven.

Perhaps it's the March heat or maybe it's the raised blood pressure from his encounter with Landow earlier, but Harris has left the coat and tie in the car. He would have left them there regardless. He doesn't feel like a professional, doesn't feel like a detective. He's frustrated with Landow and the "system", he's frustrated with himself. During the drive to Megan's place, he questioned why he would have said Miranda's name in place of Megan's. Was he seeking pseudo justice for Miranda and cost Megan hers? He's reexamined the last several months, trying to determine if he made a mistake, if he became blinded in some way, got tunnel vision and missed something. Maybe he should have refused the case. Maybe he should have taken that retirement.

He knows that plea agreements are common place in the justice system, so common that they account for over ninety percent of convictions. This one, however, is hard for him to swallow. He's standing at the gate off of Touro Street, watching silently as Megan works on the Bronco in her garage. She seems content. She seems herself again. Now he has to tell her that Donny will be released in two months, that the man that stalked and, despite her best efforts, found her, the man that tried to kill her, will soon be walking the streets of New Orleans a free man. He could have opted to let the D.A.'s office notify her. He could have. But he has things to do, things that are his responsibility. Telling her is one of them. After a few minutes of building up his nerve, he calls her. She steps to the door and pushes a button to open the gate, then returns to the engine compartment of the Bronco. He hesitates for a moment, and then makes his way toward her.

"I've got a classic out there in the street, could use a brake job. Think you could help me out?" he says as he approaches the garage.

"If it's pre-'75, you're in luck," she says without looking up from her task.

"Can I come in or does your shop insurance not cover that sort of thing?"

She looks up to him and smiles. "I think you're a safe risk."

He walks up to the Bronco and inspects the new engine as Megan works to finish the installation of a carburetor.

"You got it in! Looks nice. What is this? 302?"

"351 Windsor," she says, finishing her task.

"Nice."

"Yeah, she's looking good. I've beefed her up a bit. She's a lot meaner now," Megan says with a smile as she begins collecting her tools.

Harris nods and surveys the Bronco up and down.

"You know, honestly, I'm surprised you kept her—considering."

"Are you kidding? What doesn't kill ya makes ya stronger, right? She means too much to me. Plus, it gave me something to do and keeps me in a… productive and positive state of mind."

He watches her as she turns and places some of the tools into their box.

"You're looking good. How you feeling?"

"You know… I feel good. I think being back here has actually been good for me."

"That's good to hear."

There's a long pause filled only by the sound of wrenches banging against each other as Megan drops them in their place. She stops and stares down at the tools. She can feel the tension.

"Al, while I've grown fond of you, I don't think you came here just to bullshit about cars," she says without looking back at him.

After a long moment, she turns to him. He doesn't need to say a word; his face says it all. He fights to maintain eye contact with her, struggling to force his mouth to form the words. She beats him to it.

"I knew it."

"Megan, I'm so sorry. I don't know what to… Maybe if I had—"

"You did everything you could do. You did everything right."

"I don't know that. If we could have tied him to the house maybe it—"

"This had nothing to do with case, Al. It was political," she says as she turns back around and begins fidgeting with the tools, moving them from one position to another and then back.

"Political?"

She fidgets with the tools harder, slamming them down into place. The emotion begins to bleed through her voice as she speaks.

"Max called earlier. Donny's testifying for Landow in the Elliot trial."

He watches her, stunned and shocked. He thinks of the case, that Donny had minor drug possession charges on his record, that he used cocaine. Caleb Elliot is being tried for cocaine distribution. He recalls a news report... something about the prosecutions main witness had been killed while in Orleans Parish prison. He recalls a campaign commercial for Landow and that moment of clarity hits.

"Son-of-a-bitch."

"Amazing what you can remember from inside a jail cell, huh?" Megan says, her voice cracking with emotion.

She drops her head, her back still to him. He watches as her hands begin to shake. The walls of the garage seem to shake as she screams and slams the lid of the toolbox over and over again, catching her fingers several times causing them to bleed. She picks it up and throws it in a rage across the garage and into a wall, tools spilling across the floor. She places her bleeding hands over her face and begins to cry.

Harris grabs her, spinning her around and into his arms as she collapses on his shoulder, sobbing uncontrollably. Tears build in his eyes and then flow freely. She isn't the only one that's been wronged by the system.

Chapter 34

RELAUNCH

After Megan calmed down, Harris bandaged her fingers. He told a story from his youth of thinking he had blown his thumb off when he was nine after having a firecracker explode in his hand. She laughed at the mental images he painted of running through the streets of Brooklyn screaming, holding his hand, only to get home to a terrified mother and find that it was simply a blood blister. He helped her pick up the tools that had scattered across the garage but left saying he would check on her later, after she told him she just wanted to be alone.

Her eyes still red from the tears, she slowly reorganizes the tools. She's numb and stops often staring into nothingness, devoid of emotion and lost somewhere in her mind. She knows all about plea agreements but she's never been on the other side, on the victim's side. She feels like a number, a statistic, a pawn sacrificed in a game of political chess. She feels humiliated, that her pain, her life and happiness, was worth so little.

She picks up a hammer and begins to place it back in the toolbox. She pauses, holding it up in front of her as she examines it closely. She looks to her phone which lies on a nearby work bench then away, back into the darkness. After a long moment, she calmly lays the hammer down and picks up her phone and dials a number. She stares at the hammer as she listens to the phone ring a few times before the call is answered.

"I need to talk to you," she says calmly.

Harris sits in his office, door closed, and light off. He stares out the window looking over the city, his home. He reflects on the case, on Megan, on Jeff, on Kyle. It's been a journey that took him places he never expected. One that boiled up emotions that he thought he controlled, and stirred fears he didn't realize he had. The phone on his desk rings. He doesn't bother answering it.

He rises and walks to the window, looking down at the small park outside the offices. He watches people as they go about their day, minding their responsibilities. He considers how one unforeseen and uncontrollable incident, can drastically change any of their lives, throwing their sense of normal into a state of chaos.

A young boy walking in the park catches his eye. He looks for the mother, expecting to see her calling him to catch up. He notices a man, perhaps the boy's father, walk up and extend his hand, which the boy takes as they begin walking together. The man reaches down and picks up the boy, carrying him in his arms. The boy repeatedly slaps the man's shoulder and he obliges, lifting him up and setting him atop them.

Harris turns back to his desk and picks up a picture of Miranda and a six-year-old Kyle, taken at a children's festival a year before Miranda was killed. In it, Kyle smiles widely as Miranda kisses him on the cheek. Harris touches Miranda's image softly, remembering similar times when she was a child.

He sets the picture down and picks up another one, of himself, Andrea, and Kyle. It's a recent portrait for the church directory. He stares at Kyle's image and the sadness in his eyes. It's an image that, seeing it now, he hates.

Andrea is in the small laundry room sorting the day's wash when she hears a car pull into the driveway. Not expecting Harris home for a couple of more hours, she sets down the clothes and goes to the front door, finding him walking quickly up the sidewalk. She opens the door and meets him on the porch.

"You're home early. Everything okay?"

He puts his arms around her, hugging her tightly then kisses her. "Everything's fine. Where's Kyle?"

She steps back and looks at him, as if a stranger stands before her. "Living room, watching TV. Why?"

He doesn't answer, already moving towards the house. He walks past the kitchen and finds Kyle watching a rerun of Project Runway. Andrea follows closely behind but stops near the kitchen to watch. Something's about to happen—she can feel it—and she prays it's something good.

"Hey, what are you up to?" Harris asks, as Kyle looks up at him.

"Just watching TV," Kyle replies. He then takes the remote and changes the channel to ESPN, starts to get up from the couch.

"Whoa, hang on. What were you watching?"

Kyle looks at Harris, then at Andrea who can offer him little help.

"Project Runway," he says squeamishly. "Why?"

"Just wondering. I've never seen it," Harris says, nervously looking at Andrea, his face a wreck of nerves. Her smile encourages him. He sits on the couch and picks up the remote.

"What channel is it on?" he adds.

Kyle glances back at Andrea who shrugs her shoulders and nods for him to sit back down.

"98," he says, taking a place beside Harris.

Harris changes the channel and the fashion designer wanna-be's are back to discussing their current challenge.

"Project Runaway, huh?" Harris says, purposefully botching the name.

"Runway."

"Oh.... *Runway*. I love shows about airplanes."

"It's not about airplanes, silly," Kyle says as he slides a bit closer to Harris.

"It's this show about designers, it's a competition. Each episode they have to design an outfit and then they are judged on it," he explains.

"So what do they win?"

"This year it was a hundred and fifty thousand dollars plus a lot of other stuff including a car."

"Hundred and fifty thousand?" Harris says looking at Kyle with astonishment.

"Yeah and more."

"Hmmm," Harris says nodding then looking back to the TV for a moment before turning to Kyle.

"Think you could do that?" he asks.

Kyle doesn't answer, he just stares at this alien creature that walked into the house and sat on the couch.

"Who are you and what have you done with my Paw Paw?" he finally asks.

"I gave that old goat the boot," Harris says after a pause and a glance to Andrea.

He turns to face Kyle directly. Kyle nervously looks back, cutting his eyes between Harris and Andrea. After a long moment, Harris manages to summon the words.

"You see that woman over there?" he says, motioning with his eyes.

"Yeah."

"I know we've said this a thousand times but—she loves you, and I love you. We both love you with all of our hearts. We love *you*," Harris says stressing the last word and tapping Kyle's chest.

"And we will never abandon you. We will always be here for you, no matter what. Okay?"

Kyle nods, looks at Andrea who clutches her chest, and then back at Harris.

"Okay."

"Alright, now, fill me in on this episode of project hallway," Harris says turning back to the TV.

"It's runway, sheez," an exasperated Kyle moans as he settles into position and begins bringing Harris up to date on the episode.

Chapter 35

POETIC

It's been a week now since Donny was released from the Orleans Parish prison. He's enjoying his life of solitude now that his mother has moved out. While he was locked up, parish counselors persuaded her to move in with a family member to get away from the abusive Donny. That's all fine with him; he doesn't have to listen to her whine.

He was quite pleased with the outcome of the case. He beat the system and he knows it. He may have three years of monitored probation ahead of him but he's confident it will be a breeze. He'll lay low, doing his best to make his monthly meeting with his probation officer.

It irritates him that he has to wear the ankle bracelet tether for twelve months but it was a condition of the plea agreement. He also can't come within five hundred feet of Megan. That's fine with him. He's had the bitch already. Having to be home at a certain hour ticks him off, but he'll manage. He'll just bring the party home with him. He reaches down and moves the bracelet around his ankle while watching an episode of *The Walking Dead*. This particular bracelet is a new model, with built-in GPS location and transmission. He can't leave New Orleans without explicit permission. So as long as he stays within the city limits, it's all a playground.

Donny lights another cigarette and walks towards the hallway and the bathroom. He stops cold in his tracks as one of Victor Donkova's bodyguards, the big guy, the Russian, steps out of the darkness in the hall in front of him. Donny turns to flee but instead runs directly into the smaller one with soulless eyes, the Persian.

"Who the *fuck* are you? Take whatever you want man. There's some grass under the bed, good shit. I can't smoke it anyway," he says while looking into the Persian's dark, heartless eyes.

Feeling the big guy behind him, he turns, but it's too late. The needle is already in his neck.

"Nine, eight, seven..." the big guy says in Russian before Donny's eyes roll back and he collapses to the floor.

The Russian ties Donny's hands and tapes his mouth shut. The Persian pulls a roll of clear plastic sheeting from a backpack and spreads it across the floor and rolls Donny on top of it. As the Russian steps out the back door, his partner pulls Donny's pant leg up to the knee. He then ties a tourniquet tightly around Donny's leg just below the knee then pulls the ankle bracelet as far up the leg as he can without damaging it. He finishes by wrapping the plastic sheeting over the top of the leg. The Russian re-enters from outside and pushes the couch out of the way, giving himself plenty of room.

He positions himself in front of Donny's legs, squaring himself up as his comrade rolls the leg to position the heel straight up and foot extended out.

"Don't miss," he says.

"I won't," says the Russian, as he raises a sledge hammer over his head, grits his teeth, and slams it down hard onto Donny's heel. He strikes it several more times, turning it into a bloody pulp.

The Persian pushes the plastic back and removes the monitor bracelet from Donny's leg, holding it and looking up to the Russian who doesn't react; he simply begins to roll Donny up in the plastic, taping it shut below the feet to catch the blood. They pick Donny up and exit the same door they came in.

The house is eerily quiet except for the gunfire and hacking of zombies that emanates from the television. After a few moments the door opens and the Persian enters carrying a small, mixed breed dog, a stray picked up from the streets, and a bag of dog food. He sets the dog down and walks into the kitchen and finds a large bowl and fills it with dog food. He then finds a second bowl and fills it with water. He calls the dog to him and places the monitor bracelet over his head and around his neck.

"Every dog needs a collar," he says.

He pets the dog gently on the head then rises. He begins to leave then pauses to evaluate the situation. The dog looks back at him with sad, brown eyes and whimpers. The poor thing could die of starvation before anyone would come looking for Donny if that's all the food he leaves for him. He takes the dog food bag and pours the remainder of its contents onto the floor, stopping to pet the dog one last time before leaving.

A black Chevy Suburban rolls to a stop at a deserted intersection in Estelle, a community in Jefferson Parish just south of New Orleans. Inside, the Russian removes a handkerchief from his jacket and blows his nose, a cold setting in. He sighs and rolls his eyes as a moan, one of many over the last few miles, comes from the back. He looks over at his partner and hands him the handkerchief.

"Shut him up."

The Persian reluctantly takes the soiled linen and gets out, walking to the back and opening the rear doors. He violently pulls the tape from Donny's face and shoves the cloth into his mouth. He picks up the roll of tape that lies next to Donny and applies a fresh coat over Donny's lips, being careful not to block his nose. They don't want him dead yet.

The darkness of the May night pervades the living room of Megan's house as she sits quietly, staring blankly into the flame of nearby candle, one of many she has lit around the room. She thinks of what might be happening at this moment, of the hell that may have been released, a Russian Kraken seeking vengeance for a wronged, adopted daughter.

"He needs to pay..." she says softly to herself, considering what Victor meant when he uttered those words and the brutality that the Russian mafia is infamous for.

She looks to the angel statue which seems to glow, lit oddly by the nearby flames. The bells of St. Louis Cathedral begin ringing and she listens to all ten strokes, each seeming louder than the previous.

<hr />

A three-quarter moon begins its late climb through the skies, shining between the trees deep in a swamp south of Luling where nature plays a symphony. The chorus of frogs, crickets, birds, coyotes, and an ensemble of raccoons perform their nightly ritual amid a light fog that drifts over the swamp's waters. Their composition is interrupted by the crunching of limestone beneath the tires of the darkened Suburban as the Russian eases it down a long abandoned oil field access road. As the intruder passes into the darkness, the orchestra returns to their performance, slowly rising to a deafening crescendo.

The Suburban rolls to a stop and he turns off the engine. They sit silently as the darkness of the swamp engulfs them. In the back, Donny moans loudly. The two of them roll their eyes and get out, immersing themselves in the sounds of the swamp.

They stand, watching the waters beneath towering Cypress trees, searching for a signal. The fragrant, slightly spicy, scent of the lizard-tails plant permeates the air. A pair of Barred owls exchange their trademark "Who cooks for you, who cooks for you all" calls nearby. In the distance, coyotes howl at Selene as she races her chariot through the sky. A Barn owl, spooked by motion in the water below him, screeches its blood curdling scream and flies from its roost, moving to less disturbed grounds deep in the swamp, and startling the normally steel-nerved duo.

The Russian notices a light flickering within the fog. He pulls a small flashlight from his pocket, flashes it twice, and sees three flashes in return. He looks to his partner who nods and opens the passenger door retrieving his backpack.

The Russian moves to the back doors and opens them. He laughs as a steadily awakening Donny, eyes filled with terror, tries in vain to kick him. He picks him up; carrying him like a bale of hay to the water's edge and throws him face first into the soft earth, sending a team of bullfrogs leaping into the dark, murky waters. As Donny screams muffled cries, a mud-boat pushes its bow through the fog and onto the bank.

They have little trouble catching Donny, who with hands and feet bound crawls snake like in a vain attempt to elude them. The Russian picks him up, tossing him into the front of the boat and delivering him to its two attendants. No words are spoken as a thick envelope is tossed on top of Donny. As the two of them silently return to the Suburban, the mud-boat pushes away from the bank, into the fog and into the darkness.

In the early morning hours of Sunday, in a rough part of New Orleans, citizens of varying degrees of respectability mingle in the shadows along a street's edge. The Suburban rolls to a stop at a red light and a Chrysler 300 pulls up beside it. The Russian exits the Suburban, leaving the engine running and door open, and enters the Chrysler which pulls away into the night. He's already replaced the license plates with the actual plates for the Suburban, which was reported stolen five hours ago.

Several of the less reputable elements study the prize as it sits empty, awaiting a driver. They nervously scan the street, looking for signs of a trap. After several minutes, the bait proves too enticing and the Suburban is soon on its way to meet its own fate.

St. Louis Cathedral's Sunday mass begins at nine, a fact that Megan had to look up online as it's been years since her last attendance. She walks quickly down Chartres Street besides the Lower Pontalba building and across the fog draped plaza in front of the Cathedral.

She arrives early, knowing the confession occurs before mass. She enters through the front doors, stopping to light a candle for her father and recite a prayer. She enters the main sanctuary and steps to the cherub held, clamshell stoup and touches her finger in the holy water. She makes the sign of the cross then genuflects to the cross behind the altar.

She hasn't heard a Gregorian chant in years and this morning, it's particularly soothing to her. She turns back and finds an available confessional and steps inside, closing the door behind her and kneels. Tears form in her eyes as the priest speaks with a voice that seems of God.

"May the Lord be in your heart to help you make a good confession."

She makes the sign of the cross once again and her voice quivers.

"Forgive me father for I have sinned."

Chapter 36

THREADS

On his way to Bobby's, Andrea's cousin, in Boutte in St. Charles Parish, Harris drove south on I-310. When he crossed over St. Rose Road and looked down on it, he couldn't help but think of Megan. He's spoken to her a few times on the phone over the last couple of months and she seemed to be doing okay. He scolded himself for not going by to check on her when Donny was released, if for no other reason than to be there for her as moral support.

As he pulls into the gravel parking lot in front of Bobby's shop, he wonders again what could possibly have Bobby so panicked. He called earlier, insisting that Harris drive down and that he didn't know who else to call. So out of family obligation, he's driven the forty minutes it's taken to get here.

He parks his car next to one of the large air-boats and gets out. He's met by Bobby, who looks like he's seen a ghost. It's not the usual appearance of the man who catches alligators in the wild and rumored to be the inspiration for a popular cable show about life in the Louisiana swamps

"Al, thanks for coming. I didn't know who else I could call," Bobby says as Harris closes the door on his car.

"It's not a problem, Bobby. What's all the fuss about?" he asks as they begin making their way to the back of the building.

"Cuz, you know I do everything by da books. I don't want no trouble. I took a gator Al, a big one. Whooee, he's a monster you know. Mean sonabitch too. He was causing problems down by Esther's place, you know Esther, Billy's momma. He had come up outa d' swamp into the canal you know, few folk missing some dogs. These guys are hungry this time of year."

"Bobby, you took a gator out of season. It's not that big of a deal."

"Al, it's not the gator," Bobby says as they step around the corner to the back of the shed.

"It's what he have inside 'im."

At the edge of the shed, on a small concrete slab that Bobby uses to harvest the alligators he catches, lies a twelve-foot beast, its belly split open and contents poured onto and across the surface.

"I ain't touch noth'n since I cut him open and found dat."

Harris kneels beside the mess of intestines and the contents of the beast's stomach, grimacing at the stench of rotting flesh. Mixed among the bits of fish and other poor creatures, lies a human hand, distinctive tattoos on the knuckles: F, U, C, and K. Adorning the top of the hand is another tattoo of a cross. He picks up a stick and moves the contents around, discovering a portion of a finger and knuckle, the letter Y tattooed on it. He knows, without a second guess, he's looking at the hands of Donny Herbert.

"That a real hand, Al?"

"I think so."

He moves the pile of rotting flesh further revealing an ear which proves too much for the tough Bobby who loses what lunch was left in his own stomach.

Harris notices a piece of rope, some scraps of tape, and a piece of beige fabric that stands out, it's woven texture reminding him of the tie he got for Christmas, an unusual fabric for a piece of trash like Donny. He uses the stick to pull the remnant from the pile. Holding it up to examine it closer, he sees what appears to be some sort of monogramming on it.

"I ain't never seen nothing like this, Al. I been doing this a long time and I done heard stories, but I ain't never seen it wit' my own eyes," Bobby says, still nauseated and pale.

"Bobby, can you get me a baggy?"

Bobby exits into the shop and returns with a small sandwich bag.

"It's the best I got."

"That will work fine," Harris says, taking the bag and dropping the fabric into it. He seals it and places it in his coat pocket, then pulls out his phone and calls the incident in. Someone from St. Charles Parish will handle it from here on.

In the week since the trip to Bobby's, a feeble search has been initiated by St. Charles parish, but the odds of finding any further remains are not in their favor. The range of an adult alligator can be several square miles. Complicate the search by having it occur inside a cypress swamp and the odds of finding a body begin to approach that of winning the lottery.

Harris sits at his desk, working through a file folder for a new case, a drive-by shooting. His cell phone rings. It's a former colleague who was part of the department's forensic lab but left last August to take a professorship at Tulane. Harris took the fabric sample to her and called in a few chips, asking her to analyze it off the record.

"Liz, how are you? Got anything for me?"

"I do," she says through the phone.

He closes the case file and opens his notebook.

"Okay shoot."

"Your guy has expensive taste. It's Latvian linen, some of the best in the world."

"I thought it might be linen," he says proudly.

"You thought right. And that monogram, looks like the Russian letter for L. There's just not enough of it for me to be certain though."

"Okay, thanks Liz. I owe you. And say hello to Grant for me," he says.

He puts his cell phone down and sits silently, considering the possibilities. Megan, Russians. Megan, Donny. Russians, Donny. The letter L. He opens a desk drawer and removes the Donkova case file. He sets it on his desk and flips through it, stopping when he reaches a profile sheet. He stares at the picture, remembering the face from the courtroom. He looks at the name, Leon Barkov, the big guy, the Russian. He removes the page, closes the case file and rises. He walks to the window and looks out across the city, as the puzzle pieces fall into place. He looks down at the profile sheet, staring through it as he recalls the conversation with Ellen the first day he went to Memphis.

"Good Lord that girl was a mess, never afraid to get her hands dirty..." she had said.

He remembers the discussion with Megan in the barn when she was working on the Bronco, hands covered with grease.

"My father was one that taught his daughters to be self-sufficient, take matters into our own hands," she had said.

"You'd be amazed how handy I am with the right tool in my hands," he recalls her saying as she pulled the water pump from the engine.

"I've beefed her up a bit. She's a lot meaner now," Megan had said immediately before he told her of the plea agreement. He considers the possible meaning of those words.

He looks back out over the city as a feeling of satisfaction washes over him, a feeling that he hasn't felt in some time.

"I'll be damned," he says as a smile creeps across his face.

"Don't fuck with Megan Callahan," he says softly to himself.

He turns and looks at his wallet and badge lying by the phone. He gazes at the pictures of Kyle, Andrea, and Miranda. He folds the profile sheet and places it in his pocket, picks up his wallet and badge and exits his office, pausing to look back at it nostalgically, then turns off the light and closes the door.

Later this afternoon, Blanchard will return to his office and find the badge and service weapon of Albert Harris laying on his desk. His time is done.

It's been a week now since Harris took retirement. The time was right, something that Blanchard himself ultimately conceded after trying, not so convincingly, to persuade Harris to stay with the force. He had quietly offered that perhaps it was time for him to consider retirement too, and the two of them joked that they would start a private investigation firm.

Andrea and Kyle have retired for the evening, and Harris is up late. He's been thinking of Megan a lot lately. He heard she quit Flannigan's firm entirely. He needs to go see her.

He sits at his desk and wakes the computer from its slumber. He navigates to the poetry site and Megan's profile. He notices that almost all of her work, particularly the erotica, has been removed, save for the love poetry between her and Jen and one new posting from a few days earlier titled "Here and There". He opens it and begins silently reading.

Somewhere between here and there
I lost myself,
forgetting who I was,
adrift between realms of reality.

Existence became a spider,
spinning its web of entrapment,
its silken death of suffocation.

Thread by thread,
I discard my past lives.
Each segment of myself
exposed before you,
to observe,
to use,
to love.
To wrap me back up,
when I've come undone.

To find my real self
when too many faces
were staring back.

He sits for a moment, reflecting on her words. He hopes that perhaps, in some small way, she thought of him when she wrote it and that he in a backwards, accidental manner, helped to wrap her back up when she came undone. He sighs and scolds himself for getting soft in his old age.

He looks back at the monitor, reading the author's comments.

Thank you, Albert.

He smiles and laughs heartily, so much so that he lets out a tear.

"Oh, Megan. Thank *you*," he says, turns off the monitor and heads to his bedroom.

The rough, coarse, jagged metal that composes the angel statue is haunting yet beautiful. Its chaotic edges force the eye to examine them, seeking form and ultimately shaping beauty from that chaos. Jen stands, admiring the work while she waits for Megan to finish getting ready. They have a movie date night with Anna and Michelle.

Megan emerges from the hallway, her characteristic pony tail gone, replaced by free flowing waves of strawberry-blonde. Her tall, sleek form is stunning even at her most casual. Jen is mesmerized by her. Megan steps to her, a worried look on her face.

"Does this look okay?"

"You could make a potato sack look like Versace."

"Ah, you're biased," she says looking down at her shoes.

"Seriously, are these shoes okay?"

"Eh. What about those booties, the Frye's, tan with the wings?"

She looks away, picturing them in her mind, mentally modeling them. She looks back at Jen, grins and nods.

"Be right back."

She returns moments later, Frye booties with wings in place.

"Yeah, nice. What size are those?" Jen asks, eyeing the leather goodness.

"They won't fit you. Get your own."

Megan walks to her, putting her arms around her neck, looking deep into her light green eyes.

"God, I love your eyes."

Jen opens them widely, giving them all to her.

"I love *you*," she says

"I love you too, Jen."

Their soft, passionate kiss is disturbed by the ringing of Megan's phone. She sees that it's a call from Anton Donkova, Victor's son, and worry washes over her face.

"Anton, how are you?" she says in her most serious voice.

Her worry changes to sadness as she listens intently to what Anton tells her.

Victor's death from a heart attack came as little surprise to most. It was odd for Harris when he first heard the news. Part of him was happy to see that such a vile man had gone to his final judgment. On the other hand, he felt a degree of loss, of comradeship with a man, who he suspected, helped deliver Donny to meet his maker.

Harris sits in his car, parked near the back of other funeral attendees at Metairie Cemetery, the final resting place of choice for the rich and powerful of New Orleans. Victor could have chosen to be taken back to Russia and buried in his hometown of Ekaterinburg, but chose instead to lie for all eternity within the veritable plaza of black and red granite, his stateliest image etched forever into the towering black granite tombstone. It's a message to New Orleans that the Russians are here to stay.

Harris had no desire to ask Megan directly about Donny but his curiosity, or perhaps a small degree of newfound respect for Victor, drove him here today. If Megan owed Victor, she would be at his funeral and he sees her now, standing behind Victor's family.

As the funeral ends and the attendees begin to disperse, he exits his car and walks towards her. She sees him and smiles as they meet.

"I hoped I would find you here," he says with a smile.

'Yeah? Well, the old fart got to me," she says before looking around to make sure no one can hear her. "Mobster or not, personally he was good to me."

"I'm not here to judge. I just wanted to check on you. How you holding up?"

"I'll survive."

"How's your mom? Kristi?"

"They're good. Mom's busy with the ranch. Kristi lives at the hospital."

"How's Jeff...," Harris says before stopping himself. "Jen? Haven't seen him... her in a while," he adds, doing his best to adjust his pronoun usage.

"She's good. She's going back to school."

"Really? What's she studying?"

Megan just looks at him, expressionless. "She can't decide," she says after a moment.

"Women," Harris says with a grin.

"I know. Oh my God, she's horrible, Al," Megan says with a sigh. "Maybe I should encourage her to go into fashion design. God knows she knows shoes."

"I've been there," Harris says as they both enjoy a laugh.

"What's the future look like for you?" Harris says after catching his breath. "Heard you quit Flannigan. What are you going to do?"

She looks around for a moment, thinking it through, considering that she's in a place of death. She looks back to him and sighs softly.

"Live," she says with a smile.

He nods and smiles as he considers how simple, yet how brilliant and wonderful that sounds.

"What about you? I heard you finally took that retirement."

"Yeah, finally took the leap. It feels good. Not sure what I'm gonna do for now, just take it easy I guess. Spend time with Kyle and Andrea."

"How is he?"

"He's good," he says.

He surveys the graveyard, with its symbols of love and loss. He thinks of his new understanding of Kyle and that if Miranda were alive, she would be proud of her dad.

"You know, we're all doing great," he says with a grin.

Megan smiles and nods and they begin walking towards their cars.

"I don't know if you have plans this Saturday but Andrea and I... if you want... we would like to have you over... for dinner."

"Can I bring a friend?"

"Sure."

She smiles, choosing her words for maximum effect.

"Great. Jen's been looking for a reason to wear her new dress."

He raises his eyebrows, not expecting that response.

"I'm kidding," she says with a laugh, letting him off the hook.

A relieved Harris smiles as they reach Megan's car and she steps to the trunk, popping it open with her key.

"I'm glad you stopped by. I've got something for you."

She reaches in and removes the protective wrapping from a small statue, a pair of angel wings with small gears as the base. A rusty red cross adorns it from the base to center of the wings.

"I made this for you. Something good from something bad," she says, handing it to him.

He turns it in his hands, admiring it and then looks away, turning his eyes from her.

"It's beautiful, but you didn't—" he says after a long moment.

"I know, but I wanted to. The wings are from that fender and the gears are from the rear differential... if that matters."

He steps to her and they exchange a hug. He feels a surge of fatherly pride, knowing that she made it through the valley.

"Thank you," he says, choking back the emotion.

She nods and smiles, closes the trunk lid and then opens the door and gets in, rolling down the window.

"Okay then. We'll be in touch," he says.

He turns to leave but stops himself. He has to ask, somehow.

"Say, you been fishing since up there at your mom's place?"

She hesitates, and looks away for a moment, then back at Harris. Their eyes meet, exchanging the truth.

"Once," she says after a brief moment.

"Catch anything?"

She smiles, looks away, then back at him.

"A scrawny little catfish."

He attempts to hide his smile, but it bellows out into a wide grin. He nods and turns to return to his car. She calls to him.

"You still believe in Angels? That they're among us?" she says.

He turns back, pondering the thought as he looks down for a moment at the statue she gave him then looks back at her.

"More than ever. They come in many forms, for many reasons. We can't always see them, but we see what they do, how they change our lives," he says.

She nods and smiles then begins to pull away before he yells to her.

"Megan."

"Yeah?"

"Thank you."

"For what?"

"For you," he says.

He smiles as he watches her drive away, not sure if he will ever see his angel again.

It's Sunday morning and Harris, Andrea, and Kyle sit in their pew at New Hope. Harris has received several compliments on the tie he wore this morning, the one that Kyle made and gave him for Christmas. The national dialogue regarding transgender rights has the pastor worked into a lather.

"I know there aren't any of them here in the fellowship of the believers. We, the Christians, they the LGBT community. You can't be lesbian, gay, bisexual, transgender or whatever they add next... *and* be a Christian," the pastor says.

Harris looks over to Kyle, who hangs his head and leans into Andrea as if trying to hide from the hateful words. Andrea shakes her head, seemingly trying to shake the words from her mind. His thoughts drift back to that Sunday morning, much like this one, when his world changed. He recalls the scripture from First Corinthians he read then, its words replaying through his mind.

Love is patient, love is kind. It does not envy, it does not boast, it is not proud. It does not dishonor others, it is not self-seeking, it is not easily angered, it keeps no record of wrongs. Love does not delight in evil but rejoices with the truth. It always protects, always trusts, always hopes, always perseveres.

He looks down at his tie, holding in his hand the intricate patterns of winding vines highlighted by roses. As he follows the threads twisting path, his thoughts drift to another place; he's led down a darkened hallway to an ancient wooden door. Behind it, a scared girl, Kylie, sits on a cold floor wearing a mask of what looks like Kyle's face. She hears footsteps beyond and calls out. "Hello?"

She hears nothing except the movement behind the door.

"Hello?" she says again before the door opens slowly. Her eyes widen when she sees who is on the other side.

"Paw Paw?" she says as tears stream down the mask.

"Kylie?" he says softly, extending his hand into her cell and offering it to her.

She rises and takes his hand. He removes the mask from her face with his other hand, casting it back into the cell as they walk away into what is now a hall filled with sunlight.

Harris, standing now in the aisle at church, finishes helping Kyle from the pew. He lets go of him and offers his hand to a shocked Andrea who takes it and steps out of the pew into the aisle with the both of them. She looks at him, seeking an answer.

"We're finding a new church," he says to her.

They make their way, hand in hand, out of the building, to their car, to a house on Desoto Street. It's a house in a city of segmentation, in a society seemingly intent to dissever itself, in a country marked by engrained dissolution, in a world characterized by division.

It's a home that, no matter the trial, stands united.

THE END

Made in the USA
Monee, IL
21 March 2021